MEDICAL

Pulse-racing passion

Therapy Pup To Heal The Surgeon
Alison Roberts

Pregnancy Surprise In Byron Bay
Emily Forbes

MILLS & BOON

THERAPY PUP TO HEAL THE SURGEON
© 2024 by Alison Roberts
Philippine Copyright 2024
Australian Copyright 2024
New Zealand Copyright 2024

First Published 2024
First Australian Paperback Edition 2024
ISBN 978 1 038 91739 3

PREGNANCY SURPRISE IN BYRON BAY
© 2024 by Emily Forbes
Philippine Copyright 2024
Australian Copyright 2024
New Zealand Copyright 2024

First Published 2024
First Australian Paperback Edition 2024
ISBN 978 1 038 91739 3

MIX
Paper | Supporting
responsible forestry
FSC® C001695
www.fsc.org

Published by
Harlequin Mills & Boon
An imprint of Harlequin Enterprises (Australia) Pty Limited
(ABN 47 001 180 918), a subsidiary of HarperCollins
Publishers Australia Pty Limited
(ABN 36 009 913 517)
Level 19, 201 Elizabeth Street
SYDNEY NSW 2000 AUSTRALIA

Cover art used by arrangement with Harlequin Books S.A.. All rights reserved.

Printed and bound in Australia by McPherson's Printing Group

Therapy Pup To Heal The Surgeon

Alison Roberts

MILLS & BOON

Alison Roberts has been lucky enough to live in the South of France for several years recently but is now back in her home country of New Zealand. She is also lucky enough to write for the Harlequin Medical Romance line. A primary school teacher in a former life, she later became a qualified paramedic. She loves to travel and dance, drink champagne, and spend time with her daughter and her friends. Alison Roberts is the author of over one hundred books!

Dear Reader,

My love for dogs has been lifelong, despite being bitten as a toddler because I stuck my arm through a gate to pat a Jack Russell terrier. I've had the most amazing canine companions over the years, and I'm currently lucky enough to be sharing my life with an adorable black-and-white Cavoodle called Abby, who thinks she's a small, fluffy border collie.

I have to confess that being asked to write a story featuring a therapy dog was a dream for me—especially when I discovered an elite group of dogs that are trained to go into spaces you wouldn't think they'd ever be allowed, like a procedure room, to support and comfort children.

Hugh, my hero, still thinks they shouldn't be allowed, but Molly is passionate about her work as a pediatric nurse and the handler for her beloved therapy dog, Oreo.

There's a good reason Hugh is afraid of letting either Molly or Oreo get too close to him, but once they fall in love with *him*, he really doesn't stand a chance.

Happy reading!

Alison xxx

DEDICATION

For Megan

With the deepest appreciation for so many years of
your exceptional editorial skills and wisdom xxx

CHAPTER ONE

IT WAS ONE of those days.

The ones where there wasn't a minute to spare and it felt like you had to focus that much harder to ensure that no time got wasted and, more importantly, that no attempt to get as close to perfection as possible got sacrificed by taking short cuts.

The kind of day that Hugh Ashcroft liked the most. When his life was exactly the way he had worked so hard to make it. The fresh appreciation for it after the interruption of taking annual leave only made a pressured routine more enjoyable. Not that he'd been lazing around on holiday. Hugh had only flown back to arrive in New Zealand yesterday afternoon, after delivering a whirlwind lecture tour in several major cities in the United States—a world away from this children's hospital in the South Island's largest city.

It was also pleasing to find he had a new, senior registrar assigned to his team. Someone who was already following his own career pathway to becoming a paediatric orthopaedic surgeon. Even better, Matthew was someone who was particularly interested in his own subspecialty of oncology.

'So I only met this seven-year-old girl yesterday.' Hugh broke the strings of the mask dangling around his neck and pushed open the doors to the operating theatre they were leaving after the successful pinning of the complicated fracture a teenager had given himself when his skateboarding trick hadn't quite worked. 'She fell over in the playground at school and came in late in the day because her leg was still painful. She had an X-ray, which ruled out any fracture, but I got an urgent call to ED.'

Hugh didn't mention that he had still been in his office at ten o'clock last night, catching up on the paperwork that had accumulated in his absence. It wasn't anyone else's business that his work filled the vast majority of his life, was it?

He pulled a clean gown on backwards to act as a coat over his scrubs and looped his stethoscope around his neck. 'I couldn't get a slot for CT and a PET scan until tomorrow morning and an MRI is booked for the afternoon but I managed to get a slot in Radiology to do an urgent bone biopsy under ultrasound and they'll be waiting for us now.'

'So you think it's an osteosarcoma?'

'Certainly looks like it. Huge lesion, just above her knee. Size of an orange. I can't believe she hasn't had problems before this.'

'The family must be terrified. What's her name?'

'Sophie Jacobs. And yes, the family is, of course, extremely concerned.' Hugh headed for the stairs rather than waiting for a lift, shoving open a heavy fire-stop door to the stairwell. 'Which is why we need to be able to give them answers as quickly as possible.'

He wasn't quite quick enough to shut down the echo of Sophie's mother's voice in the back of his head.

'But...but she's just passed her first ballet exam. She lives for her dancing...'

Yeah...'terrified' definitely summed up the parents' reaction he had witnessed last night but Hugh would never use such emotive language. He knew all too well just how devastating a diagnosis of cancer could be for a child and their family.

He knew that, if he let himself, he could be sucked back to a time when another young girl had received such a diagnosis. He would remember realising why the fight for life was called a 'battle' and the crippling toll it could take on everybody involved for months. Years, even. And, if he was careless enough, he might also get an unwelcome glimpse of that darkest of spaces when the battle was lost.

But that wasn't going to happen. Because Hugh also knew that his ability to avoid tapping into the emotions of personal memories was what made him so good at his job that getting asked to be a guest speaker all over the world was now a regular occurrence.

There were plenty of people available to provide the empathy and psychological support that was, admittedly, badly needed, but what seven-year-old Sophie Jacobs and her family needed even more were the specialists like him and his esteemed colleagues in the paediatric oncology team, who could provide the science and skill to follow through on tough decisions and provide the best quality of life for the child in a worst-case scenario and a complete cure in the best.

He was still moving fast as he reached the procedure room in the radiology department, which was another very familiar clinical space for Hugh. A glance at his watch told him he would most likely find his patient on the table with either her mother or father beside her and she might already be sedated and under the care of a team of medics and technicians. He pushed open yet another door and stepped into the room with Matthew hot on his heels.

And then he stopped, so abruptly that his new registrar very nearly collided with him.

Because he was staring at something he'd never seen in any procedure room.

Ever.

'Can somebody please tell me…' Hugh Ashcroft kept his voice quiet and he spoke slowly and very clearly so that nobody could miss the significance of what he was asking '…why there is a *dog* in here?'

Uh-oh…

Molly Holmes caught the gaze of the black and white dog sitting by her feet but if her border collie, Oreo, had picked up on the dangerous tone of this man's voice, she wasn't bothered. Why would she be, when she was so well trained to cope with anything that could happen in a clinical environment like this? Alarms going off, people moving swiftly, children screaming—none of it would distract Oreo from her mission in comforting and supporting a child. She didn't even move her chin from where it was resting on a towel on the edge of the bed, in just the perfect place for a small hand to be playing with her ear.

Molly, however, *was* bothered. Because this was the first time this was happening here and the last thing she wanted was for it to be a disaster. Thank goodness the clinical director of the entire hospital, Vivien Pryce, had chosen to observe what was going on this afternoon and she was smiling as she took a step closer to the person who'd just spoken. Molly would have thought twice about getting that close to someone who looked like a human iceberg but Vivien actually touched his arm.

'Oreo's here to help Sophie with her biopsy,' she said softly. 'Just give us another moment, would you please, Hugh? I can fill you in then.'

So...*this* was Hugh Ashcroft—the orthopaedic surgeon that everybody said was the best in the country when it came to dealing with any skeletal tumours? One of the best in the world, even? Of course it was. Molly had also heard that he insisted on doing any biopsies of his patients himself, rather than leaving it to the very capable radiology department's doctors and technicians.

Mr Ashcroft had been away on leave when Molly had started working here, having moved back to her hometown of Christchurch a few weeks ago after working in Australia for several years. Had no one informed him that the new programme of using therapy dogs in the children's hospital had been approved after apparently waiting in the wings for too long? Perhaps it had been Molly's arrival—with Oreo—that had finally tipped the balance in favour of getting the project under way?

The radiologist was on the point of inserting the cannula in Sophie's hand that would allow them to administer the sedation needed for this invasive procedure. The little girl was lying on the bed on her side. She hadn't even noticed the doctor peeling off a sticky patch on the back of her right hand, revealing skin that would now be numb from the anaesthetic cream that would make the insertion of a needle painless, because she was stroking Oreo's silky ear with her left hand.

'She's *so* pretty…' Sophie whispered.

'She thinks you're pretty too,' Molly whispered back. 'Look at the way she's smiling at you.'

'How do you know she's smiling?'

'It's her ears. See the way she pulls them down?' Talking was another distraction for Sophie from what was going on. 'You can see her teeth, too, and the way her tongue is hanging over them a bit. That's how a dog tells you they're happy and that they like you. They're smiling…'

Sophie was smiling too. So was the doctor, as she slipped the cannula into a tiny vein and taped it into position. A nurse handed her a syringe.

'You're going to start feeling a bit sleepy,' the doctor told Sophie. 'You'll be awake again very soon, okay?'

'Will Oreo still be here when I wake up?' Sophie's gaze was a desperate plea as she looked up at Molly. 'Like you said she would be?'

Molly wasn't completely sure about that now but she chose to ignore the waves of hostility she could feel coming from Hugh Ashcroft's back as he scrubbed his hands at a basin. A nurse was waiting with the gown and gloves he would need to wear to perform a sterile procedure.

'Yes,' she said, firmly. She even raised her voice a little. 'We promised, didn't we? We're not going anywhere.' She could see Sophie's eyes drifting shut as the medication was injected. 'Sweet dreams, darling.'

Oreo didn't move as Sophie's hand slid away from her ear. She would be quite happy to sit here beside the bed, as still as a rock, to guard Sophie while she had her biopsy taken, but when Molly moved back the dog followed instantly. Molly headed for the far corner of the room to tuck herself into a corner amongst the big metal blocks of X-ray machinery. Surely that would be acceptable so that she wouldn't have to break her promise to be here the moment Sophie began waking up again?

Vivien's nod suggested approval.

Hugh's glare did not. But he was glaring at Oreo, so Molly didn't get the full effect.

'We can discuss this later.' Hugh's tone was dismissive but his tone as he turned to Sophie's mother was noticeably warmer. 'Hi, Joanne. I'm sorry I couldn't get here any sooner.'

'It's okay.' Joanne stroked her daughter's wispy blonde curls. 'I can't believe how easy it's been with having Oreo able to be with her. Sophie just adores dogs… Dancing and dogs are her two favourite things in the world.'

'Mmm.'

The sound from Hugh was strangled enough for Molly to start feeling nervous about the upcoming discussion that she would, no doubt, be part of. She caught Vivien's glance as Hugh, now gowned and gloved, stepped towards the table and the older woman's expression was reassuring. Moments later, however, the beeping of a pager saw the clinical director reaching for the message and then mouthing an apology to Molly as she slipped out of the room.

Sorry…have to go…

Molly would have loved to have followed her but she'd made a promise to Sophie and wasn't about to break it. She knew she had Vivien's support. It had been Vivien who'd signed off on Molly using her highly trained dog for an extension of duties that went quite a long way above any simple animal therapy programme that allowed dogs to visit public areas of a hospital or even within the wards. Using medical assistance dogs, or 'dogtors' as they were affectionally known, was happening more and more overseas but Oreo was one of the first dogs in this country to be approved to enter clinical areas like this procedure room, recovery areas and even the intensive care unit to assist children. Molly had made the dog version of a gown Oreo was wearing to cover her back and the elastic topped booties for her paws, which were a smaller size of the disposable ones available for staff to put over their footwear.

Sophie was lying on her back now with an area of her upper leg being prepped. An ultrasound technician was manoeuvring her equipment into place and a nurse was uncovering the top of a sterile trolley that had all the instruments and other supplies that would be needed, including the jars to hold the fragments of bone tissue about to be collected.

'You don't have to watch this bit, Joanne, if you'd rather not.' Hugh looked away from the screen as the technician located the bone lesion. They were ready to begin the procedure. The biopsy needle would show up on the screen to let him position it so that they could be confident the samples would be coming from exactly the right spot.

'I won't watch,' Joanne said quietly. 'But I'd like to stay close. Just in case Sophie might know if I'm not here.' She turned to face the head of the bed so she couldn't see what was happening and she bent down so that she was curled protectively over her daughter, her lips touching Sophie's hair. 'Mummy's here, sweetheart. It's okay... I'm here...'

Molly blinked back a tear but she could feel herself nodding at the idea that Sophie might be aware of her mother's touch. During the later stages of Oreo's training in Australia, she'd seen children respond to the dog's presence even when they were deeply unconscious and on a ventilator in ICU. She'd seen their heart rate and blood pressure drop after just a few minutes of their fingers being in contact with the soft warmth of Oreo's body.

She couldn't see the screen of the machine monitoring Sophie's heart rate and blood pressure so Molly watched Hugh instead. He certainly seemed to know what he was doing and she knew he was so focussed he'd totally forgotten her—and Oreo's—presence in the room. He was calm and confident, making a small incision on Sophie's leg and inserting the device that placed a cannula down to bone level.

'Drill, thanks.' Hugh smoothly removed the stylet and went on to the next stage of the procedure to make an opening in the bone, his gaze on the screen to get right inside the tumour. 'This won't take much longer,' he told Joanne. 'I'm about to start collecting the samples. I'll have an eleven-gauge biopsy needle, please,' he said to his scrub nurse.

Molly could see the care he took to remove several samples of tissue and ease them into the collection jars. She knew some would be used for tissue-based diagnosis and others for molecular analysis. If this tumour was malignant, they would soon know just how dangerous it might be. Again, her heart squeezed painfully enough to bring tears to her eyes. Molly might not be a mother herself, yet, but she was an aunty to nieces and nephews whom she adored and she had chosen to become a paediatric nurse because of her love for children. The joy of sharing their journey back to health was the best feeling ever but being part of the challenge of caring for them when they faced—and sometimes lost—a battle for life was as much of a privilege as it was heartbreaking.

She could feel a tear tickling as it ran down the side of her nose. Without thinking, she reached up to wipe it away with her fingers. She knew she hadn't made a sound, like a sniff or something, so it had to be purely coincidence that Hugh Ashcroft looked in her direction at that particular moment as he stepped back from finishing the procedure.

Molly could only see his eyes between the top

of the mask and the cap that was covering his hair, but that was enough to know that he was even less impressed than he had been when he'd seen Oreo in here.

The sedation for Sophie was already wearing off as a nurse put a dressing over the wound on her leg. The little girl was turning her head.

'Where's Oreo…?'

'Right here, darling…' Molly moved back towards the bed with Oreo glued to her leg. 'We're going to go back to the ward with you.'

Oreo put her chin on the edge of the mattress again. Her plume of a tail waved gently as she felt the touch of Sophie's hand on her head.

'Can she sleep with me tonight?'

A sound that was reminiscent of a growl came from Hugh's direction but maybe he was having trouble stripping off his gloves and gown. Or perhaps he was simply clearing his throat before speaking quietly to Sophie's mother about how long it would take for the pathology results to come through.

Molly had to shake her head. 'Sorry,' she said to Sophie. 'We can come back to the ward with you for a bit but there are special rules for dogs that visit in the hospital and Oreo's got to come home with me to sleep.'

Behind her, she could hear Joanne being told that an MRI and PET scan were booked for tomorrow and her heart sank. The surgeon had to be already very confident of his diagnosis if he wanted the kind of diagnostic tests that would let them stage the cancer by checking for its spread to other parts of the body like the liver or lungs.

Molly made her tone bright. 'Hey…did I hear your mum say that you love dancing, Sophie?'

Sophie's nod was drowsy.

'So does Oreo.'

Sophie dragged her eyes open again. 'Dogs can't dance…'

'Oreo can. We'll show you when she comes to visit one day.'

'Promise…?'

Molly didn't shift her gaze but she could hear that the conversation with Sophie's mum had ended and she could feel the stare coming in her direction from the orthopaedic surgeon, who was now listening to what she was saying.

It was already clear that Hugh Ashcroft didn't like dogs. Or women crying. But it wouldn't be the first time that she'd encountered a surgeon who found it difficult to show a bit of compassion. Maybe it was because their patients were unconscious for most of the time they spent with them so it was easier to be aloof? To see them as simply patients needing surgical treatment without the complications of their own lives and families or their dreams and fears that could make a situation unbearable. And maybe it was just as well there were people like her around to balance the equation.

'I promise,' she whispered to Sophie.

She looked up as she heard another pager beeping, just in time to see Hugh Ashcroft leaving the procedure room.

He spotted her heading through the hospital foyer towards the main doors.

It wasn't hard. Not when she had that large black and white dog walking beside her. At least the animal wasn't still dressed up in a ridiculous version of a human's theatre gown and booties now. It was wearing a red coat with white writing that advertised its status as a service dog. It also had the medical logo of a heart divided by a stylised ECG trace. And…good grief…small dog paw prints beneath it?

'Excuse me…' It was a command rather than a query.

She turned. She'd been wearing a hat and mask in the procedure room so he hadn't really seen what she looked like and Hugh's first impression was of very curly dark hair that was almost shoulder length and quite uncontrolled looking. Wild, even…

He got closer. 'I'm Hugh Ashcroft,' he introduced himself.

'Yes, I know.'

She had hazel-brown eyes and he could see the flash of wariness in them, which was understandable, given that he'd heard her making a promise to a sick child that—when Vivien had heard his misgivings about the access her dog had been granted in visiting *his* patients—she might no longer be able to keep.

'I'm just on my way to find Vivien Pryce. I saw you and realised I don't actually know your name.'

'Molly,' she said. 'Molly Holmes. But I think you'll find that Dr Pryce is not available. I was supposed to meet her myself so that we could talk about our first session with a dogtor.'

'With a...*what*?'

'Medical assistance dogs. Calling them "dogtors" differentiates them from the pet therapy dogs that don't have the level of training needed to go into a clinical environment.'

The dog at her feet was looking up at Hugh and he got the strange notion that he was being approved of. Being smiled at, even? Perhaps that was because the dog was wagging its tail as it stared at him—a slow, thoughtful sweep against the polished linoleum. Its ears were pulled back as well, which made its eyes crinkle, just as a person's might if they were really happy to see someone they knew. Hugh didn't smile back. He avoided direct eye contact and stared at the dog's owner instead.

'Dogtors' was just the kind of cute title he might have expected people involved with this sort of organisation to have come up with. People who probably also spent a significant percentage of their lives helping to save whales or persuading farmers to play classical music to their cows as they got milked. People who wanted an excuse to make it acceptable to take animals into totally unsuitable environments. It was also an insult to anyone who'd gone through many years of tertiary training to earning the title of 'doctor'.

'First session…and *last*…' he heard himself muttering.

'Excuse me…?'

Molly Holmes' echo of his greeting was definitely a query. An outraged one, in fact. She wasn't nearly as tall as Hugh but she seemed to have just grown an inch or two. 'Dr Pryce might have something to say about that. She assured me that all HoDs were on board with the idea. And Christchurch Children's Hospital is now registered as an active participant in an international research trial looking at the benefits of therapy dog visits for paediatric patients.'

'We were on board with *visits*, yes…' Hugh shook off the impression that this woman seemed well spoken. Intelligent. And very defensive…?

'In a ward playroom, perhaps. Or other public areas. Not contaminating an area that needs to be as sterile as possible.'

'We were nowhere near a sterile field while the procedure was happening,' Molly snapped. 'And we follow clear protocols when it comes to hygiene. "Visits", as you call them, are certainly beneficial to sick children but these dogs can make clinical differences in the most distressing situations for children. Procedures like the one Sophie was having today. Or when they're having an anaesthetic induced or they're in Recovery. Or ICU.'

Her words were blurring. 'Recovery?' he echoed. 'ICU? *Theatre...?*'

'Only the induction room. The kind of spaces that parents are also allowed to be in.'

But Hugh held up his hand. 'This is worse than I thought. I don't want to discuss this with you any further, Ms Holmes. No doubt you'll hear more about my concerns from Vivien Pryce in due course.'

'I'll look forward to it,' she said. 'Have a good evening, Mr Ashcroft.' She turned away but then flicked a glance back over her shoulder. 'You might find you'll enjoy it more if you loosen that straitjacket you're wearing first. It might even help you to consider things from a point of view that isn't solely your own.'

Hugh found himself simply standing there, watching the pair of them walk out of the main doors of this hospital.

Shocked…?

Not so much at being told he was so uptight he might have difficulty enjoying his time away from work. He was quite well aware that people considered him to be a workaholic to the point of being antisocial and enough of a recluse for it to be a waste of time inviting him to parties. He didn't care that he might be considered selfish in thinking that his own point of view was the most important, either. It didn't matter to Hugh what they thought of him on a personal level as long as they also considered him to be the top of his field in his chosen specialty.

Which they did.

People weren't normally this rude directly to his face, however.

This was *his* patch. So it was his point of view that carried the weight here.

Any doubt that it would be worth his time and energy to influence the decision the clinical director of this hospital had made in his absence had just been removed.

Maybe Molly Holmes wasn't as intelligent as he'd thought. Did she not realise that smart re-

mark might have just sealed the fate of both herself and her dog?

With a bit of luck, he might never have to set
eyes on either of them, ever again.

CHAPTER TWO

DAWN WAS ONLY just breaking as Molly drove her classic 1960 Morris Minor van over the winding road in the hills that bordered the entrance to the city's harbour and the view was enough to make her catch her breath.

'It's going to be a gorgeous day,' she told Oreo. 'Good thing I'm on mornings this week because that means I can take you to the beach after work.'

Molly had moved into the family's much loved holiday house on her return from Australia recently and it was only a short walk to Taylors Mistake beach, which was now Oreo's favourite place to go. Or maybe the real favourite was one of the challenging walking tracks that went for miles through these hills.

No…judging by how excited Oreo was to jump out of the van at the old villa overlooking the harbour where Molly's mother, Jillian, lived, having finally moved off the family farm in the hills, it was the best place in the world to be when she couldn't be at home or with Molly. Of course it was. Molly's mum's young dog, Milo, was Oreo's new best friend and they got to play all day while Molly was at work. Not that she had time to stop and watch the joy with which the dogs greeted each other this morning. An overweight golden retriever was watching the game of chase and roll from the villa's veranda.

'I need to keep going,' Molly told Jillian. 'I want to get in early today.'

The shift handover started at six forty-five a.m. and Molly was always there early. It wasn't simply because this was a new job and she wanted to impress, it was because of her position. As a nurse practitioner, she had spent years in advanced training that gave her a scope of practice well above a registered nurse. Her authority to prescribe medications, interpret laboratory tests, make diagnoses and instigate interventions and treatments meant that she worked closely alongside the consultants and registrars in her area. She was part of every ward round and family meeting, knew every patient under their care and was sometimes the only medical practitioner available on busy days or in an emergency.

It was a position that carried enormous responsibilities and Molly was passionate about doing her job to the very best of her capabilities.

But, okay…there was that bit of extra motivation today.

Because Hugh Ashcroft was back in town and it was only a matter of time until their paths crossed again.

'No worries.' Jillian was fishing in the pocket of her apron for the small treats she always kept there. Oreo and Milo came racing to sit in front of her, being the best-behaved dogs ever.

'See?' she called as Molly was closing the gate behind her. 'Milo's got to do everything Oreo does now. He's going to be another dogtor, I'm sure of it.'

'I'll do some more training with him on my next days off.' Molly nodded. 'See you later, Mum—and thanks so much…'

'You know how much I love providing doggy day care. Hey…how did it go with Oreo yesterday?'

'She was perfect. And the little girl who was having the biopsy just loved her. The surgeon not so much.'

'Oh? Why not?'

'I have a feeling he wasn't expecting to find us there. Or it might be that he's a control freak that would never consider bending a rule.' Molly bit her lip. 'I told him he might need to loosen his straitjacket.'

'Oh, Molly…you *didn't*…'

'Could have been worse.' Molly grinned. 'I could have told him he needed to take the stick out of his bum.'

Her mother laughed and flapped her hand to tell Molly to get going, so she turned to open her driver's door. Her brother had stored the car in a barn in the years she'd been away and the porcelain green shade of paintwork was still perfect. With the sun having risen further and now shining on the vehicle, she realised its olive-green colour was reminding her of something.

Oh…dear Lord…

It was Hugh Ashcroft's eye colour, wasn't it? An unusual shade of green in a human, which was just a bit darker than the traditional colour she'd chosen to repaint the van.

'How did he take that?' Jillian wasn't laughing any longer. 'The surgeon, I mean?'

'I'm not actually quite sure.' But Molly was also unrepentant. He'd deserved to hear that his attitude wasn't appreciated. She shrugged as she pulled the door shut. 'Guess I'm about to find out.'

It was far too early to expect to find the hospital's clinical director in her office but Hugh had sent an email message to her secretary, giving her his timetable for the morning and asking for a meeting to be set up in either her office or his own, with some urgency, but there was no reply by the time he needed to prepare for his first surgery of the day.

Hugh looked into an anaesthetic induction room where an anxious mother was holding a crying toddler. Thirteen-month-old Benji's oral sedative had clearly not been quite strong enough to make what was happening to him tolerable.

'He'll be asleep in just a minute or two, Susan,' he assured the distressed mother. 'Are you okay? Have you thought of anything else you wanted to ask me since I saw you and Benji's father yesterday?'

She shook her head. 'I just want it to be over,' she said. 'Shh…it's okay, Benji. It's not going to hurt.' She cuddled her baby harder as he shrieked in fear and writhed in her arms when the anaesthetist reached towards him with a face mask. 'This part is the hardest…' Susan was losing the battle to hold back her own tears and Hugh could feel himself backing away from the increasing tension and noise level. It was past time he scrubbed in, anyway.

'Try not to worry,' he said briskly. 'We're going to take the very best care of Benji. I'll come and find you as soon as the surgery is finished.'

Matthew was already at the sinks scrubbing his fingers with a sponge. He tilted his head towards the noise coming from the induction room, which was, fortunately, diminishing rapidly.

'Not a happy little camper next door,' he commented.

Hugh's response was a dismissive grunt. He took his watch off and dropped it into the pocket of his scrub tunic. He opened the pack with the soap-impregnated sponge but left it on the ledge while he lathered his arms with soap and used a nail pick. A pre-wash before scrubbing in for the first surgery of the day was mandatory and he rinsed off the soap suds thoroughly before using the sponge to begin a routine that was so familiar and automatic, this could be considered time out. Relaxation, even...

Or maybe not...

'He might have been happier to have that dog in there with him.' Matthew was scrubbing his forearms now. A theatre assistant was hovering nearby with a sterile towel ready. 'That bone biopsy yesterday was quite cool, wasn't it? I've never seen pet therapy used like that before.'

Hugh ignored his registrar's comment this time. He was scrubbing each individual finger now, moving from the little finger to the thumb, a part of his brain quietly counting at least ten strokes on all four anatomical sides of each digit. He had no intention of discussing an issue that had already taken up far too much of his head space. Good grief...his brain had even produced images of that impertinent woman and her scruffy dog as he'd been drifting off to sleep last night.

'So what can you tell me about our first case?'

Matthew dropped his towel and pushed his arms into the sterile gown the assistant was holding for him. 'Benji's parents noticed a bump on his collarbone when he was about four months old. It's got steadily more prominent and imaging has revealed a congenital pseudoarthrosis of the clavicle.'

'Which is?'

'A "false joint". Where a single bone, such as a clavicle or tibia, grows as two bones.'

'Cause?'

'Most likely due to a birth injury.'

'And why is it an issue?'

'The bump can become pronounced enough to be unsightly but, more importantly, it can cause pain and affect the function of the shoulder, which is what's happening in Benji's case. He's developed an odd crawling style because he's avoiding using his right arm.'

Hugh nodded. He was holding his arms under the stream of water from the tap now, letting suds run off from his fingers towards his elbows. 'And what are we going to do?'

'An open debridement of the bone ends and

then fixation with clavicle plates and, if necessary, a bone graft with cancellous bone harvested from the iliac crest to fill the gap.'

'Good.' Hugh took the sterile towel from the tongs held by the theatre assistant and dried his hands carefully. 'I'll leave you to stay and see how they apply a wrap-around body and arm cast when the surgery's completed. I'll be popping down to my office on the ward for a meeting with Vivien Pryce before we get started on our second case for this morning.' He turned to put his arms through the sleeves of his gown. 'It shouldn't take long. I expect I'll be back by the time young Benji has gone through to Recovery.'

Baby Chloe giggled as Molly used a fluffy soft toy to tickle her tummy.

'What a gorgeous smile. She doesn't seem that bothered by having her legs strung up in the air like this, does she? We'll see how she goes today now that the weight on the traction's been increased.'

'I hope I can still breastfeed her.'

'It's possible. Not easy but if you can wriggle under the strings and lie sideways beside her, she'll be able to latch on. I've seen mums do it.' She smiled at Chloe's mother. 'It's amazing how you can find a way to do the things that are really important. I love that you're not giving up on the breastfeeding.'

The traction mechanism attached to each end of the cot was gradually stretching ligaments to try and position a congenitally dislocated hip so that it could then be held in the correct place by a splint for months to come.

'She's going to need surgery if the traction doesn't work, isn't she? That's why we're in this ward?'

'It's certainly a possibility.' Molly checked the baby's case notes. 'She's due for an X-ray tomorrow so we should have a better idea of how things are going after that. Would you like me to get the surgeon to come and have a chat to you before then?'

'Yes, please… I always try and hope for the best but being prepared for the worst is kind of an insurance policy, isn't it?'

'I couldn't agree more.' Molly was writing on Chloe's chart. 'I've finished my ward round so I'm going to go and leave a note for the surgeon to come and see you as soon as possible.' She flicked a page over. 'Oh…' An odd knot suddenly formed in her stomach. 'Chloe was admitted under Mr Ashcroft's team, yes?'

'Yes. I haven't met him yet, though—only his registrar. They told me he was away doing a lecture tour in America but he'd be back in time if Chloe did end up needing an operation.'

'He's back now. I met him for the first time myself yesterday.'

'What's he like? He must be very good at his job if he's asked to give international talks.'

Molly swerved the question by making a sound that could have been agreement. Or perhaps it was encouragement, as she picked up the fluffy toy to try and make Chloe giggle again.

The delicious sound of a happy baby stayed with Molly as she scribbled a note to ask Hugh Ashcroft to visit his potential patient's mother. She could have left it with the ward manager to deliver or put it in the departmental pigeonholes for mail but she was due for a break and wanted a breath of fresh air. Heading for the access to the courtyard garden that opened off the foyer area just outside the ward entrance took her very close to the consultants' offices, so she decided to put it on his desk herself. That way, she could make sure he saw it immediately.

She opened the door without waiting for a response to her polite knock because she knew he was upstairs in Theatre with a full list for the day. The shock of seeing him standing behind his desk peering at his computer screen was enough to make her jaw drop.

'Oh, my god,' she said. 'You're not supposed to be here.'

'It's *you*…' It was a statement rather than a question but he was looking as startled as she was. 'I could say the same thing,' he added, slowly. 'You're certainly not supposed to be in *my* office.'

He was staring at the scrubs she was wearing. At her hair, which, admittedly, was probably already trying to escape the clips she used to try and tame it during work hours. His eyebrows rose as his gaze flicked down to the stethoscope hanging around her neck and the lanyard that made it obvious she was a staff member. And then that gaze shifted again, to look straight at her. 'Who the hell *are* you?'

Oh…the intensity in those olive-green eyes that could be due to either suspicion or anger was…well, it was disconcerting to say the least. It had to be nerves that were pinching deep in Molly's gut right now because she knew what was coming—a well-deserved bollocking for having been so rude to a consultant surgeon yesterday?

'My name's Molly Holmes.' She lifted her chin. 'I started work here as a nurse practitioner last week.'

'But…what were you doing here yesterday? With that dog?'

'I've been involved in pet therapy for years. It's what I do on my days off.'

There was a moment's silence during which Molly noticed something was changing in that gaze she was pinned by. Was it softening? Because Hugh Ashcroft was now seeing her as a colleague and not a layperson who volunteered to bring her pet dog into a hospital occasionally? Or could he be just a little impressed that she chose to spend her days off in the same place she worked? That she cared enough about her patients to be here when she wasn't being paid to do so?

Perhaps being impressed was a bit much to expect.

But he wasn't looking angry so much. He was looking…

Puzzled…? Or curious? As if interest might be winning a battle with irritation…?

Her nervousness was receding now that it didn't feel like she was in quite so much trouble with one of her senior colleagues but, strangely, that sensation in Molly's gut wasn't going away. If anything, it seemed to have become even stronger.

He knew he was staring.

He knew it was a rude thing to do, but Hugh couldn't help himself. It almost felt as if, by keeping a steady gaze on this woman, he might be able to find his balance.

It wasn't often that something knocked him sideways but having Molly Holmes walk into his office like that had done it. He'd left the hospital yesterday quite confident that he would never see her—or her dog—again but…here she was. In his work space. His *happy* space. Not only that, she was a nurse practitioner. Someone who was highly trained enough to be filling gaps and monitoring his patients, possibly better than his more junior registrars.

Someone that he would expect to have a close working relationship with.

Vivien Pryce, the clinical director, who was going to arrive in his office at any moment, according to the email he'd just read, might not be very happy if Hugh said everything he'd been planning to say to her about yesterday's incident with the dog in his procedure room.

Hugh cleared his throat.

'About yesterday…' he began. 'About your dog…'

And then he stopped because he couldn't think of what to say next.

He was still staring. At her brown eyes that were fringed with lashes as dark as her hair. Her skin was tanned enough to make him think she spent a lot of time outdoors and…

…and she was smiling at him.

'Oreo,' she supplied to fill in the gap. 'She liked you, Mr Ashcroft.' Her eyebrows lifted as if she had found this quite surprising. 'And I have to admit that my dog is usually a very good judge of character.'

Hugh remembered the way the dog had been looking up at him yesterday and waving its tail in approval. Smiling at him… He actually shook his head to get rid of the image of those brown eyes, as warm as melted chocolate, fixed on him. Not unlike Molly's eyes, come to think of it.

The list of objections he had been more than ready to discuss with Vivien seemed to be getting less defined. Hugh found himself frowning as he tried to focus.

'It wasn't that I didn't know a pet therapy programme was being considered for our ward,' he said, a little curtly. 'But nobody said anything about allowing animals to have access to the kind of areas you mentioned, like an intensive care unit. Or a procedure room, for that matter. I was…surprised, to say the least.'

Molly was nodding. 'I'm sorry about that. And I take full responsibility. There was a meeting last week, while you were still away, and because I've already been involved with a similar programme in Australia I was invited to bring

Oreo in. It was only going to be an orientation but then Radiology let us know about Sophie's appointment and Vivien asked if we could visit and it just sort of grew from there. Sophie fell in love with Oreo and asked if she could go with her for the biopsy and I said she'd love to if she was allowed and...' Molly finally paused for breath. 'Anyway... I do apologise. I can try to ensure that everyone's aware she's going to be present next time.'

Next time...? I don't think so...

Hugh wasn't aware his thought had been audible until he saw Molly's expression change. Until he saw the fierce gleam in her eyes that told him she was quite prepared to fight for whatever she was passionate about.

'There are some articles you might like to read when you have a spare moment,' she said. 'There aren't too many peer-reviewed studies that have been written up yet but anecdotal evidence is gaining quite a following. The trial that Dr Pryce has enrolled us in will be hoping to reproduce the kind of results being seen overseas, where people are reporting quite dramatic improvements in parameters like anxiety levels and pain scales in children who have animal companions in stressful medical situations. Measurable results with blood pressures and heart rates dropping, which is a pretty good indication that pain or stress levels are diminishing—'

The knock on the door interrupted her and Hugh saw her eyes widen when Vivien Pryce entered his office. He also saw the flash of something that looked very much like fear and…

…and he suddenly felt guilty because he could have caused Molly some serious problems that might have ruined the start of her new job if he'd gone ahead with his complaints.

He also felt quite strongly, and very oddly, as if he wanted to protect her, which was both very unexpected and just as unwelcome.

Oh, no…

Molly saw the apologetic expression on the clinical director's face as she entered Hugh Ashcroft's office.

'Sorry, Hugh. I've been putting out fires so far all morning and I've only got a minute or two now but my secretary said it sounded like you wanted to talk to me about something urgent.' Her sideways glance was curious. 'Is it about our first dogtor consultation yesterday? Is that why Molly's here, too?'

'No…' Molly edged towards the door. 'I just came to leave a note for Mr Ashcroft.' She hurriedly put the now rather crumpled piece of paper, asking Hugh to go and talk to Chloe's mother, on the edge of the desk. 'I'll leave you to it.'

'Don't go.' Hugh's tone sounded like a command. 'You probably need to know what I was about to say to Vivien, anyway.'

Molly bit her lip. If he wasn't about to tell Vivien how inappropriate he considered it to be to have animals in a procedure room, he was intending to tell her that their new nurse practitioner was lacking the kind of respect a senior consultant surgeon was entitled to expect.

She had to agree that he should be able to expect some privacy in his own office without having people barging in uninvited. And he certainly shouldn't have been told that he was so buttoned up he couldn't bend far enough to consider that the opinions of others might actually be as valid as his own.

But Hugh was nodding at Vivien as Molly held her breath. 'That was, in fact, what we've just been discussing,' he said. 'I was explaining that I wasn't aware there was any mention of allowing animals in areas that most clinicians wouldn't consider to be remotely suitable for pet therapy when we had that initial departmental meeting on the subject.'

'That is true. Personally, I wasn't aware of the most recent literature concerning the therapeutic benefits of allowing dogs in those kinds of areas until I was having a chat to Molly after her job application interview. It was, admittedly, an addition that should have been more widely discussed before we put it into action.'

The sound Hugh made was a cross between agreement and annoyance. Then he shrugged. 'Perhaps it's not too late. You might like to send me the links to those papers when you have a spare moment.'

Vivien flicked another glance in Molly's direction. There was curiosity in that lightning-fast glance as well—as if she was surprised that Molly had somehow defused the bomb that had been about to be hurled?

'I'll do that. But if it's more information you need, Hugh, it's Molly you should talk to. She's got far more experience in this field than anyone here. I'll also forward the memo I got from the research technician who was recording vital sign measurements on Sophie yesterday. If you compare them with the control case we monitored last week, you can see a rather startling difference. I know it's early days but I think this is going to be a very exciting trial to be part of.' She was smiling at Molly now. 'And we have our recently appointed nurse practitioner to thank for getting it off the ground.'

Hugh might have resisted the opportunity to get Molly into trouble but he wasn't about to go

as far as being friendly to his new colleague. He
was reaching to pick up the note Molly had put
on his desk and he scanned it swiftly. 'Tell them
I'll be on the ward as soon as my surgery list is
complete for the day,' he said. 'That should be
around four o'clock if we have no emergencies or
complications to deal with. And if I'm not holding everyone up by having unscheduled meetings.' He glanced up at the clock on his wall.
'Which means I need to be scrubbed in again in
less than five minutes.'

His nod signalled the end of this unscheduled
meeting with Molly. He moved towards the door
and Vivien turned to follow him out.

'Keep me posted on Sophie's case, would you,
please, Hugh? I was thinking about how hard this
is going to be for her family last night. Did you
know she's the star of her ballet class? Her dad
just put up a rail in her bedroom to be a barre for
her to practise with.'

It was no surprise that this aloof surgeon ignored such a personal detail. Molly could hear
the clinical detachment in his voice as he walked
away with Vivien. 'She's scheduled for a PET
scan about now. I'll forward the results...'

Molly headed back to pass on the message for
Chloe's mother. The handover for the afternoon
shift would be over long before Hugh was due
to be back on the ward so it was very unlikely

that she would see him again today, which would probably be a relief as far as Mr Ashcroft was concerned.

It was a relief for Molly as well because she was quite sure that she had, somehow, dodged a bullet.

There was no reason at all to feel disappointed. Molly had a busy few hours ahead of her dealing with whatever challenges arose in a surgical paediatric ward. Her pager was beeping right now, in fact, to alert her to a potentially urgent situation.

Moments later, she was on her way to replace an IV line that a toddler had managed to pull out. She could hear the two-year-old boy's screams already as she sped down the corridor. This could keep her occupied for quite some time but it was just the kind of challenge she enjoyed the most— winning the confidence of a terrified child and succeeding in a necessary intervention with the least amount of trauma. It was a shame she didn't have Oreo here to help, mind you.

But, by four o'clock, she would be back at her own mother's house to collect her beloved canine companion. She'd do some training with Milo before she went home but the days were lengthening nicely now that summer wasn't far away. There would be time for a walk on the beach with Oreo before it got dark.

Feeling disappointed that she wouldn't be seeing Hugh Ashcroft again today was…
…weird. That was what it was.

CHAPTER THREE

SUNSET WASN'T FAR off but there was still enough time to go and play on the beach, especially when they only had to go through the gate at the bottom of the garden and run along the track through the marram grass on the sand dunes to get past the driftwood and near the waves, where there was enough space to throw the frisbee.

Molly kicked off her sandals and got close enough for the last wash of the waves to cover her feet. She flicked the frisbee and laughed as Oreo hurled herself into the chase with a bark of delight and then leapt into the air to catch the plastic saucer and bring it back to drop at her feet. This time with her dog was a world away from the stress that could come from her work and completely different from the focus that came from the training sessions she did with Oreo and now Milo on a daily basis. It was simply hanging out. Loving each other's company.

Pure fun.

She wasn't the only person taking advantage

of the last of the sun's rays to have some fun. A lone surfer, protected by a full body wetsuit, was well out to sea, waiting for a bigger wave.

For a disquieting moment, Molly was taken back in time. She was a teenager in love for the first time, watching her boyfriend and her brother out catching waves on a summer evening, and she'd never been so happy. The pain—and shock—of her first romantic disaster when she was dumped a few months later had never been forgotten.

On the positive side, the pain was never *quite* that life-shatteringly bad when it happened again.

On the negative side, it had happened too often.

Okay…sometimes it had been her decision to call time on a relationship that wasn't going any-where but, more often, it hadn't been her choice. It was usually an amicable ending because they were great friends but, quite understandably, the guys moved on because they wanted something more in a life partner. And sometimes, it came too close to an echo of that first heartbreak.

Molly had given up trying to work out why she always seemed to be put in the 'friend zone'. The men she liked didn't seem bothered that she wasn't blonde and blue-eyed. Or that she had the solid, healthy kind of body that suited a girl from the farm. It certainly wasn't that she wasn't good company or intelligent enough to be able to have an interesting conversation.

She told herself for years that she just hadn't met the right person. That she'd know when she did and she wasn't going to settle for less. That she might be surprised to find him around the very next corner in her life. But the last break-up—the one that had persuaded Molly it was time to go home to New Zealand—was taking a bit longer to get over.

Getting settled again and starting a new job were good excuses to have no interest in even looking for male companionship but, to be honest, Molly was almost ready to embrace single-dom. If she wasn't looking, maybe the 'one' would come around that corner and find her. If he didn't, it wouldn't be the end of the world. It wasn't as if she were alone, after all. She bent to pick up the frisbee Oreo had dropped hopefully in front of her and threw it again.

Oreo's joyful bark as she chased after the toy made her smile.

This was the kind of happy she could trust to last…

When she straightened up, she saw the surfer catch the wave he'd been waiting for and when he leapt to his feet, Molly found herself slowing to watch him. She didn't even notice the frisbee being dropped within easy reach.

Wow...

This guy was seriously good at surfing. Molly liked to swim in the sea but she'd never got bitten by the surfing bug. Her older brother had, though—which was how she'd met her first boyfriend—and she'd heard and seen enough over her teenage years to know how much effort and skill went into making it look this easy. This graceful.

Right from the moment he got to his feet, he was in control and there was no way Molly could look away before he reached the end of this wave. To be able to sense the power and purpose in his movement from this far away was something special. This person was passionate about what they were doing—totally oblivious to any audience, living in the moment and loving it.

He had done an aerial move within seconds, flipping his board into the air above the lip of the wave and then landing to twist and turn along the wave face. As the height and strength of the wave collapsed he even did a flashy re-entry turn off the end of it. And then he dropped down to lie on his board and paddle back out to sea, as if he couldn't wait to catch another wave. As if his life depended on it, even...

Oreo's bark made Molly realise she had ignored the frisbee for too long and she turned her attention back to the game, but as she reached the end of the beach and turned back towards home she caught sight of the surfer again—now a dark blob against the increasing colour in the sky behind him, reflecting the sunset happening on the other side of the hills. He wasn't showing off this time. He was simply poised on his board, at one with the limitless ocean he'd just been flirting with, as he rode the wave right to the wash of shallow foam so close to the beach he could step off and be only ankle deep. He picked his board up at that point, slung it under his arm and walked out of the sea…straight towards Molly.

Oreo was normally wary of strangers and stayed protectively close, often touching her legs, so Molly was astonished to see her take off and run towards the surfer. When she got close, she dropped her frisbee and then put her nose down on her paws and her bum in the air to invite the man to play. When he walked straight past her, she looked confused for a moment but then grabbed the toy and ran after the man. This time she got right in front of him before she dropped it. Molly increased her pace, ready to apologise for the annoyance her dog was creating.

But then she stopped dead in her tracks, completely lost for words.

Blindsided…

Never, in a million years, would she have guessed that the man whose longstanding passion for what he was doing on the waves showed in his level of skill and every confident, graceful movement of his body could possibly be someone who could also be so lacking in an emotional connection to other living creatures that he couldn't embrace the pure joy of being able to provide comfort to a small, scared child.

Did Hugh Ashcroft have an identical twin?

Or had she stumbled into the private life of a person who was actually the opposite of who he appeared to be in the company of others?

How—and *why*—could someone be like that?

Curiosity was quite a powerful emotion, wasn't it?

'Hullo, Molly.'

So, there was definitely no identical twin, then.

'Hullo, Mr Ashcroft…'

Even a tiny shake of his head released droplets of sea water from his hair. Hair that was very neatly cut but was so wet and full of salt, it was spiky, so even his hairstyle was utterly different.

'Call me Hugh, for heaven's sake,' he said. 'There's no need to be so formal, at work *or* away from it.'

He was staring at her, but this was very different from how it had felt when he'd given her a look of this intensity at work, when he'd demanded to know who the hell she was. He wasn't wearing his surgical scrubs, he was encased in skintight neoprene that was almost as sexy as seeing him wearing nothing at all. And he was dripping wet.

Okay…maybe it did feel pretty much the same. Because Molly could feel that curl of sensation unfolding in her gut, not unlike one of the large waves still breaking offshore, and, this time, she knew it had nothing to do with being nervous.

It didn't have anything to do with her confusion, either, although the burning question of which person was the *real* Hugh Ashcroft wasn't about to go away.

No. This was something else entirely. Something even more powerful than that curiosity.

It had everything to do with…attraction.

Sexual attraction…

Dear Lord…she had the hots for someone she was going to be working with? Someone who had made no secret of his disapproval of her taking her dog into sacrosanct areas of the hospital. Who'd even looked vaguely disgusted when he'd caught her shedding a tear?

'Fine…' Molly was pleased to manage to sound so offhand. 'Hugh it is.'

She reached down to pick up the frisbee and flicked it towards the sea. Oreo bounced through the shallow water to catch it before it hit the waves.

'I've forgotten your dog's name,' Hugh said.

He was moving again, towards where a towel had been left on the sand, neatly rolled up.

'Oreo.'

'Like the cookie? Of course…he's black and white. Great name.'

'*She*… Oreo's a girl.'

The correction sounded like a reprimand but Hugh ignored it. He wasn't really interested in her dog, was he? Or her? And that was just as well. It meant that Molly could dismiss that moment of inappropriate attraction and make sure it didn't happen again.

Oreo was back with the frisbee. Molly held out her hand but Oreo dropped it right beside Hugh's bare foot. He bent down but didn't pick up the toy. Instead, he picked up the towel and started walking again, towards the car parking area that also had a facility block.

'I'd better get a shower before I get too cold,' he said. The glance over his shoulder felt like a question.

'I'm heading that way myself.' She nodded. Oreo picked up the frisbee and followed them.

'I can only see my car,' Hugh said, a few steps later. 'Where did you park?'

'I live here,' Molly told him. 'See that little white cottage with the red roof and the big chimney up on the road?'

'You live right by the beach? Lucky you…'

'It's not exactly my house. It's the family bach. I grew up on a farm and this was where we came for holidays.'

'You still count as a local, then. I've always wondered how it got its name. Someone told me that there was a shipwreck here and that was the mistake.'

Molly laughed. 'I think getting the ship stuck on the beach was the second mistake that Captain Taylor made. The first one was thinking he was going into the harbour in Lyttleton, I believe. It was back in the early settler days of the eighteen-fifties.'

Good grief…did she think Hugh might want a history lesson? Molly didn't dare look at him. She glanced sideways at the waves, instead.

'My older brother, Jack, got into surfing when he was just a kid and was going to competitions by the time he was a teenager.' She bit her lip. 'Don't think he's as good as you are, though.'

The sudden silence made her look back to find Hugh blinking as if he was startled by the compliment but then he turned to look at the waves again himself. 'Did you surf, too?'

'No. It's always been about animals for me. I rode horses and did dog trials—you know? Rounding up sheep and getting them into a pen?'

Oreo was walking beside them, clearly resigned to the fact that the frisbee game was over for the day. Curiously, she was walking beside Hugh rather than Molly.

'I think you've got an admirer.'

'Excuse me?'

Oh, help…did he think she meant herself, after she'd told him how good he was at surfing? She tilted her head and he glanced down to follow her line of sight. Oreo looked up at him and waved her tail.

It was Hugh who broke a still awkward silence.

'Vivien sent me those articles,' he said. 'I had time to browse one of them when I went back to the ward to talk to Chloe's mother this afternoon.'

'Oh…?'

'I didn't realise quite how extensive the range of therapies is that animals can be involved with. Like physiotherapy.'

Molly nodded. The turnoff for the track up to her house wasn't far ahead of them but she didn't want this conversation to end quite yet. Not when she could talk about something that might make a real difference to how enjoyable her new job was going to be.

'I love working with physios. It's amazing how reaching out to pat a dog or taking one for a walk, even if it's just to the door of their room and back, can get them past the pain barrier of starting to move again after surgery. Oreo's good at pretending to take medicine with kids, too. She'll drink liquid from a syringe or take a "pill" that's actually one of her treats. And it's not just beneficial to the patients. Most staff members love having a dog around and the parents and siblings of patients can get a lot of comfort out of it...' Molly sucked in a breath. She had too much she wanted to say and not enough time. 'What could be better for anyone who's having a tough time than to be able to cuddle a dog?'

'I wouldn't know.'

But Hugh's response sounded merely polite. He was looking past Molly, towards the house she'd pointed out as being where she lived. She knew he would be able to see the track leading away from the beach and, if she kept walking with him, it would be obvious that she was doing it for a reason and not simply because they were going in the same direction. Heaven forbid that it might occur to him that she'd had even a moment of being interested in him as anything other than a colleague.

'See you tomorrow, Hugh.' Molly turned away. A glance was all it took for Oreo to follow her.

'Have a good evening, Molly.'

Hugh's farewell was an echo of what she'd said to him—good heavens, was it only yesterday? Just before she told him that he might like to loosen his straitjacket. In retrospect, after seeing the way he'd moved his body in response to the force of the waves, it had been an astonishingly unfounded accusation to make. Worse, remembering what it was like watching him reminded Molly of her physical reaction to having him standing in front of her, dripping wet, in that skin-tight wetsuit. She was actually feeling that twist of sensation in her gut all over again.

And that was disturbing enough for Molly to avoid looking back at him at all costs as she walked away.

Oreo looked back, though. And when she looked up at Molly again, it felt like her dog was asking the same question that was filling her own head.

'I don't know,' she heard herself saying aloud. 'We'll just have to wait and see, won't we?'

The meeting room was full of people.

There were representatives from the paediatric oncology, radiology and surgical departments. The head of physiotherapy was here, the ward manager, Lizzie, a senior pharmacist, a senior nurse specialist and the nurse practitioner, Molly, and a child psychologist and family counsellor.

Oh, yeah…and one dog. It must be one of Molly's days off. She had probably been intending to bring Oreo into the hospital anyway but, oddly, it felt quite appropriate that the dog and her owner who'd been there at the beginning of this case were also present at such an important family meeting. Oreo was lying very still, her nose on her paws, on the floor beside Molly's foot.

It was very quiet.

Quiet enough to hear Sophie Jacobs' mother, Joanne, pull in a shaky breath, as if she was trying to control the urge to cry. Her husband, Simon, was staring at the ceiling and it was possible to see the muscles in his jaw working to keep it clenched. He was also trying not to cry in public, wasn't he? Sophie's grandmother had also been included in this meeting to discuss the diagnosis, ongoing treatment and prognosis for their precious seven-year-old girl and she had a wadded tissue pressed beneath one eye.

Hugh glanced at the paediatric oncology consultant who, along with the paediatrician who had been the admitting physician, had delivered the results of all the tests they had done and confirmed the devastating news that Sophie did, indeed, have a malignant osteosarcoma. He'd provided details of the staging process and prognosis that had, no doubt, been too much to understand at this point and would need to be talked about again, probably more than once.

The oncologist had also explained her role to care for Sophie as she received an intensive period of neoadjuvant or pre-operative chemotherapy before the surgery to remove the tumour.

The pharmacist had finished an outline of the kind of drugs that would be used for the chemotherapy and answered questions about how side effects such as nausea and hair loss might be managed. The family had been warned early on in the investigations that if the tumour was malignant then amputation, rather than any limb-saving surgery, would very likely be necessary.

The oncologist met Hugh's glance and gave a discreet nod. It was the right time for him to say something about the upcoming surgery for Sophie.

There was a screen at this end of the room and Hugh tapped the mouse pad on his laptop to bring up an image.

'This was the very first X-ray we took of Sophie's leg,' he said quietly. 'And it was immediately obvious that she had something significant going on at the distal end of her femur—almost directly on top of the knee joint. We have a lot more information now, thanks to the biopsy, MRI, the PET and CT scans and all the other tests that Sophie has very bravely put up with over the last week or two.'

Joanne blew her nose. 'Thanks to Oreo,' she said. She smiled across the table at Molly. 'I don't know how we could have coped without you.'

'It's been our pleasure,' Molly said. 'I'm going to take Oreo to visit her again in a few minutes, to let you have more time to talk to everybody today. I just wanted you to know that we consider ourselves to be part of this team and we'll be here whenever I have my days off.'

Sophie's father simply nodded brusquely.

'The good news—even though it might not seem like that at the moment—is that this is a primary osteosarcoma and not evidence of metastatic disease from somewhere else. Even better, the PET scan, amongst the other tests, has shown us that the clinical stage is early and the tumour is still intracompartmental, which means that it hasn't extended as far as the periosteum, which is the membrane of blood vessels and nerves that wraps around the bone.' Hugh was putting up images from the scans now. 'The lymph nodes are clear and there's no sign of any hot spots at all in the lungs or any other bones, which are the most likely targets for metastases. This is all really good news because it gives us confidence that the cancer hasn't spread. At all...'

Hugh paused for a moment to let that positive statement sink in. He saw the glances exchanged between Sophie's parents and, if he let himself, he knew he would be able to feel the beat of hope in the room. Not that he was going to indulge in sharing anything close to joy when he still had the hardest part of this meeting to get through.

'We still need to treat this cancer aggressively

enough to try and ensure we get rid of it completely and it can't recur—or spread—and that
means that the surgery Sophie is going to need
will be amputation. The procedure that we will
be recommending is the one I mentioned to you
as a possibility the other day—the rotationplasty
salvage procedure.'

'*No...*' Joanne pressed her hand to her mouth
to stifle a distressed cry and her husband put his
arms around her.

Hugh clicked onto a new image but as he
shifted his gaze he caught the way Molly had
dropped her hand to Oreo's head—as if she
needed a bit of comfort herself? He could understand that the concept was confronting but it
was, without doubt, the best option for Sophie.

'As I explained, what happens is that the bottom
of the femur—where the tumour is located—the
whole knee joint and the upper tibia are surgi-
cally removed, with the cancer and a wide clear
margin around it also removed. The lower leg is
then rotated one hundred and eighty degrees and
attached to the femur.'

Hugh could see that Joanne Jacobs still hadn't
glanced up at the image on the screen of a young
boy who'd had this procedure. With no prosthesis
on, he had the unusual appearance on one leg of
a foot pointing backwards at knee level.

'Because the foot is on backwards, it can function as a knee joint,' he continued calmly. 'A special prosthesis is made that the foot fits into and it provides much greater mobility and stability than a full leg amputation would. It also lowers the risk of phantom leg pain.'

He put up a new image of the boy with the foot hidden inside his artificial lower leg and perhaps Sophie's father had murmured some encouragement to his wife because Joanne finally looked up as well. The next image was of the boy kicking a football—a wide grin on his face.

'The bone will continue to grow as you would expect in a young child and, of course, the prosthesis will be adjusted to fit.' Hugh closed his laptop. 'Younger children have another real advantage in that their brains learn more easily to use their ankle as a knee and adapt their walking patterns.'

The physiotherapist at the meeting was nodding. 'I can answer any questions when you're ready to talk about it,' she said.

Joanne shook her head. She wasn't ready. She folded herself further into her husband's arms and it was obvious she was sobbing silently by the way her shoulders were shaking.

There was no point in trying to reassure these distressed parents any further at this time. Hugh caught the counsellor's gaze with a raised eyebrow and the silent communication suggested that she would stay here a little longer but, yes, it would be better for everyone else to leave and give this couple some private time to deal with their initial reactions. Others had seen the silent message and, as a group, they were beginning to leave the room.

Hugh picked up his laptop as he saw Molly and Oreo leaving. He wanted to catch a moment of the oncology consultant's time for a chat about the chemotherapy regime that would be started for Sophie, hopefully today. He had cleared a good space of time this afternoon so he would check back to see if Sophie's parents wanted to talk to him about anything, but he suspected he might be the last person they'd want to see again today.

When he walked back past the meeting room, Joanne and Simon were nowhere to be seen and the psychologist was shutting the door behind her.

'I suggested they went for a walk outside and got some fresh air before they went to see Sophie so that she wouldn't see how upset they were,' she told Hugh. 'But we've made a plan to discuss how and when to talk to her about the amputation. I'm going to see if I can set up a meeting with the parents of that boy in your photos. I know they'll be happy to offer their support and it could be a game-changer for everybody. He's a few years older than Sophie now but maybe he'd be up for coming in to visit and show her his leg?'

'Good idea.' But Hugh's response was brisk. Everyone involved on the team assigned to this case had different roles and thank goodness there were people who were more than willing to immerse themselves in the social, psychological and emotional side of a life-changing diagnosis like the one Sophie Jacobs had just received. His job was to make sure he gave her the best chance of, not only survival by completely removing the tumour, but the best quality of life possible, going forward, by advocating for a procedure he knew was the best option. His role was all about the surgery and the most important part of his role would be inside an operating theatre with a patient who was sound asleep and any emotional family members completely out of sight—and mind.

Just being in the tense atmosphere of that family meeting had been enough for Hugh to be hanging out for a bit of private time for himself to prepare for the rest of his day. He didn't need a walk in any fresh air, though. The peace and quiet of his office with the door firmly closed would be quite good enough and the close proximity of that small, personal space was too tempting to resist.

Between the paediatric orthopaedic surgical

ward and the row of consultants' offices was a courtyard roof garden, opening off the foyer space that housed the stairway and bank of lifts. It wasn't huge but it provided the nice aesthetic of an open space with some lush greenery and seating. The concrete pavers were smooth enough to make it easy for IV poles to be pushed or beds to be rolled outside for a bit of sunshine.

As Hugh walked past the floor to ceiling windows to get to his office, he saw a wheelchair parked to one side of the central square of pavers. And then he saw that it was Sophie Jacobs who was sitting in that wheelchair. The wide door to the garden hadn't been completely closed so he could hear music that was being played outside. An old tune he remembered from high school discos back in the day—Abba's 'Dancing Queen'.

Sophie had a huge grin on her face and her arms were in the air as if she were dancing to the music, but she wasn't alone. Both Molly and Oreo were out there with her.

Hugh's steps slowed and then stopped. What on earth were they doing?

Skipping…that was what it was.

But it wasn't just Molly skipping. Oreo was holding up one front paw as she hopped and then the other. And then Molly made a hand signal and Oreo stood on her hind legs and went around in a circle.

Molly turned in a circle as well and Sophie clapped her hands.

Then Molly started moving in a diagonal line across the square, straight towards where Hugh was standing, but she didn't notice him. She was watching Oreo as she took long steps, her legs very slightly bent, which seemed to be a signal to the dog to go in figures of eight, her own gaze fixed on Molly's as she was weaving through the space between her legs from one side and then the other.

It was only when dog and owner paused a beat before they started skipping again in the opposite direction and he realised that it was in time to the music that Hugh remembered Molly telling her that Oreo loved to dance.

This was what she and her dog were doing, wasn't it?

Dancing...

And obviously loving doing it as much as Sophie was loving watching it.

It was kind of cute, Hugh conceded.

But it was also...

Mesmerising?

His feet were certainly glued to the floor. His gaze was glued to Molly. To the changing expressions on her face and her hand gestures that were a language all of their own and the lithe movements of her body as she bent and twisted, reached and curled.

It was…

Okay…it was damned sexy, *that* was what it actually was.

Hugh could feel his body waking up, as fixated as his gaze had been on this woman and what she was doing. He could feel tendrils of a sensation that was both physical and mental and, while he might not have felt it to quite this degree since he was an adolescent, he knew exactly what it was.

Attraction…

Desire…?

A want that was powerful enough to feel like a need.

And the shock of that recognition was more than enough to break the spell that Hugh Ashcroft had fallen under. He could move his feet again and that was exactly what he did to escape from the disturbing realisation that he was sexually attracted to the new nurse practitioner.

Not that it was a problem. Hugh was more than capable of both keeping his own feelings completely private and making sure that something professionally awkward simply wouldn't be allowed to reappear.

But he did need the privacy and time out of his own office for a few minutes even more now than he had a few minutes ago.

CHAPTER FOUR

'I CAN'T SEE this working.' The older woman watching what Molly was doing with a young patient and his mother was shaking her head. 'It's never going to stay properly clean, is it?'

'Don't be so negative, Mum. That's why I'm getting as much practice in as I can before we take Benji home this afternoon.'

'I know it's going to be a bit of a challenge at times,' Molly conceded. 'Especially in the first week or two.' She offered the anxious grand-mother a smile. 'I'm sure your help is going to be very much appreciated, Louise, but Susan is a very competent mother and I know she's going to cope brilliantly. Look at how well she's doing this nappy change.'

Susan's baby, Benji, was in an unwieldy plaster cast that wrapped around his chest and one arm to keep it completely still after the surgery he'd had to remove the false joint on his clavicle. He was also coping well with the nappy change, waving his unrestrained arm in the air, trying to grab his mother's necklace as she leaned over him.

'You're doing a great job,' Molly said. 'Tuck the edges of the first nappy right under the cast and then we'll put another one on top. We want to avoid the cast getting wet or dirty if at all possible. You may find it easier to use a smaller size than usual for the first nappy.'

'What do I do if it does get dirty or wet?'

'Use just a damp washcloth to clean it. If it's really damp, you can use a hairdryer on a cool setting to speed up the drying process or take Benji outside to get a bit of sunshine on it. Another good tip is to use a towel as a big bib when he's got food or a drink in his hands.'

'He must weigh twice as much with that cast on.' Louise sighed.

'He'll certainly be top heavy and won't be able to sit up by himself,' Molly agreed. 'He'll need to be propped up with pillows and cushions and don't let him try and walk by himself. The last thing you want is a fall, so he'll need to be carried everywhere.'

Louise made a tutting sound. 'You're going to have to be careful when you pick him up, Susie. You'll be in trouble if you put your back out again.' She turned to Molly. 'How long is he going to be in this cast?'

Molly opened her mouth to answer but stopped

as she saw Benji's surgeon coming through the door of the room. Hugh Ashcroft was wearing scrubs and still had a mask dangling by its strings around his neck. Had he left his registrar to finish up in Theatre after the actual surgery was completed and ducked down to the ward for some urgent task?

Hugh acknowledged Molly with a brisk nod but his gaze went straight to Susan.

'Benji's discharge papers are signed,' he told her. 'I've reviewed the X-ray he had taken yesterday and I'm happy that he doesn't need to stay in any longer. The clavicle is exactly where it needs to be and it should heal very fast.' He shifted his gaze to Benji's grandmother. 'In answer to your question, this cast will need to stay on for five to six weeks. We'll see Benji well before then, however, and monitor his progress in our outpatient clinic.' He was turning to leave. 'You'll find a phone number on the discharge information to call if there are any problems, so please get in touch with the team if you have anything you're worried about.'

'Thank you ever so much for everything you've done, Mr Ashcroft,' Susan said.

'Ashcroft...' Louise was staring. 'You're not Claire Ashcroft's boy, are you?'

'Ah...' Hugh had taken a step towards the door. 'Claire was my mother's name, yes...'

'You probably don't remember me. I used to work for the same house cleaning company as your mother. Spick and Span? Goodness, it must be more than twenty-five years ago. Susie here was still in kindergarten when I had that job but you would have been at primary school.'

'Ah…'

The sound from Hugh was strangled. The sudden flick of a glance in Molly's direction gave her the impression that Hugh was taken aback enough to be having difficulty deciding how to react. He looked as if he was merely going to acknowledge the information and escape but Louise kept talking.

'We only worked together until your poor sister got so sick, of course. We all understood why she had to give it up and go on a benefit to look after her.' She was making that tutting sound again. 'Such a tragedy…she never got over it, did she? Your mum? And it was so hard on you when you were just a little boy yourself…'

Molly was watching Hugh's face as Louise prattled on but when she saw his head beginning to turn as if he wanted to know if she *was* watching him, she hurriedly looked away.

'Let me help you get Benji's clothes back on, Susan,' she said, a little more loudly and firmly than she would usually. 'Or maybe your mum would like to help.'

She was hoping that Susan's mother would take the hint and stop talking. Because Molly had seen the horror washing over Hugh's face and the rigid body language that was like a forcefield being erected and it was patently obvious that this was a subject that was not only private, but it was capable of causing anguish.

Molly could actually feel that pain herself, her heart was squeezing so hard. Something else was gaining strength rapidly as well—the urge to try and protect Hugh Ashcroft.

'Louise?' This time her tone was a command. 'Could you help us with Benji, please?'

'Oh…yes, of course…' Louise looked towards Molly, then swung her head back to the door but Hugh had vanished. Louise shrugged. 'It *was* a long time ago,' she muttered. 'Maybe he doesn't want to talk about it.'

Molly's smile was tight enough to advertise that she didn't want to talk about it, either, but Louise didn't seem to notice.

'Dear wee thing, his sister, Michelle. So pretty, with her golden hair that hung in real ringlets. Until it all fell out from the chemo, of course,' she added sadly.

Molly's response was a request. 'Could you get the hoodie jacket with the zip that matches these dinosaur pants, please, Louise? That will keep Benji nice and warm and it'll be easy to get on and off.'

Benji started crying as his mobile arm got lost inside the larger size tee shirt that had been purchased to fit over the cast.

'Got cancer, she did,' Louise continued as she went to the pile of clothing in the cot. 'When she was only about three, poor kid. Can't remember what sort it was but she was in and out of hospital for years and years and then she died. Never really saw Claire after that.'

She handed the jacket top to Molly, who was showing Susan how to position her hands to lift her top-heavy baby, who was now crying loudly. Susan looked as if she might start crying herself.

'She died not that long after. There were rumours that she'd taken some kind of overdose but I reckon it was down to her heart being broken so badly.' Louise must have realised that nobody was listening and gave up. 'Rightio…let Nana help you get your jacket on, Benji. We need to get you back home, don't we?'

Molly helped with getting the baby dressed and then left the women to pack the rest of their belongings to be ready for Benji's father, who was coming to collect them.

It wasn't that she hadn't been listening to Louise. Molly was professional enough to hate gossip but she couldn't deny that she had been listening avidly to every word. It explained so much, didn't it?

That aloofness.

The way he could be a completely different person when he thought he was totally alone and doing something, like surfing, that provided such an effective escape from the real world.

She could forgive the control he kept over himself. She could understand the distance he preferred to keep from others. How could he not have learned to protect himself from getting too involved?

Molly was still thinking about what she'd heard as she went to the next patient needing her attention. Thinking about the little boy that Hugh Ashcroft had been. A child who'd had to live with a terrible tragedy? It was the kind of story that would touch anyone's heart, but Molly Holmes had always been a particularly soft touch for a sad story.

And this one had already captured her heart completely.

Hugh stayed well away from the ward for the next few hours. Until he could be completely sure that Benji's grandmother would be nowhere on the grounds of Christchurch Children's Hospital.

It helped that, after a morning of scheduled surgeries, Hugh had a fully booked outpatient clinic for the afternoon. There was no time at all to dwell on the unpleasant pull into the past that Hugh had experienced in his visit to Benji's room and plenty of cases that were complex enough to need his full focus. Concentration that worked a treat until the last patient to be ushered into the consulting room for today's clinic.

Fourteen-year-old Michael had been a patient under Hugh's care for some years now.

'You've had a bit of a growth spurt, haven't you, Mike?'

'Just over eight centimetres,' his father said proudly. 'He's going to end up taller than me at this rate.'

'It's making his scoliosis worse, though, isn't it?' Michael's mother looked pale and worried. 'Is that why he's getting so short of breath lately?'

'It is,' Hugh agreed. 'Lung function is compromised because the diaphragm and chest wall muscles can't move the way they should. Is getting short of breath interfering with what you want to do, Michael?'

The teenager nodded. 'I can't go to the gym… I can't hang out with my mates at the skate park… It's hard to even walk…'

Listening to him speak made it very clear how far his lung function had deteriorated since Hugh had last seen him.

'His brace is hurting him, too,' his mother added.

'I'm not surprised,' Hugh murmured. He clicked his keyboard to bring up scan images taken only days ago. The screen showed a spinal column distorted enough to resemble a letter S.

'See that?' Hugh talked directly to Michael. 'You've now got a sixty-five-degree curve on the top of your spine and nearly eighty degrees on the bottom. Surgery is recommended when the scoliosis is over fifty degrees and, with the effect it's having on your breathing, I think it's becoming urgent.'

Michael's nod was solemn. 'You said this might happen one day—that I'd need an operation. I'm ready for it. You have to put rods and screws in my back, don't you?'

'And maybe some bone grafts. It's called a spinal fusion and it will straighten your back enough to make it easy to breathe again. I think you'll find you can do a lot more at the gym—and on your skateboard—but you'll have to be patient while you recover properly, okay?'

'Sure…' Michael's eye contact was brief and his tone just a little off-key. 'How soon can I get it done?'

He was scared, Hugh realised, but he didn't want anyone to know—his friends, his family or even his surgeon. He was young enough to crave comfort but old enough to know that adults had to be able to look after themselves. Maybe he didn't want his mother to be any more upset than she already was.

For a moment that was even briefer than that eye contact, Hugh remembered what it had been like when he was fourteen.

Being that scared even though it was for different reasons.

And being unbearably lonely at the same time. *Dammit*...

This was because of Benji's grandmother. She'd known enough to invade his privacy and make it public that his younger sister had died from her cancer. That it had broken his mother irreparably. How much more did she know? And would she think it was so long ago it didn't matter if she shared it with others?

Like Molly Holmes...?

Hugh had the horrible feeling that Molly had seen more than he would want anybody to see but he'd been ambushed, hadn't he? He hadn't even known that he might need to be ready to protect himself from what had felt like a potentially lethal attack.

Hugh squashed the thought ruthlessly. This wasn't about him.

It was never about him. Not at work or away from it.

'Let's have a look at my schedule,' he said to Michael. 'It's a four-to-six-hour operation but you'll only need a few days in hospital. It'll be a bit longer before you can go back to school, though. When do the summer holidays start?'

'First week of December. But my exams will all be over in November.'

'Sounds like a plan,' Hugh said. 'It would be nice if you were back home and well into your recovery by Christmas, wouldn't it?'

Michael's mother was reaching for her husband's hand. 'That would be the best Christmas present we could get.'

It was nearly five o'clock by the time Hugh put his last folder of patient notes on the desk for the clinic administration staff to sort out.

Benji would have been discharged hours ago.

Molly would have finished her morning shift about the same time so there was no danger of being reminded of what he'd spent the whole afternoon trying to forget. It should be quite safe to go and check on his post-op patients from this morning. He needed to see the teenager who'd torn his anterior cruciate ligament playing a game of rugby and received a hamstring tendon autograft to repair it. He was a day-surgery patient and his registrars would have been monitoring him since he came out of Theatre but Hugh preferred to see all his patients himself before they were discharged.

'Have you had a chat to the physio?' he asked him. 'Did they check your brace and size the crutches for you?'

'They made me go up and down the stairs to make sure I know how to use them.'

'Good. And you've got an orthopaedic outpatient appointment set up?'

'Yes.'

'Excellent. You can go home.'

Hugh could go home, as well. He might even have time to get out to the beach and catch a wave or two before it got dark. Not at the beach where Molly lived, mind you. He wasn't planning to go back there any time soon.

Maybe it was because he was thinking about her that Hugh turned his head as he walked past the courtyard garden. She wasn't out there, of course, but it was all too easy to conjure up the memory of her dancing with her dog.

All too easy to feel a frisson of what he'd felt when he'd been watching her.

No. He certainly wasn't going to go back to that beach to surf again. He didn't want to meet Molly out of work hours again.

He wasn't too sure he wanted to meet her *during* work hours, in fact, so it was an unpleasant surprise to turn back from that glance into the garden to find her walking straight towards him.

As if he'd conjured *her* up along with that memory.

After this morning, he had more to worry about than a fleeting moment of attraction. She knew something about him that was personal. Something he didn't want to become common knowledge.

Hugh could feel his eyes narrowing. Because attack was the best form of defence, perhaps? 'What are you still doing here?' he demanded. 'I thought your shift finished a long time ago.'

'I stayed a bit longer,' Molly said. 'I was talking to Joanne Jacobs. Sophie's mother?'

'I know who she is.' Hugh was still watching her carefully but he couldn't see any sign that this was anything but a professional exchange. There was nothing to suggest she was interested in—or possibly had taken note of—anything personal about him at all.

'I'm just heading back to see her again. It was a pretty intense conversation. They're still struggling with the idea of the rotationplasty.'

Hugh's frown deepened. 'So I heard.'

'Well… I thought of something that might help—especially when they're talking to Sophie about it. I worked with a girl who had the procedure in Australia and she was a very keen dancer as well.'

'Oh...?'

It was there again, unbidden, in his head. A private video clip of Molly with her arms in the air, making a circle and then gracefully bending her body to bring the circle low enough for the dog to jump through.

'So... I went to print something out but then I wondered whether I should be getting this involved.' Molly was fishing in the pocket of her scrub tunic. 'Can I show you? I don't want to overstep boundaries or anything and she is your patient.'

Hugh blinked. Surely Molly had overheard what Benji's grandmother had said this morning? Was she just going to pretend it had never happened? That she wasn't aware of any personal information that was going to change their professional relationship?

Well...that was fine by him...

'What is it?' He had to admit he was curious.

Molly had rolled the sheet of photocopy paper so it didn't get creased. She unrolled it and Hugh's eyes widened.

It was an astonishing picture. A small girl—maybe eleven or twelve years old—was doing one of those ballet leaps that could make them look as if they were suspended in mid-air, with their arms and legs stretched out wide, if the photo was taken at precisely the right moment. The girl in this photo was looking straight at the camera as she jumped and she had a smile as wide as the reach of her arms, but what was truly remarkable was that one of her legs was a prosthesis.

Hugh could see in an instant, by the scarring high on her leg, that the girl had undergone the procedure of using the ankle as a new knee joint. The back-to-front foot was hidden inside the structure of the artificial leg and...there was a pale pink ballet shoe on the foot to match the one on the girl's normal leg.

'Her name's Amber,' Molly said. 'I don't feel like I'm invading her privacy because she—and her family—were so proud of this photo. Amber's the poster girl for the orthopaedic and prosthetic departments and this picture's on the website for the hospital I worked at in Australia.'

'So Sophie's family could find it themselves with an Internet search?'

'Yes...but Sophie's only seven and I thought she might like a real picture so that she could look at it whenever she wanted to.'

Hugh was having another one of those strange moments, like he'd had with Michael, when he'd been whisked back into the past to remember what it was like being a teenager. Now he was going even further back. To when his sister was so sick and she'd lost all her hair. She'd loved her ballet class, too, when she'd been well enough to attend. Would she have felt better if she'd seen a picture of a girl with no hair, doing a leap in the air like this, with the happiest smile in the world on her face?

His throat felt oddly tight. How good would *he* have felt as a big brother if he'd shown her that imaginary photograph and told her that it could be *her* doing that in the future? Michelle would have probably slept with the picture under her pillow and put it on the wall when she was in hospital, as she did with the one of Fudge—the family's chocolate brown Labrador.

Would Molly feel that good if it helped Sophie?

Hugh suspected she'd probably have to wipe a tear off her face—as he'd seen her do in that radiology room when Sophie had had her biopsy—except it might be a much happier tear this time.

He swallowed past the sudden lump in his own throat.

'I don't think you're overstepping any boundaries,' he said. 'Show it to Joanne first or perhaps the psychologist who's working with them.'

'Okay...thanks, Hugh.' Molly was rolling the paper up again.

'No...thank *you*...' he responded.

She caught his gaze, her eyes wide. 'What for?'

What for, indeed?

For going above and beyond any part of her job description—working overtime after an already long day without any financial reward for her efforts—to help the patients she was caring for on a very personal level?

For being the kind of person who would spend their days off doing the same thing by being a handler for a pet therapy programme?

Or was it deeper than that for Hugh? Was he thanking her for respecting his privacy? For making it clear she wasn't about to display curiosity, let alone try to get more information about his past?

Maybe it went even deeper than *that*.

Perhaps what Hugh was really thanking Molly for was making him feel that she was someone who could be trusted on a personal level, because people like that were few and far between in his life.

Pretty much non-existent, in fact.

And that made Molly Holmes rather special.

Not that he was about to tell her any of that. What he did do, however, was smile at her. A smile that felt like it was coming from somewhere he hadn't been in…what felt like for ever.

From right inside his heart?

'For doing something that might make a real difference,' was all he said. 'Good job, Molly.'

CHAPTER FIVE

THE OUTPATIENT CLINIC had finished long ago.

Almost all the department's ancillary staff members—the receptionists, technicians and nurses—had already left for the day. Hugh's registrars were up on the ward doing a final ward round and sorting any clinical issues.

Julie, the charge nurse manager, poked her head around the door of the consulting room Hugh had stayed in to snatch a few extra minutes of peace and quiet.

'Haven't you got a home to go to, Hugh?'

'I've got my last case notes to update. On Benji?'

'Oh, yes…isn't he doing well? He's crawling properly now instead of scooting along on his bottom to avoid putting any weight on the other shoulder.'

'Definitely a success story.'

'I didn't envy his mum having to look after him in that cast for so long, though I guess it's not as bad as a spica cast for hip dysplasia.'

'That's certainly harder to keep clean.' But Hugh turned back to the computer on his desk to indicate that he wanted to get on with making notes about how well Benji's clavicle had healed, not discuss how well his family had coped with the recovery period.

Julie took the hint and left but Hugh was aware of a remnant of thought about that patient interview that had nothing to do with anything clinical. Thankfully, Benji's grandmother hadn't come to this last appointment with her daughter but that hadn't stopped Hugh from remembering that encounter the day the toddler had been discharged after his operation.

And, as usual, that made him think about Molly Holmes.

He saw her all the time when she was working in his ward, mind you. He'd seen her quite often in the hospital on her days off when she brought her dog in for pet therapy sessions. He'd even seen her in the theatre suite once when she'd been with a child who was having a general anaesthetic induced and he had no problem with that. Hugh was more than happy that they were both far more comfortable around each other now than they had been when they'd first met but…

…but it was always just a bit disturbing when she entered his mind when she was not physically present in his environment.

When something reminded him that she had tapped into a space that nobody was allowed to enter by making him believe he could trust her. If anything, that feeling had grown a lot stronger because, in all the intervening weeks, Molly had never said or done anything to suggest that she intended to cross boundaries. She hadn't even given him one of those 'knowing' looks that women seemed to be so good at delivering.

It was getting less disturbing, however. Possibly because it happened so often? It was only yesterday when he'd gone to the paediatric oncology ward to see how Sophie Jacobs' latest round of neoadjuvant chemotherapy was going that he'd had a double whammy of being reminded, in fact. Sophie had that piece of A4 paper stuck onto the wall above her bed. The one Molly had printed out with the ballet dancer doing the leap with her prosthesis.

That reminded Hugh not only of that conversation they'd had about the image of someone dancing but of Molly herself dancing, with that dog. But that was exactly what Hugh needed to think of to flick the 'off' switch. Preferably before he was reminded of an attraction he had managed to gain complete control of.

He channelled that control into his fingers as he typed into the digital patient records.

The surgical intervention of the resection

and excision of the clavicular pseudoarthrosis, in conjunction with bone grafting using autograft tissue from the iliac crest and then internal fixation, has resulted in a very satisfactory bone union. The cosmetic result is pleasing and the patient is rapidly gaining full function of his shoulder joint.

That summed up the consultation well, along with the radiologist's comments on the latest X-rays and notes from the physiotherapist. There was only one thing to add.

There are no indications that further follow up is needed at this point although a second surgery in the future to remove the plates may be an option if implant prominence or irritation occurs.

Hugh saved his notes, logged out of the access to medical records and closed down the desktop computer.

Closing the door of the consulting room behind him, Hugh was startled by a clattering noise coming from the reception area. Surely he hadn't taken so long it was time for the cleaners to come through the deserted department?

And then he heard something so unexpected he couldn't quite place it.

Someone coughing?

A *dog's* bark?

And, dammit…there was Molly Holmes in his head again.

He walked past the reception desk and into the waiting area and somehow he wasn't even surprised to see that she was here in a physical sense as well.

With her dog.

No…make that *two* dogs…

Milo wasn't too sure about this.

He barked again and then crouched to deliver a growl that sounded way more playful than ferocious.

Was there really something scary about the spokes on the wheelchair parked in the corner of the waiting room? Or maybe it was being in the hospital environment with all its strange smells and noises and too many people and things on wheels.

'It's okay, Milo.' Molly reached into the pouch that was attached to a belt around her waist and took out a tiny treat to give to the young dog. 'I know it looks scary but it's just a wheelchair. Look—Oreo's not bothered at all, is she?'

But when she looked up, Oreo had uncharacteristically deserted her post where she was sitting at the end of a row of chairs and was heading straight for the person emerging from the back of the department. Fortunately, Oreo didn't bounce at Hugh Ashcroft. She just stopped in front of him and waved her tail in a polite greeting. His expression, however, was reminiscent of when he'd walked into Sophie Jacobs' bone biopsy appointment and had seen her there with Oreo.

Was this going to undo the growing ease that seemed to have developed between herself and Hugh in the last weeks? An edging closer that could possibly develop into a real friendship?

Sometimes, recently, when Hugh had smiled at her in passing, and even more when he'd caught her gaze deliberately, Molly had had moments of dreaming that something more than friendship could evolve. The way he was looking at her right now, however, suggested that any thoughts in that direction were purely one-sided.

'I'm so sorry.' Molly grimaced. 'My friend Julie told me it would be fine to bring Milo in for some training when the department was empty and before the cleaners came in. I thought today's clinics finished more than an hour ago.'

'They did. I stayed late.' Hugh stepped around Oreo without acknowledging the greeting he was being given. 'You have *two* dogs?'

'This is Milo. He's my mother's dog but I'm going to adopt him, at least for a while. Her retriever, Bella, has just had another litter of pups and it'll be too much for Milo when they get mobile. She kept him from the last litter because she thought he could be a good candidate as a therapy dog and I think she's right. He just needs to get some more exposure to clinical spaces and I knew that Orthopaedic Outpatients would have plenty of wheelchairs and walkers and crutches to make things interesting.'

While she was talking, Milo had bravely taken a step towards the wheelchair and stretched his nose out to sniff the unfamiliar object. Then he cringed and jumped backwards. Molly bit her lip. And then she glanced at Hugh.

'Have you got another minute or two to spare?'

'Why?'

'I think the wheelchair might be less threatening if it had someone sitting in it.'

'You want *me* to sit in the wheelchair?'

'You're a stranger. It would make it more realistic. I can go out and come in again and if you encouraged Milo, he might come and say hullo and realise the chair isn't going to bite him. He's very friendly and it'll only take a minute.' She gave Hugh her best smile. *'Please...?'*

She saw the hesitation but she shamelessly held his gaze because instinct told her that this was an opportunity to add something much more personal to their professional relationship and that was the only way this could turn into any kind of a real friendship.

Hugh shrugged. 'Why not? I owe you a favour.'

'Why?'

'Sophie Jacobs' parents signed the consent forms for the rotationplasty today. She's going to have the moulds of her foot made in the next few days and we can schedule her surgery after she's recovered from this round of chemo.'

'Oh…' Molly forgot about Milo's training for the moment, catching her bottom lip between her teeth again. 'That's *such* good news. And she'll be back in the orthopaedic ward for a while. I'll have to bring Oreo in to visit again.'

'It is good news. Having a visit from a lad who had the procedure a few years ago helped the decision making but it was that picture of yours that started the ball rolling in the right direction. Did you know that Sophie said "I want to be just like her" as soon as she saw it?'

Molly nodded. 'I was there. I knew that Joanne and Simon wanted to get her through the initial chemo before making a final decision, but I had a feeling they just needed the time to get used to what Sophie's leg was going to look like.'

Hugh was walking towards the wheelchair. Molly patted her leg and Milo obediently followed her into the side corridor without pulling on his lead. Oreo's gaze was on Hugh.

'Oreo, *down*,' Molly commanded. *'Stay.'*

With an audible thump, Oreo dropped to the floor and put her nose on her paws. Hugh sat in the wheelchair. When Molly walked back in she casually approached Hugh and he clicked his fingers at Milo.

'Hullo,' he said. 'Who's a good boy?'

Milo went straight towards him, his whole body wiggling with happiness at being noticed. Molly reached for a treat but Milo didn't notice because he was poking his nose around the wheel, trying to reach Hugh's hand for a pat.

She expected Hugh to pull back but, to her amazement, he was smiling at Milo, who nudged his hand so that it was automatic to fondle the dog's head and ears and then his neck.

'It's not so scary, is it?' Hugh looked up at Molly. 'Want me to roll around?'

'If you've got time, that would be fabulous.'

Milo leapt back as the wheelchair moved and Molly just let him watch. Oreo got up as the wheelchair went past her and started walking beside Hugh but Molly didn't tell her to stay again. It felt like she was showing Milo how it was done and, when Molly gave Milo some more length on the long lead, the young dog went straight towards them and walked behind Oreo.

They both got treats a few minutes later.

'Thank you so much,' Molly said to Hugh. 'I couldn't have done that by myself.' She smiled at him. 'I won't make you hop around on crutches or use a walker.'

Hugh made a huffing sound that was almost

laughter. 'I think I'd prefer to put off giving a walker a trial run.' He got up out of the wheelchair. 'I do happen to know when orthopaedic gear like this goes when it's out of date or deemed not worth repairing. Would it be helpful if you had some rusty crutches or an ancient wheelchair at home for training purposes?'

Molly nodded enthusiastically. 'That would be awesome. Let me know if there's anything available and I can pick it up. I've got a van.'

Oreo was following Hugh towards the doors that led from the outpatient department into the main corridor that joined the front foyer of the hospital.

'She really likes you,' Molly said. 'Sorry... I realise it's probably a one-sided attraction.'

Oh, *help*...had she really said that aloud? It sounded as if she was talking about herself and Hugh.

But Hugh didn't seem horrified. 'I don't dislike dogs,' he said. 'I grew up with one.' He paused and gave Oreo a pat. 'Fudge, his name was. He was a rather overweight chocolate Labrador. He lived to be fourteen, which was the same age I was at the time he died.'

'*Oh*...' Molly could feel her face scrunching into lines of sympathy. 'It must have been devastating to lose him. He'd been there for your whole life.'

Hugh was staring at her and Molly's heart sank. She'd crossed a line, here, hadn't she? Pushed herself into a personal space where she was definitely not welcome? Maybe this wasn't as bad as asking about his sister who'd died but it was pretty close. His dog would have been a huge part of his life. As important as another sibling, even…?

But Hugh's gaze dropped to Oreo again.

So did Molly's. She watched the gentle touch of his fingers as they traced Oreo's head and ear.

She could actually *feel* that touch herself and it was doing strange things to her body. No wonder Oreo's eyes were drifting shut in an expression of ecstasy.

'It was devastating enough to make me know I never wanted to do it again,' Hugh added quietly.

Molly swallowed. 'It's unbearably hard to lose dogs,' she agreed.

Hugh's hand lifted abruptly as though he'd just realised what he was doing. A look from Molly was enough to get Oreo to move back to her side and she clipped a lead onto the harness that was part of her service dog coat.

'But, for me,' she added, 'it would be even harder to live without them.'

The sound Hugh made was no more than a grunt. He was heading towards the doors again.

'I'll let you know if there's any unwanted mobility aids available.'

'Thank you. And thanks for your help. You don't owe me any more favours.' Molly wasn't sure if he could hear her as the doors swung shut behind him. 'You never did…'

He didn't owe her any more favours.

She'd told him she had a van and could collect any large items like an unwanted wheelchair. Maybe if it hadn't been a lightweight, easy-to-fold kind of wheelchair that still left space in the back of an SUV for a battered, old walking frame and some elbow crutches that had seen better days, Hugh wouldn't be driving out to Molly's house.

Except that it was something he wanted to do enough to overcome any doubts about whether or not it was something he *should* be doing.

It was a warm, late spring evening and, while it was too late to rope his surfboard to the roof rack and try to catch a wave, there was always a pull towards the beach and the sea for Hugh. Even filling his lungs with the smell of the ocean could be enough to tap into the freedom of being in the water—or, better yet, skimming the face of a wave that took him to a place where nothing else mattered.

Where there was nothing but the joy of utter freedom.

If Molly was on an afternoon shift she wouldn't be at home but that wasn't a problem. He knew which house was hers, having had it pointed out to him from the beach, and he would just leave the items on her doorstep. It might be better if that was the case, in fact, because one of the doubts Hugh had entertained—the *main* doubt—was that Molly might think he was coming on to her by turning up out of the blue.

Had that disturbing recognition of attraction not been completely quashed?

Was he coming on to her?

No. Hugh turned up the steep road that wound over the hill to Taylors Mistake beach. Of course he wasn't. The last thing he wanted was a relationship that would interfere with his life and he was confident that Molly probably felt the same way. Even if she was single, Molly had quite enough going on in her own life and, anyway— she wouldn't have the slightest interest in a man that she'd considered so uptight he might as well have been wearing a straitjacket.

So that made it feel safe.

And…it would be nice to have a friend.

Someone he could trust.

It was oddly disappointing when his knock on the door of the little white cottage with the red roof and the big chimney went unanswered but Hugh simply shrugged and went to unload the back of his vehicle. He could have a quick walk on the beach before he went home and that would make the journey more than worthwhile.

As he propped the elbow crutches inside the walking frame, however, he heard Molly's voice.

'*Yes…* Good girl, Oreo. Go… Go, go, *go…*'

It was a happy shout. There might have been some hand clapping going on as well and there was definitely an excited dog bark.

Hugh told himself he wasn't being nosy. It would simply be polite to let Molly know that he'd delivered the mobility aids, so he walked around the side of the house, stopping as he came to a long back garden that morphed into the marram grass covered sand dunes between the row of houses and the beach.

There was some kind of obstacle course laid out on the coarse grass of a beachside lawn.

Molly was still shouting.

'*Jump…* Good girl… And over the seesaw… *yes…*'

The jump was a tree branch of driftwood set on top of two wooden crates. The seesaw was a long plank of wood balanced on an empty forty-gallon drum that must have come from a farm. So had that tractor tyre that was suspended above the ground to make a hoop that Oreo had been jumping through as Hugh stopped to watch. Neither dog nor handler noticed him. Oreo raced up the thin plank of wood on the drum, stopped for a moment to let the wood tilt down on the other side and then she was off again. Over the jump from another direction, through a bending tunnel that was the only part of the course that didn't look homemade and then she was weaving through a set of poles in the ground.

Molly was as focussed as Oreo and clearly loving it just as much. She ran beside her dog, making a hand signal to encourage a jump, clapping to emphasise something good—even running with her head down herself as Oreo went flat to run through the tunnel.

She was wearing ancient denim shorts that looked like cut-off jeans judging by their frayed hems, and a tee shirt that was knotted on one side to make it fit close to her body. Her hair was loose—a wild mop of black curls—her face was pink from exertion and she was out of breath when she held out her arms to Oreo to jump into for a hug.

She was laughing as she put Oreo down and straightened, which was the moment she saw Hugh standing there.

And…it made Hugh suddenly feel as happy as he felt when he was riding a particularly good wave. As if he were flying.

As if there was nothing he needed to worry about in this moment.

As if he was free…

'Oh, my goodness… *Hugh*…?'

Oreo went straight towards Hugh and sat in front of him.

'Sorry to interrupt,' he said. 'I brought some old mobility gear for you, like the wheelchair you wanted. They're by your front door.'

'Oh, wow…thank you *so* much. That's fantastic.' Molly was pushing curls damp with perspiration back from her face. That wild hair was framing a face that clearly didn't have a scrap of makeup on it and…

…and…she looked absolutely gorgeous.

Stunning, even…

Oreo barked at Hugh as if she were trying to cut his train of thought and he was grateful enough to smile at the dog and reach down to pat her head.

'She wants to play,' Molly told him. 'She wants you to do her agility course with her.'

Hugh shook his head. 'I wouldn't know how.'

'She'll show you.' Molly was grinning at him. 'You'll love it, I promise. It's more fun than surfing.'

'Impossible.'

'You won't know until you try. Go on… I *dare* you…'

A tumble of thoughts raced through Hugh's mind. That Molly was encouraging him the way she had been urging Oreo on? That if he ever wanted a chance to prove he wasn't as uptight as Molly thought he was, this might be the best opportunity ever. That this was the kind of light-hearted stuff that friends could enjoy doing together and…

…and that smile was simply irresistible.

'Fine.' Hugh loosened his tie and pulled it off. He rolled up the sleeves of his shirt. 'Come on, Oreo.'

Molly called directions. 'Over the jump. Follow Oreo to the A frame… Now get ahead of her, point to the jump and then head for the seesaw…'

It was only Hugh who needed the directions. Oreo knew the course by heart and was so happy to be showing off to Hugh that she kept barking, even as she disappeared into the tunnel and then weaved at incredible speed back and forth through the poles.

Hugh was laughing himself by the time he got back to Molly, despite being completely out of breath.

'Hold out your arms,' Molly commanded. 'It's not finished until Oreo gets her cuddle.'

Without thinking, Hugh held out his arms and suddenly they were full of the warmth and hairiness of a large dog. He was getting licked on his neck and…this was another kind of happy, wasn't it? He hadn't been this close to a dog since he'd hugged Fudge before he went to school.

The day he'd come home to find he wasn't lying there at the gate with his ball safely between his paws, waiting for their game. And he never would be again…

Hugh crouched to let Oreo slip from his arms to the ground. Molly's smile was still doing something unusual to his brain. For the first time ever, he was thinking of Fudge and remembering the joy of being with him was overriding the sadness of losing him.

'Well…that *was* fun,' he admitted. 'But it doesn't beat surfing.'

'I can't believe you actually did that.' Molly was biting her lip as if she was trying not to grin too widely. 'I was so wrong about you…'

Her smile had faded and her gaze was fixed on his. He could see the way her bottom lip almost bounced free of her teeth and the appreciation in Molly's eyes made him want to turn back and do that obstacle course with Oreo all over again.

No…

What it *really* made him want to do was to kiss Molly.

For a long, long moment, Hugh couldn't breathe. It felt like he didn't need to because time had stopped. He couldn't look away from those golden-brown eyes, either. It was probably only for a heartbeat—maybe two, but it was long enough for something to force its way into his head.

A cloud that was dark enough to obliterate any sunshine.

Fear...?

He jerked his gaze away from Molly's. He pretended to look at his watch.

'Is that the time?' What a stupid thing to say. 'I have to go,' he added. 'I've got a lot of prep to start getting done tonight.'

'Oh...?'

Molly sounded slightly bewildered. When he sneaked a lightning-fast glance as he turned away, she wasn't looking at him.

'Yes. It's Sophie's surgery the day after tomorrow. We've got a full team meeting to plan the surgery in detail tomorrow and I want to be well prepared for that.'

'It must be a big deal. You're basically reattaching an amputation, aren't you?'

'Yes.' This was better. Professional conversation. And Hugh was on his way to escape.

'Do you have vascular surgeons involved? And neuro?' Molly asked.

'It's a huge team. And there's a lot of interest with it being an unusual procedure, so it's in the main theatre with the gallery.'

Hugh was feeling almost safe again as he got closer to his car. He was also feeling a bit embarrassed. How rude did Molly think he was, running off like this?

'Why don't you come and watch as well, if you're not working?' he suggested. 'It's a long surgery but not something you get to see every day.'

Molly's intake of breath was an excited gasp. '*Could* I? It *is* a day off for me.'

'You're part of the extended team involved in Sophie's care and I know that this surgery might not be happening if it hadn't been for you. I can make sure there's a front row seat saved for you.'

There…the movement of time and tide were completely back to normal.

If Molly had been aware of any inappropriate and/or unwanted notions that had entered Hugh's head when he'd been staring at her like some lust-struck teenager, she had forgotten all about it now.

She was biting her lip again and her eyes were shining. 'I can't wait.'

CHAPTER SIX

HE'D ALMOST KISSED HER.

Hugh Ashcroft had actually been thinking about *kissing* her.

Oh, *my*…

As she slipped into the seat on one end of the front row in the gallery above Theatre One, the only thing Molly would have expected to be thinking about was how exciting it was going to be watching some extraordinarily rare orthopaedic surgery.

'Scalpel, please.'

Hearing Hugh's voice through the speakers on either side of the enclosed gallery area should have been enough to focus absolutely on what she could see on the screens beside the speakers, which gave a close up, 'surgeon's eye' view of what was happening below them. Having an audience was clearly no distraction for Mr Ashcroft but, even through the glass, perhaps he was aware that everyone was holding their breath, waiting for the first incision. He had to know they would appreciate every bit of detail he was able to share.

'So our first incision is longitudinal below the groin and this gives us access for the dissection of the femoral artery and vein.'

Yeah…the ultimately professional, *impersonal* tone of his voice should have made Molly sit forward and focus on what she had come to see. But what she was, in fact, thinking about as that first incision was made was that the gowned and gloved surgeon standing beside the small, draped shape on the operating table had been so close to kissing her the day before yesterday that she could still feel her toes curling.

'I'm clamping the femoral artery to prevent bleeding during the surgery and now we'll extend the incision.'

Molly needed to clamp the direction her thoughts were going in. She focussed on the screen as vessels and nerves were slowly and painstakingly revealed and the specialist microvascular surgeon working with Hugh took over, giving a commentary on everything she was doing, such as the continuous dissection of the sciatic nerve behind the leg muscle. These important structures would be kept separated and completely intact while the middle section of the leg was removed.

This was a surgery that would take from six

to eight hours and there were long periods of intense and often silent work going on.

And Molly couldn't stop her gaze drifting from the close-up screen back to where Hugh had his head bent, looking into the actual operating field. He was completely covered with sterile fabric and a hat and mask and eyewear but, with his head bent like that, Molly could see a patch of skin at the back of his neck and she could feel a sensation deep in her belly as if something was melting.

She couldn't stop her thoughts drifting back to what could have ended up being a kiss.

Had she *wanted* Hugh to kiss her?

Judging by the sharp spear of sensation that obliterated the melting one, the answer to that question was resoundingly affirmative. The sexual attraction was real.

In retrospect, Molly was surprisingly disappointed that Hugh *hadn't* kissed her.

How ridiculous was that?

Even if she was ready to start looking for someone to fill the life partner-shaped gap in her life, Hugh Ashcroft would not be a contender.

Why not?

Molly ignored the little voice at the back of her mind and tuned back into what was happening on the screen. More incisions were being made and the surgical teams were discussing where to cut the bones of the upper and lower legs to leave sufficient margins to healthy tissue.

Minutes ticked on and turned into hours. People around Molly in the tiered seating, mostly wearing surgical scrubs themselves, came and went as they got paged or finished their breaks or needed to grab something to eat but Molly didn't move from her privileged spot in the front row. And, as fascinated as she was, her focus definitely faded at times.

Enough for that little voice to make another attempt.

Why not? You mean you don't believe that the right man might be just around the next corner in your life, like you keep telling yourself? Does Hugh not even make a shortlist?

No, Molly told herself.

Give me one good reason.

I can give you more than one. The first is that we work together and you know as well as I do that my last relationship was with Jonathon who I also worked with and that was the most spectacular disaster in my entire history of relationships that haven't worked out. I walked away from my job as well as that relationship. It felt like my life was completely broken.

Maybe that was because he didn't want Oreo as part of his life and that was just a cover for not wanting kids and then it turns out that he never wanted an exclusive relationship. You were just part of a harem...

Thanks for the reminder.

Molly shut the conversation down.

She didn't need reminding that she'd come home to her family and a place she loved in order to try and repair her life once and for all.

She didn't need reminding that her heart was too easy to capture.

Too easy to break.

Molly was actually scared of that happening again. What if it was the last straw and she could never put the pieces back together again?

That fear should be more than enough to silence any notion that she might want to be kissed by Hugh Ashcroft.

Besides, it was getting to the most fascinating part of this operation anyway.

'So...those are the wires in place to mark where the incisions will be made. They'll allow me to pass a suture around the exact level I want to cut the bone and we'll clamp that to the Gigli saw.' Hugh turned to his scrub nurse. 'I'll have a tonsil clamp, thanks, and then I'll be ready for the braided suture.'

Molly found she was holding her breath as she watched the absolute focus Hugh had on his task—so much so, she could sense it in every muscle of his body. She could watch his hands close up on the screen and was riveted by the precision and care he was taking to do everything perfectly and make clean cuts through both the femur and the tibia, protecting the surrounding tissue as much as possible.

And then came the most astonishing moment of this surgery as the middle section of the small leg, which contained the tumour, was lifted clear and then sent to the laboratory for examination. In the space on the table, the arteries, veins and nerves that had been so painstakingly detached from the section that contained the tumour still joined the top of the leg to the ankle and foot.

'Now comes the part that will determine the success of this surgery.' Hugh's serious tone of voice came quietly through the speakers. 'We'll rotate the foot and ankle one hundred and eighty degrees in the axial plane and then join the femur and tibia with a dynamic compression plate. I'll hand over to my microsurgery colleagues at that point to re-join the blood vessels and nerves.'

The microsurgery was fascinating to watch and Molly had no intention of leaving until everything was finished, but she found herself sneaking glances to where Hugh was assisting rather than leading this part of the surgery instead of watching only the screen where so many tiny stitches were being placed to join structures that were so small it was hard to see exactly what was happening.

It was no surprise that her attention span was getting harder to maintain. That her thoughts, along with her gaze, drifted back to Hugh yet again.

Reason number two for Hugh to not make any shortlist for a potential life partner popped into her head with startling clarity. It wasn't simply that they were colleagues that made him similar to her last spectacular error of judgement.

He didn't like dogs any more than Jonathon did.

Oh, yeah? You didn't think so when he and Oreo were having the time of their lives running around the agility course.

Molly couldn't argue with herself over that point.

Both dog and man had clearly been enjoying themselves and that had shown her another glimpse of a very different Hugh Ashcroft. Like seeing him at one with the ocean when he was surfing had done.

She was beginning to think that she might be seeing the *real* Hugh through cracks in the persona that the majority of people in his life were permitted to see.

And what about Fudge? A dog he'd lost in a vulnerable part of his adolescence and it had hit him hard enough he was never going to go there again. He didn't even want to connect with someone *else's* dog. Had Oreo sensed that? Was that why she'd been so polite—gentle, even—in her approach to Hugh? Sitting there like a canine rock when he probably didn't notice the way he was stroking her ears as he talked about Fudge?

Well…both man and dog had let go of the barriers stopping them connecting when they'd done the agility course together, hadn't they?

Had that been the reason Hugh had done something as unexpected as almost kissing her?

Oh…

There it was again…

That delicious flicker of attraction. A flame that was resisting any attempts to douse it. The sensible part of her head hadn't stopped trying, however.

I don't even know if he's single, it announced. He could be married for all I know—not everybody wears a ring. Maybe he's even got a few kids.

But the part of herself she was arguing with didn't even bother to respond. They both knew how unlikely that was. With the kind of hours Hugh worked and his dedication, it seemed far more likely that he was married only to his job. Watching him at work like this had been impressive and Molly could be absolutely certain that he hadn't been distracted for a moment by her presence in the gallery or any memory of what had—almost—happened between them.

Her interest in this surgery hadn't been exaggerated, had it?

Hugh hadn't expected Molly to stay and watch the entire operation but he'd been aware of her presence from the moment he'd entered this theatre and had seen her sitting on the end of the front row.

The awareness was far enough in the background of his consciousness to have no bearing on his focus. It was just there, like a faint hum that added something extra to his normal determination to do the best possible job that could be done. This was someone who had cared enough about this patient to have gone to the trouble of finding that picture of the girl dancing with her rotationplasty prosthesis. To happily give the time and effort that bringing her dog in to dance for Sophie had required.

This mattered to Molly.

She was still there when Hugh was checking the perfusion of the reattached foot, feeling for a palpable pulse and noting the acceptable skin colour, but she had gone when Hugh glanced up to the gallery after the final closure of the wound.

He stayed to supervise the final dressing where

they would be using soft, orthopaedic wool as a thick bandage under the plaster cast to prevent too much pressure on repaired vessels and nerves as they healed. He was still there in the recovery room a while later as Sophie regained consciousness enough for him to be able to check for the first indication that nerve function was still intact. It was a very satisfying moment when the drowsy, heavily medicated little girl managed a tiny movement in her ankle joint when asked.

Hugh went to meet her anxious parents, able to tell them that the surgery had gone as well as they could have hoped for.

'She'll be taken up to the intensive care unit soon and will stay there for twenty-four to forty-eight hours.'

'Can we go and see her?'

'Of course. I'll get a nurse to take you in. The ICU consultant who'll be in charge of her care while she's in the unit is in with her now.'

'Thank you *so* much, Mr Ashcroft. You must be exhausted after being in Theatre for so long today.'

'It's what I do,' Hugh said simply. 'And when it goes this well, it's the best job in the world.'

He had to admit he *was* exhausted after so many intense hours of concentration—on his feet, and under the glare of artificial light—and Hugh knew he should really take a break after he'd done a brief ward round of his inpatients. He would have his phone by his side at all times and he'd come back in an hour or two to check on Sophie again, but she was stable enough to make any complications unlikely and there was a huge team of specialists in intensive care and paediatric oncology who had already taken over the primary care for this little girl in the post-operative phase of her treatment.

Going home to his inner-city apartment for a break wasn't attractive. Hugh needed some fresh air and whatever real daylight was left for the day. He could have headed into the centre of the city to the huge park and had a walk but, as he drove out of the hospital car park, he found himself following the line of hills on the southern city border. Heading for the place that would restore his energy levels and alertness faster than anywhere else.

He could have turned to his left a short time later to get to the beach that was closest to work but it seemed a no-brainer to turn right. To get to a beach that was far less likely to be crowded by other people shedding any stress from their working day. A beach that was his favourite but that he hadn't been back to since that surprise meeting with Molly after he'd gone surfing. And, after his visit to her little white cottage, he hadn't expected to ever come here again. Because he was sensible enough to heed an alarm when it sounded. Especially when he knew exactly *why* it was sounding.

Not that Hugh had consciously given it any thought since then, but he was well aware that if he hadn't grappled control back from the brink of losing it, he would have ended up kissing Molly Holmes completely senseless.

Because a tiny part of him suspected that she might have wanted him to?

Not that it mattered right now. Because control had been regained and he was far too drained after a marathon surgery to be remotely interested in thinking about something that would be disturbing.

Surfing would have been the best option but that wasn't possible when Hugh needed to be within earshot of his phone in case he had a call regarding Sophie's condition, but just a barefoot walk on the sand and some deep breaths of sea air should do the trick. It wouldn't take long.

Had Molly felt the same way after her long day in the gallery?

Was that why he could see the black and white shape of her dog running in the shallows as he stepped onto the beach?

But where was Molly?

Oreo was barking now and, instead of scanning the beach to look for a woman holding a frisbee, Hugh looked in the opposite direction. Thanks to following Oreo's line of sight, he could see past the break of the first wave and…good grief…was that Molly swimming? Without a wetsuit? At this time of the year the water would still be icy.

She was on her way back to shore but it wasn't until she reached the shallows and a relieved Oreo that Hugh realised how much less than a figure covering wetsuit Molly was wearing. She was in a rather scant bikini that showed off every curve of her body.

Every rather delicious curve…

She came out of the water at a run, heading straight for a crumpled towel on the sand and, even at this distance, Hugh could see how cold she looked.

Oreo was shaking water out of her coat as Molly snatched up the towel.

'Hey…' Hugh was close enough to call a greeting. 'That was brave. You must be absolutely freezing.'

'*Hugh*…' Molly stopped rubbing at her hair and held the towel in front of her. There were goosebumps on the skin of her arms and he saw her suppress a shiver. 'What on earth are you doing here?'

'I needed a break and some fresh air.'

'I'll bet… I was drained enough from just watching what you've been doing all day.' Molly was clutching the towel in front of her body now.

Hiding…?

But she was grinning. 'If you really want to wake yourself up, go and have a dip in those waves. It's gorgeous.'

'I haven't got anything to swim in.'

Her eyes widened in mock shock. 'Are you telling me you don't wear any undies, Mr Ashcroft?'

Nobody ever talked to him like this. Probably because he looked—and behaved—like someone who couldn't take a joke or a bit of teasing? Hugh's lips twitched. Maybe being unexpectedly teased like this was almost as good as fresh air and sunlight for getting rid of accumulated tension. But old habits died hard, as they said.

'I'm not about to put my underwear on public display,' he said.

Uh-oh…that was the kind of thing someone who was uptight enough to be repressed and prudish might say, wasn't it?

'I haven't got a towel,' he added, realising that sounded just as lame the moment he uttered the words.

But Molly was still grinning. 'I'll share mine,' she offered. 'Go on…you know you want to.'

And, astonishingly, Hugh knew she was right. He *did* want to. He wanted to shake off the tension and stress of an extraordinarily intense day by doing something a bit crazy.

But he still shook his head. He could never be tempted enough to turn his back on the most important thing in his life. 'I can't leave my phone. I'm on call in case there are any complications with Sophie.'

'Are you expecting any?'

'No. She was looking great when I left Recovery. She could even move her ankle for me.'

'No *way*...' Molly's jaw dropped. 'That's amazing. I'm so happy to hear she's doing well. And hey... I can guard your phone and answer it if necessary. I can guarantee you won't need more than about sixty seconds in that surf to get the full recuperative benefits.'

The Hugh who'd never met Molly Holmes and her dogs would never have been so impulsive. He would have simply found another excuse not to do something as unconventional and potentially humiliating as running into the ocean in his underwear but...

...it appeared that Hugh wasn't quite the same man as he'd been a couple of months ago.

Because he handed his phone to Molly and stripped off his clothes. He didn't unbutton more than the second button of his shirt—he just yanked it over his head. Even Oreo seemed to be staring at him in disbelief but then she barked her approval and ran with him as he splashed through the shallow water until he could dive under a wave. And Molly was right, sixty seconds would have been more than enough to wash off every ounce of fatigue and pang of discomfort in overused muscles, but he stayed in twice as long, just to make sure.

If he'd stayed in any longer, he might have acclimatised to the chill water and been able to enjoy a swim, but Hugh was too conscious of needing to be near his phone so he came out of the water and got hit by the wind chill, even though it was only a mild sea breeze.

He reached for the towel Molly held out to him.

'No calls,' she told him. 'I was right, wasn't I? It was worth having a dip.'

'So worth it.' Hugh nodded.

'Better than surfing?' she suggested.

He shook his head. 'No…and I'll let you know later if it was really worth the hypothermia.'

Molly's towel was already damp so wasn't very effective in drying his skin, so Hugh was shivering uncontrollably before he'd rubbed more than half his body with the towel and Molly, who now had an oversized jumper on over her bikini, was biting her lip and looking—a little repentant?

Cute…

'You'd better come and stand under a hot shower for a minute,' she told him. 'Otherwise you'll never get properly warm again. Come on...' She didn't give him the chance to respond through his chattering teeth. Worse, she swooped on his pile of clothing and grabbed his shirt and trousers and then took off towards the sand dunes and the row of houses.

And she was still in possession of his phone!

Oreo looked torn for the space of two seconds and then took off after Molly.

There was nothing Hugh could do, other than pick up his shoes that had his socks stuffed inside them and go after them. By the time he went inside the cottage, Molly already had the shower running.

'Help yourself to shampoo or anything,' she invited. 'I'll get you a clean towel.'

The shower was over an old, clawfoot bath with just a curtain to stop the water splashing into the room. Hugh didn't peel off his sodden boxer shorts until he was safely behind the curtain, under the rain of water that felt hot enough to scald his chilled skin. He stayed under it for about as long as he'd been in the ocean and then reached to turn off the tap.

'Don't turn it off...' Molly was back in the bathroom. 'I need to jump in myself and the plumbing can be a bit temperamental. I'll put your towel by the basin, okay?'

'Thanks.' Hugh poked his head around the

edge of the curtain to see Molly about to drop
the towel near where she'd left his phone beside
a glass that held a toothbrush and tube of tooth-
paste.

Her toothbrush. Hugh could suddenly imagine Molly wearing nothing but a towel herself,
standing in front of that mirror to clean her teeth
last thing at night. And then two things hit him
like a ton of bricks.

Molly was still wearing nothing but those two
rather small scraps of fabric under that jumper.

And *he* was no more than a few inches away
from her and was wearing absolutely nothing at
all…

No…make that three things. Because now
Hugh was thinking of the gorgeous curves of
her body and the perfection of her smooth, olive
skin being marred by goosebumps. In retrospect,
he knew he'd been wondering what it would feel
like to run his fingers, oh, so lightly over those
goosebumps.

Would they reappear if he helped her peel that
woollen jumper off?

Oh…*help*…

In the same instant a wave of that attraction
that had almost made him kiss her—something
he'd thought had been dealt with and banished—
washed over him with even more of a shock than

plunging into the icy sea so recently, Hugh noticed that Molly was watching *him*.

In the mirror.

It still felt like direct eye contact when he met her gaze, though.

Until she turned to face him and the touch of their gazes became suddenly searing. She still had the towel in her hand and, instead of dropping it, she held it out so that he could take it before he stepped out from behind the curtain. He knotted it loosely around his waist the moment his feet hit the floor.

Because he needed to hide the reaction his body was having to that wash of attraction that had somehow morphed into a level of desire like nothing Hugh had ever experienced in his life.

Molly couldn't move.

She couldn't breathe.

The universe seemed to be holding its breath as well as she simply stood there, holding that gaze for moment after moment after moment…

Until Hugh took one step closer, slid his fingers into her salt-tangled curls to hold her head and leaned down to cover her lips with his own.

Of course he knew it was what she wanted. A whole silent conversation had just been held in that prolonged eye contact. Questions asked…

Permission given…

No…maybe Molly had actually begged a little for this to happen…

The shower was still running behind him, which made it sound as if they were standing in a heavy rain shower, and the small room was filled with the warmth and steam of it. It was filled even more with the astonishing power of what was overwhelming every one of Molly's senses.

Hugh…

The taste of him.

The pressure of his lips.

The sliding dance of his tongue as he deepened a kiss that had already woken up every cell in Molly's body.

She felt his hands beneath the hem of her jumper now, sliding up her skin towards her breasts. Her hands followed his so that she could pull this unwanted piece of clothing off. To clear away a bulky obstacle, hopefully before he changed his mind and vanished again.

Hugh's lips and tongue were on the skin of her neck and shoulder moments later.

'You taste like the sea…'

Molly shivered. Partly because of the shaft of desire taking over her body but also because she was still wearing a damp bikini and her skin was sticky with sea salt. Chilled enough for it to be making Hugh's lips and tongue feel like flames licking her skin.

'You're cold…' Hugh's towel was falling to the floor as he took her hand. 'Come…'

He helped her step over the edge of the bath into the rain of the hot water. He helped her peel off her bikini top and bottom. And then he kissed her again.

A fierce kiss…

A need like none she had ever experienced took over Molly's body—and mind. There was danger here but there was no turning back. The sound Hugh made as she pressed herself even closer to his body could have been one of frustration—as if he was about to make this stop because he, too, had recognised it wasn't safe?

'No…'

It wasn't really a word. More like a sound of desperate need as Molly ran her hands down Hugh's back until she found the iron-hard muscle of his buttocks and shaped them with her hands. Pulled them closer.

The sound Hugh made then was more like a sigh of defeat. Or submission?

His hands were gripping Molly's bottom now. Lifting her so that she could wrap her legs around him. Holding her so they could find their balance and rhythm and give in to the waves of desire that were building to a climax like no other.

It was over too soon.

But not quite soon enough because the hot

water that Molly's cottage had available was running out and the shower was already cooling down fast.

At least that interrupted what could have been an awkward moment as Molly's feet touched the enamelled surface of the bath. Even eye contact was avoided for a few seconds as she climbed out and Hugh turned the tap off, she handed him his towel and reached for another one on a towel rail.

When they did finally make eye contact again, Molly raised her eyebrows. She wanted to lighten what was threatening to become an atmosphere they might both find too much, too soon.

'Better than surfing?' The words came out as a husky kind of whisper.

Hugh had to clear his throat before he could speak.

'Maybe…' he said.

His smile and tone suggested that it was possible he might need to experience it again to be sure.

And Molly smiled back. She wasn't about to object.

Maybe it could have happened then. In a comfortable bed. If the sound from Hugh's phone hadn't changed everything.

'It can't be anything urgent.' He picked up his phone. 'It's only a text message.' He looked up from the screen a moment later. 'Sophie's properly awake,' he told Molly. 'She's just moved the toes on her reattached foot.'

The very personal ground they had been on was being blurred into something professional and it felt…uncomfortable? Molly was quite certain that the last thing Hugh would want to talk about now was sex.

'I'll let you get dressed,' she said quietly. 'You'll want to go in and see her.'

She let her gaze graze his as she slipped out of the bathroom to find her own clothes. Less than a split second of contact but it was enough to let her know that Hugh appreciated that she understood.

His work always came first.

CHAPTER SEVEN

MAYBE SHE'D IMAGINED that unbelievable encounter in her bathroom.

She'd certainly *re*imagined it, more than once, during the somewhat sleepless night she'd just had.

But the version of Hugh Ashcroft that Molly encountered when she took Oreo into the children's hospital the next afternoon bore no resemblance at all to the man with whom she'd had the sexiest, most passionate encounter of her life less than twenty-four hours earlier.

He was back to being the version of the distant and disapproving surgeon she'd first encountered in that radiology procedure room.

Did he regret what had happened between them?

He certainly hadn't appeared to feel like that when he'd paused long enough to place a lingering kiss on her lips before he'd left the cottage.

Was he concerned that the information might be welcomed into the gossip mill with even more fascination than what Molly already knew about his private life?

No…surely Hugh knew that any trust in her was not misplaced?

Molly was the one who should be concerned. She'd allowed this gorgeous but complicated man to capture her heart and now she'd allowed him close enough to capture her body. They had to be the most significant building blocks to falling head over heels in love with someone and Molly wasn't at all sure she was at a point where she could halt that process if—or *when*—it became a matter of self-protection.

If she had her heart broken again this soon, she might never find the courage to let someone else this far into her life. Ever.

Perhaps that look was simply because Hugh felt it was a step too far, taking Oreo into the paediatric intensive care unit where Sophie Jacobs was in the early stages of her post-operative recovery? Oreo was on her very best behaviour, thank goodness, and she had waited for a signal that it was a time no other patients in the unit or their families might be disturbed. They had probably not even noticed her arrival because the rooms that opened onto the central space with the nurses' station and banks of monitoring equipment were very private, especially when the curtains were drawn across the internal windows.

The unit staff had also been consulted about this visit but…

…maybe Hugh was being reminded of the first time he'd seen a dogtor near one of his patients and maybe he was a bit shocked by how much had changed between himself and Molly since then…

Sophie was in a nest of soft pillows, her leg well supported and stable. Molly could just see an oxygen saturation probe clipped to the big toe of her reattached foot. She had electrodes on to monitor her heart and an automatic cuff to take her blood pressure. There were IV lines to deliver medications including the pain relief she was having and other tubes snaked from beneath a light, brightly coloured bed cover. With no hat on to cover her bald scalp, Sophie looked so incredibly vulnerable, it would be no surprise that some people might think it was totally inappropriate to have an animal in here who could potentially disrupt such a delicately balanced, technical set up.

But Sophie's mother was crying softly when she saw Molly and Oreo. 'I'm so glad you could come,' she said. 'Soph made me promise that she'd be able to see Oreo as soon as she woke up. I wasn't sure you'd be allowed in here but I said "yes" because that was what she wanted more than anything…'

'We can only stay for a few minutes.' Molly glanced over her shoulder, knowing that they were being carefully watched by staff members, including Hugh, who was talking to one of the intensive care consultants. 'This is the first time pet therapy has happened in the ICU here.'

She held Oreo's leash close to the clip on her harness and made sure the dog didn't get near any tubes or lines. She put a towel on the edge of Sophie's bed and tapped it to tell Oreo where to put her chin.

'Sophie?' Joanne was on the other side of the bed, stroking Sophie's head. 'Are you awake, darling? Guess who's come to see you…'

Eyelashes fluttered but Sophie was reaching out with her hand before she opened her eyes.

'Aww…' Her lips were curving into a smile. 'It's Oreo…'

The small hand had found Oreo's nose and fingers traced their way up to find her head and ears. Her dog might have been poked in the eyes on the way because Molly could see her blinking, but Oreo didn't move a muscle. She barely waved her tail and she didn't take her gaze off Sophie's face.

Molly had to fight back tears. She was *so* proud of Oreo.

She could see the emotion on Joanne's face as her daughter got the gift she'd wanted the most in this difficult time. Even Sophie's nurse, who was taking photos of this visit, was using a tissue to blot her eyes.

Molly didn't know whether Hugh had witnessed the joy. By the time Molly led Oreo quietly out of the unit a few minutes later, he could have been long gone. She didn't head straight back to her van in the car park, however. Because it had been such a short visit to the ICU, Molly thought she'd leave via her ward to see if there was another child who might like a visit from Oreo. And, when the doors of the lift slid open on the ward floor, she saw Hugh walking away from his office in the company of a very distressed looking woman.

Oreo picked up on the emotional intensity the moment she stepped out of the lift. She sat down, refusing to move any further towards the ward, and waited for Hugh to get closer.

He'd never been so relieved to be offered such an irresistible distraction.

Not only was his own mind diverted by a flash of how it had felt, albeit briefly, to be in a parallel universe with Molly Holmes yesterday evening, the distraught woman with him—Annabelle Finch—seemed to be having a reprieve from any aftermath of the awful conversation he'd just had with her.

She was veering towards Oreo.

'Oh…aren't you gorgeous?' Annabelle still had tears on her cheeks as she looked at Molly. 'Am I allowed to pat him?'

'Of course.' Molly smiled.

'She's a girl.' It was Hugh who made the correction. 'This is Oreo, Annabelle. She belongs to Molly, here, and she's trained to visit children as an assistance dog.'

He was also looking directly at Molly and had to ignore an odd squeeze in his chest as she shifted her gaze to catch his. This was definitely not the time to allow any pull towards what had happened between himself and Molly.

'This is Annabelle,' he said. 'She's Sam's mum. Sam is one of my patients.'

Annabelle was on her knees now, her cheek on Oreo's neck as she hugged the dog. 'Sam would love you,' she said. 'He's been begging me for a puppy for months now and…and I was planning to get one after the end of his chemo—in time for Christmas…' She turned to bury her face in Oreo's thick coat just in time to stifle a sob.

Hugh could feel his whole body tensing. Trying not to be pulled into this mother's pain. It was quite noticeably a much harder ask than normal. Because Molly was standing so close and his body was desperate to remind him of how it felt to be even closer to her?

He cleared his throat. 'Maybe Molly's got time to take Oreo in to visit Sam for a few minutes?'

'I have.' Molly nodded. 'That's why I came down. We could only be in the ICU for a very short time so we'd both appreciate a chance to make another visit.'

Annabelle lifted her face. 'Really? You could do that?'

'Why don't you go and see how Sam feels about it?' Hugh suggested. 'Come and tell us if he's awake again and his pain levels are under better control. Otherwise, it might be a bit much for him. Check with his nurse, too?'

Annabelle nodded, but an almost smile was hovering on her lips. 'Where will I find you?'

Hugh thought fast. 'I'm sure Oreo could use a breath of fresh air. We'll just be out in the garden here.'

We...?

Did Hugh want to be alone with Molly when he'd have no chance of *not* thinking—and probably saying something—about last night?

No.

Yes...

He held the door open for Molly. 'I thought you might need a bit of background,' he said quietly.

Oreo looked delighted to be back in the garden where she'd danced with Molly and, with no one else there, she could be let off the lead for a few minutes.

Molly sat on one of the benches and Hugh sat down beside her. Close enough for his thigh to be touching hers and it was inevitable that memories of last night came flooding back in a kaleidoscope of sensations that were enough to make Hugh catch his breath.

It wasn't just the sex that had been a revelation, was it? He'd never felt like this *afterwards*, either. As if his body were watching a metaphorical clock and counting down every second until he could do it again.

Molly seemed to be avoiding catching his gaze. She'd closed her eyes, in fact, and she was taking in a slow, deep breath—as if *she* were aware of that clock as well? The thought that she might be feeling the same way he was about repeating the experience was enough for Hugh to know this definitely wasn't the time to say anything. Their body language might already be enough to catch the attention of someone walking past the windows and… Hugh had no intention of turning his back on what had been disturbing enough to welcome the distraction that Molly and Oreo's arrival had provided.

'So…' His deep breath mirrored Molly's. 'Sam is four years old. I saw him about eighteen months ago when he fell off his scooter and broke his arm. His humerus. Like Sophie, the X-ray that was taken was the first indication that he had something serious going on.'

Molly's face was very still. Her eyes wide. She was absolutely focussed on what Hugh was saying. 'An osteosarcoma?' she breathed.

'No. In Sam's case it was a Ewing sarcoma. Rare. And incredibly aggressive. He had equally aggressive chemotherapy and radiotherapy and I did a limb-saving surgery to remove the diseased humerus and replace it with a bone graft that we took from his fibula.'

Molly didn't say anything when he paused for a breath this time, but Hugh could feel she was holding her own breath.

'He seemed to be doing well for some time. We thought we'd caught it. Annabelle told me she felt like she could finally breathe again. She's in her early forties. She chose to become a single mother and is totally devoted to Sam.' Hugh swallowed carefully. 'The first metastases showed up a few months ago and further chemo has been ineffective. The tumours are right through his body—in his lungs, bones, spine, brain...'

Hugh didn't bother continuing the list. 'Surgery's not an option unless it's palliative...which is why he's been transferred to my team. He broke his femur yesterday due to the bone damage from a fast-growing tumour. His leg is in a cast but it needs surgery to stabilise it effectively so I was consulted about whether removing the lesion and plating the fracture could significantly improve his level of comfort. I think it probably could but it's a much higher risk operation in his condition so it's got to be Annabelle's choice whether or not the risk is worth it. We're keeping a theatre slot free for later today, just in case.'

Hugh had been watching Oreo exploring the garden as he spoke quietly. Perhaps instinct had been protecting him from making direct eye contact with Molly, because now, when he turned his head, he could see a level of emotion in her face and eyes that he would never let himself feel for a patient.

Yes, this was an incredibly sad story and it was reaching an even sadder ending but that only made it vital for Hugh not to be sucked into an emotional vortex. He had to stand back far enough to offer support and make the best decisions for both Sam and his mum, Annabelle.

'So…' The word was crisp, this time. Decisive. 'If you—and Oreo—can handle it, it might be… you know…'

He didn't finish his sentence. It was too heartbreaking to think about a small child finding even a moment of joy in what could be his last days alive. Or a memory being made that his mother might treasure for the rest of her life. He didn't need to finish it...

'I know,' Molly whispered. She was blinking hard and then she lifted her chin. 'And it's precisely why I got into this in the first place. Oreo's at her best with children like Sam. My job is just to put her in the right place at the right time.'

Maybe Oreo heard her name. Or maybe she'd picked up on Hugh's tone of voice. She'd given up exploring and come to lie quietly at their feet. When the doors to the garden opened and Annabelle came out to find them, Oreo wasn't looking at the newcomer. She was gazing up at Molly, waiting for her cue.

And Molly looked down at her dog. It was a moment of silent communication. A warning perhaps that they were about to do something difficult but it would be okay because they would be doing it together.

It was a message carried on an undercurrent that felt like...

...like love. A love so strong it was palpable.

It was only between Molly and Oreo but, for a heartbeat, before he could definitively shut it down, Hugh felt as if he was included in it.

Or perhaps he'd just *wanted* to be...

Oh...*man*...

Emotional moments were part and parcel of

a job working with sick kids and their families. Being with a mother who was facing the final days of her precious child's life took it to a whole new level. Adding all the feels that bringing a dog into the picture could provide made it…

…poignant enough to be a pain like no other.

How much easier would it be to be able to put up a wall to protect yourself from that kind of pain—the way Hugh Ashcroft seemed to be able to do with ease? Molly hadn't heard any wobble of emotion in his voice when he'd been filling her in on Sam's case out in the garden earlier. He'd avoided looking at her as he'd given her the clinical facts. He was concerned with weighing up the benefits versus risks of a surgical procedure and making sure the mother was able to make an informed consent. Or not.

And yes…knowing that he'd lost his sister to a childhood cancer gave her an insight into why he was like he was but…but it still didn't make sense. Not when she knew that beneath the cool, professional persona that Hugh put on in public there was a man who was capable of feeling things.

Passionately feeling things…

Things you might expect like the satisfaction of saving a young life or ensuring a better future for a child.

But unexpected things, too—like the power of the ocean.

Like the sensual pleasure of the intimate touch of another human.

It had been surprisingly hurtful to find herself shut out again, so when Molly saw Hugh also heading towards the lifts from the direction of his office, she increased her pace.

'Hugh? Have you got a minute?'

He looked up from the screen of his phone and Molly's heart sank. She could swear he was dismayed to see her and Oreo.

'Is it important?'

'I think so.' Molly tried to keep her tone calm. 'I've just come from being with Sam and his mum.'

Hugh glanced at his watch. 'Really? You've been in there for more than an *hour*?'

'Sam was so happy to have Oreo there. We let her lie on the bed beside him and he went to sleep with his arm around her. We didn't want him to wake up and find she'd disappeared.'

Because Annabelle had known he would start crying instantly. From the pain he was in and because his new friend was no longer beside him.

'We got some lovely photos.' Molly pulled her phone out. 'Would you like to see them?'

'Not right now.' Hugh was turning towards the lift. 'I've got a lot to get on with.'

'You'll probably have even more soon. Annabelle's decided that she wants Sam to have the surgery on his leg. If he gets enough analgesia to cope with the pain, he's completely knocked out.'

'Thanks for the heads-up.' Hugh was frowning now. Thinking about what might be a difficult surgery? 'Is she certain about that?'

Molly nodded. 'She said that if it could keep Sam comfortable to enjoy his favourite food or a bedtime story or even one more visit and a cuddle with Oreo, then it would be worth it.' Molly was staring at Hugh's profile. 'I've promised I'll bring her to see him every day I can, depending on my shifts. Either here, or when they get home again.'

'*If* they get home.' Hugh's words were a mutter that nobody nearby would have overheard. They would have heard the disapproving tone in his next words though. 'I don't think that's a good idea.'

Molly blinked. He didn't want to see the photos and that was fine. She understood that images of a frail child with no hair, IV lines in his arms and oxygen tubing taped to his face could be confronting for Hugh when they had nothing to do with anything medical. But to deny that child the moments of joy—of forgetting that life could be unbearably hard—that was also so apparent in those photos was…well…it was unacceptable.

'Why not?' Molly demanded.

It wasn't surprising that the challenging note in her voice was enough for Hugh's registrar, who was stepping into the lift, to turn and stare at them. Or that Molly could see a flash of…what was it? Annoyance? Anger, even?…on Hugh's face.

'Not here,' he said coldly. 'Come with me.' He turned away from where Matthew was holding the lift door open. 'Go ahead without me,' he told him. 'I'll be there in a few minutes.

He strode back to his office, held the door for Molly and Oreo to enter and then closed it behind them, with a decisive click.

'Sam may not survive this surgery,' he said, without preamble. 'If he does, it might make him more comfortable but it will not prolong his life. He's on palliative care and Annabelle knows that the probability is very high that he won't make it home again.'

'I'm aware of that,' Molly said.

'Are you also aware that you're at risk of getting too involved in this case? On a personal level?'

'I know what I'm doing,' Molly said. 'It's not the first time I've worked with a terminally ill child, Hugh.'

He was staring at her as if she'd just stepped off a spacecraft from another planet.

'Why?' He sounded bemused. 'I don't understand how—or *why*—you would choose to get so involved in a case like this?'

'And I don't understand how *you* can avoid it,' Molly said quietly.

Maybe that was it in a nutshell. Why they could never be together, no matter how tightly Molly's feelings for Hugh had entwined themselves around her heart.

'I *learned* how. So that I could be capable of doing my job properly, without having decisions affected by unhelpful emotional involvement with my patients *or* their families.'

Hugh met her gaze and the shutters were firmly down. It felt like Molly was being given a reprimand. That she should also do what it took to acquire this skill?

'It's better to keep an appropriate, professional distance,' Hugh added as if she had somehow agreed with his viewpoint.

She stared back. It wasn't going to happen. She wasn't even going to try and make it happen.

'Distance from what? Or whom?' she asked, enunciating her words clearly. 'Just from the patients and their families? From your colleagues?'

Like her…?

'From *life*…?' Molly forgot that she was speaking to a senior colleague, here. Or that they were in the place they needed to be able to work together in amicably, never mind what had happened between them away from the hospital. Perhaps it was the hurt caused by realising that their time together out of hours was not significant that was making her angry. That he could have sex with her and then push her away to protect that precious distance…

Hugh opened his mouth and then closed it again, clearly unable to find the words he wanted. Oreo was pressed against Molly's leg and she could feel the shiver that ran through her dog's body. She put her hand gently on Oreo's head to let her know she wasn't the one who was doing anything wrong.

'Who's it better *for*, Hugh?' Molly wasn't done yet. 'It's never going to be better for the other person, or people, in the equation. So let me answer that, if you haven't already figured it out for yourself.' She narrowed her eyes. 'It's better for *you*. And only you. Me? I'll continue to let people know how much I care about them because…in the end, that's better for *me*.'

Molly didn't give Hugh a chance to respond. She turned and walked out of his office, Oreo glued to her side.

She knew she'd crossed a rather significant boundary line but she hadn't said anything that she didn't believe in. Being distant was never going to be better for someone like Sophie Jacobs and her family. Or for Sam and his mother, who was going through unimaginable pain right now.

And yeah…keeping that kind of distance was never going to be better for herself, either. Or Oreo. Even as they reached the staircase, Oreo was looking back towards the office they'd just stormed out of. Hoping to see the man she, for some inexplicable reason, had decided she was devoted to.

Okay…maybe it wasn't inexplicable. Because Molly's heart had been equally captured, hadn't it?

And that was when Molly changed her mind. Hugh keeping this distance he'd learned to do so well *might* actually be better in this case.

For both of them.

CHAPTER EIGHT

'So what actually happened, Tane?'

The lanky thirteen-year-old that Hugh had been called into the emergency department to see made a face that hinted at how enormous this catastrophe could be for him.

'It was the final moments of the game, bro. I had the ball and it was the only chance for us to break the tie before the whistle went. And I did the highest jump shot ever...got it through the net...crowd goes wild...but then I landed...'

'Did you hear anything go pop or feel it snapping as you landed?'

'Felt like someone shot me in the back of my foot, you know?' He had his hand shielding his eyes now. 'They had to carry me off the court.'

Tane was still wearing the boxer shorts and singlet with his number and the name of his team.

'Can you turn over so you're on your stomach?' Hugh asked. 'Hang your feet over the end of the bed...that's it. And now relax your feet and calf muscles as much as you can.' He took hold of the calf muscle above the ankle on Tane's uninjured leg, squeezed it firmly and watched the foot move downwards. The same stimulus on the other leg provoked no movement whatsoever in the foot.

'You've definitely ruptured your Achilles tendon,' Hugh told him.

'Oh, *man*… How long am I going to be out for?'

'Depends on the severity, which we'll find out when I send you for an ultrasound and an MRI scan. If it's a minor or partial tear, you'll be in a cast or walking boot for six to eight weeks. If it's severe or a complete rupture, it'll need surgery and it will take a lot longer to heal.'

'But there's a sponsors' tournament that's part of the national team's selection series next month…'

Tane was on the verge of tears so Hugh didn't tell him he thought this injury was quite likely to be on the severe end of the spectrum. Time enough to do that when the results of the scans came through. Right now, it was time for Hugh to be somewhere else. Before the tears started.

'I'll be back to see you as soon as you've had the scans done,' he said, turning away from his patient. 'We'll talk about the next steps then.'

Sometimes, it was kinder to give people the chance to prepare themselves for bad news, but if Tane needed surgery to reattach the tendon to his heel or possibly replace part of it with a graft and it was going to take six months or more to heal, then Hugh would tell him. If the lad got tearful or angry he wouldn't let it affect him on a personal level, or change whatever management he advised.

That was what keeping an emotional distance enabled him to do. And yes, it was better for Tane as well as for himself. How would it help anyone if he sat here, holding this boy's hand and sympathising with what a disaster this was for his hopes of making the national team? Or worse, letting himself be persuaded that it might be okay to try a conservative approach with a few weeks' rest in a cast first and then finding it could be harder to achieve the best result from a surgical repair.

Molly was wrong.

His complete opposite, in fact.

Hugh was at a loss to understand why he'd been attracted to her in the first place, but at least he could be confident it wasn't going to get any more complicated. From now on, he was going to keep an emotional distance from Molly Holmes as well as his patients.

Preferably, a physical distance as well.

He hadn't even gone into the induction room the other day, when he'd learned that Molly had stayed on so that Oreo could be with Sam as he was taken to Theatre and given his anaesthetic. He hadn't seen her in the ward since that surgery despite knowing that Sam had not been discharged and it was unlikely to happen as they kept the little boy comfortable in a private room away from the main bustle of the ward.

If Molly was keeping her promise and taking Oreo in to see him every day possible, perhaps she was avoiding him as well now that it was obvious they had so little in common?

Hugh should be happy that it was going to make it easy to forget the unfortunate lapses of his normal self-control that had led to doing things as outrageous as running around an agility course with a dog.

And having *sex* in a shower?

The fact that he wasn't happy and that it was proving surprisingly difficult to forget anything about Molly was enough to give Hugh a background hum of something unpleasantly reminiscent of anger. And that only made him even *less* happy.

Mr Hugh Ashcroft wasn't looking aloof when Molly saw him walking briskly past the windows when she was giving Oreo a toilet break in the roof garden.

He was looking as if he was in a decidedly bad mood.

He was actually scowling!

Thank goodness he didn't look outside and see her because that would, no doubt, make him even grumpier. They hadn't spoken since she'd unleashed on his lack of connection with his patients the other day. They hadn't even made eye contact. And…

…and Molly was missing him.

Okay, she knew perfectly well that they were totally unsuited to being with each other but that didn't change the fact that Molly's heart had been well and truly captured—even before he'd given her the best sex she'd ever had in her life.

Even now, as she saw the tall man with the scowl on his face striding past the garden, she could also see a lonely boy who had not only been grieving the loss of his sister but had lost his beloved dog as well. Molly could almost see the barriers he'd built to prevent himself feeling that much again and her heart ached for him because she knew, all too well, that those barriers were also preventing him from feeling the joy that life could offer.

She'd already pushed him too far, though, hadn't she?

She wasn't going to get another chance and that made her feel sad.

Almost as sad as she felt every time she and Oreo quietly slipped into Sam's room to spend some time with him. The sweet little boy was being kept pretty much pain free now but the complications with his lungs and heart were making his care too complex for Annabelle to be able to manage at home.

She knew she was going to be saying goodbye to her precious son in hospital within a short period of time but she was making the most of every moment she still had with him, and the way Sam's face lit up when he was conscious enough to know that Oreo was beside him was enough for Molly to make sure she came in every day. She enlisted the help of her mother one day when she was on duty to bring Oreo to the hospital to make a brief visit during Molly's lunch break and on another day she came back in the evening after she'd finished her shift.

There were many other patients needing her attention, of course.

Sophie Jacobs had gone home a week after her rotationplasty surgery. She would need crutches and a wheelchair until her leg had healed enough to be fitted for her custom-made prosthesis and she would be spending a great deal of time with her team of physiotherapists to learn to use her ankle joint as her new knee, but she left the ward with a huge smile on her face and the picture from her wall, of the other little girl doing her ballet leap with her prosthesis, folded up and in her pocket. She gave Molly a copy of one of the photographs the nurse had taken when Oreo visited Sophie in the intensive care unit after her surgery. Sophie had been just waking up and the smile on her face as she'd been able to touch Oreo's head was enough to melt anyone's heart.

Maybe even the heart of the man who'd done Sophie's surgery?

Molly pinned the photo, with pride, to a long corkboard on the wall near the entrance to the ward. She—and her beloved canine partner— were becoming a part of the fabric of this hospital and nobody—other than Hugh—had questioned the wisdom of their frequent visits to a small boy who was dying.

Molly had been invited to attend a very sombre meeting where an end-of-life care plan was discussed for Sam. Hugh was apparently caught up in Theatre but his presence wasn't considered necessary given that Sam would not be having any further surgery. His oncologist and cardiologist were there, along with Molly representing the nursing staff and the support of Sam's grandmother and aunty for Annabelle. At the end of the meeting, Annabelle signed consent forms for a process known as Allowing a Natural Death or AND, which meant keeping Sam as comfortable as possible for as long as possible but restricting the interventions to prevent death, such as CPR including intubation or defibrillation. She also made what was, for this hospital, the first request of its kind, ever.

'I know it's a lot to ask...' Annabelle's words were choked '...and maybe it won't be possible but... I think Sam believes that Oreo is *his* puppy now. If she could be there at...at the end...'

She broke down completely then and Molly was the first to get up and go to give Annabelle a hug. She knew that any comfort Oreo could provide would be for Annabelle as much as for Sam.

'If it's possible,' she said softly, 'we'll make it happen.'

It *was* a big ask. Not because Molly wasn't willing to be there if it was at short notice or in the middle of the night but because it was quite likely that Sam's heart function or respiratory efforts could cease without any warning. What did end up happening, however, was a more gentle progression with signs that Sam's small body was giving up the fight. His blood pressure dropped and his body temperature began fluctuating. His skin became slightly mottled as his circulation slowed down and Annabelle found she couldn't tempt her son to eat, even with his favourite treats.

Molly took Oreo in during the afternoon. Assistant dog protocols meant that she had to stay in the room with Annabelle, *her* mother and her sister but, having positioned Oreo on the bed beside where Sam was being held in his mother's arms, she made herself as inconspicuous as possible in a corner of the room. Oreo looked as though she was asleep, with her eyes shut and Sam's hand just resting on top of her body and Annabelle stroking her sometimes, but, occasionally, the dog would open her eyes and her glance would find Molly's, as if seeking reassurance she was doing the right thing as she stayed there, motionless, for an hour and then another. And Molly would smile and sometimes murmur quietly, telling her that she was a good girl and to stay where she was.

Oreo still didn't move even after Sam quietly sighed and then didn't take another breath. Molly waited until Annabelle's mother and sister closed in to share the holding and grieving for Sam and then signalled Oreo, who slipped off the bed unnoticed by the family.

The charge nurse on duty, who was in the room at that point, followed Molly and Oreo out of the room.

'Are you okay?' she asked Molly.

Molly could only nod. She didn't trust her voice to work yet.

'Take Oreo home.' The charge nurse gave her a quick hug. 'And look after yourself. You're both heroes, you know that, don't you?'

Molly tried to smile but it didn't work. It was time for her to take Oreo home and she knew that Sam's family would be well cared for and allowed to stay with him as long as they wanted to. Her own tears were making everything a bit of a blur as she walked out of the ward, but Oreo knew the route well by now and was leading Molly towards the stairwell beside the lifts. In a few minutes they would be outside and then in the familiar privacy of the old van. Maybe she knew how important it was that Molly needed to get somewhere where she could have a good cry.

She didn't see him.

She probably wouldn't have recognised him if he'd been standing right in front of her because Hugh could see that Molly was half blinded by tears.

And he knew why.

He'd been heading towards his office when someone had intercepted him and told him quietly that little Sam Finch had died. Hugh had simply nodded acknowledgement and thanked the messenger and it was then he'd spotted Molly leaving the ward with Oreo.

There was no reason not to continue to his office, where he had an article on an experimental surgical technique for bone grafting waiting for him to peer review for a leading journal of paediatric orthopaedics.

Yes, the news was sad but it was part and parcel of specialising in orthopaedic surgery for children with bone cancer and, fortunately, they seemed to be winning more and more battles these days. Hugh had learned long ago how to protect himself from being sucked too deeply into a case like Sam's.

But Molly clearly hadn't.

A short time later, Hugh found the image of her struggling to control her grief as she escaped the hospital was interfering with his focus on the article.

Where had she gone? Was she alone in that little cottage by the sea?

Was she okay?

Did she have someone to talk to?

Someone that could help her get past what could be a damaging level of emotional involvement rather than wallowing in it?

Someone like himself...?

Hugh shook the notion off and tried harder to focus on what was a well-written paper, on the advancements in biomaterials and methods for bone augmentation, but he couldn't prevent his thoughts drifting back to Molly.

He couldn't get rid of the odd tightness in his chest that was unusual enough for him to wonder if he might have an undiagnosed issue with his heart.

No. He knew what the problem was.

He was worried about Molly. He'd warned her about how unwise it had been to involve herself in this case but that didn't mean he wasn't sympathetic to her finding out the hard way that he was right.

He wasn't going to say 'I told you so'. He wasn't expecting her to take back the things she'd said about his ability to distance himself being selfish because he was the only person to benefit and that he was living less of a life than others.

To be honest, Hugh had no idea what he was going to say or what Molly might say back to him. He just knew he needed to see her, which was why he closed his laptop and reached for his car keys.

This was better.

Molly had cried her eyes out at the same time as throwing the frisbee for Oreo again and again. The background of waves breaking on the beach was soothing and a soft evening sea breeze was enough to dry the tears on her cheeks without becoming too cold. When Oreo was panting so hard she had to drop her toy and head into the waves to cool off, Molly sat to simply watch for a while and that was even better because she could feel the edges of her sadness being softened by the comfort of being in a place she loved.

With the dog she loved with all her heart.

Oddly, it wasn't surprising to look up and see Hugh walking towards her. Molly knew that he would have heard about Sam and he'd warned her how hard it might be to have involved herself so much. But the fact he was here told her that he wasn't being judgemental or righteous because being like that would be far more effective in their working environment. His expression suggested that he was feeling concerned.

Concerned about her?

That was a kind of involvement on his part, wasn't it?

That meant he wasn't keeping himself as distant as he might think.

And, for some reason, Molly felt a spark of something that felt like…hope…?

'I thought I might find you here,' he said.

Molly just nodded.

'I thought you might like a bit of company.'

Molly nodded again and Hugh sat down on the sand beside her. For a minute or two they both watched the waves endlessly rolling in and then receding. And then Hugh spoke quietly.

'You okay…?'

Oh… Molly could hear how difficult it was for him to ask that question. He knew he was inviting a conversation that might include something emotional. Something a long way out of any comfort zone of his.

She needed to reassure him that she wasn't going to stamp on any personal ground so she managed to find a smile as she nodded slowly.

'I'm okay,' she said. 'I'm incredibly sad, of course. I'm gutted for Annabelle and her family but I don't regret my involvement. And Oreo was an absolute angel. I know she helped...'

'I'm sure she did.'

Molly had to brush away a few leftover tears. She could feel Hugh's gaze on her face and the increase of tension in his body language.

'I really am okay,' she told him. 'It's okay to feel sad sometimes, you know. And it's okay to cry...'

Oreo was still playing in the shallow water. They had the beach to themselves and the only sound was the soft wash of small waves breaking.

'I haven't cried since I was fourteen.'

Hugh's words were not much more than a whisper and Molly knew he was telling her something he had never told anyone else.

'When you lost your sister?'

Hugh was silent for so long that Molly thought she might have crossed too big a boundary but then he spoke again and his voice was raw.

'And Fudge...' The way he cleared his throat

made Molly wonder if he was close to tears himself. 'My mother had him put down a few days after Michelle died.'

Molly gasped in total shock. 'Oh, my God… what happened to him?'

Hugh was staring out to sea. 'Nothing…my mother just said he was too old. I came home from school and he…just wasn't there…'

Molly was staring at Hugh. Horrified. Imagining that boy who was dealing with the loss of his sister and having the lifelong companion who could have offered comfort like no other simply snatched away for no good reason. Her heart was breaking for fourteen-year-old Hugh. But it was also breaking for the man who was sitting beside her.

Who'd learned not to love any people—*or* dogs—because the world would feel like it was ending when you lost them.

All Molly wanted to do was to hold Hugh in her arms. To offer, very belatedly, all the understanding and comfort that *she* was able to bestow.

She knew not to touch him, however. That Hugh had stepped onto an emotional tightrope by telling her something so personal and, if he was touched in any way, verbally *or* physically, he could fall off that tightrope and she'd never be allowed this close again.

And she really didn't want that to happen.

Because it was in this moment that Molly realised just how much in love with Hugh Ashcroft she had fallen.

She knew he was never going to feel the same way. That if she didn't back off she would be setting herself up for total heartbreak but…it didn't feel like she had a choice, here. It was a bit like being with Annabelle and Sam today. There was something powerful enough to make dealing with that level of pain worthwhile.

That she—and Oreo—could help.

'I've got a spot in my garden where you can watch the sea while the sun sets,' she said, as if she were sharing something secret. Or perhaps just completely changing the subject? 'I've also got a bottle of wine in my fridge and I'd really like a glass of it but you know what they say about not drinking alone, don't you?'

Hugh nodded carefully. 'I *do*…'

'I know I'm not technically alone when I've got Oreo with me.' Molly bit her lip. And then she smiled. Properly this time. 'But she hates wine.'

The soft huff of laughter from Hugh was a surprise.

A definite win.

'I did come out because I thought you might need some company.' Hugh got to his feet and held out his hand to help Molly up. 'I didn't realise it was to drink wine but…hey… I'm willing to go with the flow, here.'

Molly put her hand in his, loving the strong grip and tug that made it so easy to get up and stay this close to Hugh.

It would have been easy to keep moving. To lean in so close it would be an invitation to be kissed.

But Molly didn't do that. Because if offering him an opportunity to get closer—to build a friendship, or even a relationship—was going to work, it had to be completely Hugh's choice how far he closed any distance between them.

Safety.

That was what this felt like.

He had been pretty sure Molly would have been filled in by Benji's grandmother about his family tragedy, but nobody had known about Fudge. That look on Molly's face when he'd dropped that emotional bomb had made him realise that this was the first time anyone understood exactly what it had been like for him.

It felt like Molly might be the only person in the universe who *could* understand that. More than understand, even. It felt like she could *feel* it herself.

And she didn't say anything. It was enough that he knew she understood. He certainly didn't want to revisit the past in any more detail and Molly seemed to get that, too.

So yeah...

Hugh felt safe. He could sit on a comfortable, old wicker chair with Oreo lying on the grass by his feet, drink a very nice Central Otago wine and still hear the waves as the day drew to a close and he could relax more than he remembered being able to do in...well...in for ever, really.

Perhaps that was why it felt okay to have Oreo's head resting heavily on his foot. Why, when he looked down and found the dog looking back up at him with those liquid brown eyes, he could feel a melting sensation deep in his chest. He didn't dare look up to where Molly was sitting, in the matching chair that was close enough to touch his, in case *she* was watching him, too.

'I was nine years old when Michelle... Shelly... got diagnosed with a brain tumour,' he said. 'She was only three so she never really remembered a life without being sick. She died at home when she was eight. Fudge stayed on the bed with her that day. He refused to get off even when I tried to take him outside for a wee. I think he knew...'

Oh, dear Lord...even mentioning that last day was taking him too close to a space he had successfully avoided for so long. He'd even managed to keep it locked away when he'd been trying to warn Molly that being with Sam at the end might have repercussions that could haunt her for life. If she said anything about Shelly now, he might lose something he could never get back.

His safe space...

'Dogs are amazing,' Molly said softly into the silence. 'They understand far more than we give them credit for and they have this astonishing ability to supply limitless, unconditional love...'

Her voice trailed away as if she felt like she'd said too much and when Hugh lifted his gaze he could see she had tears in her eyes.

'Grief is the worst feeling in the world, isn't it?' she murmured. 'I heard it said once that grief is love that has nowhere to go.'

Hugh had no words. He was lost in what he could see in Molly's dark eyes. They were sitting so close that all he had to do was lift his hand to touch her cheek. If he leaned towards her he would be able to kiss her.

Especially if she leaned a little, as well.

Which was exactly what she did a heartbeat after he'd moved. Hugh cupped her cheek with his hand, tilting her jaw as his lips found hers.

He didn't need any words, did he?

Not even to tell Molly how she had made such a difference in his world just by being there to hear him talk, even so briefly, about his beloved little sister. And his dog. To understand how devastating it had been to lose them both but not to ask him to say anything more. To allow him the dignity of maintaining control. One day he might tell her how his mother had disappeared, inch by inch, into the depression that eventually claimed her life. That *he* had largely disappeared for her over the years when her sick daughter was the total focus of her life.

But not now. All he wanted right now was to thank Molly for being here.

For understanding.

And he didn't need words.

Because he could touch her.

He could hold her face as he kissed her until they were both short of breath. He could stand up and take her hand and lead her into her little house and find her bedroom this time.

And he could touch her whole body—with his hands and his lips and his tongue. He could feel her skin against his own. He could make sure that this was as good as it could get—for both of them. And he could take his time because this was about more than simply a fierce physical attraction.

It was about being safe. In a world that only the two of them could inhabit.

Because Molly understood why he was so different.

CHAPTER NINE

As THE NURSE practitioner on duty, it was part of Molly's job to accompany the consultants and their registrars as they made their ward rounds. Prior to that, she needed to collect all the most up-to-date clinical information on the patients and be ready for the 'board round' before the ward round. This was where the team would gather around the digital whiteboard on the wall of the nurses' station, which had details of all the inpatients, and decide the order of priority. The most unwell were seen first, then the patients who were ready for discharge that day, followed by the more routine visits to everyone else for the monitoring of charts and medications, physical examinations and any adjustments to treatment plans.

It was Hugh, his registrar Matthew and two junior doctors doing their rounds this morning and Molly had been completely focussed collecting all the latest blood test results and notes from the handover, until Hugh and his colleagues walked towards the nurses' station for the board round.

Her stomach did a weird flip-flop then and, for a moment, Molly struggled to clear a sudden flash of images from her brain—like a movie on fast-forward—of last night. Of her body being... good heavens...*worshipped*...?

But that was what she had decided it had felt like later in the night, after Hugh had gone home. The focus he'd had on her... As if making this the most profound sexual experience she'd ever had was the only thing on his mind?

Maybe it wasn't images that flashed through her mind in that heartbeat of a moment. It was more like a reminder of physical sensations like none she had ever had before in her life. The sheer delight of the whispers of fingers against her skin. The delicious spears of desire. Anticipation—and need—building to a point that was actually painful and the blinding ecstasy of release.

No...it was more than that. It was like the physical form of emotions that were so intense and unfamiliar Molly couldn't even find words to describe them. And she certainly wasn't about to try right now.

This was work and Molly knew perfectly well that it came before anything else in this surgeon's list of what mattered the most. If there was a way to ensure that what had happened between herself and Hugh Ashcroft last night never, ever happened again, it would be to let it interfere with how either of them did their jobs. That deal-breaker was closely followed by putting any kind of pressure on Hugh to build on how well they knew each other, but at least that was easy to put aside, especially when Molly wasn't at all sure she was ready for even attempting a new relationship. The reminder was useful, however, because suddenly any personal thoughts evaporated.

The blip in focus had been so momentary hopefully nobody else could have noticed. Especially Hugh. Molly took a deep breath as she looked away from him and flicked open the notepad where she'd scribbled the information she needed to communicate with this team that wasn't on the whiteboard yet.

The first patient whose condition was causing some concern was twelve-year-old Gemma, who had had surgery two days ago for a slipped upper femoral epiphysis—where the ball at the top of the femur had slipped out of position due to damage to the growth plate—that had happened after a collision and fall in a soccer game.

'So, Gemma was doing very well with her crutches and was flagged for discharge today but she spiked a temperature during the night and is feeling unwell this morning,' Molly reported. 'She's got some redness and is complaining of increased wound pain. Preliminary results on the bloods and wound swab I took first thing after handover shouldn't be too far away.'

'Thanks, Molly. Is the ward pharmacist available? I'd like to run through our initial management of any infection.'

'I'll get someone to page her.'

Hugh's glance told her that he was impressed with her initiating tests that would determine the course of treatment needed to combat the surgical complication of infection.

It also told her that they were both now safely in a totally professional arena. That Hugh had no idea of that momentary lapse she'd had. But perhaps he hadn't been entirely wrong in telling her it was better to be able to keep a personal distance from others. Sometimes.

Like for the rest of this ward round. With Gemma examined, antibiotic treatment started and her family reassured that she wouldn't be discharged until this setback had been sorted, there were enough patients to keep the team busy until it was time for a morning tea break. Not that Hugh or his team stayed for a coffee in the ward staff room. They were gone, heading towards Radiology for a scheduled biopsy, a family meeting in the oncology ward for a patient who had just been diagnosed with a bone cancer and was about to start chemotherapy before surgery, and then an outpatient clinic that was apparently so packed it would keep both himself and his registrars largely unavailable all afternoon.

'I know you won't page us unless it's urgent,' he said to Molly as they left the ward.

She might have deemed the smile she received to be as aloof as she'd once thought Hugh actually was himself, but she could see past that protective barrier now. Or maybe it was just something new she could see in that graze of eye contact. Something that acknowledged there was a lot more than simply being colleagues between them but that Hugh was trusting her with much more than overseeing the care of his patients for the rest of her shift.

He was trusting her not to trespass across boundaries.

Especially at work, because this was his safe place.

Molly's smile in return was just as polite. 'Of course not,' she murmured.

He *could* trust her. On both counts. He'd never know that she had a totally *un*professional thought as he walked away from her. That, as she carried her mug of coffee out to the garden for a minute's peace and quiet, she was reminded—oddly—of a pony club camp she'd been to as a teenager, taken by a local legend in horse whispering.

At first Molly couldn't understand why her

brain had dredged up something she hadn't thought about in more years than she could count.

'Every horse lives with a mindset that's like a human with PTSD,' she remembered the course leader saying to them as he gave them a demonstration. *'They have eyes on the sides of their heads. They've always been prey, not the predators. They're hypervigilant. Always looking for danger...'*

Molly found herself catching her breath, as she slowly sat down on a bench and put her coffee down beside her. That was Hugh as far as relationships went, wasn't it? Hypervigilant. A kind of prey because a relationship was something that could hurt him. Destroy him, even.

The emotional trauma from his childhood must have left huge scars. Remembering what he'd told her about his baby sister's last day alive brought a lump to her throat that was sharp enough to be painful as she imagined how terrible that day must have been for a boy and his dog.

And how hard had those five years before that day been? All the attention would have been on the sick little girl to start with. Had that become a way of life? Had Hugh been left feeling abandoned? Molly had the odd urge to reach back through time and give that boy a hug. To make sure he knew how important he was, too. That he knew he was loved.

The unbearable heartache of losing Fudge before he'd even had a chance to process the loss of his sister was unthinkable.

So yeah…it wasn't a crazy analogy that he was like the horse running around the edges of that round pen with the trainer standing in the centre. That Hugh had learned to keep that distance from any kind of relationships that the trainer represented.

But he'd circled closer to Molly, hadn't he? Close enough to tell her a little bit about that childhood trauma. Close enough to make love to her, even if he hadn't realised that was what it was.

Just the way that horse had circled closer to the trainer when it had had time to read the signals, accept the newcomer in its life and trust that this person wasn't a threat.

'Then you can turn your back and walk away and the horse will come up behind you.' The trainer had slowed and then stopped and the horse had nudged his shoulder. *'Now I can walk away and the horse gets to choose where he wants to be and…look…he's right behind me. He wants to be with me…'*

Good grief…it was time to stop this before it got silly. Before Molly could imagine Hugh following her around like some sort of lovestruck puppy. Her coffee was too cold to be desirable now so shc tipped it out into the garden behind her and stood up. It was time she went back to work now, anyway.

She did feel more at peace, she realised. She'd already known instinctively that Hugh needed the time and space to make his own choices. He'd already come close enough for it to be meaningful and that was…

…it was huge.

And very, very special.

Molly could wait. If anything else was going to happen between them, it would be well worth waiting *for*.

Working together made things so much easier.

If Hugh didn't see Molly at work, either when she was on duty or there with Oreo to visit sick kids and sometimes with Milo as a training exercise, the pressure might have been unwelcome.

It would certainly have been unforgivable not to make contact with her after the evening of the day that little boy, Sam, had died. When he'd opened a door into his personal life that was never opened to anyone—even to himself, if he could avoid it. The evening that had included sex that had been somewhat disturbing in its level of intimacy.

Not that Molly had given any hint of it being a problem for her. That next morning, when they'd met in the ward, had made it seem like it was no big deal. That it could have been simply an evening with a friend that had happened to end up in bed. That she didn't necessarily expect it to happen again and definitely wasn't going to let it impinge on their professional relationship.

Gemma, who'd had the unfortunate complication of a nasty post-op infection, had needed a bit more time in hospital to get it under control and for her to then catch up on the skills she needed with her crutches before she could go home but she'd been discharged yesterday. It was during that ward round, when Hugh had signed off on the discharge, that he'd realised how easy this was.

It felt like he and Molly were friends now. Even better, that there was no pressure for it to be anything more than that. He didn't have to ask her out on a formal date or anything but he didn't have to avoid her company, either, and that was a relief.

He didn't have to give up on one of his favourite beaches to go and catch a wave. With the days getting longer and the weather more reliable, Hugh was hoping to get into the sea as often as his work schedule would allow. Because there was nothing better than surfing to escape… well…everything, really.

Except…maybe there was *one* thing better than surfing.

And, as the days ticked past and the smiles and quick chats, when his path crossed with Molly's, became something familiar and welcome, Hugh was starting to wonder if she might like to spend some more personal time together again.

He didn't want to ask because that might make it seem more significant than he wanted it to be. And, anyway, hadn't all the time they'd had together happened without any prior arrangements? When he'd discovered her in the outpatient department with Milo after hours and ended up helping with the young dog's training. When he'd taken that old equipment out to her house and ended up running around the agility course with Oreo. When he'd gone to the beach for a breath of fresh air and ended up swimming in sea that was so cold he'd needed that hot shower and…

Hugh blew out a breath. If he went too far down that mental track he might get lost in a level of desire that could ring alarm bells. But was there a theme here? He'd gone to find Molly on the beach the day Sam had died.

He'd met her away from work for the first time on that beach, come to think of it. Maybe all he needed to do was head for Taylors Mistake again to find out what fate had in store for him?

Whether Molly *did* want more of what had

happened the last time he'd gone in that direction? No pressure, of course. On either side. And definitely no strings attached either.

No...

It couldn't be.

Which was a silly thing to think because this was exactly where she'd met Hugh Ashcroft more than once and, like the very first time, he was wearing his skintight wetsuit again and that was enough to know exactly who he was given that Molly was taken straight back to that first wave of the sexual attraction she had felt for this man. The one that had been powerful enough to make her stomach curl and her knees weak.

Both Oreo and Milo had recognised him as well and were running towards the figure with the surfboard slung under his arm but the curl in Molly's gut this time felt very different from a wash of attraction.

It felt more like...trepidation...?

It felt as though he was walking right into the middle of her life this time.

Which, in a way, he was. The Holmes family was celebrating the birthday of Molly's niece, eight-year-old Neve. Christchurch had turned on one of its spring evenings that felt far more like summer so they were all on the beach, including the dogs, having some playtime with the chil-

dren before going back to the house for a barbecue dinner.

Molly was sitting on the sand, making castles
by filling a moulded bucket and turning it upside
down so that her youngest niece could flatten it
with a toy spade. She paused, with the bucket in
mid-air, as she took in the moment Hugh recognised the dogs and then realised she was part of
this family group.

Even from this distance, she could feel the eye
contact.

She could feel how torn he was and that made
it feel like this was a very significant moment.

A make-or-break kind of moment?

Hugh had obviously come to do some surfing
but it was quite possible—probable, even—that
he'd been hoping that he would find her here.
Molly's heart sank as she wondered if this was
the moment she'd been waiting patiently for—
when Hugh felt safe enough to make the choice to
be with her because it was something he wanted
as much as she did?

Would this be the end of any such opportunity?
Hugh was cautious enough of a one-on-one relationship. Would the dynamics of a whole family
be his worst nightmare? Molly could understand,
all too easily, why he was taken aback. He was
probably considering turning back to the car park
and escaping but she knew he wouldn't do that.

How much courage had Hugh had, as a child, to face up to what life had thrown at him?

He'd learned to get through anything, no matter how hard it was.

And he'd learned to do it alone.

Molly's heart took another dive. Not just because it was aching for someone who possibly didn't even know how much it helped to *not* be alone when facing the tough stuff in life, but because Hugh didn't know the worst of what he was walking into right now. He didn't yet have any idea that her niece was celebrating her birthday.

Her eighth birthday.

Neve was now the same age as Hugh's sister, Michelle, had been when she died...

Molly got to her feet, knocking over the half-filled sandcastle bucket in her haste. The toddler beside her waved her toy spade.

'More...' she demanded. 'Aunty 'olly...*more*...'

But Molly was walking towards Hugh.

'Oreo... *Milo*...stop harassing Hugh...'

Her brother, Jack, paused in his cricket game with his son. 'You know this guy?'

'Friend of mine from work.' Molly smiled. 'And an ace surfer. You'll be impressed. Hugh, this is my brother, Jack. I think I told you how keen on surfing he used to be.'

Jack grinned at Hugh. 'Wish I could join you out there, mate. There're some awesome waves but we haven't even finished our first innings, have we, Liam?' He turned back to the impatient boy standing with his bat in front of the plastic wickets stuck into the sand. 'Come and have a beer with us when you're done.'

Molly's mother had come to get Milo and she didn't wait for an introduction.

'I'm Jill, Molly's mum. And this is Neve. It's her birthday today.'

'I'm *eight*,' Neve announced proudly.

Hugh's gaze flew to Molly's, as if he couldn't help checking to see if she remembered the significance of this. She tried to hold his gaze. To send a silent message.

I know, Hugh... I know exactly how hard this is and I'm sorry...

But Hugh was breaking the eye contact too soon. Before the most important thing Molly wanted him to know.

You don't have to do this alone. I'm here... and... I love you...

Hugh was oblivious. He was smiling at Neve. That distant kind of smile that he used with his young patients. It didn't mean he didn't care.

It meant he knew what could happen when you cared *too* much.

'Happy birthday,' he said. 'I hope you have a wonderful party. Maybe I'll be able to see all those candles on your cake from out on the waves.'

And, with that, he excused himself with another smile and strode off into the sea.

The waves *were* awesome.

It was close to a high tide and, as often happened close to sunrise or sunset, there was a decent swell and the offshore breeze was enough to smooth things out. Best of all, the swell was on an angle so that the wave was peeling off instead of breaking all at once.

Hugh wasn't the only surfer making the most of the fading daylight but it was far from crowded, in the sea or on the beach. Molly's family celebration was, by far, the biggest group of people and Hugh was acutely aware of them each time he finished a ride and prepared to paddle back out to find another wave.

He could see Jack playing cricket with Liam and even heard the little boy gleefully shout *'Howzat?'* having presumably bowled his father out. He could see Molly building sandcastles with a toddler who was happily knocking them down with her small, red spade and, after a later wave, he saw her taking the youngest child into the shallow foam of the waves to wash the sand off her hands. The birthday girl ran to join them and they both took a hand of the toddler, lifting her up to jump the foamy curl of a spent wave.

Hugh could hear the shrieks of excitement from the baby and he recognised both Molly's laughter and Oreo's happy barking.

He saw them gathering up the toys and towels and wending their way back to the family's holiday house. He knew he would be welcomed if he chose to join them in the garden for a drink. They were probably going to start cooking sausages on the barbecue and, at some point, a cake with burning candles would appear for Neve to make her birthday wish.

But Hugh paddled back to catch another wave.

And another.

The other surfers left. Daylight was almost gone and, despite the wetsuit, Hugh was getting really cold.

He told himself that each wave would be the last one but then he decided to try just one more…

Because he wanted it to be dark enough when he got out that Molly wouldn't notice him leaving.

She knew too much and he didn't want to be at her niece's birthday party and feel her understanding. Her sympathy. To know that she genuinely cared about how he was feeling. He needed some distance.

And Molly needed it too, even if she didn't realise that.

She was in the place she needed to be. With the people—and animals—she loved so much. With her whole family and those gorgeous children who loved her back. This would be Molly's future, wouldn't it? The heart and soul of a new branch of the family with the chaos of kids and dogs and big celebrations for every birthday and Christmas.

It was never going to be Hugh's future.

How hard had it been to walk into that family scene?

Molly had known that it would be another blow to any defence mechanism he had honed to learn that it was Neve's eighth birthday. That he would be reminded of Michelle. Getting to know Oreo had been enough of a pull back into his past. To where he and Fudge had been an inseparable team. They'd both adored Michelle and had been so protective of her. They'd both comforted each other on the darker days.

There were splashes of sea water getting into his eyes and blurring his vision as he flipped out of the end of the wave and dropped onto his board to paddle back out. Or were they tears?

Hugh wasn't sure. What he was sure about, however, was that he'd come closer than he'd realised to losing any of the hard-won protection he'd built for himself in the years since Michelle had died. Seeing Molly with the children in her extended family was sounding a warning that he couldn't ignore. This might be his last chance to avoid any more echoes of a pain he never wanted to experience again.

And maybe Molly had been right and he *was* creating a distance from living a life that was totally fulfilling.

Maybe it *was* only better for himself.

She'd made it so very clear that she would never want to live *her* life like that.

They were complete opposites and getting close to Molly Holmes was...well...he'd always known how dangerous it was. But it had been a risk he'd been—almost—willing to take. Until now, when he could see it might be dangerous for Molly as well as himself and he couldn't allow that to happen.

Because *he* cared about her.

One day, she would be grateful for him keeping them both safe.

CHAPTER TEN

THE SAME BUT DIFFERENT.

That was how Molly began to describe the relationship she had with Hugh Ashcroft to herself as the days slid past after that family gathering on the beach to celebrate Neve's birthday.

The day that she wished had ended so very differently.

If only they could have met on the beach with nobody else there to complicate things. Or Hugh had come and knocked on her door after he'd been surfing and they could have gone for a walk in the hills with Oreo or shared a glass of wine and watched the sunset.

As Molly replayed that evening in her head time and time again, adding the fantasy of what she'd wished had happened, it always ended up with the same kind of love making as last time. The kind that had taken everything to a completely new level and made Molly realise how much she wanted to take the next step towards a relationship that could change both their lives and give them a future.

Together.

But it hadn't happened like that and Hugh had obviously seen enough to make him back away and Molly just knew it was about her family.

About the children in her life.

He'd only ever seen her interacting with the children she worked with and their patients were part of the professional life she shared with Hugh. He'd never seen her with the children who were such an important part of her personal life—and always would be. Had it made him think that Molly saw children of her own as part of her future? Had Hugh ever got close enough to think about a permanent relationship with someone and imagine creating a family of his own? Had he made his mind up at that point that it was never going to happen? Like the way he'd decided he never wanted to have another dog?

She couldn't blame him for making the choices he had in life, but it did make her feel sad.

Maybe Hugh didn't see how good he was with kids? Or dogs, for that matter. Or that both children and dogs were instinctively drawn to him?

He was currently with fifteen-month-old Jasper, on their ward round, who was due to be discharged after the surgery he'd had on a badly dislocated and fractured elbow.

The adventurous toddler, who'd managed to climb onto a kitchen chair and then fall onto his outstretched arm, was now in a long arm cast with his elbow fixed at a ninety-degree angle but it didn't seem to be bothering him. He was grinning up at Molly as she stood beside his mother and he was trying to lift the heavy cast on his arm so that he could reach for the stethoscope she had hanging around her neck, attracted by the bright green, plastic frog head clipped to the top of its disc.

'Can I borrow that for a sec?' Hugh asked. 'Could be just what the doctor ordered for checking the range of movement and capillary refill of those fingers.'

Molly handed him the stethoscope and Jasper's gaze followed the frog's head as it got closer.

'Ribbit-ribbit,' Hugh growled.

Hugh's registrar exchanged a grin with Molly. 'We learn that in medical school,' he said.

'True,' Hugh agreed, but he didn't look up to catch Molly's gaze.

He was watching Jasper's fingers move as he played with the frog and then he quickly checked limb baselines like skin temperature and colour. Jasper's frown as he pressed a fingernail to check blood flow suggested that his ability to feel touch was not compromised, but he didn't start crying.

Instead, the frown turned to a grin as he caught the frog and he gave a gurgle of laughter.

He liked this surgeon.

Yeah… Kids and dogs could sense things that people might not even know about themselves, couldn't they?

And yes, she could totally understand where his wariness of choosing to have a child—or a dog—of his own came from but wouldn't it be easier to accept having the joy of them in his life when they were someone else's? Molly had seen Hugh patting and playing with her dogs. He would be just as good with nieces and nephews and, in time, he might even be very grateful to have them in his life.

'I'm happy for him to go home.' Hugh nodded at Jasper's mother. 'You'll get outpatient appointments and we'll be looking at removing the cast and pins at around the four-week mark.'

'Are there any long-term complications we should be worried about? I've heard that elbows can be tricky with all the nerves and things in there.'

'I don't think you need to worry.' Hugh was trying to gently prise the disc of his stethoscope from a small but determined fist. 'There may be some limitation in the range of movement but we'll encourage him to work through that as soon as he's out of the cast. Elbows are the most complex joint in the human body and we're very careful about them because of how important they are for arms and hands to function but, if there *were* any long-term complications, like disruption to the ulnar nerve, perhaps, we can deal with them.' He smiled at the anxious mother. 'And there's no point worrying about crossing bridges like that when we may never get anywhere near them. Let's take it one step at a time and be happy that Jasper's doing very well so far.'

They moved on to the next patient on their ward round but Hugh got distracted on the way by the arrival of a new patient who was waiting by the reception desk.

'Michael… I'll come and see you later today. You've got a few appointments for things like a chest X-ray and blood tests to make sure we tick all the boxes before your surgery tomorrow. How did your exams go at school?'

'Good…'

'I'll bet you smashed them. We'll talk later, okay?'

Molly had been expecting the arrival of this teenager, who was being admitted for the surgery scheduled to correct his spinal scoliosis that was affecting his breathing. She also knew that when the surgeon visited later, he would be talking about what was going to happen tomorrow. The prospect of having bone grafts and metal rods

and screws being put into his body to fuse his
spine had to be terrifying, no matter how brave a
face this lad was showing to the world right now.
Michael's mother was certainly looking as if she
was on the verge of tears as they waited to finish
the admittance process paperwork.

'Hi, Michael.' Molly paused to smile at him.
'I'm Molly and I'm one of the nurses who'll be
looking after you while you're with us.' She low-
ered her voice as if she were imparting a secret.
'I've earmarked the best bed for you. You'll get a
great view of all the helicopters landing and taking off from the helipad on the next-door roof.'

'Cool.'

Michael's smile was tentative but at least it was
there. Hugh had seen it as well and it felt like he
had deliberately kept his head turned for long
enough to catch Molly's gaze and send a private
message of appreciation for her attention to his
new patient.

And that ability to communicate silently was
something else that was different even though
they were still the same colleagues. Their opinion of each other had also changed and grown
into something completely different from initial
impressions. They were now people who could
work together with genuine respect that was personal as well as professional. Trust had been established.

In fact, they knew each other *too* well to be considered simply friends, but it was a grey area when nothing had actually been said and Molly had no idea whether Hugh even wanted to see her again. She was, in fact, on the point of giving up her patient wait for Hugh to come and find her out of working hours.

It felt as if that initial distance between them that had become the most different aspect of their relationship was being reinstated.

Slowly but surely.

With kindness. The way someone who was so good with kids and dogs might approach something that needed to be done but could be hurtful.

Someone who'd make a great father even though he never wanted to have his own children.

Someone who had probably been the best big brother in the entire world to a little girl whose heartbreaking life was the reason he never wanted to have his own children.

And okay… Molly had been trying to follow the advice Hugh had just given Jasper's mother in taking things one step at a time and being happy with how well it was going but…

…that bridge was right there in front of her and she couldn't ignore it.

Because her heart was already aching and it would be completely broken if—or when—she had to cross the bridge that might be the only way out of a dead end.

She wasn't quite there yet, mind you. And the possibility of discovering a detour came into her head as she saw Hugh walking away having signed Jasper's discharge paperwork.

What if Hugh knew that not having children of her own was not a dealbreaker as far as a relationship with him was concerned?

And, yeah…that had been a dream once but, by the time she'd moved back to New Zealand, she'd already made peace with the possibility that it would never happen, hadn't she? She'd decided that she could be happy with the children she had in her life through her family and her work. That the fur children she would always have at home would be enough.

Perhaps she just needed to find a way to let him know that? A way that didn't put any pressure on Hugh, of course, because that would send her straight across that bridge she really, really didn't want to cross.

He heard the sound of her voice before he'd turned the corner to where the reception area bridged the two main corridors in the ward.

'Show me again…? Oh, *wow*…look at you.'

Hugh could hear the smile in her words and he knew exactly what Molly's face would look like—lit up with genuine warmth that brought a glow to everyone around her. He could feel himself taking a deeper breath, his muscles tensing, as if they could form the forcefield he needed to not feel that glow.

Because it made him remember that Molly had implied he was missing out on life by keeping himself closed off and he suspected that that glow might be one of the things he was going to miss most about not allowing himself to get too close to her.

He was somewhat blindsided, however, when he did turn the corner to find who Molly was praising with so much enthusiasm. Sophie Jacobs, wearing a cute beanie with pompom ears, was standing in front of her on her crutches and, for a split second, Hugh's head was full of the image of Molly and her dog dancing for the little girl and every cell in his body was trying to remind him of how attracted he'd been to her.

He knew he would remember the physical connection they'd discovered for the rest of his life. That he was almost certainly never going to experience anything quite like that ever again.

Sophie almost looked like she was trying to dance herself, on those crutches, but then Hugh realised that was demonstrating the range of movement she had now that she was free of her plaster cast.

'And I can do it sideways, Molly…look… I can play a game where I can hit a ball with my foot. But sometimes I just lie on a mat on the floor when I do it. It's called a hip ah…ad…'

'A hip adduction,' Hugh supplied as he came up behind Molly. 'That's great, Sophie. Do you remember to keep your heel knee pointing straight up when you do that exercise on your back?'

Sophie nodded. 'And when I walk with my crutches, I have to have it pointing in front of me like it's a torch and it's shining a light for me to see where to go.'

'That's a good way to think of it.' Molly nodded. 'Did your physio give you that idea?'

'Yes. His name's Tom and he's really nice. I'm going to physio almost every day now that I've got my brace and we're going to go swimming soon when my scars are properly joined up.'

'When did you get the cast off?'

'Last week.' It was Hugh who responded. 'I saw Sophie in Outpatients that day.' He looked around. 'Where's Mummy?'

'She went to get a coffee. Molly said I could stay with her until she gets back. We're going to see somebody else after that. The man who's making my new leg that will be like the one the dancing girl has.'

'Your prosthesis?'

'Yes… I can't say that word.' But Sophie's smile

was stretching from ear to ear. 'I can't wait…it feels like Christmas…'

Hugh found his own smile was feeling oddly wobbly and he knew that Molly was watching him. He could feel the touch of her gaze on his face but it felt as if she could see way deeper than that—as if she could see how much this child's happiness was touching his heart.

'I'd better go,' he said briskly. 'I've got a patient to see who had a big operation on his back a couple of days ago.'

'Michael's looking forward to seeing you,' Molly told him. 'He wants to ask you about when he can go home. He's been in and out of bed three times already today.'

Hugh stepped towards the desk to ask for Michael's notes.

'Want to see some more of my exercises, Molly?'

'I sure do. I might even see you in the gym this week. I take Oreo in to help children with their exercises sometimes and her friend Milo is going to start soon, too.'

'Have you got *two* dogs?'

Hugh had to wait for the ward clerk, Debbie, to find Michael's notes so there was no distraction from Sophie's excited question that was an echo of one that Hugh had asked himself that day he'd found Molly in Outpatients with both Oreo and Milo and he'd been persuaded to help with training the younger dog.

'I do,' Molly told Sophie. 'Let me show you a photo of him. He's really fluffy and he's got lot of spots.'

Hugh could see her scrolling for photos on her phone. 'Here we go… This was when Milo and Oreo were at the beach last night. They found a stick they both wanted so they decided to share and, look…they're each holding one end of it…'

'Aww… They're so *cute*…' Sophie sighed.

'I'm so proud of them,' Molly said. 'They're my fur kids.'

'Best kind to have.' Debbie grinned as she handed Michael's notes to Hugh.

'Absolutely,' Molly agreed. 'The only kind *I* really need.'

There was something in Molly's voice that made Hugh look up from where he'd flicked the notes open. She didn't look up from her phone as she kept scrolling. 'Let me find some of my mum's puppies to show you, Sophie.'

'I want a puppy,' Sophie said. 'Do you have a dog at home, Mr Ashcroft?'

'No.' Hugh closed the patient file and took a deep breath. He was still trying to identify what it was in Molly's tone that had sounded like…

What…? A warning bell…?

She needed to know, didn't she? That he couldn't give her what was going to make her happy.

Ever.

This might be the perfect opportunity to let Molly know that. Before it went any further and someone—i.e. *Molly*—got hurt. And perhaps he could do it in a way that would make it her choice as well as his own to avoid spending any more time together out of work hours.

Sophie was making it easy.

'Why not?' she asked. 'Why don't you like dogs?'

'I do like dogs,' he told her. 'But only when they're someone else's. I just don't want to live with any. I spend way too much time at work so it wouldn't be fair on them, would it?'

'But…'

Sophie's eyes were wide. She couldn't understand.

Molly could. Hugh could sense that by the way she had become so still. Pretending to be so focussed on her phone but he could tell she wasn't looking at anything in particular. She was simply avoiding looking at him.

She probably needed some time to let his words sink in and Hugh was only too happy to provide it. He walked away without a backward glance.

Maybe he needed a bit of time, too.

CHAPTER ELEVEN

A DEALBREAKER.

There was no getting past that.

It didn't matter how much in love with Hugh she was. Being prepared to forgo having her own children didn't make enough of a difference, either.

Molly simply couldn't imagine not having dogs in her life. *And* in her home.

Which meant that there was no future for her and Hugh Ashcroft.

Maybe they could be friends. Eventually. They might even laugh about it over a wine or two at some staff function in a distant future.

'I had such a crush on you back in the day, Hugh...'

'Did you? You must have known it could never have worked.'

'Yeah...we both dodged a bullet, didn't we?'

'Well... I wouldn't say that, exactly, but look at you... Happily married and with those gorgeous kids of yours—and all those dogs!'

'And look at you, Hugh. Still alone...'

'Just the way I like it. Cheers, Molly...'

Molly's breath was expelled in something that sounded like a growl. Flights of conversational imagination weren't ever going to help. If anything, they had contributed to how difficult it had been for Molly to deal with the aftermath of what had felt like a significant break-up. Which was ridiculous, really. How could she have allowed herself to get in that deep when it hadn't even been a real relationship?

Except, it had been, hadn't it?

On her side, at least.

There was nothing fake about how she'd fallen in love with Hugh.

And something told her that, even if he hadn't realised it, the attraction on Hugh's side had to have been more than purely a physical thing.

They'd connected on a level on which she just knew Hugh had never connected with anyone else.

He'd told her about his sister.

About Fudge.

They'd made love.

There hadn't been any distance at all between them that night. Every touch had been as full of an emotional connection as much as anything physical. But now, the distance between herself and Hugh felt even further than it had been the first time she'd met the aloof surgeon in the radiology procedure room. Because of how close they'd been that night, the barrier between them felt...

...impenetrable, that was what it was.

Not that the solidity of that barrier mattered when neither of them were going to make any attempt to break through it because there was no point. For both of them, what lay on the other side was not something they wanted in their future and there was no compromise that could make it work.

Molly hadn't been pushed to cross that bridge to walk—yet again—into her future alone. She had chosen to cross it because she realised that the road she'd been on with Hugh had been a dead end all along.

And she was going to be okay.

She'd spent as much time as she could playing with Bella's adorable litter of pups in the few weeks since then and she'd poured hours into stepping up Milo's training as he settled in to living with her and Oreo in the beach cottage. They all spent time walking in the hills or on the beach every day but, while there were more and more surfers there when there were some decent waves, Hugh had clearly crossed Taylors Mistake off his list of preferred beaches.

Milo was living up to his promise to become

a valuable assistance dog and would graduate to being in work rather than training on his visits to the hospital, but it was Oreo who was by her side when Molly headed for the ground floor of a wing of Christchurch Children's Hospital that was becoming one of their regular destinations.

The state-of-the-art physiotherapy department included a full-sized indoor basketball court suitable for wheelchair rugby to be played and a gymnasium crowded with exercise equipment and soft mats, walking tracks with rails on either side and even a small staircase. It also had a twenty-five-metre heated swimming pool with hoists and waterproof equipment that could cater for any level of disability. Community groups and staff members had access to some of the facilities, like the basketball court and pool, outside normal hours but Molly and Oreo weren't here today to take advantage of that privilege.

They were here to be a part of Sophie's first session of learning to walk with the custom-made prosthesis that she'd been anticipating with such excitement because it would represent a big step on her long journey back to being able to dance. Oreo took no notice of the children in wheelchairs and on beds who were working around the edges of the gymnasium. She was heading straight towards the small girl sitting at one end of a walking track with a small cluster of people around her.

'Hey, Sophie…'

'Oreo…'

Sophie's mum stepped to one side to allow Oreo to get close to Sophie's wheelchair to say hullo. Her smile was apologetic.

'We're happy to see you too, Molly—not just Oreo.'

'I'm happy that I'm allowed to be here *with* Oreo,' Molly responded. 'How exciting is this?'

Tom, the physiotherapist, was helping one of the technicians from the prosthetic department to encourage Sophie to push her foot into the first version of the artificial lower leg that would enable her to walk without needing her crutches.

That would, hopefully one day, enable her to dance again.

Sophie's face was scrunched into lines of deep uncertainty, though. Disappointment, even?

'It feels…weird…'

'It'll take a bit of getting used to.' Tom nodded. 'This is just a try on to see how it fits. And it's just your training leg so it doesn't have the brace that will fit around the top of your leg.'

Sophie's head bent further as she stared down at the leg.

'Her hair…' Molly whispered to Joanne. 'Look at those gorgeous curls coming through.'

'I know.' Sophie's mum had tears in her eyes but she was smiling. 'It's like her baby hair used to be. So soft…'

Sophie lifted her head and she was smiling now, too. 'My new foot's got a shoe the same as my other leg.'

'Of course,' Tom said. 'You can always do that with your shoes.'

'Even ballet shoes?'

'Even ballet shoes,' Tom agreed. 'Like in that picture you showed me. Now…let's see if you can stand up, sweetie.'

Sophie looked suddenly fearful but, with a determination that brought tears to Molly's eyes as well as Joanne's, she let herself be helped up to stand on her normal foot and then, very tentatively, put some weight onto the artificial foot. Then she let go of Tom's hands and held onto the rails of the walking track instead.

'Do you feel ready to take a step?' Tom asked.

Sophie shook her head. Her bottom lip wobbled.

Molly quietly signalled Oreo, who moved to where she pointed, going under the rail to sit on the track a short distance from Sophie.

'Do you want to give Oreo a treat?' Molly asked.

Sophie nodded.

Molly took a tiny piece of dried beef from the

pouch on her belt. She put it on top of the rail just out of reach for Sophie.

'Oreo really wants that treat,' she said. 'But she's not allowed to have it unless you give it to her. One step will just about get you there.'

Sophie stared at the treat. Then she looked at Oreo, who had her mouth open and her tongue hanging out and her ears down. She was smiling at Sophie. Encouraging her.

And everybody held their breath as she moved her prosthetic leg in front of her, put some of her weight onto it and then moved her other leg. She could stretch out her hand now and pick up the treat.

'It's for you, Oreo,' she said proudly. 'You're a good girl…'

'Take it nicely,' Molly reminded her dog. Not because Oreo needed reminding but because she needed to take a breath and say something so that she didn't end up with tears rolling down her face at the joy of seeing Sophie—quite literally—taking her first step into a new future.

Giving up her free time to do something like this was no hardship.

It was, in fact, inspirational and Molly knew she could channel this little girl's determination and courage to move on with her own life. She would get over missing seeing him at the beach or remembering what it had been like to have him touch her. She would learn to respect his boundaries and have no more than a polite friendship at work. There was no point in continuing to feel grief of losing what could have been with Hugh Ashcroft because it had never really been there in the first place, had it?

It took two people to want a future with each other.

Maybe her imaginary conversation with Hugh hadn't been that far off base, either. It wasn't beyond belief that she could still meet someone who would want to share her life and her dreams of a family of her own—dogs included—but, if that didn't happen, it was up to her to make sure her life was as full of joy as possible.

And, with moments like this in it, how could it not be?

Despite the fact that the physiotherapy department became like a second home for many of his patients during their rehabilitation, there was no need for Hugh Ashcroft to go into that wing of this hospital. He was very familiar with what went on in the department and he could follow up the progress his patients were making after their orthopaedic surgery by reading reports written by the physiotherapists or speaking to these experts when they attended team meetings in the ward. What was most satisfying, however, was simply observing the changes in his patients for himself during their follow up outpatient appointments.

He had to smile when he saw the way Michael was walking into the consulting room, only weeks after his spinal fusion to correct the scoliosis. Even better, the teenager had a grin that was shy but still enough to light up his face.

'Look at you,' Hugh said as he got to his feet. 'I don't think I need to ask how you're doing.'

Michael's mother looked just as happy. 'He's taller than I am now.'

Hugh clipped the X-ray films to the light boxes on the wall. 'Everything's healing very well. Look, you can see how straight things are now and where the fusion is happening between the discs in your spine. Let's get your shirt off and get you on the bed so I can have a good look at your back.'

His examination was thorough but he stopped towards the end when Michael winced.

'Does that hurt?'

'A bit.'

'Your body is having to adjust to the change in the position of your ribs. You'll find there are bits that hurt, like here in your shoulder, that didn't used to be a problem. It'll get better. Is the paracetamol enough for pain relief now?'

'Yes.'

Hugh scribbled in Michael's notes as he got dressed again and then came to sit in front of the desk with his mother beside him. 'How has the gentle exercise programme they gave you been going at home?'

'Okay.' Michael nodded.

'He gets frustrated at how tired he gets,' his mother added.

'Don't forget you've had a big surgery,' Hugh told him. 'It can take longer than you expect to recover from a general anaesthetic and blood loss. There's a lot going on in that body of yours that isn't just adjusting to a new shape—like the healing around the implants that you can see on the X-rays. That sucks up some of your energy. There are things you can't see, as well. It's a lot more work for the muscles in your trunk to be holding up a spine that's suddenly straighter and longer and that takes more energy than it used to. It's really important to pace yourself and rest as often as you need to. Full recovery can take anywhere from six to twelve months.'

'Can I start driving lessons during the summer holidays? My uncle said he'd start teaching me on his farm when I'm there for a holiday.'

'I'll leave it up to your physios to decide when you're good to do something like that but I'm happy to sign you off to start physiotherapy sessions in the department here. They've got a hot

swimming pool you're going to love and you'll
get some one-on-one sessions in the gym as well.'

'Cool,' Michael said. 'I like swimming. Can I
stop wearing my brace now, too?'

'Not just yet. I'll have a meeting with your
physios before your next outpatient appointment
and we'll talk about that then, okay?' He turned
to Michael's mother. 'Have you got any questions
or worries about how everything's going?'

She shook her head. 'That nurse practitioner
in the ward has been so great. You know Molly?'

Hugh gave a single nod of agreement. He
dropped his gaze to Michael's notes again so that
he could hide the way it made him feel when he
heard Molly's name.

Uncomfortable, that was what it was.

As if he'd done something wrong. Or stupid.
Something that he should apologise for?

Something that he had the disturbing feeling
that he might regret for the rest of his life?

He had pushed her away. They were simply
colleagues now. He'd made sure they didn't meet
by chance out of work hours. He'd even gone as
far as not going surfing. Anywhere...

Because thinking about going surfing made
him think about Taylors Mistake beach and that
made him think about Molly.

'She called us every day when we were first at
home.' The list of things that Molly had helped

with felt like a muted background to Hugh's thoughts but he nodded occasionally, to make it look like he was listening. 'And if Mike ends up being a helicopter pilot it'll be Molly's fault.'

Oh…now he could see her in the ward on the day that Michael had been admitted. Taking the time to ease his fears and to make him feel special by telling him she'd saved the best bed for him where he'd be entertained by watching the helicopters come and go.

It was only a tiny example of how kind a person Molly Holmes was.

She'd made Hugh feel special too. As if he'd met the only person in the world who could understand what he'd gone through when he'd lost both his sister and his dog.

She had really cared about him and he'd pushed her away.

Yeah…he needed to apologise…

Hugh pasted a smile on his face. 'Is that what you want to do, Michael?'

'It was pretty cool, watching them taking off and landing on the roof,' he admitted. 'And I love flying…'

'I'll tell Molly she's inspired you,' Hugh said. 'I'm sure she'll think that's a brilliant plan.'

They weren't just empty words, he decided, as he gave Michael and his mother directions to get to the physiotherapy department and make their first appointments.

He would tell Molly at the first opportunity he got. It might even provide an opportunity for that apology that he needed to make.

Molly was later than she'd intended to be leaving the physiotherapy department after sharing Sophie's first walk with her prosthesis because she'd bumped into Michael and his mum and they'd had a chat.

She was in a bit of a rush, now, to get Oreo back to the van in the hospital car park and head home. Molly needed to pick Milo up from her mother's, take some time to admire Bella's puppies and play with them, of course, and she was hoping to still have enough daylight for a walk on the beach. She had her head down, sending a text to her mother to let her know she was finally on her way, when Molly thought she heard her name being called.

She hadn't imagined it because Oreo had suddenly gone on high alert with her ears pricked and every muscle primed for action.

And there it was again, coming from behind her.

'Molly...'

Two things happened in a tiny space of time as Molly swung her head to see Hugh coming towards her, framed by the backdrop of the hospital's main entrance.

Oreo—very uncharacteristically—did a U turn and took off, bounding towards Hugh as if he was a long-lost friend she couldn't wait to reconnect with.

And a car came racing along the stretch of road that led to both the car park entrance and the emergency department of Christchurch Children's Hospital.

Hugh's voice was much louder this time. 'Oreo…*no*…!'

Like it did in the movies, sometimes, everything became slow-mo and, to her horror, Molly could see it happen in excruciating clarity. Oreo had her focus so completely on Hugh she was unaware of the vehicle speeding towards her. A split second either way and it probably wouldn't have happened.

But it did.

Oreo ran in front of the car. She got hit square on her side and knocked flat. Even worse, the car went over the top of her and for another split second she vanished. Then she rolled out from beneath the back of the car as the driver slammed on the brakes.

And she wasn't moving.

At all.

* * *

The car screeched to a halt and the driver was starting to climb out of the car as Molly ran towards Oreo.

'Oh…my God…' The man was halfway out of the driver's seat, clearly distressed. 'I didn't see her… I've got my son in the car and he's having a bad asthma attack…'

Hugh arrived at the same time Molly did.

'*Go…*' he told the man. 'Get your son into the emergency department.'

The man drove off, his car door still swinging half open.

Molly sank to her knees. Oreo's eyes were only half open and she couldn't tell how well her beloved dog was breathing. She could see injuries that made her feel sick to her stomach. An open fracture to her front leg with bone visible. Missing skin and bleeding on her flank. A lot of bleeding. Molly's vision was blurring with tears and her breath felt stuck in her chest beneath an enormous weight.

Hugh had one hand on the wound. He put his other hand on Oreo's chest. 'She's breathing,' he told Molly. 'Her heart rate's strong but rapid— maybe two hundred beats per minute. We need to get her to a vet. *Stat…*'

We…?

Molly blinked to clear the tears in her eyes.

She could feel them rolling down her face as she looked up to meet Hugh's gaze. She wasn't alone in what felt like the worst moment of her life.

For just a heartbeat—a nanosecond—Molly remembered being on the beach that evening when everything had changed. When she'd known Hugh was confronted with memories of the worst moments of *his* life, when he'd lost everything that mattered the most to him. She remembered the silent message she'd tried so hard to send him.

You don't have to do this alone. I'm here... and... I love you...

It felt as if she was the one receiving that same message right now and it was cutting through her fear and shock.

'I need to keep pressure on this wound and stop any more blood loss,' Hugh said. 'Do you know if there's a vet clinic near here?'

'Yes...there's a big one only a few minutes' drive away.'

'Can you go and get your van?'

Hugh still hadn't broken that eye contact and it was giving Molly a strength she wouldn't have believed she had.

'*Yes...*'

'Hurry...'

Molly ran. She was out of breath and her hands were shaking so it took two attempts to get the key into the lock and open the driver's door. It took less than another minute to drive down the hospital's entranceway to where a small crowd had now gathered around Hugh and Oreo. Someone had supplied a dressing and bandages—maybe from ED—and it looked as if the bleeding was under control. Oreo was panting but her eyes were closed as if her level of consciousness was dropping and Molly had a moment of absolute clarity as she opened the back door of the van and Hugh gently picked Oreo up to put her on the soft blanket on the floor.

There was no way she could let Hugh come with her to the vet clinic.

No way she could put him through possibly having to witness Oreo being euthanised because her injuries were too severe to survive with any quality of life.

She loved him too much to put him through something he'd spent most of his life trying to escape.

'We'll be okay now,' she told Hugh. 'You don't need to come with us.'

'Are you sure?'

She loved that he looked so torn. That he was prepared to go through this for her sake. But she could see the flash of relief in his eyes when she gave a single but decisive nod of her head.

'I'm sure.'

* * *

Hugh stood where he was, watching the little green van speed off.

The crowd was beginning to disperse. A couple of people helpfully picked up the wrappers from the bandages and dressings he'd used to keep the worst of Oreo's wounds covered and under pressure to help stop the blood loss. He could hear the shocked tone of the things they were saying to each other but it sounded as if it were muted. That someone else was listening to it or it was a part of a dream. A nightmare.

'I know his kid was sick but he shouldn't have been going so fast.'

'His kid was sick. He wouldn't have been thinking about anything else.'

'And why was that dog here, anyway?'

'It had a coat on. Maybe it was a guide dog.'

'Its owner wasn't blind. She was driving a van!'

'I hope that kid's okay...'

'I hope the dog's okay...'

Hugh could have added to that conversation to echo those comments and say that *he* hoped Molly was okay.

But he didn't want to share his feelings with strangers.

He didn't want to think about them, either.

Maybe if he made himself move he could somehow wake up from this daytime nightmare.

For some reason Hugh turned to walk back into the hospital rather than continuing towards the car park. Because he couldn't imagine going home to stare at the walls of his apartment and think about what had just happened? Or maybe it was because he needed the comfort zone of being at work rather than in a personal space?

He got as far as the stairs he could take to get up to the level of his ward and his office but he didn't push the firestop door open. He pressed the button to summon a lift, instead, but he wasn't thinking about what he was doing or why he was doing it. His head was full of something else.

The knowledge that Molly couldn't possibly be anything like okay.

She *loved* Oreo. Adored her, even. She was able to love fiercely and without reservation and she could give everything she had—heart and soul—to the things she loved that much.

He'd been like that, once.

He'd loved Michelle like that.

And his mother.

And Fudge.

Before he knew just how destructive it could be to have your heart shattered in an instant. Or chipped away at slowly so that it felt like it was bleeding to death, the way it had when his mother had become lost for ever in the depths of her grief and depression.

But Molly knew how hard it was to lose someone or something you loved that much and yet she was still prepared to do it again. She had no hesitation in throwing herself into everything she chose to love in her life. To her family. To her dogs—her fur kids...

He could hear an echo of her voice.

It's unbearably hard to lose dogs...but, for me, it would be even harder to live without them...

She was that passionate about her job, as well. To those children she gave so much to in and out of her normal working hours, like she had when little Sam Finch was dying.

Maybe she would love *him* that much, if he ever let her get close enough. Or maybe she would have but he'd destroyed that possibility by pushing her away so decisively.

The ding announced the arrival of the lift. The doors opened and people got out. And then the doors closed again but Hugh hadn't stepped inside.

He was thinking about Sam again.

About how he'd known Molly wouldn't be okay and how he'd had that urge to go and find her. Not to tell her that she should have heeded his warning about the dangers of getting so involved.

He'd gone because he'd needed to see her.

To make sure she wasn't alone because…

…because he needed to *be* there with her.

And he finally knew why. It was because he *loved* her. As much as he'd ever loved anything in his entire life.

Hugh turned away from the lift. He was scrolling his phone to find the address of the closest veterinary hospitals.

He was running by the time he reached the car park.

He knew exactly where he was going now.

Where he needed to be.

CHAPTER TWELVE

THERE WAS NOTHING more Molly could do.

Staff from the veterinary hospital had rushed into the car park as soon as Molly stumbled through the doors, begging for help. They had carried Oreo into one of the clinic's treatment rooms and they were doing everything they could to help the badly injured dog.

It could have been a trauma team in the emergency department of Christchurch Children's Hospital working on a child who'd been rushed in by ambulance after being hit by a car, Molly thought as she listened to them going through a primary survey. It felt like she was watching from a huge distance even though she could almost have reached out and touched Oreo.

'Is her airway open?'

'Yes.'

'Is she breathing?'

'Tachypnoeic. Breath sounds reduced on the left side. Potential pneumothorax. Feels like at least one rib's fractured.'

'What's her heart rate?'

'Two hundred. Gums are pale. She's in shock.'

'Let's get an IV line in, please, and fluids up. Forty mils per kilo over the next fifteen minutes or so.'

'What's her weight?'

'I'd guess around twenty kilos.'

Molly knew it was eighteen kilos but the vet's guess was close enough. She couldn't make her lips work in time because they, along with the rest of her body, felt completely numb. Things were happening too fast and this was simply too huge. These strangers were fighting for Oreo's *life…*

'I think we should intubate and ventilate. Her oxygen saturation's dropping.'

'Is that external bleeding under control?'

'As soon as we've got her airway secured, we need to set up for X-rays. I want an abdominal ultrasound, too, thanks. We can't exclude major internal bleeding from a rupture with that mechanism of injury…'

They knew what they were doing, this team, as they worked swiftly and effectively to get Oreo's airway and breathing secured and fluids up to maintain her circulation and blood pressure. They started antibiotics, took X-rays of the fracture in her front leg and cleaned and dressed the wound on her flank. The ultrasound showed some free fluid that could be internal bleeding but, as the head vet explained, they wouldn't know the extent of all the damage until they got her into Theatre.

Oreo was heavily sedated and dosed with pain killers so she probably wasn't even aware of where she was or what was happening but Molly had to press her lips to the silky hair on her head and whisper something only her dog could hear before they took her away to Theatre. She had signed a consent form that included a statement to the effect that if it was clear that the likelihood of Oreo surviving or that her quality of life would be unacceptably diminished, they would not wake her up again.

A nurse took her back out to the waiting room. She touched Molly's arm and her expression couldn't have been more sympathetic.

'Is there someone I can call for you?'

Molly shook her head. She could have called for her mum or her brother or a friend to come and stay with her while she waited for the call that would tell her whether Oreo was still alive but she couldn't do it.

Not simply because she was still feeling so frozen.

She knew she would need all the comfort and understanding that her family could give her soon but, right now, there was only one person who would be able to hold her hand on a level that was so much deeper than merely physical.

Only one person who could touch her soul in a way that would give her the strength to get through anything.

Even this…

But she had pushed him away. She'd put up the same kind of barrier he'd put in place himself not so long ago. Except that she'd done it for very different reasons, hadn't she? She'd wanted to protect him from pain because she loved him *that* much.

He'd put the barriers up to protect himself…

Was that why Molly felt so utterly alone?

So…*lost…*?

'You could wait here but it could be hours,' the nurse said. 'We've got your number. I'll call you as soon as we know anything. It might help to be somewhere else. Or to go for a walk or something?'

But Molly shook her head again. She didn't want to leave.

But she didn't want to stay, either.

She had absolutely no idea what she wanted, to be honest.

Until she heard the doors sliding open behind her and heard a voice that filled the air around her and she could breathe it in and feel it settle close to her heart.

'I'll look after her,' Hugh told the nurse.

And then he folded Molly into his arms and she pressed her head into the hollow beneath his shoulder. She could feel the steady beat of his heart beneath her cheek.

'I've got you, sweetheart,' he murmured against her ear. 'I'm not going to let you go...'

There was a river that meandered along the foothills on the south side of the city and it had wide enough borders to provide walking tracks, picnic tables, children's playgrounds and lots of benches for people to sit and enjoy the kind of serenity that moving water and the green space of trees and grass could bestow.

Hugh would have preferred to take Molly to a beach to watch and listen to the waves rolling in but he knew she would hate to be taken too far away from where Oreo was fighting for her life. Luckily, like Christchurch Children's Hospital— a mile or two downstream—this veterinary hospital was just across the road from the river so Hugh led Molly across a small, pedestrian bridge to where there was a bench on the riverbank— a two-minute walk at most from the front doors of the veterinary hospital and he'd told the nurse where they would be. That way they could come and find Molly to give her any news, rather than making a more impersonal phone call.

For the longest time, they simply sat side by side. In silence.

There were ducks on the river who were diving to catch their dinner and then popping up again to bob on the surface like bath toys. People walked past, some walking their dogs, but they were too far away to intrude.

It was Molly who broke the silence.

'Thank you…' she said softly. 'For coming.'

'I had to,' Hugh said.

'No…' Molly shook her head. 'You didn't *have* to.' But her sideways glance was anxious. 'I hope you don't think what happened was your fault. I should have had Oreo on her lead. She's never run off like that before.'

'It was because I called you.'

'No…' Molly shook her head again but this time there was a poignant smile playing around her lips. 'It was because she loves you. She's been missing you.'

Hugh swallowed hard. 'I've been missing her. And you.'

Molly was staring at the ducks on the river again. 'Same…'

Hugh reached for Molly's hand and she let her fingers lace through his and be held. Silence fell again and he knew they were both thinking about what was going on in the operating room of the veterinary hospital across the river. About how much Oreo would be missed if she didn't make it through this surgery. This waiting period was more than anxiety. It felt like a practice run for grief.

'You told me once that grief is love that has nowhere to go,' he said softly. 'I know how overwhelming your love for Oreo is right now. I can *feel* it.'

Molly's voice had cracks in it. 'But you're so good at *not* feeling things like that. At protecting yourself.'

'I used to be,' he agreed quietly. 'And, if it ever got hard, all I needed to do was remind myself that grief can kill you, like it killed my mother. It didn't matter that I was there and I loved her. She just took herself somewhere else and never came back. She died of a broken heart but she never told me how bad it was.'

'Maybe she was trying to protect you,' Molly suggested. 'By shutting you away from her pain?'

'I didn't want to be shut away,' Hugh said. 'I wanted to help.'

'I know. I'm sorry…'

Hugh had to pull in a slow breath. 'I'm sorry, too…' he said.

'For Oreo?'

'Of course. But for more than that, too. For the way I've been shutting *you* away.'

'I pushed you,' Molly admitted. 'I pushed my

way into things that you wanted to keep private. I said things I shouldn't about you being selfish when you were only doing what you needed to do to protect yourself.'

'When I was coming to find you, I found myself remembering the day that Shelly died,' Hugh said quietly. 'Mostly, the way that Fudge refused to get off her bed. The look in his eyes that told me he knew what was happening and, no matter how hard it was, he didn't want to be anywhere else.'

Molly nodded. And brushed away a tear that rolled down her cheek.

Hugh squeezed her hand that he was still holding.

'I remembered you saying how hard it was to lose a dog but that it was even harder to live without them. That dogs have the ability to supply limitless, unconditional love.'

She nodded again. 'They do...'

'I think you do, too.' Hugh had to swallow past the lump in his throat. 'I never wanted to become dependent on any kind of love again after losing everything I cared the most about. I didn't think that I could even get close to feeling like it could even exist for me again.'

He could feel an odd prickling sensation at the back of his eyes.

'Until I met you,' he added.

He could feel Molly's fingers tightening around his own. Looking up, he found her gaze fixed on his face.

'Until I realised that you could not only understand the kind of grief I went through with Shelly—and Fudge—but that you were still brave enough to get in there and do it all again. And… and I think that maybe you're right. That it is harder to live without that kind of love in your life. Emptier, anyway…'

'I think of love as being a kind of coin,' Molly said. 'There's lots of different kinds—or values, I guess, like real coins. There are the ones for friends and siblings and others for, say, your mum or a child. And dogs, of course. And really special ones if you're lucky enough to find your soul mate.'

She paused to take a breath but Hugh didn't say anything. He knew she hadn't finished yet.

'They have two sides, too, like real coins,' Molly added. 'There's love on one side but there's grief on the other side and if it gets dropped and spins you don't know what side it's going to land on. And yeah…there are some coins you don't have a choice to hold, like your family, but there are others where you get the choice of whether or not you pick them up and it's safer not to, because some of them are the wrong coins and some of them might lead to heartbreak again, but if you don't pick them up, you'll never know the joy it can bring if you've found the one you were always meant to find—or were lucky enough to be given.' She offered him a smile. 'Like your Fudge coin?'

'I remember.' Hugh nodded. 'The joy I felt when I came home from school and Fudge would be there, lying just inside the gate, his ball between his paws. Waiting...just for me. And how it felt when he sat on the back step with me late at night sometimes and I could put my arms around him and hide my face in his hair while I cried...'

Oh, *God*... He was crying now. For the first time since the day his sister had died, he knew he was crying.

Okay...maybe he had been crying that day in the surf when he'd made the decision that he had to stay away from Molly—and Oreo—because he couldn't risk loving them and he wasn't going to risk hurting them. But it had been easy to think it was sea water.

This time, there was no hiding the fact that his walls had completely crumbled.

'I get that feeling with you,' he whispered. 'Only it's even bigger. I love you, Molly. And, when I touch you, I think I can feel a kind of love that's so big it's...well, it's a bit terrifying, that's what it is.'

* * *

Molly let go of his hand but only so that she could reach up and brush away the tears on Hugh's cheeks.

'You can feel it because it's there,' she said, softly. 'I do love you, Hugh. *So* much. I fell in love with you ages ago. Right about the time I heard about your sister and I knew there was a reason why you had walls up to stop anyone getting close to you.'

'My walls don't seem to be working any longer.' Hugh was blinking his tears back. 'I've tried to stay away from you and it's not working.' A corner of his mouth lifted. 'Do you really love me, Molly?'

'More than I can say.'

She still had her hand on his cheek as she lifted her chin and Hugh bent his head and their kiss was as tender as it was possible for any kiss to be. And then Molly pulled back.

'When they took Oreo into Theatre, the nurse asked me if she could call someone to be with me while I waited and I said "no" because there was only one person I wanted to be with me and I didn't want to call you. I couldn't ask you to do something this hard…for *me*…'

'I will always be with you,' Hugh said. 'Today and tomorrow and for ever. No matter how hard it is, I will always be here and I will always love you.'

'Oh…' Molly was going to cry again. She tried to smile instead. 'That sounds like it could be a wedding vow.'

'Maybe I'd better write it down.' Hugh was smiling, too. 'Just in case we need it one of these days.'

They hadn't noticed the figure coming across the bridge until the nurse from the veterinary hospital was close enough to clear her throat and warn them of her approach.

Molly's heart stopped. She felt Hugh's hand close around hers and then she felt a painful thump of her heart starting again. But she still couldn't breathe. Even though the nurse was smiling.

'Oreo's okay,' she said. 'She's come through the surgery like a champion and she hasn't lost her leg. We're going to keep her well sedated and in intensive care for a while but do you want to come and see her for a minute or two?'

Molly was already on her feet.

So was Hugh.

And his hand was still holding hers as if he had no intention of letting it go.

Ever…

'We do,' was all he said.

It was all he needed to say. Because that one tiny word said it all.

We...

Molly was never going to be alone again. She had found her soul mate.

EPILOGUE

Three years later...

'WHY DOES YOUR dog walk funny?'

'A long time ago, she had to have a big operation on her leg.'

'Like I'm going to have?'

'Just like you're going to have, darling.'

'But she got better?'

'Yes, she did.'

'Does it still hurt her? Is that why she holds her paw up like that?'

'Do you want to know a secret?'

The small boy lying on the bed nodded. He was reaching out to touch Oreo's nose and wasn't taking any notice of the anaesthetist who was getting ready to inject the sedative needed for this procedure.

'I think when Oreo was getting better from her operation she learned that if people thought she had a sore paw, she would get lots of cuddles.'

The child's eyes were drifting shut. 'I like cuddles…' he murmured.

His mother leaned closer to squeeze her son, but she was smiling at Molly. 'Thank you,' she whispered.

'You're so welcome.'

'It can't be easy making the time to do this when you've got a little one of your own to look after.'

Molly adjusted the warm, sleeping bundle that was her newborn daughter, tied close to her body in its comfortable sling. 'Oh, it's easy at this stage. It's when they get mobile that it gets harder. That's why I've got our toddler in the great crèche we have here. I'm so happy that I get to use that even when I'm on maternity leave.'

An ultrasound technician had manoeuvred her equipment into place and a nurse was ready with all the instruments and other materials that would be needed, including the jars to hold the fragments of bone tissue about to be collected. Molly moved Oreo away from the table as the surgeon who was about to do the bone biopsy moved towards the table. She knew he was smiling at his patient's mother by the way his eyes crinkled over the top of his mask.

'How are you feeling, Sue?'

'Okay. You were right—it's been so much easier having Molly and Oreo in here with us. I had no idea that dogs would be allowed somewhere like this.'

'Not only allowed. We encourage it.' Hugh was smiling at Molly as she prepared to slip out of the room. A heartbeat of time that was too relaxed and warm to be entirely professional. A beat of eye contact that was even more personal. 'We all love Molly and Oreo.'

Molly paused for a moment as the room's lights were dimmed enough to make the ultrasound images on the screen clearer and Hugh shifted his focus entirely onto the procedure he was about to perform.

She just wanted to let her gaze rest on her husband for a moment longer. To feel the sheer joy that this man was sharing every bit of this amazing life they were building together. That, so often, there was something extra special to be celebrated in the private moments they had together when their two adorable daughters were finally both asleep at the same time and Oreo and Milo just as content.

Like they had last week when Hugh had told her about his outpatient appointment with Michael, who'd come to ask him to contribute to the medical assessment he needed to gain the Class Two certificate that was a necessary part of the process of qualifying for his private pilot's licence. His parents had given him the first hours of his dual instruction in flying as his seventeenth birthday gift and, apparently, they were planning to invite Molly to his graduation ceremony.

And this afternoon, when Molly had gone to visit her ward before Oreo was scheduled to be the dogtor for this bone biopsy, she'd been lucky enough to catch a visit from Sophie Jacobs, who had been on her way to an appointment in the prosthetic department. The now cancer-free ten-year-old, who still had a smile that looked like it was Christmas, had wanted to show off the diploma she'd just received for passing her Grade Two ballet examination.

Molly couldn't wait to share that news with Hugh this evening.

No…actually, it wouldn't matter if she didn't have something interesting or exciting to share with him.

She would be just as happy to simply *be* with him.

Today, tomorrow and…for ever.

* * * * *

Pregnancy Surprise In Byron Bay

Emily Forbes

MILLS & BOON

Emily Forbes is an award-winning author of Medical Romance novels for Harlequin. She has written over thirty-five books and has twice been a finalist in the Australian Romantic Book of the Year Award, which she won in 2013 for her novel *Sydney Harbor Hospital: Bella's Wishlist*. You can get in touch with Emily at emily@forbesau.com, or visit her website at emily-forbesauthor.com.

Visit the Author Profile page
at millsandboon.com.au for more titles.

Dear Reader,

Thank you for picking up this book—my 40th! I'm not sure that I ever imagined this number when I first put pen to paper, but it's been an incredible adventure, and I am so grateful to everyone who has read one or more of my novels.

My stories have been set everywhere from Antarctica to Canada, Hollywood to London, and Coober Pedy to Sydney, but this is the first one I've set in Byron Bay on Australia's east coast. Australia has such diverse landscapes, but the quintessential beachside locations are high on my list of favorites. Sun, surf, sand and sex are the perfect recipe for a romance, and summer in Byron was the perfect time and place for Molly and Theo to reconnect.

I'd love to hear from you if you've enjoyed this story or any of my others. You can visit my website, emily-forbesauthor.com, or drop me a line at emily@forbesau.com.

As always, happy reading.

Emily

DEDICATION

For Ned and Finn

In the time it has taken me to write forty books, you
have grown from babies to young adults.
I am so proud of you both. You are amazing men:
kind, intelligent, handsome, polite and funny.
You would both make fabulous heroes, and I hope
you each get your own happily-ever-after one day.

All my love,
Mum

CHAPTER ONE

MOLLY PRESCOTT CHECKED the time as she stepped out of the surf at Clarkes Beach and picked up her towel. She cursed softly to herself. She'd need to hurry if she was going to make the meeting on time.

Who was she kidding? She was definitely going to be late, she thought as she dried her face and wiped her arms with her towel. The clinic manager, Paula, had organised a quick breakfast meeting to introduce everyone to the new locum doctor who was coming up from Sydney to provide cover in the Byron Bay clinic for a few weeks. But there would be enough staff for him or her to be introduced to until Molly arrived. She wasn't the most senior doctor on staff, she'd only been there for six months, and maybe no one would even notice if she was late. Or maybe they had come to expect it. Timekeeping was one thing she had difficulty with. She was always trying to squeeze too much into her day and time was constantly getting away from her as a result. It was a perpetual struggle. She hadn't won the battle yet but she hoped that one day she'd miraculously develop a time-management gene.

Punctuality had been one thing, along with resilience and independence, that she'd hoped might improve with her move to Byron Bay. Here in the northern New South Wales coastal town she had only a short commute to work—nothing like the fifty-minute trip she'd made twice a day back in Sydney—but instead of improving, she'd just filled that extra time with another activity—her daily swim.

She quickly towelled her blonde hair before throwing a T-shirt over her swimsuit and jogging up the beach. She still had to get home to the apartment she rented with Gemma, one of her colleagues, shower and then make the quarter of an hour walk from Lighthouse Road into town. She would have liked to have taken a detour past The Top Shop to grab some breakfast but she didn't have the extra ten minutes that would take.

She really should have cut her swim short today but it was her favourite way to start the day, she needed it for her mental health and it was an important part of the process of finding herself. Swimming gave her time to reflect on what she wanted out of life. After wasting years of her life with her ex-boyfriend, finally saying goodbye to Daniel was supposed to be a turning point in her life. Her plan had been to move to Byron Bay and to make time and space to work on herself. She no longer wanted to worry about pleasing others. She no longer wanted to seek attention. From her father. From her ex. From anyone.

She shook her head. She didn't want thoughts of Daniel encroaching on her mind. She was putting her past behind her, moving on from a bad relationship. Moving in general, she reminded herself as she checked her watch again, hoping her tardiness would be forgiven. Her consulting list didn't start until ten o'clock on Wednesdays so no one should expect her to be there at quarter to eight.

Molly's shoulder-length hair was still damp when she arrived at the clinic and she knew the humidity of the summer air would make it kink but she certainly couldn't have spared the time to blow-dry it. She sneaked into the staffroom a few minutes before eight, quite pleased with her effort, and relieved to hear Tom Reynolds, the senior doctor whose leave necessitated locum cover, still going around the room introducing the staff to the new locum.

She could smell coffee and she headed for the machine to grab a cup, along with a muffin, sending a silent thank you to Paula for organising food. She added milk to her coffee and took a bite of her muffin just as she heard Tom say, 'And, last but not least, is Dr Prescott.'

The room was full and many of the staff were standing, as there weren't enough chairs for everyone. Molly could hear Tom but, being only five feet four inches tall, she couldn't see to the front of the room. But Tom had obviously seen her tardy arrival.

She quickly tried to swallow the muffin and school her expression to casual nonchalance in an attempt to convey that she'd been at the back of the room all along as opposed to sneaking in thirty seconds before.

'Molly, this is Dr Williams.'

All she could see was the top of what she assumed was a man's head, although it could have been a tall woman. She waited for her colleagues to part, not expecting them to reveal a familiar face.

'Theo?'

She hadn't seen him for four years, but he looked just the same. Tall, close to six feet, with broad shoulders that belied his otherwise slim physique. His thick black hair, cut short at the sides, was swept away from his forehead above dark eyes that widened a little, the only indication that he was as surprised as she was.

'Hello, Molly. It's been a while.' He nodded slightly but only managed a half-smile. He didn't look all that thrilled to see her and she couldn't blame him.

Four years had passed but all of a sudden it felt like yesterday. And not in a good way.

She felt the long-forgotten heat of embarrassment, could feel the blush creeping up her neck and into her face, and knew her cheeks were now stained pink.

She tried to school her features to mirror his. Trying on a mask of pleasant surprise rather than abject embarrassment as she wished the floor would open up and swallow her.

She dropped her gaze, focusing on her coffee, as Tom continued speaking. She let her colleagues close the space and shield her from view as the colour faded in her cheeks.

'While I have you all here, I had a call from the organisers of Schoolies Festival. They need a few more volunteers for the weekend so if any of you can spare a few hours they'd love to hear from you. I think any clinical staff would be qualified to help, but, for any admin staff who are interested, as long as you have a police clearance and your first-aid accreditation, you can sign up too. Paula has the contact details.'

Her mind drifted as Tom continued speaking about the imminent influx of teenagers who would be descending on Byron Bay for the next ten days to celebrate the end of their school lives.

She threw her unfinished muffin into the rubbish, her appetite deserting her as the memories flooded in. She hadn't seen Theo since their university graduation ceremony and she hadn't spoken to him since they both attended the same party to celebrate the end of their final exams prior to graduation. The last words they'd exchanged had come just after she'd unceremoniously kissed him.

Mortified about her behaviour and still feeling the sting of rejection, she had avoided him at graduation as she'd tried to pretend nothing had happened. She'd been immensely relieved when he'd appeared reluctant to seek her out too.

But the feeling of embarrassment returned now as she remembered her foolishness. She knew she'd behaved badly. Drunk and emotional, she'd acted impulsively and then tried to pretend nothing had happened. Theo had treated her with kindness and compassion and she'd repaid his kindness with the assumption that he'd welcome her impulsive kiss, even though she'd been in a relationship. Albeit an emotionally complicated one.

He had kissed her back—she hadn't drunk so much that she'd forgotten that—but when he'd asked if she would take Daniel back if he had cheated on her she hadn't replied. She'd known she would. She'd done it every time. And Theo had known it too. He'd stood up and walked away.

She didn't want to be twenty-five again. She hadn't always made good choices four years ago but she had matured; life had a way of forcing you to grow up. She was rebuilding herself and she didn't really want to see someone who knew the old Molly, who knew the mistakes she'd made in the past, on a daily basis. Someone who she felt had judged her and found her lacking.

After four years she was still embarrassed and ashamed of her behaviour. Of the kiss. She'd acted carelessly and then realised she didn't want to be the girl who cheated on her boyfriend. She didn't want to be the cliché. Her boyfriend had cheated on her—often—but she didn't want to play tit for tat. She wanted to be the bigger person and kissing Theo had been a mistake. She shouldn't have put him in that position.

She could feel herself being watched and she lifted her eyes to see Gemma grinning at her from the other side of the room. Gemma raised her eyebrows, darted her eyes in Theo's direction and mouthed one word. *Wow.*

Molly glared at her and Gemma started to cross the room as Tom wrapped up the meeting and the rest of the staff began to disperse.

Molly had been vacillating over whether or not she should approach Theo. If she did, how should she behave? What should she say? Four years was a long time. Especially considering what had happened between them. So, at least Gemma's arrival meant she didn't have to make that decision. She could talk to Gemma instead. That would give her time to compose herself and work out how to manage this unexpected turn of events.

'Oh. My. God. Talk about tall, hot and handsome,' Gemma said as she reached Molly's side.

Molly glanced around, hoping Theo wasn't within earshot, and was relieved to find he'd actually left the room. She really didn't want to have this conversation with Gemma in the middle of the staffroom but it looked as though that was what she was getting.

'Where have you been hiding him?' Gemma asked.

'Theo?' Molly feigned indifference, knowing she felt anything but. 'I haven't been hiding him anywhere. I haven't seen him for years.'

Gemma was watching her closely. 'He's not a skeleton in your closet?'

Molly shook her head and turned away to gather the left-over breakfast items. Wrapping the platters of muffins and fruit and putting them into the fridge for later gave her an excuse to avoid Gemma's gaze as she tried to stop the blush from returning to her cheeks.

'So, you don't know if he's single?' Gemma continued.

Molly felt a twitch of jealousy. *Theo was hers.* But that was ridiculous. *She* was ridiculous. Gemma was quite entitled to fancy Theo.

'I have no idea, but I thought you were taking a break from dating?' she replied as she closed the fridge and started stacking empty coffee cups into the dishwasher.

Gemma had recently been dating a pilot but it turned out he had a girl in several cities and she was currently single. 'It only takes one man to change my mind. But tell me if he's off limits.'

'Why would he be off limits to you?' Molly

asked as she closed the dishwasher and switched it on.

'Several reasons. If you fancied him, for one. After all, you saw him first. Or if he's an ex of yours then I'm not going there.'

'I told you, he's not an ex. There's no history between us,' she said. She knew she was massaging the truth very slightly but she wasn't about to share all the embarrassing details. 'We studied together, that's all.'

'You've never mentioned him.'

'Why would I?'

'Because he's gorgeous and he works for Pacific Coast Clinics.'

'I didn't know he did.' She'd only been employed at the clinic for six months. She knew there were several associated clinics throughout New South Wales, and she knew the locum was coming from one of them, but she hadn't bothered to look at the staff list across all the different locations. There'd really been no need. 'You'll have to work fast—he's only here for six weeks,' Molly said, trying to sound light and breezy. It sounded like no time but Molly feared it might feel like an eternity.

'No.' Gemma shook her head. 'Looking like he does, I bet he's not single and I'm not going to get burned again.'

Molly didn't try and persuade her friend otherwise. Besides, she could be right, Theo could be spoken for already.

Molly wiped the bench, dried her hands and she and Gemma headed for their consulting rooms. She planned to use the extra time before her list started to follow up some of her patients, check their results and organise referrals. But her mind kept drifting.

She and Theo had studied medicine at university together but they hadn't been close friends. They'd moved in different circles. He'd spent a lot of his time in the library, she'd spent a lot of time in the university bar with Daniel, when they'd been 'on' again.

When their circles had overlapped she'd got the impression that Theo had judged her choices. She knew they'd been questionable but, at the time, her choices had made sense. At least in the world she knew.

She remembered Theo had a way of quietly watching people, taking stock, and once, in just a few moments, he had accurately summed up her and her relationship with Daniel, which had frustrated her. She hadn't wanted to hear his opinion. She'd wanted to be seen as strong and confident, not weak or scared, and she definitely hadn't wanted to admit that he'd been right.

There were so many things in her past she'd rather not think about. The present was about making better decisions. She was using her time in Byron Bay to find herself. To work on herself. She'd grown up, the middle of three sisters, always feeling as though her father would have preferred to have sons. She was constantly trying to prove that girls could do anything boys did, trying to be the perfect daughter. Then the perfect girlfriend. She'd been desperate for attention, desperate for affection.

She realised now that had been a big factor in her relationship with Daniel. Her father had ignored her mother, herself and her sisters and Molly had been flattered by Daniel's interest in her. He was intelligent, good-looking and popular and she'd been so desperate for attention she'd overlooked the negatives—his lies, his unfaithfulness, his unkindness. Her younger self had been happy just to have someone take notice of her and she knew she'd been conditioned to believe that everyone cheated—her father had certainly been guilty of the same offence on several occasions—and so the young Molly hadn't stopped to think about whether Daniel's attention was positive or negative. She hadn't cared. But not any more. She knew now that she didn't need someone else's validation—especially not whcn it was thinly-disguised emotional abuse. Now, away from her family and single for the first time in years, she was just trying to be the best version of herself. Whatever that was.

Here in Byron, she wasn't a sister, a daughter, a girlfriend. She was just Molly. A doctor. A friend.

But seeing Theo reminded her of the old Molly, the one she was trying to leave behind. She didn't want to be reminded of that girl.

She'd need to avoid Theo. And seeing as he was only in Byron Bay temporarily, it shouldn't be too hard.

Theo Chin Williams tried to concentrate as Tom Reynolds showed him around the clinic. He schooled his expression to make it look as if he was listening but he wasn't sure he would retain any of the information. His mind was too busy going back over old times. Back to Molly. He'd been stunned to see her at the clinic today. He hadn't seen her profile on the Pacific Coast Clinics website and he knew he would have noticed it, which meant it wasn't there. She must be new to the practice.

Four years was a long time but Molly hadn't changed. At least, not in appearance. She looked exactly the same—petite, blonde, shiny. Theo had always seen an aura of lightness and joy about her. With the exception of one memorable occasion, she'd always presented as a happy person. She'd been popular at university. She'd been fun and people had been drawn to her. He knew he had been. But they had mostly moved in different circles and Molly had barely noticed him. Except for that one night.

He remembered their last encounter. Their only intimate encounter in the seven years they'd been acquainted. Molly had cried on his shoulder, confided in him, kissed him and they hadn't spoken since.

He had admired her from afar for many years before that fateful night. He'd put her on a pedestal and hadn't been able to resist kissing her back when she'd abruptly and unexpectedly kissed him, but he'd been convinced she would never choose him over Daniel and so he'd walked away, wishing he were brave enough to stay.

At the end of the staff meeting he'd wondered if he should approach her, but what would he say after four years? They weren't friends, they were acquaintances at best. And then Tom had steered him out of the staffroom to embark on a tour of the clinic, taking the opportunity away from him.

Which brought his mind neatly back to the

matter at hand. Back to the reason he was in Byron Bay—to work. He was here for the next six weeks in a locum capacity but he'd also been tasked with some problem-solving. The Byron clinic was the newest addition to the Pacific Coast portfolio, a group of medical centres owned by his parents and managed by his mother, and she had flagged some issues, which Theo had been entrusted with sorting out. Between treating patients and going over the clinic's books and operating procedures he had enough on his plate. He didn't need to add Molly Prescott to his list. His mother was a perfectionist who expected nothing less than one hundred per cent effort at all times. He knew he was expected to return to Sydney with answers, and possibly solutions, to the issues she'd raised. He had plenty to focus on and his mother would not be pleased if he let himself get distracted. She wasn't interested in excuses, only in results.

Molly was a blast from the past but one that didn't need revisiting. He didn't need the distraction. Reminiscing wasn't a priority for him and he got the impression it wasn't high on her agenda either.

He forced himself to concentrate on the guided tour he was being given. He knew Tom's leave started today and he knew he would be expected to step up to the plate and take on a patient load immediately. He needed to focus. He hadn't seen Molly for four years. He could put her out of his mind for another few hours, at least while he was at work. He was older and wiser now, no longer infatuated. They had both moved on.

He could ignore the fact that she still glowed, still made the air around her shimmer. He could ignore the fact that his heart rate had escalated when their colleagues had parted to reveal her standing there and he could ignore the fact that his hands had perspired and his mouth had gone dry.

He could ignore her.

Molly scrolled through patients' test results on her computer screen but couldn't find the headspace to pick up the phone to pass any results on. She was being extremely unproductive. She was unsettled and she hated to admit it but Theo's arrival was responsible. She really thought she'd been making progress since she'd moved to Byron Bay. She was growing in confidence, no longer having to wonder what life with Daniel would have in store for her, whether she would be in or out of favour, whether she'd be fighting for attention or battling for his affection. She was on the path to independence and she didn't want Theo's arrival to pull her backwards. But she was stronger now, she wasn't the same girl any more, and she would show Theo that. Or just avoid him and allow him to see that for himself.

She nodded to herself, encouraged that she'd found a solution. She earmarked a couple of patients for the receptionists to call with non-urgent results and decided she'd go and grab another coffee before her consulting list started. Perhaps that would kick her brain into gear. Into the present and off the past.

On her way to the kitchen, she passed Paula's office. The practice manager had a large internal window looking out to the reception area. Molly glanced through the window and saw Theo leaning over Paula's desk, deep in conversation and pointing at a computer screen. What on earth could they be discussing? She paused briefly as her curiosity got the better of her, before realising she didn't want to be caught peering in at the unexpected tableau. It was none of her business and if it had been anyone but Theo she wouldn't have given it a second thought. Why did she find him so interesting?

Not wanting to go down that rabbit hole, she continued on to the kitchen but couldn't resist glancing through the window as she returned with her coffee. Theo was still there.

Molly kept walking and just as she reached the reception desk the front door to the clinic burst open and a very distressed middle-aged woman barrelled in, holding the door for her male partner. The man was overweight and sweating, not unusual in the humid air of Byron Bay, but Molly could see he was having difficulty breathing.

The woman plonked him on a seat and rushed to the desk, ignoring the other patients waiting to be attended to. 'Please, we need to see a doctor. My husband isn't well.'

'Are you a patient of the clinic?' the receptionist asked as Molly hurried around the desk and into the waiting room.

The woman shook her head. 'No. We're here on holiday. My husband has been complaining of indigestion, over-indulging I think, but it's got so bad this morning he's finding it hard to breathe.'

The clinic was not technically an emergency clinic but because they were right in the centre of town they got a lot of walk-ins. Despite the sign on the door giving the hospital's details, if the clinic was open people just turned up. The hospital had recently undergone extensive upgrades but, being a ten-minute drive out of town, it wasn't nearly as convenient. Especially for the tourists.

Molly sat down next to the man. 'My name is Molly, I'm one of the doctors.' He turned towards her but she could see he was having difficulty taking her words in. He was rubbing his sternum but it seemed to be an unconscious movement. 'Why don't you come with me and we'll get you looked at?' she continued.

She was concerned he was displaying symptoms of a cardiac episode. She could call for an ambulance but she knew from experience that dealing with any emergency was better done behind closed doors and out of the reception area. She wanted to get him somewhere with some privacy. He'd walked into the clinic, she just hoped he'd be able to walk into her consulting room. She didn't fancy her chances of breaking his fall if he toppled over.

'I'll take him, if you can get some details,' Molly told the receptionist.

The man stood, unsteadily, and Molly instinctively gave him her arm for support. 'What is your name?'

'Warwick,' he replied breathlessly.

Molly took him into the examination room where they had an ECG machine, just in case she needed it. She pressed on the footplate under the treatment bed, lowering it so Warwick could sit down. She lifted the back support and helped him to lift his feet.

'Can you describe to me what you're experiencing?'

'I'm having trouble breathing. It feels like someone is squeezing my lungs.'

'Does it hurt?'

Warwick nodded.

'Is this the first time you've had this pain?'

'It's the first time it's been this bad,' he said, not without some difficulty.

'Are you seeing a doctor for any chronic health conditions? Do you have any allergies? Any heart issues? Angina? Diabetes? Anxiety?'

Warwick shook his head.

'Are you taking any medications?' Molly asked as she wrapped a blood-pressure cuff around his arm and pressed the button to inflate it.

'Tablets for high cholesterol.'

Did he not think that was a condition worth mentioning? she thought as she looked at the reading on the monitor. She was surprised to find his blood pressure was within normal limits but noted his heart rate was rapid.

'I'd like to take a closer look at your heart. Have you ever had an ECG done before?'

Warwick shook his head again.

'I need to stick some electrodes onto your chest. Can you undo your shirt for me?' Molly asked as she turned her back to prepare the ECG machine.

'I don't…' Warwick's sentence faded away behind her. She spun around.

Warwick's eyes were closed. Was he breathing?

Molly looked for a rise and fall in his chest.

Nothing.

'Warwick?' She shook his shoulder before grabbing his wrist and feeling for a pulse.

Nothing.

She dropped the back of the bed, lying him flat.

She suspected he was in cardiac arrest.

She needed help.

She darted out of the room, snatching the defibrillator kit from the box on the wall outside Paula's office, and yelling instructions to Crystal at the reception desk as she flew past. 'Call an ambulance. Code blue.'

Through the window of Paula's office she could see Theo sitting by the desk.

She needed help and there was no time to go looking for it. She scanned the corridor, hoping someone else might materialise but, of course, no one did.

It would have to be Theo.

She stuck her head through the door. There was no time to worry about the past. She'd have to shelve her plans to avoid Theo.

She needed help.

She needed Theo.

'Theo!' She all but shouted his name, barely waiting for him to look up before she was already turning back to her exam room. 'I need you. Patient in cardiac arrest.'

CHAPTER TWO

THEO LIFTED HIS head as he heard Molly call his name. She'd already turned on her heel and was heading along the passageway by the time he moved. As he stepped into the corridor, he was immediately enveloped by the scent of oranges hanging in the air and he was transported straight back to the night Molly had kissed him. Her hair had smelt of oranges then too. It was the scent of her shampoo. Now was not the time to be distracted, though. He hurried after her, catching up to her as she ducked into a clinic room. Her words trailed behind her. 'Middle-aged male, sudden cardiac arrest. No reported prior history.'

Theo nodded and said, 'I'll start compressions.' This wasn't how he'd imagined their first conversation would go but there was no time to waste. There was no time for the past.

Molly was avoiding eye contact, which piqued Theo's curiosity. Four years ago, they hadn't been friends, but they hadn't been enemies either—at least he hadn't thought so. But a cardiac event was a stressful situation. He couldn't expect her to spend time making him feel welcome.

Pushing his curiosity aside, he ripped open the buttons on the patient's shirt, exposing his chest and belly as Molly quickly opened the defibrillator kit and pulled out the pieces she needed. He leaned over the patient and placed his hands on his sternum, beginning chest compressions as Molly worked behind him.

Theo counted out loud and tried to ignore Molly as she moved around him. But it was difficult. She was hard to ignore. Each movement she made disturbed the orange-scented, perfumed air; he could feel where she was even when he couldn't see her. She squeezed behind him, putting her hands on his hips, obviously trying to keep him in position, trying not to disturb his rhythm, but her touch nearly made him lose track of his count.

'Fifteen.'

Molly's arm brushed his as she reached across to press the sticky pad onto Warwick's chest and a spark of awareness surged through him.

'Twenty.' His voice was husky. He cleared his throat and focused hard. Now was not the time to be thinking about Molly Prescott as anything more than his colleague.

He continued compressions as Molly placed the second pad onto the patient, this time without any further contact with Theo. She connected the pads to the machine and it began to issue instructions in its automated voice.

'Stop CPR, analysing rhythm.'

'Shock advised.'

Theo could hear the whine as the power built up in the defibrillator unit.

'Stand clear.'

'Clear.' Theo lifted his hands, holding them in the air, and repeated the machine's instructions. Molly stepped back from the bed and pressed the flashing red button. Theo stayed close. The patient was large and he was worried he could fall when the shock was delivered.

The patient lifted off the bed as the machine delivered a charge, trying to shock his heart out of fibrillation and restore its normal rhythm.

Theo and Molly waited but there was no change.

'Continue CPR.'

The machine continued its instructions.

'Are you okay to continue and I'll do the breaths?' Molly asked.

Theo nodded and resumed chest compressions. He knew the AED machine would expect two minutes of continued CPR before performing another analysis.

Molly opened the face-shield container and placed the shield over the patient's mouth and tipped his head back. Her left hand cupped his chin and Theo noticed her fingers were bare. She wasn't wearing a ring.

As Theo approached the count of thirty, Molly was preparing to give two breaths. Despite the fact they'd never worked together before their movements were smooth and coordinated. Theo reached thirty counts and paused and Molly bent her head and breathed into their patient. The transition from compressions to breaths was seamless.

Molly was standing opposite Theo now, keeping out of his way, and he watched the top of her head as she bent over the patient, her blonde hair falling over her face. She tossed her head to shift the hair from her eyes as she tilted her head to check for the accompanying rise of the patient's chest, making sure her breaths were reaching his lungs. Theo had to stop himself from reaching across and tucking Molly's hair behind her ear. He didn't think she'd appreciate the help but his fingers ached to touch her.

He returned his focus to his patient's chest

as Molly finished her second breath, making sure he wasn't caught looking at her when she straightened up.

They continued administering three more rounds of CPR. Two more long minutes before the machine interrupted them again.

'Stop CPR, analysing rhythm.'

'Shock advised.'

'Stand clear.'

Another jolt. But still nothing.

Theo continued with a fifth round of compressions. His shoulders were starting to complain—the patient was large and Theo was using a lot of effort, but he couldn't quit.

'Analysing rhythm.'

The defibrillator deliberated a possible third shock.

'No shock advised.'

'Check pulse.'

Molly checked for a pulse. 'I've got something!'

Her eyes met his. She was grinning, her smile was wide, full of relief and achievement, and Theo felt something tug at his heart. He smiled back. A proper smile this time, not the uncertain half-smile he'd bestowed on her earlier in the staff kitchen.

He let his hands drop and breathed out as Molly cried, 'We've got him!'

Theo could hardly believe it as the patient's eyes opened, a look of confusion on his face.

'Hello, Warwick.' Molly turned her attention to their patient and Theo felt a chill as her smile was directed at someone else. 'You gave us quite a scare.'

Warwick. That was the patient's name, Theo thought as Molly picked up the phone and buzzed the reception desk, asking Crystal to send the paramedics in when they arrived.

'We're going to send you off to hospital now and get you sorted out,' Molly continued as the door opened and Paula ushered the paramedics in, followed by a woman who Theo assumed was Warwick's wife. She made a beeline for their patient but Molly, who had her eyes trained on the woman, inclined her head slightly in Theo's direction. He understood her gesture—he needed to keep the wife out of the way while Molly did the patient handover. He steered the woman to a chair in the corner.

'Is he okay?' she asked. 'What happened? Why is the ambulance here?'

Theo didn't have much information but he had enough to pass on to the wife and hopefully ease her concerns.

'He's all right now but he needs to go to hospital.'

'For indigestion?' The woman was frowning.

'He went into cardiac arrest,' Theo explained gently. 'Your husband's heart stopped. We had to resuscitate him. He needs to go to hospital and he'll need further tests done.'

'He had a heart attack?'

'Cardiac arrest,' Theo repeated. 'It's a bit different from a heart attack.' Technically they were two different things but he didn't have time to go into that detail and he doubted if she'd remember much of what he told her anyway. 'Warwick will be seen by a cardiologist. They'll be able to give you more information.'

In his peripheral vision Theo could see the paramedics slipping an oxygen mask over Warwick's face as Molly took a final blood-pressure reading and removed the sticky pads from his chest. Warwick was transferred to the paramedics' stretcher as Molly removed the cuff.

'Can I go to the hospital with him?' Warwick's wife asked.

'Of course.'

Molly and Theo remained behind as the paramedics wheeled the stretcher out, followed by Warwick's wife.

Theo went to the sink in the corner and filled

two disposable cups with water. He handed one to Molly as she sat on the edge of the bed and let out a large sigh of relief.

'Thank you,' she said as she took the cup from him.

'Are you okay?' he asked.

She nodded. 'You?'

He smiled. 'Yep. Can't say I was expecting that on my first day though. Is Warwick a patient of yours?'

Molly shook her head. 'I've never seen him before. They're tourists, here on holiday.'

Theo frowned. 'But there's a hospital in Byron Bay. Why did they come here?'

Molly sipped her water. 'It happens a lot. We're in the centre of town. We're a lot more convenient.'

'But you're not an emergency clinic.'

'I know. But they thought it was indigestion.'

Theo wondered how often this occurred and what impact it had on the practice. On the staff. GPs weren't emergency physicians and the clinic certainly wasn't equipped like a hospital ED. Warwick had been lucky today.

'Warwick was lucky you knew what you were doing,' Theo said.

'I was lucky you were here too. Sorry, to throw you in the deep end. That's the first real emer-

gency I've had to deal with in the six months
I've been here.'

Six months—that was one question answered.

'What brought you to Byron Bay?'

She shrugged. 'I needed a change of scenery.'

He wanted to ask about Daniel. He wanted
to know if he was there too, if Molly was still
with him, but there was no subtle way to phrase
that question so he let it lie. Her bare ring finger
was no clue. Lots of doctors didn't wear rings
for practical reasons. It was easier to keep your
hands clean if you didn't wear jewellery.

Molly finished her water, stood up and began
to tidy the room. She threw out the used sticky
pads and packed the defibrillator away after
checking that there were more pads in the kit.
'Would you mind putting this back for me?' she
asked as she held out the kit, back to avoiding
eye contact. 'It goes on the wall outside Paula's
office.'

Theo took the kit and left the room, unasked
questions still swirling in his brain. But he'd
been dismissed. Sent away by Molly. No longer needed.

He returned the kit before heading to the consulting room that had been allocated to him. He
ran the cold water in the basin and rinsed his
hands to cool them down. He stared into the mir-

ror as he let the water run into the sink, looking at his reflection and wondering if Molly had seen the changes he saw in himself.

He knew he had grown as a person over the past four years but would anyone else notice? Would Molly? Did it matter?

Theo had grown up caught between two cultures, on the outside looking in at kids like Molly and her friends, kids who were comfortable in their skin, who knew where they belonged. He'd never felt completely at ease. He'd often felt he was drifting lonelily between his Asian heritage and his Aussie upbringing. Fitting in nowhere.

His mother was Taiwanese. She'd moved to Australia as a teenager and had met his Australian father at medical school. But although his parents came from different backgrounds their goals were almost identical. Their level of contentment was directly proportional to their level of success—they aspired to successful careers and to raising successful children. But there was some irony there, Theo knew, given that his maternal grandparents had emigrated from Taiwan to look after his sister and him while their parents established their careers and then grew their businesses, having little to do with raising their own children.

Theo was bilingual. Speaking Mandarin with

his grandparents, he'd worked hard to cultivate an Australian accent so that he'd fitted in at school, but he'd known there were more differences between him and his classmates than just an accent. He and his sister were officially Chin Williamses, but Theo had refused to use Chin on his paperwork, preferring to stick with the more Anglicised Williams. Even that hadn't seemed to help. He hadn't eaten the same lunches, he hadn't played sport, his parents and grandparents had never attended assembly or the Christmas concerts and had only occasionally made it to a music recital. He'd given up wishing for attention beyond what he'd garnered by his results. If anything, he knew that was partly what had motivated him to do well at school—it was the only time he'd got any recognition. Any positive attention.

A stint working overseas after graduation had taught him a lot about himself and the world. He had returned knowing the importance of his skills and the importance of human relationships and as he'd settled into his career as a doctor he'd found an identity that had started to fit him. It didn't matter what grades he'd got at school or university once he had his degree. It didn't matter if he played sport, had gone to parties or out on dates. All that mattered was whether he could help his patients. And he had no difficulty with that.

Seeing Molly had thrown him momentarily. He had never expected to run into her here. He'd had no idea she worked for Pacific Coast Clinics. The company was owned by Theo's parents but managed by his mother, a general practitioner, while his father concentrated on his career as a plastic surgeon. They had added the Byron Bay clinic to their stable eighteen months ago but Theo had never given the practice on the upper New South Wales coast much consideration. His time was consumed by his job in Sydney and by his parents' expectations. He was always expected to work harder and longer than the other employees, to prove his value, his skills and his suitability as heir apparent.

He knew he was expected to take over the clinics one day, and he wanted that. But he also knew it wouldn't be handed to him on a plate. He was expected to work for it, and work hard. His parents could just as easily look for an outside investor or one of the other staff members to take over as they could hand him the reins. But they wouldn't be happy. Failure was not an option for a Chin Williams.

When other children had been playing sport and joining teams he'd been doing extra homework or attending tutoring. Not that he'd found schoolwork difficult, but his parents had wanted him and his sister to excel in everything. To be the best. When he was a teenager and school-mates had been going to parties he'd been at home doing practice exams. His only hobby was playing the guitar and that had developed from the piano lessons he'd been made to take as a child. As a teenager he'd taught himself the gui-tar and he had entertained fantasies of playing in a band until that dream had been squashed by the demands of university.

His parents and his maternal grandparents had told him, repeatedly, 'You'll never get any-where without hard work,' and he had to admit, they had a point. He was good at his job and was working hard to establish himself, work-ing harder than the next doctor, trying not only to meet his parents' expectations but to prove to everyone else that he wasn't getting by on his connections.

Personal relationships were another story. He'd had one serious relationship since finish-ing university, but she had wanted more of his time than he'd had to give. He was only twenty-nine. He figured there was still plenty of time for relationships in his future.

Now, thinking about relationships led him

back to thinking about Molly. He was curious to know what her life had looked like for the past four years. But curiosity was dangerous. It was distracting. Besides, did it really matter? He'd be gone in six weeks and Molly would be firmly back in his past. He needed to stop thinking about her and remember why he was here.

His mother had put her faith in him, her trust, and Theo knew that wasn't easy to come by. He had a job to do in Byron Bay—two jobs: one as a doctor and the other to evaluate the clinic. Its profits had been falling and he had six weeks to figure out why. Normally his mother would have looked into this herself. She'd told him as much. She'd looked over the books but she wanted to see how the clinic functioned in person, but an upcoming overseas conference where she was a keynote speaker had made that impossible so she'd sent Theo in her place. Killing two birds with one stone. He would fill the locum position and get her some answers. Failure was not an option.

Finding out he'd be working with Molly Prescott was a surprise but he wouldn't let it be a complication. They had worked well together today but they weren't friends. They had never been friends and there was no reason to think things would be any different now.

Yes, he'd had a major crush on Molly at university. Yes, he had admired her from a distance. She always seemed so sure of herself and her place in the world and he'd been a little envious of her confidence back then. She was pretty and positive and popular, but there had been one night when he'd found out that she was vulnerable just like anyone else.

He could only remember seeing her let her guard down that once, and it had stayed with him. Not just because of her vulnerability, but because of what else had happened.

He knew the kiss Molly had bestowed on him had been spontaneous, he knew he'd just happened to be the man in front of her when she'd needed comfort, but that hadn't stopped him from kissing her back. And he couldn't pretend the kiss hadn't been incredible. And for a fleeting moment he'd imagined it could be something more than what it was. But just because he wished it didn't make it true.

She'd chosen to kiss him that night, but he knew she wouldn't choose him again permanently. She'd made that much clear. And so he'd walked away.

It had hurt at the time. He had always had Molly on a pedestal, wanting her to notice him, and for a brief moment in time she had.

None of that mattered now. The past was the past. Four years later they were equals. Colleagues. What Molly thought of him now shouldn't matter. He didn't usually care what people thought of him. He was used to existing in his own world. He expected to be judged on his achievements, not for who he was. Molly had been the exception; he had wanted her to see him. For her to see Theo. For some inexplicable reason Molly Prescott had been the only exception in his world.

But as much as he'd like Molly to see the new, confident Theo, she couldn't be an exception again. He wasn't going down that path. He wasn't going to bring up the past. They weren't friends. They were temporary colleagues.

He'd do his job and be gone in six weeks, putting Molly Prescott behind him for the second time. He'd be in and out of Byron Bay before she even had time to notice.

Molly sat down as Theo left her room. She wondered if he'd noticed that she'd almost pushed him out of the door, but she needed a moment to catch her breath alone. All thoughts of tidying up were forgotten as she sat and gathered herself together. She closed her eyes and took a deep breath. Her hands were shaking and she clenched her fists to control the tremor. She knew it wasn't just Warwick's medical episode that had got the adrenalin racing around her body. It was Theo.

All it had taken was a look, one smile, the briefest contact, and she was catapulted right back to the night of their kiss. Everything she'd tried to ignore, how he'd listened, how he'd smelt as he'd held her while she'd cried, how he'd made her feel when he'd given her his attention and how he'd tasted when she'd kissed him, all came rushing back. She liked to pretend she'd forgotten but she knew that was a lie. And now he was here she knew she'd been kidding herself if she'd thought she could pretend it was all in the past.

Molly stared into space as she thought about that night.

She'd had a few drinks, everyone had, but she'd mostly been exhausted and emotional after their final exams. And when she'd seen Daniel in a suspicious embrace with another girl she'd completely lost her temper. It wasn't the first time she'd caught him cheating on her, and she'd been furious. She'd confronted him and they'd gone into the garden and had a massive argument. He'd denied any wrongdoing, she'd been positive he was lying, and he'd left her alone and gone back to the party.

Theo had found her sobbing and he'd sat with

her while she'd blubbered all over him. She hadn't been so drunk that she didn't remember every little detail of their encounter. She'd talked and cried and he'd listened. And then they'd talked to each other. For hours, it had felt like. Molly couldn't remember anyone talking to her for that long. Couldn't recall anyone taking what she said seriously. She was so used to being the life of the party. Being fun. Hiding her insecurities behind a smile and a laugh. But Theo had been interested in what she had to say. And gradually she'd started to feel better. She remembered leaning on his shoulder and then she'd looked up and he'd been watching her with his dark eyes and she'd known he was really seeing her. And then she'd kissed him.

She hadn't asked, she'd just done it, and he'd kissed her back.

She remembered everything. From what they'd talked about to the kiss. Especially the kiss. It had been amazing. Incredible. As if he'd known her for ever, as if he were another half of her. They'd been so in tune, as if they'd kissed a thousand times before, in a thousand different lifetimes. There had been no awkward clashing of teeth or noses. No hesitation.

She'd never been kissed like that.

And then he'd walked away.

And in the months that had followed she'd wondered if she should have grabbed his hand as he'd walked away. If she should have made a different choice. But she'd made the same mistake she'd always made and had forgiven Daniel. And had let Theo go.

She'd been insecure, meticulously curating an image of a girl content with her life, and she'd always been so careful not to let her guard down. Theo had seen her at a weak moment. He had seen and heard too much. She'd never told anyone what happened and she had never spoken to Theo again. She'd moved on with her life, moved on with Daniel and pretended that night had never existed.

She was a different person now. She was finding her independence and didn't need reminders of the past. The spontaneous late-night kiss they'd shared would have to stay consigned to history. And history shouldn't be repeated. Some things needed to be let go. Several years and many reincarnations of her relationship with Daniel had come and gone before she'd finally learned the value of leaving things behind and divesting herself of bad mistakes. It was a lesson she'd do well to remember.

CHAPTER THREE

AFTER THE RATHER dramatic start, the rest of Theo's first day went smoothly. A couple of billing enquiries had come up that he'd discussed with Paula, leaving him feeling as if he was already making headway with his mother's task. He saw a few patients of Tom's, easing himself into the locum role, before heading to the pub for something to eat.

He sat at the bar nursing a pre-dinner beer. He'd have to find time to get to the supermarket tomorrow. He couldn't eat out every night and he didn't want to eat out alone.

'Hey, Theo.' He was jolted out of his musings by the sound of his name. Matt, one of the physios from the clinic, was standing beside him. He nodded in the direction of Theo's drink as he ordered a beer for himself. 'Can I get you another one?'

'Sure, thanks.'

'I heard you had an eventful first day.'

Theo laughed. 'Yeah. Luckily it turned out okay, but I'm hoping it's not always like that.'

'It's usually pretty chilled here in Byron. This place is all about a good work-life balance.'

'Work-life balance.' Theo laughed. 'I'm not sure what that means.'

'Well, let's hope you have time to find out while you're here. Six weeks, right?'

Theo nodded.

'Have you been to Byron before?'

'Never. Born and bred in Sydney but never been here.'

'You went through med school in Sydney with Molly?'

'Yes. Did she tell you that?' Theo was surprised. He'd got the impression Molly hadn't shared their history.

Matt shook his head as he paid for their beers. 'Gemma did.'

That still meant Molly had told someone. 'I didn't know Molly was in Byron Bay.' He hadn't seen Molly since their graduation ceremony. When it was obvious she and Daniel had patched up their differences. She'd avoided him. He'd left her alone.

He'd felt both disappointed and vindicated when he'd seen them together at graduation. He'd guessed correctly that she would take Daniel back after the party and he hadn't wanted to get caught in the middle of their on-again-off-again romance. He didn't need the headache. As much as he'd been attracted to Molly, and he could admit that he was, he didn't want to be a pawn in her game, cast aside when she went back to Daniel, as she'd done several times throughout university. Being rejected was a form of failure in Theo's eyes and failure was unacceptable, therefore, the sensible thing to do was to reduce his exposure to that risk by removing himself from the situation.

But now he thought again about her bare finger, the lack of a ring, engagement or wedding, and wondered if she was still with Daniel or if she'd come to her senses over the past four years. He hoped for her sake that she had.

'I managed to convince her to make the move up here after she broke up with Daniel,' Matt said.

Theo bit back a smile. Hearing that Molly had broken up with Daniel was good news, but he wondered if it would be like all the other times she'd broken up with him. Was it going to be short-lived or was this it? 'They were still together?' He knew he was fishing for information but he was curious to know what had happened and he took some small measure of satisfaction in hearing Molly and Daniel were no longer a couple.

'Yeah, they were. It's been almost a year since they broke up this time so I'm hoping she's finally done with him. He's not a mate of yours, is he?' Matt added, as if suddenly realising he might be stepping on toes. 'He would have been at university with you too.'

Theo nodded. 'He was in our year but we weren't mates.' Theo and Daniel couldn't have been more different. Theo's parents had worked hard, built a successful business, but they had started with nothing. Theo didn't know Daniel well, but Daniel had clearly been born with a silver spoon in his mouth. He had the arrogance and general disdain of others less fortunate. He had a strong sense of self-importance, an expectation that people would listen to him—not because he had good ideas but because he had grown up having people tell him that he was special. He wasn't Theo's type of person. Theo had never been told he was special. He'd been brought up to work hard, to let his achievements speak for him, but that meant he didn't dare to fail because if he wasn't achieving, then who was he?

He did wonder, though, what it was that had finally made Molly see the light and break up with Daniel. Or had he broken up with her? At university it had always been something that Daniel did that had triggered their breakups. But Molly had taken him back time and time again.

But he wasn't going to ask Matt those questions. It really wasn't any of his business. Molly wasn't his friend; she was just a part of his past. That was where she needed to stay.

Fortunately, Matt had moved on from the topic of Molly. 'What's your trivia knowledge like?' he asked. 'We've got a regular team together for the weekly pub quiz if you'd like to join us. We're down a player—it's usually Tom.'

Theo hesitated. He wasn't sure how Molly would feel if he joined the group. He'd got the impression she wasn't that thrilled to see him.

'No pressure, we're not playing for sheep stations,' Matt said when Theo didn't reply straight away. 'And in the interests of full disclosure, we don't expect to win. We order pizzas and have a few drinks, that's it.'

Theo was assuming Molly would be there. She might not. He made a decision. 'As long as you don't expect me to answer any sports questions,' he replied.

'That's my area of expertise.'

A contest where there were no expectations on him to excel? To be the best? To win? That was a novelty for Theo and one that had some appeal. Perhaps it was time to embrace that work-life balance Matt spoke of. 'Okay, then, sounds good.' He picked up his fresh beer and followed Matt to a table at the back of the pub. It wasn't as if he had anything better to do.

He went round the table, introducing himself to some unfamiliar faces, and as he sat down he saw Molly and Gemma arrive. Her double take when she saw him at the table didn't go unnoticed by him. She looked at the seats around the table. She and Gemma were last to arrive. There was one spare seat on the bench beside Theo and another at the other end of the table. He could tell Molly intended to sit at the far end but Gemma got there first, leaving Molly to sit with him.

Her hip bumped against his as she sat down and immediately she shifted away from him. Could she not bear to be close to him? He moved aside slightly, trying to give her more space. He didn't want her to feel crowded. She looked a little skittish, as though if he said or did the wrong thing she'd get up and leave. Flee. She gave him a smile, but it wasn't her usual full-blown, all-encompassing smile that he remembered. He could see the tension in her shoulders, in her eyes.

She chatted to Matt's partner, Levi, who was a schoolteacher, and then took charge of the answer sheet. Theo suspected that was so she could avoid having to talk to him. That was okay. He didn't need her attention. He wasn't twenty-five any more. He was comfortable in his own skin now, successful, mature. He didn't need to be in awe of Molly any more. Didn't need to be seen by Molly.

Molly knew she'd given Theo short shrift when she'd sat down. She would have preferred to sit somewhere else. She was still on edge.

Working so closely with Theo had reawakened her memory of the kiss. It had been unexpected and amazing. The way it made her feel had surprised her back then, but she'd attributed that to her heightened emotional state and the alcohol. But that didn't explain why she'd had a similar reaction today when Theo had smiled at her and when her arm had brushed against his. He triggered feelings that startled her. Feelings that were out of her control. She didn't like that. She wanted to maintain control.

She was afraid to look at him. Afraid he'd see what she was feeling in her eyes. It really wasn't appropriate and she'd needed time to gather herself together, worried that if she sat beside him he'd know what she was thinking.

So when she'd been forced to take the spot

next to him, she took it upon herself to be the scribe for the group. It gave her an excuse to avoid eye contact but just because she wasn't looking at Theo didn't mean she wasn't aware of his every movement, his every breath. He reached for his drink and his arm brushed hers and the pen skittered over the paper as her skin burned in response to his touch. She tried to focus on the others in the group as the questions began.

Levi had politics and Australian history covered, Gemma was a geography nerd and Matt was all over the sports questions. She was normally good at the trivia questions but her focus was terrible and answers she could normally give without even thinking about eluded her, putting them in the bottom third of the results with two rounds to go.

Theo had contributed a few correct answers in the early rounds but everything changed in the music round. He answered every question correctly, even arguing his case successfully with Levi about the original name of a band and insisting Molly use his answer. They scored full marks and closed the gap on the top two teams. He looked so pleased with his efforts that Molly couldn't ignore him any longer. Not when every other member of the team was so excited to be in with a shot of winning.

'Wow. That was impressive,' she said as Matt took the answer sheet up to the scorer's table. 'How do you know so much about music?' The questions had been varied, it wasn't as if they were all focused on one genre, but Theo had been flawless.

'Music was a big part of my family. My mother believes studying a musical instrument helps to develop the brain so my sister and I had no choice but to learn something. I started with the piano but eventually taught myself the guitar and I have always loved listening to all sorts of music. I really wanted to be in a band but my sister is a classical violinist with the symphony orchestra so, as one of only two children, I was expected to follow in my parents' path and study medicine.'

'You didn't want to be a doctor?'

'I wanted to do both. I spent a lot of time at live gigs, soaking up that atmosphere, until it became impossible with the time commitments and hours needed to devote to study. But it's still my way of relaxing.'

'Do you still play the guitar?' Molly asked, realising she knew nothing about him really.

He nodded.

Molly couldn't play an instrument. She could

never sit still for long enough to learn. She played netball, a lot of netball. That was much more her speed.

He had musician's hands, slender fingers, fine bones. But Molly supposed they were good doctor's hands too. Gentle. Tender. She lifted her eyes to his face. He had a shadow of a beard on his chin and jaw, slightly darker where a moustache would grow, and his eyes were almost black in the dim light of the pub.

'Molly, are you ready for the last round?'

Matt's question interrupted Molly's thoughts and she jumped and dragged her gaze away from Theo. She reached for a fresh sheet of paper to record the answers but Theo reached for it at the same time and his fingers landed on hers. A burst of heat shot up her left arm and Molly dropped the paper in a fluster. She tucked her hand under the table, opening and closing her fist until the tingling subsided and normal feeling returned and she was able to rest that hand on the answer sheet to stabilise it as she wrote. Her heart was racing and she could feel a frown of concentration creasing her brow as she struggled to keep focused and keep up with the answers her team was peppering her with. Theo's knee bumped against her thigh as he reached for his drink, disrupting her focus even further, and

at the end of the round she got up quickly, needing to put some distance between her and Theo
lest she make another silly mistake.

It was impossible to avoid Theo completely
though as the next morning, as she was rushing
into the clinic, late as usual, he was waiting for
her in her consulting room.

He handed her a coffee and a paper bag.

Molly took the coffee and peered inside the
bag to find it contained a doughnut. 'What's this
for?'

'An apology.'

Molly frowned. 'Apology?'

'I get the impression you would prefer me not
to be here.'

'Here?'

'In Byron Bay. Working at the clinic. Coming
to the quiz night. Anywhere really.'

Theo's dark eyes were flat as he watched her
closely. His eyes lacked their usual shine and
made her feel uncomfortable. Had she made him
feel unwelcome? That hadn't been her intention.

'Can we call a truce?' he asked, taking her
silence for affirmation of his thoughts. 'I don't
know why you don't want me here but I'm hoping we can get on as colleagues. I promise I'm
not going to bite you. Or kiss you again.'

'You remembered.' Of course he did. But she wasn't sure how she felt about him putting that information out there between them. She was part mortified, part pleased. She didn't want to be forgettable but she would have preferred the incident to be wiped from memory. His memory. She was no longer the insecure girl who was looking for attention and seeking validation and she worried that Theo might still see her as such. Despite her having resolved to overcome the damage that Daniel had done, that her parents had done, she feared her insecurities hadn't been erased completely, and having her past and present collide could destabilise her carefully laid plan of reinvention.

'That kiss was a lot of things but forgettable wasn't one of them,' Theo said, and Molly could feel herself blushing as he continued. 'I promise I'm not here to cause drama. I don't want to make things difficult for you.'

His dark eyes were gleaming again, his gaze gentle, unchallenging, and Molly knew he wasn't looking for an argument, he was offering her a way out. Telling her he had moved past their last encounter so she could put it behind her too.

'I'm only here for forty days. Do you think you can put up with me for that long?'

She nodded, rather unconvincingly she felt,

but she couldn't ignore his question altogether. It wasn't a case of putting up with him. It was a case of maintaining her composure. She knew she'd crossed a line the night she'd kissed him but it had been so nice to have someone ask her if she was okay, to have someone listen to her. She hadn't expected the kiss to tip her world sideways. And for one crazy minute she'd been tempted to take a chance and see what would happen if she chose Theo. But for so long she had been hiding behind a mask. One that Daniel hadn't even cared enough to see behind. She'd been the loudest in the room, the funniest, the brightest and she was terrified that if her mask slipped Theo might not like what he found behind it.

But she still wasn't sure she'd be able to handle being colleagues without being awkward. She got the feeling Theo could read her innermost thoughts. That he could see into her heart and soul, and she didn't want him to read her thoughts now. She didn't want him to know she'd never forgotten him or the kiss either. Those days were long gone.

Theo was the last one in the clinic on Friday night. He had spoken to his mother and run through the issues he'd already identified within the clinic and then returned to the spreadsheets when the call ended, but the figures were swimming in circles.

He kept thinking about Molly and wondering why it was that they found themselves together in this town. Was it fate, as his mother and grandparents would attest to, or was it simply a coincidence, as his father would say? And, either way, did it mean anything?

His logical side told him it didn't, but he still couldn't concentrate. Work could wait for another day, he decided as he shut down his computer.

But now the weekend stretched ahead of him. He had no plans. He never did—he was normally working.

He wondered what Molly was doing. But if she had plans she hadn't included him, not that he expected her to, and nor had he asked her what she was up to.

He had to admit he still felt a pull of attraction, chemistry, a buzz when he was around her. She still bewitched him, that hadn't changed. But he wasn't going to make a move. He was only here for another month or so and it was almost as if they'd agreed to ignore one another for that time. Despite their truce, they'd barely said a word to each other for the past two days.

He switched off the lights and locked the clinic behind him. He walked through town, heading for the beach and home. Town was busy and loud but he assumed it was par for the course on a Friday night before remembering that the Schoolies Festival started this weekend. Hadn't Tom said the festival organisers were looking for volunteers? Perhaps he should look into that. It might fill up his time. He couldn't spend all weekend looking at spreadsheets.

Work-life balance. That was what he needed. He wasn't sure if spending his weekend volunteering in the first-aid tent counted as finding work-life balance but he didn't really know any other way to live. He'd been brought up to work hard, study hard, commit one hundred per cent to his endeavours and reach his goals. He understood the work bit but what about the life bit?

Time off was rare and he usually spent it in the gym—not because he loved it but because he knew the benefits—and to relax he turned to his music.

He unlocked his front door, picked up his guitar from the lounge, grabbed a beer from the fridge and headed out to the deck that overlooked the beach. He finished his beer and then played some chords as he looked over the ocean. He let his mind empty as the notes floated around him, accompanied by the intermittent blink of the lighthouse to his right and the stars overhead.

* * *

Molly pulled on a pair of jeans and the green T-shirt she'd been given to wear as her uniform for tonight. She and Gemma had done their regular Saturday morning walk up to the lighthouse followed by a swim, but had forgone their usual time on the beach as the sand was already being overrun by the school leavers who had arrived in town for the Schoolies Festival, which officially started today. Molly had spent the afternoon cleaning and doing the grocery shopping before she headed to the foreshore, where she would volunteer her time in the first-aid tent for the first night of the festival.

Having volunteered last year, she thought she was prepared for anything but what she wasn't ready for was seeing Theo, also wearing the green volunteers' T-shirt, walking into the tent in front of her.

'Theo! What are you doing here?'

'Volunteering.'

Molly frowned. 'Why?' Their little contact this past week had meant she was beginning to think she could navigate working with him, treating him as just a doctor she had been to university with, as a nine-to-five weekday colleague, but she hadn't counted on spending Saturday night with him as well.

'Tom said they were short of volunteers and I figured I didn't have anything better to do this weekend.'

Molly immediately felt guilty. Hadn't anyone from the clinic offered to show him around? What had happened to small-town hospitality? 'You didn't check out the beaches or the town?'

'I thought I'd avoid the beaches until after the festival—I'm not sure I wanted to share it with a thousand school leavers. I did take a drive up into the Hinterland but that still left me with a Saturday night to fill.'

Perhaps she should have sent him off with Matt. That would have meant she could avoid the situation she now found herself in, namely spending the next few hours together, she thought as they were greeted by Steph, one of the volunteer coordinators.

Steph introduced Theo and Molly to the other volunteers—Justin and Priya, both first aiders—before showing them around the large tent, which was actually several marquees joined together to create different spaces. The front section of the tent was set up as a dispensary where first aiders could hand out water, sunburn cream, painkillers and lollies to the festival-goers. A cluster of beanbags had been arranged in one corner of the tent to give kids a break-out space if they needed a chance to chill, and a couple of smaller tents at the back had been furnished with beds where treatment for minor injuries or ailments could be administered away from the crowds.

'It's fantastic to have you both here tonight,' Steph said as they returned to the front of the tent. 'We are grateful to have as many volunteers as we can get but always happy to have some with more medical experience. We've got some nurses and paramedics helping throughout the week too. Your expertise won't always be needed but occasionally we can have more serious injuries and, because the hospital is a ten-minute drive out of town, it's not easy for the kids to present to emergency, and we don't really want them turning up there as the first option for every little mishap. The first-aid tent helps to triage the load.'

'If we do need to send someone to hospital, how do we manage that?' Theo asked.

'We can call an ambulance in an emergency or, if it's not critical, someone from the Red Frogs brigade can take them.'

'The Red what?'

'Red Frogs are another volunteer group,' Steph explained. 'They're affiliated with a church group so they're separate from the first-aid crew, not all of them have first-aid skills, and they provide general support, emotional support, advice and information. For a lot of these kids this week will be the first time they've been away from home without some sort of adult supervision. Some of them get in over their heads and need support, others can find the whole experience a bit overwhelming. The Red Frogs act kind of like a big brother. Or sister. Support without judgement. They will drift in and out of our tent over the course of the night but they're around all week for the students. The kids can download an app that lets them contact Red Frogs for assistance or company, and they've been known to offer everything from pancake cookups, room visits and cleans to emotional support, walking kids home and handing out lolly frogs,' she said as she pointed to a huge bowl filled with red frog-shaped lollies that sat on one of the counters. 'Theo, why don't you take a few minutes to familiarise yourself with the treatment spaces before it gets busy? Molly can show you the ropes.'

'You've done this before?' Theo asked as Steph left them to it.

Molly nodded and headed for the treatment area, knowing it was easier to talk to Theo if she wasn't looking at him at the same time. That way she could avoid the fluttery feeling she got every time she looked into his eyes. 'I volunteered last year,' she said. 'I came up for a holiday and one week of my trip just happened to coincide with the Schoolies Festival. Matt and Levi volunteer with the Red Frogs and Matt talked me into helping out. I really enjoyed it.'

That wasn't the whole truth. Matt had invited her for a holiday when she'd broken up with Daniel and, to keep her occupied while he was at work, Matt had suggested she lend a hand during the festival. She had enjoyed it and it had kept her mind busy, given her an excuse to avoid Daniel's phone calls and given her a chance to experience life in Byron. 'I felt like I really got to know some of the locals and it was a big part of helping me to make the decision to relocate here permanently.'

'What presentations were you dealing with?' Theo asked.

'Sunburn and dehydration during the day, drug- and alcohol-affected kids later on, plus the odd broken bone and a concussion or two, but be prepared for anything,' she said. 'The first night was pretty hectic last year. The kids tend to party hard over the first weekend and then calm down as the week progresses and the excitement wears off. Once the exhaustion and hangovers kick in, they can't continue on at the same pace.'

The end of Molly's sentence was drowned out by loud cheering and yelling coming from the beach. The first-aid tent had been erected on the grassy plateau overlooking the beach, between the surf club and the pub on the corner, and the noise from the sand competed with the sound of music from the hotel. Drawn by the commotion, Theo and Molly wandered back to the front of the tent.

Sunset was approaching and the Norfolk pines cast long shadows on the lawn where several teenagers sat, feasting on takeaway. Main Beach stretched out in front of them, full of school leavers. The foreshore was an alcohol-free zone. Those who were old enough could drink at the pub, but, judging by the volume of noise and some of the rowdy behaviour, it looked as though plenty of those on the beach had made their way there from the bar. Behind them the pub was also busy, music blared from the speakers and Molly knew there would be a live band later in the night.

Her attention was drawn back to the beach where the sounds of cheering were being accompanied by rhythmic clapping. From their slightly elevated vantage point she could see a large group of kids on the sand forming a circle around four others. The circle gave the tableau the effect of a bullring. Within the circle were two boys, each with a girl sitting on top of his shoulders.

'What are they doing?' Theo asked.

The two girls each held what appeared to be long sticks but Molly knew they were actually beer cans that had been taped together.

'Playing beer-can jousting,' she said.

As the crowd cheered and clapped the two boys ran towards each other, the girls bouncing on their shoulders. The girls had the beer-can sticks thrust out in front of them, aiming at their opposition number. Molly heard Theo's sharp intake of breath as the stick of one girl glanced off the other girl's shoulder, causing her to overbalance. She tumbled into the sand as the crowd clapped and whistled. Molly held her breath until the girl got to her feet and bowed to the crowd as the other girl held her arms aloft in a victory pose.

The boys retreated to opposite sides of the circle and a new girl took the place of the one who had fallen. She waited for someone to hand her the jousting stick before the boys ran at each other again.

'Shouldn't we stop them? Someone is going to get hurt.'

Molly was watching through half-closed eyes, as if that were going to make the activity safer, but as the words left Theo's mouth she saw one girl rear backwards as the jousting stick hit her in the face. As she fell, she took all the other combatants down with her and suddenly there was a pile of bodies in the centre of the circle. The crowd, which seconds before had been loud and boisterous, fell silent.

CHAPTER FOUR

WITHOUT DISCUSSION MOLLY and Theo sprinted to the beach.

Theo pushed his way through to the middle of the crowd and Molly followed closely behind him, letting him clear a path for her. All four kids were kneeling in the sand as Theo and Molly squatted beside them. The boys appeared to have got out of the contest unscathed but the same could not be said for the girls. One had a nasty gash above her eye, which was bleeding profusely, and the other girl was clutching her mouth as blood streamed down her chin.

'Let me see.' Molly didn't bother introducing herself. Her green T-shirt identified her as a first aider and her tone implied authority. The girl took her hand away from her mouth and Molly could see a gap where a front tooth should be.

Molly looked up and saw Justin, one of the other volunteers. 'We're looking for a lost tooth,' she said, assuming the girl had started the day with both her front teeth. Looking for the tooth would be like trying to find a needle in a haystack, but it would keep everyone busy while she and Theo sorted out the injured girls.

She helped her patient to her feet while looking around for Theo. He was still squatting in the sand next to his patient. He'd ripped off his T-shirt and had it pressed against her head wound, stemming the blood. His skin was smooth and golden and his shoulder muscles flexed as he reached for the girl's elbow to help her stand. With difficulty Molly dragged her gaze away from Theo's bare back and naked chest. It was a struggle. It was a reflex reaction to let her eyes roam over his body, but she couldn't afford to get distracted.

'If you find the tooth, give it to Justin. Try not to touch the root of the tooth.' Molly issued instructions to the crowd. 'Justin, I'll send someone down with a container. If by some miracle it is found, bring it up to the tent as quickly as you can.'

She and Theo helped the girls up to the first-aid tent while dozens of kids dropped to their hands and knees and began sifting through the sand.

Molly and Theo sat the girls on adjacent treatment beds, not bothering to pull across the curtains that separated them. She pulled on a pair of surgical gloves and opened a container of saline, pouring some into a small specimen jar and handing it to Priya, the other volunteer. 'Take this down to Justin,' she said. 'If they find the tooth, get Justin to put it in there and bring it back to me.'

Priya raised her eyebrows. 'You think they'll find it?'

Molly shrugged. 'Stranger things have happened.' She had no way of knowing if they'd have any luck but they had to try.

She poured some saline into a cup and handed it to her patient. 'Rinse your mouth and spit into here,' she said as she held a stainless-steel bowl out for her. She handed the bowl to Steph, who was hovering nearby, to empty. 'Is there an after-hours dentist on standby this week?' she asked Steph.

Steph nodded as she rinsed the bowl.

'Can you give them a call and see if they'll meet us at the surgery?' Molly asked as she tore open a packet of gauze and held it to the girl's gum to soak up the blood and stem the bleeding. All the blood was coming from the gum. Her lip was intact so she wouldn't require stitches. Hopefully the tooth would be found but, either way, she needed a dental review.

Molly glanced over to Theo as Steph left the area and Priya returned, without the missing tooth. Theo put her to work helping him cut sutures as he stitched the girl's head wound. He was still shirtless, Steph would need to find him a new top, but Molly secretly hoped she wasn't in too much of a hurry. She admired Theo's physique while she admired his handiwork. His stitches were small and neat and Molly doubted anyone would be able to tell that a plastic surgeon hadn't done the job. He was applying a dressing over the stitches when Justin appeared, triumphantly holding the jar of saline, complete with the missing tooth.

'You found it!'

Justin nodded and handed the jar over to Molly. She opened the lid, put the jar on the bed and changed her gloves. She opened a fresh packet of gauze before removing the blood-soaked wadding from her patient's mouth. She carefully removed the tooth from the jar and pushed it back into the socket.

'Bite down gently on the gauze,' she told her patient as she placed the fresh wad under the repositioned tooth. 'It'll hold the tooth in place until we get you to the dentist.' Molly turned to Justin. 'Can we get one of the Red Frogs to do the transfer to the dental surgery?'

Justin nodded and he and Priya took Molly's patient, leaving Molly alone with Theo and the second girl. He was doing a concussion test before he checked on any allergies and gave her some tablets for pain relief. Once he was finished and had given her the all-clear, Molly grabbed another Red Frog to take the girl back to her accommodation to rest. Priya, Steph and Justin all drifted back to the front of the tent and suddenly it was just the two of them again.

Molly pulled off her gloves and threw them in the bin before sanitising her hands. Theo did the same and then picked up the spare T-shirt Steph had left for him and pulled it over his head. Molly tried not to be disappointed. Wasn't this exactly what she'd been trying to avoid? Letting herself get too close to Theo, letting him get too close to her. And this definitely counted as too close.

'What a stupid game that is,' Theo said as he tugged the T-shirt down over his stomach. 'They're lucky someone didn't lose an eye.'

Molly smiled. Theo was so incensed. She knew it wasn't funny but it was hard not to find his reaction a little amusing. 'Anyone one would think you were seventy-nine, not twenty-nine,' she said. 'Didn't you ever do anything stupid when you were younger?'

'No, never,' Theo replied, but he was grinning and Molly wasn't sure if he was pulling her leg or not.

'Did you go to Schoolies Week?' she asked.

Theo shook his head. 'My parents took my sister and me overseas when I finished school. I think it was their way of making sure I didn't get into any trouble. My parents both had high expectations. My sister and I didn't get a lot of freedom. It wasn't until I went to university that I really had a chance to test the waters and you'd think spending time at music gigs I'd push a few boundaries, but I was always conscious of my grades. I couldn't afford to let things slip. Failure wasn't an option in our house so I never really went wild. You?'

'Did I go wild or did I go to Schoolies?'

'Both.'

'I did go to Schoolies. And lived to tell the tale, obviously.'

'Did you have fun?'

'Definitely.' She smiled. 'It was the first time I'd been away with my friends without any parents. We had an absolute blast. But if it makes you feel any better, the police will crack down on the kids a bit later in the night. Apparently on the first night they like to take a couple of kids off to the police station on some trumped-up charges, urinating in public, underage drinking, that sort of thing, which serves to scare the majority of the kids into behaving a little better. There will still be some who want to push the boundaries but most of them don't want to get sent home or spend the night in a cell. They've paid a lot of money to spend a week here—forking out for accommodation, entertainment, meals, drinks— and they don't want to miss out on the fun, so things will calm down.'

As if to back up her point the next couple of hours were relatively quiet. Molly had to extract a nasty splinter from a boy's hand and Theo sent another to hospital for an X-ray on a suspected broken toe, and then it was mostly handing out bottles of water and vomit bags before sending kids home under the supervision of the Red Frogs.

'I'm starving,' Theo said when their shift ended at midnight. 'Is there anywhere we can grab a feed this late?'

'The pub will be open,' Molly told him. 'And they provide volunteers with a free cheeseburger and fries, or a tofu burger if that's your preference. It is Byron Bay, after all.'

'Sounds good. Would you like to join me?'

'Sure.' She justified the extra time with Theo by telling herself she was hungry so it made sense to grab some food. And it would ease her guilty conscience that no one had thought to play host and had left Theo to his own devices on his first weekend. But really, she had enjoyed his company tonight.

'That was an interesting night,' Theo said as they waited for their burgers. 'I must say I didn't expect to find myself tending to exuberant teenagers in a tent on the beach at midnight as part of my time here.'

'No, it's a bit left of centre, isn't it?' Molly laughed. 'It suits Byron Bay though.'

'I didn't expect to find you here either. I always imagined you married to Daniel and living in Sydney.'

His comment surprised her. His assumptions were probably reasonable enough, but she was surprised to hear he'd thought about her at all. 'And yet, here I am,' she said, 'neither of those things.'

'Here you are,' he agreed. He was looking at her intently and Molly could feel her heart beating in her chest as she stood in the spotlight of Theo's attention. His dark eyes held her in their thrall as she held her breath, waiting for some sort of personal declaration she felt was coming.

'Order for Molly!'

She jumped, startled out of her reverie by the

everyday sound of her name being called, and the moment was lost. Theo glanced over his shoulder and their connection was broken as he went to collect their burgers.

'Do you want to eat here?' he asked as he handed her order to her.

Molly shook her head. The pub was still busy and noisy, filled with school leavers intent on celebrating into the wee hours of the morning, and she needed some peace and quiet, some time to sort out the thoughts in her head. 'I've had enough of exuberant teenagers tonight,' she said, copying Theo's earlier description. 'I'll have mine to go.'

'Are you walking home?'

'I should be but I drove into town. I was running late.' She smiled and Theo laughed.

'Again.'

'Again,' she said. 'I parked at the clinic.'

'I'll walk with you to your car.'

Molly was about to say she'd be fine, it was only a short walk, but she realised she wasn't quite ready to say goodnight to Theo. She didn't want to admit that seeing him half undressed might have had something to do with that. But regardless of his state of dress they'd worked well together tonight and she was feeling much more comfortable with him.

'Okay, thanks.' She ate a couple of fries as they walked and then picked up the previous thread of conversation. 'Why did you assume I'd be married to Daniel?' she asked. She was intrigued to know if he'd spent a lot of time thinking about her, but of course she couldn't ask him that.

'You seemed so serious about him, so convinced he was the right man for you. I thought you might have married him. But I was pleased to find out you haven't.'

'You never liked him,' Molly stated. She knew that. Theo had made that clear.

'I didn't dislike him. I didn't like him for you. I thought you could do better.'

Molly smiled. She wasn't offended by Theo's view. She agreed with him now. 'You were right,' she said. 'But I needed to figure that out for myself. It turns out I'm not a very fast learner when it comes relationships, but I had no intention of getting married.'

'To Daniel?'

'To anyone.'

'Really? Not ever?'

'Marriage seems like a strange commitment to make. To be bound to someone until the end of time. I think it just opens you up to heartache and I haven't seen anything yet to make me change my mind. I'm focusing on myself and on my career. Taking some time out for self-reflection.'

'And what are you discovering? I assume you're not about to swap life as a doctor to move to the hinterland and grow herbs?'

'Only medicinal ones,' she teased.

'A worthy pastime, I agree,' he said with a smile that made his eyes gleam and her heart skip a beat, 'but that seems a waste of a medical degree. Or is medicine not a calling for you?'

Molly looked at Theo as she wondered how much she should admit. 'To be honest, becoming a doctor wasn't my idea. The careers advisor at school suggested it as an option. She thought I'd get the grades and I thought if I got into med school it might make my dad notice me. I am the middle of three girls and I always thought Dad was disappointed that he didn't have any sons. He never had a lot of time for us—he was the headmaster at a boys' school and he spent a lot of time at work—and I thought if I became a doctor I might suddenly become worthy of his attention. The school he taught at was very academic and there was the expectation that almost all of the students would go on to university and to study prestigious courses. Law. Medicine. Engineering. Politics. Medicine was something I could imagine doing.' She shrugged.

'Did it work?'

'Nope.' She threw her empty fries container into a council bin and unwrapped her cheese-burger. 'Turns out it wasn't our gender that was the issue. My father wasn't a faithful husband. I had always assumed he would spend more time with us if we were boys. I never considered that he was not at home because he was cheating on my mother. When I was fifteen, I saw my father with another woman. He told me my mother knew. It turned out she did know and she chose to stay with him anyway. For a long time I believed that was normal behaviour in a marriage and I decided that if that was the case, then I didn't want to get married. Marriage should be about commitment, trust, fidelity and love. I didn't see it being about any of those things.

'And then I met Daniel and he was the same, but I thought I could be the one to get him to change. To commit. I don't know why I didn't look for a faithful partner instead.' She paused, unsure how to continue, not sure if Theo would judge her but needing him to understand who she had been back then. 'Dad was a serial phi-lanterer. He had plenty of opportunity. He is handsome, charming—the mothers of his students couldn't get enough, apparently. What I couldn't understand was why my mother didn't kick him out. So, I asked her that question. She said she didn't know how to survive on her own, or as a single mother, and she was scared of what her future would look like if she left.'

Theo was looking at her and she knew what he was thinking. 'I know. I was doing the same thing with Daniel, taking him back every time he apologised and promised to be better. I'd take him back hoping this time he meant it but knowing it wouldn't last. I was repeating my mother's mistakes but at least I hadn't married him. I knew I could take care of myself financially. That was another big reason why medicine appealed to me—it was a high-income-earning job that would give me financial independence. If I was never getting married, I needed to earn my own money. I never wanted to be dependent on someone else for my financial security. Luckily for me it turned out that I love being a doctor.'

Unlike for her mother, it wasn't financial security that had influenced her decisions and kept her in a relationship with Daniel. Molly had spent most of her life wanting to be seen and she'd been afraid that if she wasn't Daniel's girlfriend any more, if she wasn't part of the cool crowd, then she'd suddenly become invisible again. That fear had been real enough to keep her going back, long after it was good for her.

She kept her eyes focused on the footpath. She hadn't expected to talk about Daniel, hadn't expected to share her thoughts with Theo, but he was a good listener and she felt safe with him. They'd worked well together tonight, and she'd been comfortable in his company while they were busy and, somehow, that feeling continued as they walked side by side in the dark, making it easy to confide in him.

'I kept telling myself I could leave whenever I wanted, but I never did. Not permanently. I'd break up with him and then take him back. Time after time after time. I'd invested so much time and effort into that relationship that it made it hard to throw it away, but I'm done now. I've been here nearly six months and I'm surviving. Better than that, I'm happy here. Away from my family. Away from Daniel. It was the best decision I ever made.'

'What made your mind up?'

'After the last time he cheated on me I realised I was exactly like my mother, just without a wedding ring. Normally the pattern would be he'd cheat on me briefly, give up the other girl and convince me to give him another chance. I suppose I'd always let him get away with his behaviour, I'd condoned it in a way. Once I became aware of the situation with my parents and had seen how my father treated my mother, and how she put up with it, I think I came to believe that it was just the way men were. The way relationships were. The way my relationship was.

'But the last time was different. He wanted me back but wanted to keep seeing the other girl as well. I had just enough self-esteem to reject that sordid offer. I had a career, my own income, no dependants. I didn't need Daniel, but it wasn't until I finally realised that I didn't want him, or the life that he was subjecting me to, any more that I did something about changing things.' She smiled. 'It's ironic really—you told me the same things years ago. But I wasn't ready to hear it then. Matt helped.'

'Have you and Matt been friends for a long time?'

'No, we met playing social netball before he moved up here, but it think it was a case of the planets aligning. He was back in Sydney for a mutual friend's engagement party when Daniel and I were on a break. Another one. Matt convinced me to come up here for a holiday and I loved it. But when I got back to Sydney I realised I needed to make the change and I left for the last time.'

'That was brave.'

Molly shook her head. 'Not really. It was well overdue but I was glad to make Daniel someone else's problem.'

'Is he still with her?'

'I don't know. I try not to think about him if I can help it.'

'Ah.'

Molly frowned. 'What?'

'Is that why you weren't happy to see me? Because I reminded you of Daniel?'

How was it possible that Theo had more insight into Molly than she'd had into herself? 'You didn't remind me of Daniel, but you did remind me of a time in my past I'm not proud of. You reminded me of the person I was then— insecure, dependent, like my mother—all the things I swore I wasn't going to be. I wanted to believe that I was growing as a person, that this move to Byron Bay was the start of a new life, a new me, and your arrival brought back some of my insecurities.

'Until I realised that I couldn't put that onto you. I'm responsible for myself and I know I'm not that person any more. I've made some tough decisions and I've made some good ones and some bad ones, but I'm starting to think the good are outweighing the bad now. Moving here has been a good one. I love the job, my colleagues and the town.'

'I'm pleased. You seem happy.'

'I am. And I've got a chance to figure out who I am now. Who I want to be and who I want to be with. I haven't been on my own since I was seventeen. This is my time to work on myself.'

'Do you think this is a permanent move for you?'

'I'm not sure. But I think it could be.'

'You like it here? You're not missing the rat race of Sydney?'

'Not at all. I love it here. The job is great, the people are lovely. It's fun. What about you? Is Byron Bay casting its spell over you yet? I would have thought the rock star part of you would like the vibe of Byron.'

'You know what, I kind of do. It's a lot more relaxed here, isn't it? I feel like even the drama of tonight will be forgotten by tomorrow. People seem to live in the moment.'

'That's a good way of putting it. I'm not sure that it's sustainable for a lot of people to live like that but it's appealing for a little while. Something to be said for being able to stop and smell the metaphorical roses.'

'Even the clinic seems a little less frenetic. Often I feel like I'd get more job satisfaction if

I could spend more time with my patients but there never seem to be enough hours in the day. But the past few days have been a revelation. I've enjoyed having more time and longer consults.'

'I think that's one nice thing about regional medicine. We get the chance to know our patients a bit better,' Molly said as they reached the car park.

The walk had taken a lot longer than it needed to and Molly realised they'd both been dawdling, so caught up in their conversation there hadn't seemed any need to hurry. Perhaps the slow pace of Byron Bay was to blame or perhaps they had been happy to spend more time in each other's company.

'This is me,' she said as she pushed the button to unlock her car. Theo reached for the door and opened it for her. She stepped into the opening and then spun around to face him. 'Thanks for keeping me company and thanks for listening.' Listening was still one of his strong suits.

'Any time.'

Molly leant her back on the car, reluctant to get in, reluctant to say goodnight. 'Can I give you a lift home?' she offered.

'Which way are you headed?'

'Up the hill.' She gestured to her right. 'Towards the lighthouse.'

Theo shook his head. 'I'm the other way. It's only a short walk.'

He was standing close, on the same side of the door as her. He had one arm resting along the top of the door, keeping it open. If Molly stood up straight, if she leant forwards and moved away from the car, she'd almost be touching him. She closed her hand into a fist and forced herself to keep it by her side, resisting the sudden and ridiculous desire to reach for him.

She maintained her position, frozen in place, too scared to move, knowing if she straightened up as she'd have to do to climb into the car it would bring her closer to him. She was scared of what she might do then.

Theo hadn't moved. He was watching her with his dark eyes and, worried that he might read her thoughts, she dropped her gaze.

But that was a mistake.

Now she was looking at his mouth.

He had an amazing mouth. His lips were full and soft and just begged to be kissed. But that hadn't ended well last time and she didn't want to repeat the same mistake, no matter how tempting. She shouldn't have kissed him four years ago and she shouldn't kiss him again. Not now. She was avoiding relationships, taking time to work on herself, but when Theo was standing in front of her it made her wonder if complete abstinence was a step too far.

But kissing Theo wouldn't serve any purpose other than to satisfy an urge and she'd learnt her lesson. It hadn't been fair of her to kiss him spontaneously four years ago and she wasn't about to do it again. Next time they kissed it would be consensual. Next time she would ask first.

Molly shook her head—what was she thinking? Next time! She was getting carried away in the moment. She needed to ignore the frisson of awareness and the shiver in her belly that she got whenever Theo smiled at her or whenever his hand touched hers or whenever he took off his shirt. It shouldn't be impossible. Even though it felt as if it might be.

Once again Molly tried to keep her distance from Theo over the next few days. The pull of attraction she'd felt had frightened her. She didn't want to get involved. She didn't want to be in a relationship. Relationships complicated life, made her part of something else, someone else, and what she really needed was time alone, time to be by herself, time to figure herself out. She'd been asked out a few times since moving to Byron Bay, but it was easy to turn down those invitations when there'd been no chemistry. But it was becoming hard to ignore the spark of awareness she felt whenever she saw Theo.

The connection she felt was strong, the pull powerful. It shouldn't have surprised her, she'd felt it before, four years ago but that was exactly why she needed to keep her distance. Her brain and her body were at odds with each other. One pushing. One pulling. One resisting. One capitulating. She was worried she'd do something stupid if she spent too much time with Theo.

It was easy enough to avoid him in the mornings because she was always dashing in the door at the last minute, and she cut down on her caffeine intake to avoid bumping into him in the staff kitchen. Thankfully there was no quiz night at the pub this week because of the Schoolies Festival, so by Thursday she thought she might make it through the whole week without seeing him. Until she found herself face to face with him at the hydrotherapy pool.

Thank God he wasn't actually in the pool, but standing beside it, fully clothed, talking to Matt. But still, her stomach flipped and her hands became clammy. If she hadn't been taking a patient through in preparation for their first hydrotherapy session she would have turned on her tail and fled.

She needed to get a grip. She was being ridiculous. She tried reminding herself why she meant to keep her distance from him but when he saw her approaching and smiled at her she couldn't remember a single reason.

She sent her patient to the change rooms and, telling herself it was just the humidity of the indoor pool making her hands clammy, she forced herself to keep walking, one step at a time, towards Matt. And Theo.

Matt was explaining the benefits of hydrotherapy to Theo. 'I'd really like to get into the pool more often, but I just don't have the time between patients,' Matt said. 'We need more staff in order to run more regular sessions.'

'Is the pool used for anything else?' Theo asked as Molly waited for her patient.

'Like what?'

'Kids' swimming lessons? Aquarobics?'

Molly frowned and wondered why Theo was asking all these questions.

'No,' Matt replied.

'So it is underutilised.'

Matt nodded as Molly waved her patient over.

'Matt, this is Susan Ford. She's got her first hydro session today.'

Matt took Susan off and Molly walked out

of the pool area with Theo. 'What's with all the questions?' she asked.

'I was just curious to see how it all works.'

She didn't understand why it mattered. He was only a locum. 'You don't have hydrotherapy in the Sydney clinic?'

'No. We don't have any allied health facilities. This clinic has a different operating structure. I'm just trying to see what works and what doesn't.'

That still didn't explain his interest, but it wasn't really any of her business. Perhaps he was thinking about offering hydrotherapy back at his clinic in Sydney. If he wanted to get to know the intricacies of the clinic, that was his choice. She just needed to worry about getting through one more day until it was the weekend, when she could relax and not have to worry about bumping into him.

Molly grabbed a handful of red lolly frogs from a bowl in the first-aid tent and sat on the edge of a treatment bed, swinging her legs as she popped a lolly into her mouth.

'I thought they were meant for the kids,' Theo teased her.

Molly's heart leapt at his voice and she almost choked on the lolly.

Her hope that he wouldn't also be volunteering on the last official night of the Schoolies Festival was well and truly quashed. There seemed to be no way of avoiding him completely. He was constantly popping up in her vicinity, so much so that she wasn't really all that surprised to see him tonight.

'I don't think they'll miss a few,' she replied. 'This is what keeps me coming back.'

'Not my company?'

'I didn't know you were going to be here.'

'I had a good time last weekend and figured I could lend a hand again. The gig came highly recommended,' he said with a smile.

He had a really lovely smile, Molly thought, not for the first time. She'd miss seeing his smile once he returned to Sydney. She'd miss the way it made her feel. But every time he smiled at her she felt her resistance to spending time with him crumbling just a little bit more until one day she feared she wouldn't have any resolve left. And where would that leave her? Throwing caution to the wind and kissing him again?

She shook her head. She couldn't do that. Perhaps she was experiencing a simple case of sexual frustration? Perhaps she needed to rethink her relationship ban—maybe she needed to go on a date and try casual sex. That might get thoughts of Theo out of her head and let her start a clean slate.

The only problem was she'd never had a one-night stand or casual sex and she didn't know if she could. But that might be her best option, she thought as she put another lolly frog in her mouth and looked for something to do to keep her hands busy and her mind engaged on something other than Theo.

The first few hours of their shift were fairly routine. They handed out plenty of water and treated a boy who'd got into a fight and broken a bone in his hand, but they hadn't been called upon much at all.

The kids were down at the beach where a DJ was playing and the rest of the volunteers were milling around the edges of the rave, handing out bottles of water and keeping an eye on things. Molly and Theo were alone in the tent, waiting for anything more serious that might need their expertise.

Though she'd been on edge initially, she'd gradually relaxed into things. Even though she sometimes felt as if Theo could read her mind, she knew that wasn't really the case. He didn't know that she'd wanted to kiss him again. He didn't know that she'd been deliberately avoiding him because of it.

She was finding him easy company. His company wasn't the issue. He wasn't the issue.

She was.

She was still worried she'd give into temptation and kiss him again.

Should she apologise for deliberately staying out of his way this week after revealing so much?

Maybe she should do that right now, she thought. They were alone. There might not be a better time.

She swallowed the red frog, ready to apologise, when two girls burst into the tent supporting a third girl between them.

CHAPTER FIVE

'OUR FRIEND ISN'T feeling well.'

Molly and Theo hurried over to the girls and ushered them to the back of the marquee. The girl in the middle was unsteady on her feet and Molly doubted she'd be able to stand without the support of her friends. Her eyes were unfocused, her pupils dilated.

'What's her name?' Molly asked.

'Tayla. Tayla Adams.'

'Let's get you up onto the bed,' Molly said as they guided Tayla through the tent to the treatment area at the back. Molly drew the curtain around them to afford some privacy as Theo helped Tayla up onto the examination plinth, physically lifting her when it became apparent that she had neither the coordination nor the comprehension to follow instructions.

'Has she been drinking?' Molly asked. She'd learned over the years never to assume the cause of a patient's symptoms. While she knew it was a fair assumption, there could be other causes, other factors at play.

But Tayla's friends were nodding. 'Vodka shots.'

'How many?'

The two girls looked at each other. 'Maybe ten.'

Molly wasn't certain they were telling the truth. Perhaps they didn't know the answer.

'In how long?'

'Since nine o'clock.'

It was now midnight.

Whatever the number of drinks Tayla had consumed it was obvious she'd drunk more than she could handle. Molly couldn't believe the girl was still standing, let alone conscious.

Molly could see Theo checking Tayla's wrist as she spoke to the friends. She knew he was looking for a medical bracelet or tattoo to indicate an underlying condition. Like her, he wasn't assuming that alcohol alone was responsible for the state Tayla was in. For all they knew she could have diabetes, epilepsy or be on medication that reacted with her alcohol consumption.

'Does Tayla have any allergies or any health problems? Is she diabetic? Epileptic?'

'No.'

'Does she take any prescription medication?'

'No.'

Molly hoped the girls' answers were correct. She looked at their patient, wondering if she should be asking her these questions. But one glance told her that Tayla was not going to be able to help her. Her eyes were glassy. She was conscious, but only just.

'Has she vomited?'

The girls shook their heads. 'She said that her hands and feet were tingling and that she couldn't breathe properly.'

'Has she taken any drugs?'

The girls hesitated. They were looking at each other, avoiding eye contact with Molly.

'It's okay,' Molly told them. 'You need to be honest. We need all the information you can give us in order to help her.'

'She had two caps of MDMA.'

'Temperature forty point two degrees.' Theo had a blood-pressure cuff wrapped around Tayla's arm and was holding a thermometer in her ear. 'Heart rate one hundred and ten.'

Molly knew that ecstasy, the common name for tablets of MDMA, could lead to hyperthermia, especially if Tayla had been dancing, which was highly likely given that most of the festival attendees had been gathered on the beach with the DJ.

'We all had lots of water. Not just the vodka,' the girls added.

Unfortunately that wasn't always the right thing to do. If Tayla's body couldn't process the water it could cause fluid to build up around her brain, which could cause headaches, dizziness, nausea, and even seizures.

'Molly.' Theo's voice held a note of warning. Molly turned around and saw that Tayla's eyes had rolled back in her head. Her mouth was open and Molly could see her tongue had swollen and she was having difficulty breathing.

'Girls, you need to wait outside.' Molly addressed Tayla's friends, who were now crying. She did not have time to deal with them as well. She drew back the curtain and ushered them out, relieved to see that Steph, the volunteer coordinator, was back in the tent. 'Steph, we need an ambulance. Accidental overdose, alcohol and ecstasy. Teenage girl, no significant medical history.'

Steph nodded in reply before Molly retreated back into the cubicle, pulling the curtain closed to block Tayla from her friends' view. She was just in time. Tayla was having a seizure, most likely related to her hyperthermia. There wasn't anything Molly and Theo could do except keep her safe. Theo was on one side of the bed and

Molly quickly stood opposite him, both of them in place to ensure Tayla didn't fall off the bed.

The seizure didn't last long, maybe thirty seconds, but it felt a lot longer. Molly helped Theo to roll Tayla into the recovery position before checking her vital signs again. Her heart rate was still high and her temperature was still elevated. The risk of another seizure was not out of the question.

'Can you grab some wet towels?' Theo asked Molly. He was wedged in behind the treatment plinth and Molly was able to get out more easily. 'We need to try to bring her temperature down.'

'Do you think we should give her a saline drip?' Molly asked when she returned with the damp towels.

Theo shook his head and took a couple of towels from her. Together they draped them over Tayla. 'No. If the seizure was due to cerebral oedema extra fluids could make it worse.' There was no way of knowing whether Tayla's convulsion was related to her temperature or fluid retention around her brain. They were simply making educated guesses and trying to minimise further harm. 'She needs to get to the hospital.'

'I'll check on the ambulance ETA,' Molly said

as they finished laying towels over Tayla. She returned moments later with the paramedics in tow.

Theo did a patient handover as Molly began disconnecting Tayla from the equipment. They reached for the blood-pressure cuff at the same time, Molly's hand coming down a fraction after Theo's, her fingers resting over his. She jerked her hand away but not before she felt the warmth of his skin flow through to her.

Her hand tingled. 'Sorry.'

'Don't be,' Theo replied as he glanced up at her. 'It's fine.' Molly's heart skittered in her chest as her pulse skyrocketed but Theo's eyes told her she had no need to be nervous around him.

She turned away to gather herself together. She was conscious that they weren't alone and disappointed and relieved at the same time. She was a mess of contradictions.

When she wasn't with Theo her resolve was strong. She resolved to be pleasant, friendly but not familiar, but when she was with him, one smile, one accidental touch sent her pulse racing and she forgot that she was going to keep her distance. All she wanted was more of him.

The paramedics had rolled Tayla onto a transfer board as Theo gathered the towels. Together they slid Tayla from the bed to the stretcher and Molly followed the paramedics as they wheeled

Tayla out, giving herself another minute to catch her breath and restore her breathing to its normal pace.

She thought Theo might remain in the treatment area but she was aware that he was behind her. Right behind her. She couldn't see him but she could feel him.

'Is she okay?' Tayla's friends were waiting in the tent and Molly turned her attention to them, letting them distract her, even as she saw Theo move in line with her on the opposite side of the stretcher.

'She should be fine,' Molly told them. 'She's asleep now but she's very lucky to have friends like you.' Molly was talking to the girls but she glanced over at Theo as she spoke. He was watching her with a smile on his face and she knew they were both thinking of the night when he had taken care of her.

Molly smiled back. He had been a good friend to her that night. Something she wasn't sure she deserved. She really did owe him an apology.

'Where are they taking her?' The girls' question brought Molly back to the present.

'To the local hospital. She'll probably need her stomach pumped.'

'Couldn't you give her something to make her vomit?' they asked.

'That's not how we do things now. And Tayla needs to be monitored overnight. She needs to go to hospital. Do you have phone numbers for her parents? They need to be told about what's happened.'

'No.'

'I'll get it sorted,' Steph said as the paramedics opened the rear doors of the ambulance. 'If you girls would like to go to the hospital I'll get one of the Red Frogs to take you,' Steph offered, leaving Molly and Theo free to return to the treatment area.

Molly busied herself tidying up, packing up equipment and throwing away discarded single-use items. The activity meant she could avoid looking at Theo.

'How will Steph find Tayla's parents?' Theo asked.

'The schools all have an emergency contact listed,' she said as she stripped the protective sheet off the treatment plinth. 'Steph can call the number for Tayla's school and they'll get in touch with her parents. It's a bit of a roundabout way to do it but it's better than nothing. Ideally if we had a contact number we could have spoken directly to the parents. Doing it this way means they'll have to call the hospital once they are notified and then chase down the information.'

'We can wait.'

Their shift should have finished an hour ago and Molly was beat. She threw the sheet into the rubbish bin and lifted her gaze to look at Theo. 'It might take them a while to get in contact with Tayla's parents. The hospital will deal with it. I don't know about you but I am exhausted.' She almost said *ready for bed*, but stopped herself at the last minute. She didn't want to complicate things. 'I'm going to head home,' she added right before she collapsed onto the treatment plinth. She lay back and stretched her legs out and let out a big sigh. 'As soon as I can make myself stand up again.'

'Are you hungry? Did you want to grab a cheeseburger from the pub?' he asked.

She shook her head. She was hungry but she didn't feel like negotiating the noise and bustle of the pub. She was exhausted but she knew the adrenalin pumping through her system would keep her awake for hours. Even so, the pub was more than she could handle at the moment. 'I'll make a cup of tea at home. I need peace and quiet. That was a bit hectic.'

Theo held out his hand, offering to help her up. 'Come on, then, I'll walk you to your car.'

She couldn't refuse his hand. That would look odd. She lifted her arm and put her hand in his.

His fingers wrapped around hers. Strong, safe, familiar. He pulled her up as she swung her legs over the side of the bed.

'I didn't drive today,' she said as she stood up, dropping his hand. 'Would you believe I had time to walk?'

Theo smiled and Molly's heart skipped a beat. 'Wonders will never cease.'

'I wish I had driven now,' she admitted. 'I'm not sure I can be bothered walking up the hill.'

'I'll walk home with you, if you like.'

She shook her head. 'You don't need to. I'll be fine.'

'I'm happy to do it. I'd feel better if you let me and, besides, I can pick you up if you collapse with fatigue.' He was still smiling and Molly found she couldn't turn down his offer. She didn't want to. Despite her misgivings, he was easy company, and she was finding she enjoyed spending time with him. She knew it was only her own thoughts that were complicating the situation.

They said goodnight to Steph and left the next shift of volunteers to man the first-aid tent. The beach party was still in full swing and the music followed them up the hill towards Molly's house. She was grateful for the background noise—she was suddenly nervous and the music disguised the lull in conversation, covering their silence.

As they walked further from the centre of town the music and the light faded. Stars shone above them and up ahead the lighthouse stood bright and white and magnificent against the dark sky as it sent its beacon of warning light across the ocean.

'Have you done the lighthouse walk?' Molly asked, desperate to make conversation to fill the emptiness. She felt uncomfortable in the dark and quiet. The silence felt far too intimate. She was afraid she was making herself vulnerable to questions from Theo that she might not want to answer. He seemed to have a knack for getting her to talk about herself and she'd already divulged more to him than she had planned to.

'No, not yet.' Theo's voice was deep, blending into the blackness of the night, and Molly felt it reverberate in her chest.

'You have to make time to do it,' she told him, 'and you should really make sure to get up early to watch the sunrise from there. That's a non-negotiable when you're in Byron. It's a pretty special experience.' The lighthouse building itself was gorgeous but, because the lighthouse stood on the most eastern point of mainland Australia, the view across the Pacific Ocean was amazing.

Theo couldn't leave Byron Bay without making that walk.

'Will you do it with me?'

She'd left herself open to that one. But the idea of watching the sunrise with him appealed to her. It was a magical experience and an iconic Byron Bay activity. She'd just ignore the fact that most people would also consider it a romantic experience. 'Sure,' she replied as they reached her apartment building. 'This is us.'

'Us?'

'Gemma and me,' she said as she entered the code and opened the building's front door. 'I'm going to put the kettle on. Did you want a cup of tea?'

'We won't disturb Gemma?'

Molly shook her head as Theo followed her inside. She headed for the stairs that would take them up to her apartment. 'She's in Brisbane for her grandparents' sixtieth wedding anniversary.'

'That's an impressive achievement.'

'I can't believe people can be happily married for that long,' Molly said as she stepped into her apartment and headed for the kitchen to flick the kettle on.

'You don't think that's normal?'

'Not in my experience.' She'd only seen evidence to the contrary, which was why she was determined not to go down that path. 'Certainly not my parents'. Are yours happily married?'

Theo shrugged. 'Mostly, I think.'

'What's their secret?' she asked as she passed Theo the tea canister, letting him choose his flavour, before filling his mug with boiled water.

'I'd like to say love, but I actually don't know if that's the truth.'

'They don't love each other?'

'I don't know. I've never heard them say they do. I don't remember them telling my sister or me that they loved us either. I guess I've just assumed they do.'

Theo's comments weren't making Molly change her views on marriage. It really didn't have a lot to recommend it, in her opinion.

'So what makes you think they're happy?' she asked.

'They don't seem *unhappy*. They have a lot in common. And common goals. As long as they're achieving those goals, I think they're happy.'

'I think people get comfortable and settle for a situation that perhaps isn't ideal. I know I did,' she admitted. She'd learnt a lot from her relationship with Daniel and she was proud of herself for getting out of it. And she had no intention of putting herself in that position again.

Theo finished his tea and stood up.

'I'm just going to call the hospital and get an update on Tayla,' she said. 'Do you want to wait?'

He nodded but moved from the kitchen and crossed the living room to stand near the front door. Molly wasn't sure if he was giving her space to make the call—he could still hear her talking and she was going to tell him the outcome anyway—or if he was just preparing to leave. She didn't want him to leave. She watched him as she waited for her call to be picked up, afraid to take her eyes off him in case he vanished before she had a chance to say goodnight.

'This is Dr Prescott,' Molly said as her call was answered. 'I sent a patient to the ED via ambulance earlier tonight. I'm just calling for an update. Her name is Tayla Adams.'

Molly had visiting rights at the hospital and she knew the ED staff would be able to tell her the basics of Tayla's condition. That was all she needed to know.

'She's stable,' she told Theo when she finished the call. 'Full of remorse and regret, I suspect, but she's okay.'

'We've all done something we've regretted after a few too many drinks,' Theo replied.

'About that—'

'I'm not talking about you,' Theo said, cutting

Molly off mid-sentence and making her wonder again how he knew what she was thinking.

Molly frowned. 'What did you think I was going to say?'

'You were thinking about the night you kissed me, weren't you?' Molly nodded and Theo continued. 'I was too but I was talking about me. About my regrets.'

'Yours?'

Theo nodded. 'I regret that I walked away. I've always wondered what would have happened if I'd been brave enough to stay.'

'Why didn't you?'

'I expected you to reject me. I didn't believe I deserved you but that didn't stop me wishing and hoping you might see me for who I was. Wishing I'd been braver. Wishing I'd kissed you a second time. I should have had the courage to find out. I was too scared of rejection, of failure, but what was the worst that could have happened? I'd get my heart broken. I was young. It could have been worth it. And I always wish I'd asked you why you kissed me.'

'You want to know why I kissed you?'

He nodded.

'Because you were gorgeous and kind and for the first time I felt like someone was listening to me and that was a powerful thing. Do you remember what you said to me?'

Theo shook his head. 'I wanted to tell you that you had terrible taste in men,' he said, 'but I don't think I did. I didn't think you would listen.'

'I wouldn't have listened,' she admitted with a small smile. 'I *should* have listened but I was determined to make Daniel love me, determined to make him faithful, so I put up with his behaviour and kept going back to him. I saw it as a challenge, something I needed to overcome. I tolerated his behaviour, his treatment of me, instead of walking away because that's what I'd seen my parents doing. Parents can have a lot to answer for. But you're right—you didn't tell me that. Do you remember talking about what we were going to do after graduation?'

'Yes.'

'You were going to work overseas. You told me I should go too. You told me I didn't need to go to work at the hospital in Sydney. I didn't tell you at the time but working overseas sounded exciting. It sounded like an adventure but I knew I wouldn't go. I wasn't brave enough either. I couldn't see myself as separate from Daniel. I made a choice. And then I wondered if you judged me for it. If you found me weak, unambitious, scared, and I was afraid I was all those things.'

'No.' He shook his head. 'I thought you were beautiful and kind and smart and funny and that you deserved so much better than Daniel.'

Molly felt tears well in her eyes as Theo's words washed over her.

'I'm sorry I behaved badly,' she said.

'It's okay. I'm just glad that you finally came to your senses. Even if it did take you a long time,' he said with a smile that took any judgement out of his words.

'I'd invested so much time and effort and energy into the idea of Daniel and me as a couple that it was hard to walk away. And I'm sorry for kissing you. I should have apologised then.' She finally gave the apology that had been haunting her. 'It was a mistake.'

'Was it?'

She shook her head. 'Not the kiss itself. I knew what I was doing. I wanted to kiss you. But it wasn't fair. I was in a relationship and I shouldn't have done it.'

'No. It wasn't fair. But I didn't handle it well,' Theo replied.

They were still standing in her doorway. He was close. If she reached out a hand she could rest it on his chest. It reminded her of this time one week ago. When they'd been standing by her car and she'd resisted the urge to touch him. One part of her knew she'd made the right decision. Another part of her regretted that she'd avoided temptation.

She wanted to touch him.

She wanted to kiss him.

She wanted to ask him to stay.

She wanted a lot of things. None of which she imagined she'd get.

The living room light wasn't on and Theo's dark eyes were hard to read in the dim light. What was he thinking? What did he want? What was he waiting for?

'But we're older and wiser now,' he said. 'And if you wanted to kiss me again it might be different.'

'Really?'

He nodded. Slowly. His gaze was fixed on her face. It was unwavering, steady and calm.

She was a bundle of nerves.

Her head waged a war with her desire. She was taking a break from dating. But she was curious to know what would happen, what a kiss might lead to. And one kiss did not mean they were dating. The chemistry was still there, she didn't think either of them would debate that. There was a spark every time they brushed past one another. With every glance they shared Molly felt as if the rest of the world ceased to exist. Theo could answer questions Molly hadn't even asked. He knew what she was thinking. They had a connection she'd never felt with any-one else.

It was only a kiss.

Her heart was racing. She could feel the blood pounding in her veins, could hear her heart beat-ing.

Was this a bad idea?

She couldn't decide.

Her gaze dropped lower, moving from Theo's eyes to his lips. There was only one way to know for sure.

CHAPTER SIX

THEO WATCHED MOLLY'S thoughts as they played across her face. He knew the attraction he felt wasn't one-sided. Their connection was real. The chemistry, the buzz he felt when their hands brushed, the buzz he felt when he made her smile, he knew she felt the same.

It had been the same four years ago. They had come together as if they were made for each other. He remembered every detail of that night. He'd tried to forget but seeing her again had brought back every memory—both painful and miraculous.

He'd been foolish to think he could ignore her this time around. The attraction was impossible to ignore.

He had been drawn to Molly from the moment he saw her on their first day at university. He'd waited seven years for her to notice him. Seven years to touch her. Seven years was a long time and the kiss had only made things worse. The kiss they had shared had been amazing but he'd known it wouldn't lead to anything more. And that had been heartbreaking.

Molly and Daniel had had a turbulent relationship but Molly always went back to him and Theo hadn't for one moment thought their one kiss would change anything.

So he'd walked away. Never knowing if things might have turned out differently if he'd stayed, if he'd taken a chance, if he'd kissed her again, if she'd realised that staying with Daniel would be a mistake.

Molly was still looking at him, her lips slightly parted. He could see the tip of her tongue. He watched as she licked her lips, watched as her gaze dropped to his mouth.

He knew she was thinking about kissing him. He just couldn't tell if she would.

He could remember how she had tasted four years ago. She'd tasted of raspberries—sweet, juicy and soft. He wanted to know if she still tasted the same.

He hadn't been brave enough to take a chance four years ago. He needed to be brave now. What was the worst that could happen? She could reject him again, but he'd survived that once before and something was telling him that this time would be different.

He didn't want to wait any longer. It had been four years and six days since he'd last kissed her. That was long enough.

'It's only a kiss,' he said before he dipped his head and claimed her mouth with his.

Molly closed her eyes and parted her lips and a little moan escaped from her throat as she offered herself to him.

Theo accepted her invitation and deepened the kiss, claiming her, exploring. Their first kiss had been tender. Their second was intense. This one was hungry and desperate and demanded a response. She clung to him and he held onto her. He wasn't going to let her go. He lost himself in the warmth of her kiss.

Theo's kiss was commanding, demanding. Gone was the reserved young man. He'd been replaced by a confident man who had seen her desire and could give her what she wanted.

Her heart raced in her chest and she could feel every beat as Theo's lips covered hers. She closed her eyes, succumbing to his touch. She opened her mouth and Theo caressed her tongue. She felt her nipples peak in response as he explored her mouth.

His hands wrapped around her back, the heat of them burning through her T-shirt. She melted against him as her body responded to his touch and a line of fire spread from her stomach to her groin. She deepened the kiss, wanting to lose herself in Theo.

She was aware of nothing else except the sensation of being fully alive. She wanted for nothing except Theo.

His touch was so familiar that it felt like she'd spent a lifetime in his arms. That made no sense but Molly felt as if she belonged there, in his embrace. She felt safe. She felt special. She felt seen.

But the kiss was over way too quickly. Between the hammering of her heart and the heat of Theo's kiss she was completely breathless. She needed to come up for air.

'I should go,' Theo said as they separated.

'You're going to run away again.'

'No. I'm not running. I'm not going anywhere. I'm giving you time to think about what you want. Giving you time to think about whether this is something you want to explore. What happens next is your decision.'

He kissed her again. Lightly this time, the gentlest of touches, so soft she wondered if it was nothing more than her imagination, before he opened the door and said goodnight.

Molly closed the door and leant against it.

Her legs were weak, her knees shaky but her mind was crystal clear, focused, certain. She didn't need time to think. She knew exactly what she wanted. She wanted Theo.

She had wanted the next time to be a mutual decision, consensual. She didn't want to take liberties, didn't want to take advantage, but now she knew Theo wanted it too, wanted her, and she didn't want to give him time to change his mind.

She spun around and flung open the door, desperate to call him back, worried he might have already disappeared.

He was standing right where she'd left him. He hadn't moved.

'You stayed.'

'I stayed.'

'I know what I want,' she told him as she reached out her hand. When he didn't reach for it Molly panicked. Was he going to turn down her offer?

Bu the moment passed and he said, 'You're sure?'

She nodded. She wasn't sure if she would regret her decision but she was prepared to take the chance. At the moment she had two choices—to invite him in or to let him go—and the first option was far more appealing. 'If we find we've made a mistake we can pretend nothing happened,' she said with a smile. 'We know how to do that.'

'We do indeed,' Theo agreed as he took her hand and let her lead him back into her apartment.

Theo pushed the door shut and pulled her to him. He spun her around and she felt the door press against her back. She was grateful for the support as her legs turned to jelly as Theo pressed his lips to the soft spot under her jaw where her pulse throbbed to the beat of her desire.

His lips covered hers as his fingers slid under the fabric of her T-shirt, warm on her skin, setting her on fire. She pulled her shirt over her head, reluctantly breaking the kiss, desperate to feel his skin against hers. She tugged his shirt out of his jeans, pressing her hands into his back.

Theo snapped open the button on her jeans and pushed them to the floor.

'Which one is your room?' he asked.

'Down the hall on the left.'

He picked her up, as though she weighed nothing at all, and Molly wrapped her legs around his waist. She could feel his erection straining against his jeans and she knew he wanted her as urgently as she wanted him.

He kissed her as he carried her to her bedroom and she was astounded that he managed not to crash into any of the walls.

He laid her down on her bed and ran his hand up her thigh. She was wearing only her underwear; he still had far too many clothes on. She reached out to him and slid her hands under his T-shirt, feeling the heat coming off his skin as she dragged his shirt up his back before pulling it over his head.

He bent towards her, kissing the hollow at the base of her neck where her collarbone ended. She tipped her head back and his lips moved down to the swell of her breast. She felt herself arch towards him, silently crying out for his touch. His hand reached behind her and with a flick of his fingers he undid the clasp on her bra and her breasts spilled free. He pushed her back, gently laying her down beneath him before he dipped his head and covered her nipple with his mouth. She closed her eyes as bolts of desire shot from her breasts to her groin. As his tongue caressed her nipple she could feel the moisture gathering between her legs as her body prepared to welcome him.

She heard him snap open the button on his jeans and opened her eyes to watch him divest himself of the rest of his clothing. His erection sprang free as his clothes hit the floor. He knelt between her legs and she slid her hands behind his back and ran them down over his buttocks. They were round and hard under her palms.

Theo moved his attention to her other breast as she moved one hand between his legs, cupping his testicles before running her hand along the length of his shaft. She heard him moan as her fingers rolled across the tip, using the moisture she found there to decrease the friction and smooth her movements.

She arched her hips towards him and he responded, removing her knickers and sliding his fingers inside her. She gasped as he circled her most sensitive spot with his thumb. He was hard and hot under her palm; she was warm and wet to his touch.

She was ready now. She didn't want to wait. She couldn't wait.

She opened her legs and guided him into her, welcoming the full length of him.

He pushed against her and she lifted her hips to meet his thrust. They moved together, matching their rhythms as if they'd been doing this for ever. She had her hands at his hips, controlling the pace, gradually increasing the momentum. Theo's breaths were short and Molly didn't think she was breathing at all. All her energy was focused on making love to him. There was no room in her head for anything other than the sensation of his skin against hers, his skin inside hers.

Theo gathered her hands and held them above her head, stretching her out and exposing her breasts, and he bent his head to her nipple again as he continued his thrusts. She wrapped her legs around him, binding them together. The energy they created pierced through her, flowing from his mouth, through her breast and into her groin where it gathered in a peak of pleasure building with intensity until she thought she would explode.

'Now, Theo, do it now,' she begged.

His pace increased a fraction more and as she felt him start to shudder, she released her hold as well. Their timing was exquisite, controlled by the energy that flowed between them, and they cried out in unison, climaxing simultaneously.

Their bodies had been made for each other and their coupling had been everything Molly had expected and more. They had been unified by their lovemaking and it was an experience Molly would treasure for ever.

Molly had fallen asleep with Theo curled against her and she woke up in the same position. Theo's hand cupped her bare breast. His breath was warm on her shoulder. He was breathing deeply, still asleep, but Molly needed to use the bathroom. She lifted his hand from her breast and slid out of bed, moving slowly, trying not to wake him.

She went to the bathroom and then looked for her phone. She checked the time even though there was nothing she needed to do today. It had been late when they'd fallen asleep and it was late now, almost eleven in the morning. She plugged her phone in to charge in the kitchen—it had spent the night on the lounge room floor in the pocket of her jeans and was almost out of power—and flicked the kettle on before going back to the bedroom.

Theo was awake and Molly was suddenly overcome with a bout of nerves. What if he had regrets about last night?

He greeted her with a wide smile and she relaxed. 'Good morning,' she said.

'It's a very good morning,' Theo agreed as he reached for her and pulled her back into bed.

He ran his fingers up her thigh, cupping the curve of her bottom. Molly closed her eyes and arched her hips, pushing herself closer to him. He bent his head and kissed her. She opened her mouth, joining them together. Theo ran his hand over her hip and up across her stomach, his fingers grazing her breasts. He watched as her nipple peaked under his touch and she moaned softly and reached for him, but he wasn't done yet.

He flicked his tongue over one breast, sucking it into his mouth. He supported himself on one elbow while he used his other hand in tandem with his mouth, teasing her nipples until both were taut with desire. He slid his knee between her thighs, parting them as he straddled her. His right hand stayed cupped over her left breast as he moved his mouth lower to kiss her stomach.

He took his hand from her breast and ran it up the smooth skin of the inside of her thigh. She moaned and thrust her hips towards him as her knees dropped further apart.

'Patience, Molly. Relax and enjoy,' he said, and his voice was muffled against the soft skin of her hip bone.

Theo put his head between her thighs. He put his hands under her bottom and lifted her to his mouth, supporting her there as his tongue darted inside her. She knew she was slick and wet, and she moaned as he explored her inner sanctum with his tongue. She thrust her hips towards him again, urging him deeper.

He slid his fingers inside her as he sucked at

her swollen sex. His fingers worked in tandem with his tongue, making her pant, making her beg for more.

'Theo, please. I want you inside me.'

But Theo wasn't ready to stop. Not yet. He had waited years for this. He wanted to taste her, to feel her orgasm. He knew she was close to climaxing and he wanted to bring her to orgasm like this. He knew this was a skill he possessed.

He ignored her request as he continued to work his magic with his tongue, licking and sucking the swollen bud of her desire. He continued until Molly had forgotten her request, until she had forgotten everything except her own satisfaction.

'Yes, yes… Oh, Theo, don't stop.'

He had no intention of stopping.

He heard her sharp little intake of breath and then she began to shudder.

'Yes. Oh, Theo.'

She buried her fingers in his hair and clamped her thighs around his shoulders as she came, shuddering and gasping before she collapsed, relaxed and spent.

'God, you're good at that,' she said, and he could hear the smile and contentment in her voice.

'Thank you.' He lay alongside her, his hand resting on her stomach as she cuddled into him.

He felt her hand on the shaft of his penis. 'Now it's your turn,' she said as she slid her hand up and down. 'And I want to feel you inside me. Please?'

'Seeing as you asked so nicely,' he replied as he gave himself up to Molly's rhythm.

She cupped his testes with one hand as the other encircled his shaft. Theo could feel it pulsing with a life of its own as Molly ran her hand up its length. She rolled her fingers over the end and coaxed the moisture from his body. Theo gasped and his body trembled.

She sat up and straddled his hips.

'Give me a second,' he said. He rolled onto his side, careful not to dislodge Molly, and found his jeans lying on the floor by the bed. He pulled his wallet from the pocket and retrieved a condom. He opened the packet and rolled it on in one smooth, fast movement.

Molly sat above him, naked and glorious, and Theo felt another rush of blood to his groin as she brought herself forward and raised herself up onto her knees before lowering herself onto him. Theo closed his eyes and sighed as she took his length inside her.

She lifted herself up again, and down, as Theo

held onto her hips and started to time her thrusts, matching their rhythms together. Slow at first and then gradually faster. And faster.

'Yes. Yes.'

'Harder.'

'Oh, God, yes, that's it.'

He had no idea who was saying what, all he knew was he didn't want it to stop.

'Now. Yes. Keep going. Don't stop.'

Just when he thought he couldn't stand it any longer he felt Molly start to quiver and he let himself go too, breathing out as his orgasm joined hers in perfect harmony. She was insatiable but their timing couldn't have been better.

They lay together looking up at the ceiling, breathing heavily as they recovered before Molly sat up suddenly, the sheet falling to her waist as she turned to look at Theo, a horrified expression on her face. 'We didn't use any protection last night!'

It had been the last thing on his mind. And obviously on hers too. They'd been too focused on their needs and desires, ignoring all practicalities.

Theo could feel the colour drain from his face. He sat up. 'You're not on any contraception?' he asked. 'Not that I'm saying it's your responsibility.'

Molly shook her head. 'I stopped taking the pill when I moved here.'

Damn. He'd been so caught up in the moment last night that he hadn't even made assumptions about contraception. He hadn't even stopped to think. 'I'm sorry. We should have had that conversation. I've let you down.'

'We're both to blame,' Molly replied, sharing the responsibility. 'I certainly didn't stop to think.'

'What would you like to do?' he asked. 'Do you want to take a morning-after pill?'

That was their best option. It wasn't perfect by any means, but it was their only choice.

Molly nodded.

'I'll go and get one,' he offered. 'And I should get more condoms too if we're going to keep doing this.'

'Are we going to keep doing this?' she asked.

'Why wouldn't we? I enjoyed it. And I hope you did too. There's no reason that I can think of to stop.' He picked up her hand and kissed her fingers, one by one.

'I'm supposed to be finding myself,' she said, 'not getting into another relationship.'

'I'm only here for four more weeks. I don't think a few weeks would qualify as a relationship.'

'Plenty of people have relationships that last less than that.'

'Well then, maybe it just depends on what we want to call it? What about hot, steamy, no-strings, no-commitment sex? Is that off limits too?'

Theo was smiling and despite the situation Molly found him impossible to resist. 'I hadn't thought about it, but you've made me realise that I miss sex.'

'I don't think you should deprive yourself, then. If it will help you sleep better at night, why don't we call it a holiday romance?'

'Neither of us are on holiday though,' she argued with a smile.

'Friends with benefits? A summer fling?' he proposed.

Molly shook her head. 'I can't think while I'm naked.'

'All right, then, you can get back to me on that. I'll go to the pharmacy now and when I come back I'll take you out for lunch.'

'You don't need to go to the pharmacy. Go to the clinic. There'll be morning-after pills in the dispensary cabinet. Do you have a key for that?'

'Yes. Do I need to sign it out?'

Molly shook her head. 'No. And there will be condoms in the nurses' room, just in case we get carried away again. They give them out at the safe sex talks they run.'

A wide grin lit up Theo's face. 'Maybe we should sign up for those.'

He kissed her before he got out of bed, affording Molly a very nice view of his bare backside as he retrieved his clothes. 'I'll go to the clinic, duck home for a shower and come back for you.'

Molly stretched her arms and legs out and felt several muscles complain. Despite her regular swims and her walks up to the lighthouse there were some muscles that obviously hadn't had a thorough workout for a while. Her sheets smelt of sex and she probably did too. But she didn't mind—the sex had been amazing and she was glad she'd given in to the temptation. It had been worth breaking her temporary vow of celibacy.

Theo had been worth it.

She finished stretching and, with a smile on her face, headed for the shower. But her smile faded as she remembered their lack of contraception. The morning-after pill worked by delaying ovulation by several days but her menstrual cycle was irregular and she had no idea where she was at. She crossed her fingers and hoped everything would be okay. Not every instance of unprotected sex resulted in a pregnancy, she reminded herself. It would be fine.

CHAPTER SEVEN

THEO STRETCHED HIS legs under the table and managed, with some difficulty, to keep a wide smile off his face. He felt good, last night and this morning with Molly had been spectacular, and he felt as if he'd won the lottery. He'd suspected he and Molly had a chemistry that was off the charts, not that he had much to compare it to, his relationship history being limited to one semi-serious one and a few short-lived, casual romances. He prided himself on being a considerate lover and knew how to please women, but he preferred it when there wasn't too much expected of him from an emotional viewpoint. He wasn't sure if he possessed those skills. That was a work in progress.

But Molly made him want to try. He imagined she would be worth it.

But he was only in Byron Bay for four more weeks. What could he achieve in that time? When he had returned from the clinic earlier this morning Molly had agreed to a summer romance, but Theo suspected that wouldn't be enough for him. Not after last night.

He breathed deeply, inhaling the orange fragrance of Molly's shampoo. He was relaxed, he wasn't thinking about work, his mind was still and quiet, which was a rarity for him. Molly's presence today was calming on his mind if not on his libido.

He wanted to celebrate but Molly didn't seem to share quite the same level of enthusiasm. He was enjoying his lunch but Molly's lack of appetite suggested she had something on her mind. The table next to them at the little café in Brunswick Heads was occupied by a family with two small children and her gaze kept flitting towards the slightly frazzled mother and the toddler in a high chair.

'Is everything okay?' he asked.

'God, I hope so,' Molly replied as her gaze flicked, yet again, to the table beside them before she turned back to face Theo, concern in her blue-grey eyes. 'I really don't want kids.'

That was a segue he hadn't expected and her comment surprised him. She sounded so adamant. 'Not at all?' he asked.

'I don't think so. Certainly not right now.'

'You and Daniel didn't talk about it?' He

wasn't sure if it was wise to bring Daniel's name into the conversation, but Molly had dated him for years and Theo was curious to know how serious they had really been.

Molly shook her head. 'Never.'

Theo looked across to the family at the adjacent table. The toddler smiled in his direction and Theo smiled back and then pulled a funny face.

Molly watched him. 'Do you want kids?'

He nodded. None of his past relationships had ever progressed to the point where he could see a future, where he could imagine starting a family, but that hadn't meant he didn't want one. He was hopeful that, one day, he'd fall in love, get married and have children. In his heart, he believed he could love and be loved and he wanted, one day, to have a family of his own.

'Why?' she asked, and he tried to ignore the slightly incredulous tone in her question.

'I want to be able to love someone unconditionally.' In his mind that was a partner and children. It was a dream he'd had but never voiced. Until now. 'I think having kids could be tremendously fulfilling and rewarding if you have them for the right reasons.'

'I'm not so sure,' Molly disagreed. 'The way I see it, mothers in particular have to sacrifice their freedom and independence to raise a family and I'm only just getting mine back. I lost sight of my independence when I was with Daniel and I have no intention of giving it up again any time soon.'

Molly was rubbing the palm of her hand with her opposite thumb in a nervous gesture. Her frown was creased, her worry obvious.

'Well, if it makes you feel any better, the chances of getting pregnant from one episode of unprotected sex are slim, and even slimmer considering you've taken the morning-after pill,' Theo said, knowing what was on her mind and trying to calm her fears. He kept his voice low, conscious of the family at the next table, and tried to pretend that her thoughts didn't bother him.

She was being honest, and he had to acknowledge and appreciate that, but her opinion surprised him and raised the first question mark in his mind. He'd pictured himself with a wife and kids one day. He didn't have a specific timeframe; he knew that was a luxury of being a male. But it was something he wanted in his future, and hearing Molly's thoughts made him wonder if perhaps they weren't as compatible as he'd like to believe.

He reminded himself they had agreed only

to a summer romance. Their compatibility past Christmas was irrelevant.

But, after last night, he wondered how hard it was going to be to say goodbye and relegate her to his past. Again.

Molly had chosen to take Theo to Brunswick Heads, fifteen minutes north of Byron Bay, for lunch. She told him it was to avoid the Schoolies Festival but, in the back of her mind, she thought it was a sensible choice. Going out in Byron, they were bound to run into someone she knew and she wasn't ready to explain why they were having lunch together.

The café she'd chosen was one of her favourites but being seated next to a young family had freaked her out a little, making her head ache with thoughts of 'what if?'. A post-lunch walk along the beach, hand in hand with Theo, the sound of the waves crashing on the sand and the feeling of the salt spray and sun on her face, had gradually calmed her mind until she felt confident that all would be well, and by the time they headed back to Byron she was feeling less panicked and more like her normal self.

She pointed out landmarks to Theo as she drove them back to town, slowing down as she approached an intersection on a narrow road as another car was headed towards them from the opposite direction. As she eased off the accelerator there was a flash of movement, a flash of red, to her right.

All of a sudden the flash of red became a person on an e-scooter. Molly saw him look to his left before careening straight onto the road. Straight into the path of the other car that was approaching from his right. The car had no time to swerve and only barely enough time to slam on its brakes. But even that wasn't enough to enable the driver to avoid the impact.

Molly hit the brakes instinctively and watched in horror as the scooter rider bounced off the other car's bonnet and was flung into the air before crashing onto the road in front of Molly's now stationary car. Thank God she'd stopped— if she hadn't she would have run straight over him.

Molly and Theo sprang from the car and rushed to the rider's side.

A second rider, a female, dropped her scooter on the footpath and ran into the middle of the road, screaming.

The driver of the car that had hit him raced over. 'Is he all right? He came from nowhere. I didn't have time to stop.'

'I know,' Molly said. The driver was obviously in shock and understandably concerned. 'We saw the whole thing. He looked the wrong way. He didn't see you.'

The rider's eyes were open, his expression suggested he was wondering what had happened, but at least he was conscious and breathing. He'd been wearing a helmet and that was still fastened under his chin. He was lucky. Most scooter riders Molly saw didn't bother with a helmet, even though the law required them to wear one. It might have just saved this man's life.

'Don't move,' Theo said as it looked as if the man might attempt to get up. 'We're doctors, let us check you over first.'

The man, who was of Asian appearance, frowned as he looked at Theo, but didn't reply. Did he have a concussion or did he not understand the question? Molly wondered.

He looked at the young girl who was squatting beside him and spoke to her in a foreign language that sounded to Molly like Mandarin.

To her surprise, Theo replied.

She'd had no idea he spoke a second language. It just reminded her of how little she knew about him.

She sat by as a spectator as Theo, the rider and the young woman had a conversation. The man was gesturing to his right arm and shoulder.

Theo was speaking now, his words accompanied by hand gestures. He opened and closed his fist before bending and straightening his elbow. The injured man copied Theo's movements, somewhat hesitantly, but he was able to complete the two actions.

Next, Theo demonstrated lifting his arm away from his body but the young man shook his head. He said a few words but Molly couldn't tell if he was refusing or unable to perform that movement.

He pointed to the tip of his shoulder where the collarbone and shoulder blade met.

'What's he saying?' Molly asked.

'It hurts to move his shoulder.'

Theo spoke to the young man again but without any accompanying actions. The man nodded and Theo ran his hands gently over the man's clavicle and shoulder blade.

Molly watched. Theo's hands were gentle, his fingers long and slender. Just a few hours ago those same hands had been tangled in her hair, cupping her breasts, between her legs, bringing her to orgasm. She closed her eyes. What was the expression? Still waters run deep. She'd always thought of Theo as being reserved but she'd definitely seen a different side to him last night and this morning. He was passionate, considerate and was it any wonder she'd found herself agreeing to a summer fling? She wasn't about to deny herself a few weeks of pleasure.

Theo spoke and then translated for Molly. 'I think he's fractured his clavicle. Can you call for an ambulance? And then we need to get him off the road.'

Molly's phone was in her car. She went to fetch it, moving her car to the side of the road in the process, while Theo helped the man, whose name was Leung, to his feet. Theo brought him over to Molly's car and let him sit in it to wait for the ambulance.

Molly dialled 000, gave their location, and explained there had been a car versus e-scooter accident.

'They're sending an ambulance and a police car,' she said as she hung up. The police would breath-test the driver of the car involved as well as Leung. Molly suspected Theo would need to explain that process too. Theo was still talking to Leung but Molly could recognise only a few words—'Byron Bay', mostly.

Theo gave a patient handover when the paramedics arrived and Molly got more information then.

'We have a twenty-four-year-old male who was riding an e-scooter when he collided with a car. He has injured his right shoulder, suspected fractured clavicle.'

The paramedics asked a question, which Theo relayed to Leung and then repeated the answer, in English, to the paramedics. 'Yes, he has travel insurance.'

Another question. Another translation. Another response, 'No allergies.'

'Will there be a translator at the hospital?' Theo asked as the paramedics prepared to put Leung onto a stretcher.

'If there's not then the hospital use a dial-in translator over the phone,' the paramedics explained.

The police arrived and Theo gave them a description of the events before they breath-tested the involved parties. The crisis over and their patient strapped securely to the stretcher, Theo and Molly were finally free to head off.

'I could use a beer,' Theo said. 'Shall we go to my place? It's only around the corner.'

They got back in her car and Molly followed his directions, driving through town and onto Childe Street where Theo's accommodation was one of a dozen or so houses. It was single storey, tucked in among the sand dunes. Theo led Molly past three bedrooms and a bathroom, a simple layout with pale wooden floors and white walls, but Molly's jaw dropped as she stepped from the passage into an open-plan kitchen living space. The back wall of the house was glass and over the top of a low hedge of native plants Molly could see the ocean. The water looked to be mere steps from the back door. Theo unlocked the large glass door and slid it back, connecting the house to a deck that led straight onto the sand. Molly could see a narrow path stretching between the salt bush giving direct access to Belongil Beach.

She was drawn to the deck and stood taking in the view. It was the same ocean that she could see from her house, but standing here it felt as if the sea were close enough to touch, as if she could reach out a hand and dip it in the water from the comfort of the house. It would be incredible to live somewhere like this. It felt a million miles away from the busyness of Main Beach.

'This is amazing. I had no idea these houses were here,' she said as Theo reappeared holding two beers he'd fetched from the fridge. He passed one to her and she took it and sat on the end of a sun lounger, facing the ocean.

'It's pretty incredible,' he said. 'I've come to love this spot in the past few weeks. Nothing beats sitting on the deck with a beer at the end of the day, watching the waves roll in. Well, almost nothing,' he added with a grin and Molly knew instinctively that he was referring to last night.

Theo took a seat behind her, straddling the sun lounger, and Molly leant on him, resting her back against his chest. 'How on earth did you find this place?'

Theo wrapped his arms around her and Molly relaxed into his embrace. 'A friend of my sister's owns it. She's overseas. She doesn't rent it out but she lets friends and family use it. I think she was pleased to have someone in it during the Schoolies Festival.'

She closed her eyes and listened to the waves breaking on the shore. She could hear the sea from her house if the windows were open, but here it sounded as if the water were lapping at her feet. The real world receded into the distance as she lost herself in the sounds of the sea, the tang of the salt air, the warmth of the sun on her face and the touch of Theo's hands on her skin.

Molly caught the yeasty smell of Theo's beer as he sipped his drink. She'd forgotten all about hers.

'I had no idea you spoke a second language,' Molly said. 'That you are fluent in Mandarin.'

'You know I'm mixed race, right?'

'Of course.'

'My dad is Australian; my mum is Taiwanese. She moved to Australia from Taiwan to finish her schooling, met my dad at university when they were both studying medicine and they married. I grew up speaking English and Mandarin. Mum's parents moved here when my sister and I were little to look after us, basically, while Mum and Dad worked. We grew up speaking Mandarin with them.'

'You said both your parents are doctors.'

'Dad is a plastic surgeon and Mum is a GP. Lian Chin.'

Molly frowned. 'Lian Chin. That's the same name as the doctor who owns Pacific Coast Clinics.' She sat up and spun around to face Theo.

Theo nodded. 'That's my mum.'

'You're the boss's son? Why didn't you say anything?'

'Why does it matter? It's not relevant. Is it?'

Molly hesitated. It felt very relevant. It felt as if he was hiding something. Why wouldn't he have told people? Told her? That was the real question. She frowned. 'Why didn't you tell me?'

'I just did.'

'I meant, why didn't you tell me earlier?'

'I don't want people to think I got where I am because I'm related to the boss.'

'Can you honestly tell me that's not why you're here?'

'The staff in Sydney were asked if anyone wanted to cover here for Tom's leave. Being so close to Christmas, no one did. I am here because no one else put their hand up so, as the boss's son, I had to fill the gap. But I didn't want to be judged by my name or by my relationship to Lian. My surname is officially Chin Williams but, because it isn't hyphenated, I usually just go by Williams. It was a habit I developed in high school, a strategy to help me fit in, to seem less Asian.'

Molly sensed there was more to this situation than Theo was telling her, but she let him continue rather than pushing for him to disclose more.

'All my life I've been judged on my achievements,' Theo continued. 'My results at school and university. My contribution. I've been expected to excel and been criticised if I fall short. I've never been praised for the person I am, only for what I've done. I don't want to be seen as the boss's son. I want people to see me. Theo. Can you understand that?'

Molly was nodding her head. 'I can. I wanted my father to see me and so I created a personality for myself—a persona—to try to make me stand out from the crowd. It became a protective mechanism. I became the person I wanted people to see. Now I'm just trying to be me. The best me I can be. So, yes, I know what it's like to feel invisible, to be judged or misjudged.'

Theo's phone buzzed with a text message.

'It's from Matt,' he said as he read it. 'Inviting me for a barbecue dinner tonight.' He sounded surprised.

'That's nice,' Molly said. It was, but she wasn't sure how she felt about it.

'You don't sound convinced. What's the catch?'

It was one thing agreeing to have a summer romance or to being friends with benefits, it was another thing spending time together in public. Did she want everyone to know what they were doing?

She knew she didn't. Just as she believed Theo's business was his, hers was hers. 'There's no catch,' she said. 'Matt and Levi host a regular Sunday night barbecue. Gemma and I usually go.'

'Are you going tonight?'

She nodded.

'Shall we go together?'

Theo didn't seem to have the same concerns as her. He seemed quite comfortable with the fact that they were sleeping together but that didn't make them a couple. They'd agreed to being friends with benefits. Did that mean that everyone else had to know what they were doing or could they keep it between themselves? How did she want to play this relationship in public? Because, no matter what they called it, and even if it was only going to be short-lived, it was a relationship of sorts. She had never had a one-night stand and anything more than that had to have some level of connection, didn't it?

What had she agreed to exactly?

'I need to go home and change. Can I meet you there?' she stalled to avoid answering his question directly. 'Their place is halfway between here and home.' She wanted to keep their dalliance between them. She didn't want to share it, she didn't want to talk about it, she didn't want to discuss it and she didn't want to hear everyone's opinions on the subject. She didn't want the others to know.

Theo nodded. He either didn't notice her hesitation or he chose to ignore it.

The night had started off well. Theo had noted that Molly had avoided arriving with him but that hadn't bothered him. This 'thing' between them was new and they hadn't discussed what, if anything, they were going to tell people. But when everyone was discussing their weekends and Molly completely wiped him from her recount, with the exception of their shift at the Schoolies Festival, he couldn't help but feel slighted. He didn't expect her to share every intimate detail with her friends, but did it matter if they knew Molly and he had gone out for lunch? Why was she pretending the day hadn't happened? Was he not good enough for her? Was he something, someone, she wanted to keep secret?

And could he be upset with her if she *was* keeping secrets?

He was keeping secrets too. He couldn't in complete honesty say that his presence in Byron Bay had nothing to do with being a Chin Williams. His mother had requested he go to Byron Bay on her behalf. He'd told a half-truth. He certainly hadn't told Molly the whole story.

He took his guitar out onto the deck when he got home and wasn't surprised to hear that the first few chords he played had a melancholy note.

Would he ever be good enough?

Would he ever be good enough for Molly?

The sad notes kept coming, his fingers seeming to find them of their own accord.

Was he prepared to be a closely guarded secret?

Was Molly worth the angst?

He was only in Byron for another month. Should he walk away now? Save himself from inevitable heartbreak?

No. He'd walked away before and regretted it, he thought as the chords he played became stronger, more determined. Failure no longer had the same hold over him. He was willing to take a chance. Molly was worth a shot. He was still fascinated by her, intrigued by her, attracted to her, and he wouldn't walk away again.

'Theo?' The intercom on his clinic phone buzzed and he heard Paula's voice. 'Do you have time to see a walk-in patient? I have an eighteen-year-old male here who's complaining of abdominal pain.'

'Sure. I'll come and get him.' Theo was pleased to fill up his diary. Too much time on his hands meant too much time to sit and think about Molly. He was still trying to figure out what had been going through her mind last night, and getting nowhere, so more work was a welcome distraction. He didn't even mind that this was exactly the sort of patient who should be presenting to the hospital ED or even the Schoolies Festival first-aid tent which was open for its last day rather than the medical clinic. As long as he was prepared to pay for a consult.

That thought reminded him again of Molly—their first shared patient, Warwick with the cardiac arrest. He hadn't been charged for his consult, but Theo needed to remember that not everything was about money. He'd become a doctor because he wanted to help people. He had worked overseas after finishing uni, in Third World countries—he definitely wasn't about the money—but he knew his mother wouldn't be happy about giving their expertise away for free. Not if patients could afford to pay for their services.

'Will?' He called for his patient.

A teenage boy stood up slowly from a chair in the corner of the waiting room, slightly unsteady on his feet. He had his right arm held across his stomach and as he stood he reached out with his left hand to stabilise himself on the wall.

'Are you okay?' Theo asked, even though it was obvious the answer was no.

'Just a bit dizzy.'

He was tall and lanky, his face pale. He was flanked by a couple of friends, one of whom put an arm around his waist and lent him support. Theo looked at the group. 'You're here for the Schoolies Festival?' They looked about the right age and all looked a little worse for wear, as if they'd had a late night and hadn't had enough coffee or fried food yet to cure their hangovers.

Will looked worse than the rest. Unable to stand up straight, his face pale and drawn, he was obviously in pain. It looked as if he was suffering from more than a simple hangover.

Theo let Will's mates help him into the examination room but ushered them out once Will was lying on the treatment bed. He seemed coherent and was able to understand Theo's conversation. He'd call the other boys back if he needed them.

'What seems to be the trouble, Will?' he asked after introducing himself.

'I've got some discomfort in my stomach, just here.' He was holding his hand over the left side of his abdomen, just below his ribs.

'Sharp or stabbing pain like a knife or tenderness like a bruise?' Theo asked.

'Like a bruise. But there's no bruise I can see.'

'You're dizzy as well?' Theo checked, recalling his comment from the waiting room.

Will nodded and then closed his eyes, the movement of his head obviously unsettling him. 'That could have something to do with my hangover.'

'When did you last have an alcoholic drink?'

'Last night probably about ten o'clock.' That

was twelve hours ago. 'I wasn't feeling too good then. We'd been drinking since lunch and I started feeling a bit off.'

Theo wasn't surprised. But he needed a better explanation as to Will's symptoms. 'Off?'

'Dizzy. I thought I'd had too much to drink.'

'And when did you first notice the tenderness?'

'This morning.'

Theo clipped an oximeter to Will's finger and then took his blood pressure.

'I was wondering if I could have alcohol poisoning?' Will asked. 'Would that give me stomach pain?'

Theo assumed Will had consulted Dr Google and wondered if he should advise him against it. 'That would be likely to make you nauseous but unlikely to present as tenderness in a specific area unless you'd strained a stomach muscle through vomiting. Have you vomited? Had any difficulty breathing? Lost consciousness in the past twelve hours?'

'No.' Will shook his head.

His blood pressure was lower than normal and his heart rate was rapid.

'I need to have a look at your skin. Can you lift your T-shirt up for me?'

Will pulled his T-shirt up, exposing his abdomen. His skin was unblemished. It was lightly tanned but not enough to camouflage any bruising.

'I'm just going to feel your abdominal organs.'

Theo started on the right, gently palpating Will's liver before moving across to the left side. His appendix didn't appear to be giving him any discomfort and Theo reached across Will and lifted the left ribcage slightly with his left hand before pressing his right hand in and up under the ribs. 'Can you breathe in for me?'

The spleen moved down, allowing him to feel the inferior margin. That was a little concerning. The spleen wasn't normally palpable except in very thin adults. If they breathed in the spleen could pop out from under the ribcage.

There were a few red flags, the elevated heart rate, low blood pressure and abdominal tenderness, but they could just as easily indicate side effects of a few days of hard partying as Will celebrated the end of his schooldays.

'Have you had a knock or blow to your stomach in the past couple of days?'

'We were playing beer-can jousting yesterday and we got knocked over and one of the girls fell and landed on me. Her knee went into my stomach. I didn't think anything of it until this morning. I looked for a bruise but I couldn't see anything.'

Theo had a sense that something else was at play.

'I'm just going to lie the bed flat,' he said as he stepped on the control pad to lower the back of the bed and prepared to do an additional test. 'I want you to lift both your legs into the air and tell me if you feel any discomfort with that movement.'

Will did as he was instructed and Theo saw him wince as he lifted his legs. Will grabbed at his left shoulder, reinforcing Theo's interim diagnosis.

'I think you might have damaged your spleen,' he told him. While Will's symptoms matched any number of things, that last test was quite specific and, combined with the other results, Theo was fairly certain he was looking at signs of a damaged spleen.

'I'd like to send you to the hospital for some tests.'

'What sort of tests?'

'A CT scan to check for damage to your spleen caused by blunt force trauma, for example, someone landing forcefully with their knee on your spleen, and an ultrasound to check for blood in the abdominal cavity. I just need to get an assessment organised.'

Theo wanted to send Will for a specialist opinion, but he had no idea whether it was something that the hospital could provide or if he needed to send his patient to a larger town with better access to specialist clinics. Gemma wasn't at work yet. He would need to ask Molly for advice.

'I have a teenage boy, a Schoolies participant, who has presented with abdominal tenderness and dizziness,' he told her when he found her in the staffroom. 'I'm concerned that he's damaged his spleen.'

'Are you sure? There are several things that present with similar symptoms.'

'I know, but there's one fairly specific test, which was positive,' he said before explaining the test.

Molly frowned. 'I've never heard of that test. How did you know about it?'

'When I was working in Cambodia and Indonesia there were lots of scooter accidents. It was fairly common to patients presenting with abdominal pain after getting handlebars in the abdomen. I was shown that test over there. We probably saw more than the average number of damaged spleens over there, caused by the blunt trauma of a handlebar into the spleen, and that test was pretty reliable. Unfortunately, there wasn't the same access we have here to scans, diagnostic tests or even blood tests. If we suspected spleen damage it was a case of monitoring and hoping that it was minor enough that it would resolve. Non-surgical intervention was our usual treatment option. Often our only treatment option. But what I wanted to know was whether I can send Will to hospital here for further tests. Can we make that referral?'

Molly nodded. 'There are general surgeons at the hospital. Make a phone call and advise that you're sending a patient for scans and review. Is he here with friends?'

'Yes.'

'If he's not critical then he can call an Uber and go with friends.'

'Okay. Thank you. Have you got another minute?' he asked, waylaying her as she was about to leave.

She waited.

'Is everything okay between us?'

'What do you mean?'

'Last night. I thought we'd have a good time together. I thought we'd agreed to a summer fling but then you brushed me off and brushed over our weekend. As if you were embarrassed.

If you're having second thoughts, please just tell me. I'd rather you were honest with me.'

Molly shook her head. 'I'm not having second thoughts, I did have a good time, but the whole thing was a bit unexpected. I didn't know how to behave and it made me self-conscious. I didn't say anything because I didn't want people to think we were in a relationship. I don't want to be in a relationship.'

'We agreed to keep it casual,' Theo said. 'Don't worry about what other people think. All that matters is how we feel. If you're not having a good time, we call it quits, okay?'

Molly nodded.

'And don't feel you have to include me in everything you do,' he continued. 'We're not dating, we're just having fun. Let's just relax and enjoy the next few weeks and make some memories. If you need space, just tell me. Promise you will talk to me, that you'll tell me if there's a problem.'

'Okay.'

CHAPTER EIGHT

MOLLY'S ALARM BUZZED, rousing her from her sleep. She reached for her phone to hit snooze, disturbing Theo in the process.

He rolled over and pulled her into him, holding her close.

He kissed her shoulder. His lips were warm and soft. He trailed his hand from her hip down her thigh and up again, sliding his hand between her legs. Molly shifted her weight and opened her legs. She seemed to be constantly aroused when she was with Theo. A glance, a smile and especially a touch of his hand, even the lightest of touches, all had the power to trigger her libido. And there was no denying how compatible they were in bed. But outside the bedroom they had been getting on just as well. Molly enjoyed Theo's company. She used to feel he was judging the old Molly—although it turned out she was her harshest critic—but she got no sense of judgement any more. He was happy in her company, as she was in his.

And she had decided that there was no point pretending otherwise. They were seeing each other casually and she'd admitted as much to her friends. She and Theo had no expectations of each other of anything bigger, anything permanent, so there really was no need to hide their summer romance from anyone. She'd been slightly surprised to find her friends were all unanimously positive in their support of the romance, but Molly had stressed that it wasn't going to be anything serious—their affair would be over almost before it began. A line would be drawn through it when Theo returned to Sydney.

She wasn't thinking about how she would feel then—she still didn't like to examine her feelings too closely. She was still telling herself it was a summer fling, although she was worried she was in deeper than she'd planned to be.

Theo's fingers were working their magic and Molly forgot about the alarm she'd set until the snooze button went off. Reluctantly she covered Theo's hand with hers and stilled his movements.

'What's the matter?' he asked.

She rolled over and apologised with a kiss.

'Nothing. But if we want to see the sunrise we need to get up.'

'It's still dark,' Theo complained. 'I'd rather stay in bed with you. There will be another sunrise tomorrow.'

'It's forecast to rain tomorrow,' Molly said. 'You can't come to Byron and not see the sunrise from the lighthouse at least once. We can come back to bed after our walk.'

'Is that a promise?'

She nodded and kissed him again before throwing off the covers and pulling him out of bed. They did need to get going if they were going to make it up the track before sunrise.

Molly and Theo leant on the white wooden fence at the top of the hill. The lookout was almost deserted save for a couple of other early risers. The lighthouse stood tall behind them. It was a gorgeous building, but Molly and Theo were focused on the horizon to the east. The sky was getting lighter, a pale azure blue tinged with pink and orange as the golden orb of the sun began to glow on the edge of the ocean.

Theo moved to stand behind Molly and wrapped his arms around her waist, resting his chin on the top of her head and inhaling the orange perfume of her hair. They stood in silence, mesmerised by the colours of nature, waiting to be among the first people to see the sun rise in Australia on this day.

Seagulls and cormorants wheeled in the sky above their heads and the tang of the sea carried to them on the warm breeze. Theo breathed deeply, taking time to feel the moment, committing it to memory. He knew this experience would stay with him always, long after he'd returned to his life in Sydney.

'This is incredible,' he told Molly. 'Thank you for bringing me here.' He had been brought up to be busy, to be achieving, and found he was always thinking about something. He was comfortable here in Byron Bay. With Molly in his arms. He felt at home. He knew he had a job to do but he still had time and space to breathe. It was a rare state for him. 'It's not often I feel completely at peace,' he added.

'What are the things that bring you peace?' Molly asked.

He could count those things on one hand. 'Playing the guitar—not performing, but playing on my own with no one to hear. It's cathartic and freeing. Watching the sunrise at the Temple of Borobudur in Indonesia—that was a very similar experience to today.' And being with Molly.

But he didn't include that last one, knowing it would be very likely to frighten her. They weren't at a point where they had serious conversations. He knew they might never be. That she might never want that.

The sun was well and truly above the horizon now. The rich pinks and oranges had faded, leaving just a cloudless blue sky and a new day.

'But every day is a new beginning. A chance to start again. What are your plans for your new future? Where do you see yourself in five years?' He tried to gently gauge her thoughts.

'Five years!' Molly exclaimed. 'I haven't really thought about it. Have you?'

'I might be running the clinics by then.'

'Is that what you want?'

'It's what's expected,' he replied. 'I've imagined other options plenty of times, but I've never seriously considered doing anything else. Maybe I should just stay here,' he said, and he was only half joking.

The sun was on Molly's face. She was glowing. Her hair was like spun gold and her eyes were the colour of the sky. She looked like an angel and he knew there was nowhere else he'd rather be.

He studied her closely, committing the vision

to memory, knowing he would take that image with him when he left.

Molly couldn't believe another week had passed. The year was rapidly drawing to a close, Christmas was three weeks away and Theo was over halfway through his stint in Byron Bay. She had to admit that she was enjoying spending time with him. She'd relaxed, realised her friends were happy for her and no one was judging her. She was free to do as she pleased. Theo gave her the space she needed and was happy to see her on her terms. It had been a fun few weeks.

The weekends had passed by in a blur of sun, the sea, sand and sex—not always in that order—and the weekdays had been filled with work and the myriad social activities that were part of the fabric of daily life in Byron. The days were busy and so were the nights.

It was Friday again and Molly and Theo were the last ones at the office. Theo's consulting room door was open when Molly went to see if he was ready to leave. It was Gemma's birthday and they were meeting friends at the Railway Hotel for an open mic night. Theo was on the phone but motioned for Molly to come in.

'I've got a few ideas. I'll talk to you again once I've got more information,' Theo said as he ended the call, but not before Molly worked out he was on the phone to his mother and they were talking about the clinic.

'Is everything okay?' she asked.

Theo nodded and switched off his computer before standing up. 'Mum just had a few questions about the clinic.'

Molly looked expectantly at Theo, waiting for him to expand.

He pushed his chair under the desk and Molly waited. 'The clinic's profits are down and she wants my opinion on a couple of things,' he said.

'What sort of things?'

'She's looked at the books but while that gives her the bottom line it doesn't indicate the reason why the figures have dropped. She wants to know what I can tell her.'

'She wants you to spy on us?'

'No.' Theo frowned. 'Why would you think that?'

'Because you were talking about getting information.'

'Why do you always think the worst of me?'

'What do you mean?'

'You accused me of keeping my relationship with the boss, my mother, a secret, when really it just wasn't relevant.'

'But it is relevant now, isn't it?' Molly argued.

'You wouldn't be reporting back to her about profits if you weren't her son.'

'This has nothing to do with the fact we're related and now you're accusing me of being a spy.'

'All those questions you were asking Matt about the hydrotherapy sessions—you were looking for information for your mother, weren't you?' Those questions that had seemed so random now made sense.

'Yes, but I'm not spying on *you* or any of the staff. I'm looking at the figures, at the way the clinic operates.'

'Does anyone else know what you're doing?'

He nodded. 'Tom was aware and Paula has been helping me with the data. I've been looking at where we can make money or save money, if there's a service we should be offering or one that isn't viable. It's not so much a staffing issue as a practice management one. I haven't been hiding this, Molly. Why don't you trust me?'

Molly thought about Theo's question. He was right, she was always questioning his behaviour, looking for reasons to push him away. 'You know trust is an issue for me. People I've cared about have let me down. A lot.'

'Have I let you down in any way?'

Molly shook her head. 'Not yet.'

'Why do you assume I'm going to?'

'Because men I care about seem to,' she admitted. 'My father. Daniel. People lie to me, people cheat and I've been gullible before, believing things I know I shouldn't, and not trusting my instincts.'

'I'm not keeping secrets from you,' he said. 'This is simply an admin issue, part and parcel of running the business. If there's anything that affects you, I'll tell you,' he added as he wrapped an arm around her shoulders and dropped a kiss on her forehead. Her hurt feelings gave way to guilt. She'd made this about her. She expected to be let down, but he hadn't done anything to her. She knew he was under no obligation to tell her about what he was doing. She wouldn't have expected Tom to tell her anything in the same situation. Theo didn't owe her an explanation just because they were sleeping together. They weren't in a serious relationship. That was her choice. She couldn't have her cake and eat it too.

'I'm sorry—again,' she apologised.

He dropped a kiss on her lips before releasing her from his embrace. 'It's okay, just remember we're on the same side,' he said as he went to the cupboard in the corner of his consulting room and retrieved his guitar.

* * *

Theo forced himself to join in Gemma's birthday festivities and leave Molly's comments for another time. But he couldn't deny her comments had upset him. Why did it always seem to be two steps forwards and one back, or maybe even one forwards and two backwards with her? She was so afraid of letting him close. He understood that she was fearful and he agreed, trust needed to be earned, but it hurt when he knew he'd done nothing to make her think she couldn't trust him. It made it difficult to prove that he was trustworthy when she was inclined to make assumptions. Inclined to tar him with the same brush as her father and Daniel.

It shouldn't matter. Their relationship wasn't serious. But he didn't want Molly to confuse him with other men in her life.

He took his guitar out of its case and began to tune it. Strumming the strings calmed him down and he was able to take some comfort in the fact that Molly had admitted she cared about him. But how much was what he wanted to know.

'Are you going to sing, Theo?' Gemma asked.

'I'm not sure,' he replied. He didn't know if he was in the right mood to sing in front of people tonight.

'These sessions are popular so you should put

your name down. You can always decline later,' Matt said. 'I reckon we'd all be keen to hear a new voice. The talent can be a bit hit and miss.'

Encouraged by their group, he signed up to sing, and when he returned to the table Gemma said, 'Molly told me you worked overseas. Can I pick your brains?'

'Sure. Did she tell you I worked with an aid organisation so we were clinic-based, not hospital-based? Is that what you're thinking of doing?'

Gemma nodded. 'I think I'd like that. Where did you go?'

'I spent two years in Cambodia and Indonesia.'

'You'd recommend it?'

Theo nodded. 'It was one of the most amazing experiences of my life.' He had loved the freedom of being away from the expectations of his parents. There were other expectations but they were manageable, he wasn't expected to be better than anyone else, he was only expected to be as good, and that had felt liberating. 'It was challenging a lot of the time, but knowing that we were actually making a difference was unbelievably rewarding. Everyone should be entitled to health care. It's a basic human right, not a privilege, and to be able to deliver that to people was incredible.'

'Why did you come back?'

'My parents expected me to go into their business.'

'What's that?'

'The clinic.'

'Pacific Coast?'

Theo nodded. 'Lian Chin is my mother,' he told them. 'My parents set up the clinic and my mother runs it.' He figured there was no point in keeping his relationship hidden. They'd find out eventually.

'That must make things hard for you at times,' Gemma said.

'It has its ups and downs,' he admitted.

He was aware of Molly watching him. She'd been quiet since they got to the pub and he wished he knew what she was thinking. Did she still think that he was hiding something from her? Or did she think, after his conversation with his mother, that he thought medicine was all about the money? That wasn't his mindset. After working overseas he knew that money was much less important than helping people. But that didn't mean it wasn't important at all.

He strummed a few chords on his guitar and, using the cover of his music to keep the others from overhearing, he said to Molly, 'Everything okay?' He wasn't going to sit there and second-guess what she was thinking.

She smiled and nodded. Her smile reached her eyes and Theo relaxed. Perhaps she wasn't upset with him at all, he thought as he was called up to the stage.

He debated whether or not to sing a love song to Molly before thinking better of it. He didn't want to embarrass Molly or himself. She might have said everything was okay, but that didn't mean she was ready to listen to him sing her a love song in public. A Christmas song was another option. Christmas was fast approaching and the streets and businesses had their decorations on display, but the audience possibly wasn't the right demographic for Christmas carols. An Aussie rock classic might be a better choice.

The crowd loved his rendition and demanded a second song as he wrapped it up. Molly was smiling and clapping along with the rest of the crowd. He'd do it for her.

'If you recognise this one, sing the chorus with me,' he invited as he launched into 'I Still Call Australia Home'.

This song had a slow beginning and as he kept his gaze on Molly and sang he reflected on how comfortable he felt in Byron Bay. He was reminded of the freedom he'd had when he'd worked overseas, where he was expected to do his job but no more or less than the other doctors working with him. Here was the same. Here he was just Theo. Not the boss's son, despite what Molly might think. Here he was just Theo, especially when he was with Molly. Then he forgot about anything else.

Molly was still smiling when he finished the next song and she welcomed him off stage with a kiss and, suddenly, all was right in his world again.

At midday on Monday Molly knocked on Theo's door and invited him to lunch in the staffroom.

'What's the occasion? Another birthday?' Theo asked.

Molly shook her head. 'No. I hope you don't mind but I asked everyone to spend some time thinking about what is working in the practice and what isn't. I thought they might have some suggestions or opinions that you haven't thought of and that you could add to your report.'

Molly was trying to make up for what she thought of as her unkindness, the accusations she'd made about Theo last Friday. He had tried to help her four years ago and she hadn't listened. He needed help now and it was her turn to listen. She wanted to help.

'You did? Why?'

Oh, God, had she got it wrong? He hadn't wanted her help at all.

'I thought it was my chance to help you. A way of saying sorry for all the times I've misjudged you.'

'Thank you.' Theo smiled and gave her a quick kiss on her cheek and Molly breathed a sigh of relief that he wasn't annoyed with her for interfering. 'Let's go.'

Paula, Matt and Gemma were already seated around the table, buzzing with ideas. Molly knew Theo had already got data from Paula, and a few suggestions regarding administrative issues, but she also knew Paula was keen to be involved further.

'Okay, let's start with what's working well.' Molly got the ball rolling.

'Our consulting lists are consistently around ninety per cent booked. For both the physios and GPs.'

'Do you think we have enough staff. Is there need for more?' Theo asked.

'We've got room for more but I don't think the demand is there. Summer is a bit busier but winter is steady also,' Paula replied.

'I think we could get more use out of the pool if we had more staff,' Matt added. 'An extra physio might let us maximise its potential in terms of rehab, but alternatively we might be able to rent it out for swimming lessons or aquarobics, as we talked about, Theo. It's an expensive asset so it would be good to get more income from it.'

'Paula, you said we have room for more staff. If we don't need more GPs or treating physio-therapists, what are some options for the vacant consulting rooms? And why are they vacant?' Theo wanted to know.

'The consulting rooms that are available to be booked by visiting specialists aren't being used as often because the new hospital is finished and they're going there instead,' Paula said.

'Who else would be willing to take on a permanent lease of some of this space?' Theo looked up from his note-taking to look around the group assembled at the table.

'I think allied health staff could be a good value add to the clinic. A podiatrist, a dietician, a psychologist. Someone like that might be in-terested in renting space on a permanent basis. Even a dentist is an option,' Molly said.

'Or we could open up those offices and make better use of the space,' Matt suggested.

'As what?'

'We could combine spaces to make a Pilates

or yoga studio. I don't think that would be hard to do. The building has been added onto over the years and doesn't present as a new modern space and doesn't work as well as it could,' he answered.

Theo was taking notes. 'All good points, thank you. There's one final issue that I think is worth raising,' he said. 'Are we billing efficiently and adequately?' He directed his attention to Paula before turning his gaze to the others around the table. 'Paula has given me access to the books and I realise this query is only a small component, but every little bit saved or earned may make a difference.'

'What do you mean?' Paula asked.

'On my first day here, Molly and I treated a walk-in patient, the gentleman who went into cardiac arrest.' Theo waited for Paula's confirmation nod before continuing. 'The reception staff told me afterwards that he was only charged the government fee for that service. Not a regular consulting fee. Why was that?'

'It's what we've always done for emergency consults,' Paula explained.

'But we're not an emergency department.'

'They wouldn't have been charged if they'd turned up at the public hospital emergency department.'

'But we're not a public hospital either,' Theo replied. 'And private hospital emergency clinics charge hundreds of dollars to treat patients. We should too. We're not a public service. We should be charging full fees.'

'Emergency presentations can be quite stressful and it seems mercenary in those times to be talking about money,' Paula responded.

'I get that, believe me,' Theo replied. 'But if people are frequently using the clinic as their emergency department instead of going to the hospital, then if they have the means to pay for our service, they should be charged.'

'What about your comment last Friday? You said everyone should have access to health care as a basic right.' Molly felt she had to ask the question.

Theo nodded. 'That is my opinion and in Australia the government provides free or subsidised health care to people who need it. But Pacific Coast Clinics is a business—it needs to make a profit. We are not funded by the government and we should expect people to pay if they are able to and be prepared to have a conversation about finances if the need arises. If the reception staff don't feel comfortable doing that, is that something you could take on, Paula?'

Paula nodded as Theo wrapped up the meeting. 'Thank you, everyone, and thank you, Molly, for instigating the meeting. I should have asked you all for your opinions earlier but I'm used to operating on my own, but I appreciate your input.'

Molly tugged on her dress as she stepped out of the car. She'd bought a new outfit in celebration of the staff Christmas function, a sleeveless shirt dress that buttoned down the front, but it felt a little tighter today than she recalled it being when she'd purchased it. Perhaps she and Theo had been out for too many meals, she thought as she undid a couple of buttons at the bottom to give her room to bend her knees—the Christmas function was barefoot bowls and she needed to be able to squat to play. She'd just have to live with the button at her waist that was a bit snug.

'Who would like a glass of bubbly?' Matt greeted Molly, Theo and Gemma on arrival. He had an open bottle in one hand and several glasses in the other.

Molly took a glass and held it as Matt poured for her. She wasn't going back to Sydney for Christmas with her family this year, she had volunteered to work between Christmas and New Year so the other doctors could take holidays, so tonight was going to be one of her main celebrations, but as she brought the glass to her lips a wave of nausea washed over her. She felt light-headed. She wondered if it was something to do with her dress being a little tight at the waist or maybe she was just dehydrated. She was feeling a little hot.

She put the glass down on a nearby table and decided to start with a water. The water helped briefly. Until the finger food was passed around. Smoked salmon, chicken sandwiches, marinated prawns, all of it made her stomach turn.

Molly tried distracting herself by joining in an end of bowls, but all the bending made her dizzy. Eventually she gave up and went home, insisting that Theo stay and enjoy the evening, and just assuming she'd picked up a virus from somewhere.

She was lethargic and felt less than one hundred per cent for the next couple of days with bouts of light-headedness but no vomiting and no temperature. She'd lost her appetite, with the exception of Vegemite toast, and reluctantly took Monday off work.

By Monday afternoon, she was feeling better, provided she wasn't looking at food and didn't stand up too quickly.

'Did you have a terribly busy day because of me?' she asked Gemma when she got home, feeling guilty because she knew her patients had either had their appointments cancelled or had been moved to Gemma's or Theo's lists.

'No, it was all fine,' Gemma replied. 'Theo says hi.'

She had told Theo to stay away but he'd phoned and messaged her during the day. There was no point in passing a virus around to more people. And in her mind a summer romance didn't include nursing care.

'I brought you something,' Gemma said as she handed Molly a bag.

Molly peered inside and her eyes widened when she saw the contents. 'What's this for?' she asked as she withdrew a box containing a pregnancy test kit.

'Just a precaution. You have to admit your symptoms fit this cause.'

'Don't be ridiculous,' Molly argued as she quickly calculated the time since she and Theo had had unprotected sex.

'When was your last period?' Gemma asked.

Molly couldn't recall. She remembered the lack of contraception two and a half weeks ago. The morning-after pill. Gemma didn't know about any of that. But was her period late? Maybe a few days late, although she couldn't be sure.

'There's no harm in doing a test,' Gemma said, and Molly gave in, knowing Gemma was unlikely to let the matter drop.

She felt the nausea return as she went to the bathroom and did the test. She left the little stick on the toilet seat, washed her hands and went back to the kitchen to put the kettle on. She needed to distract herself.

'Are you going to check it or am I?' Gemma asked as they finished the tea Molly made.

Molly wasn't sure she was game but said, 'I'll do it.' After all, it was her issue.

She returned to the bathroom. The stick was where she'd left it, looking innocent enough, until she got closer.

Two pink lines greeted her.

Molly picked up the stick before sitting down on the toilet lid. She closed her eyes and concentrated on breathing.

She heard the bathroom door open and looked up to find Gemma standing in the doorway, her eyes fixed on the stick that was still in Molly's hand.

'It's positive?' she said.

Molly nodded before promptly bursting into tears. Gemma stepped forward and wrapped her in a hug.

'Should I do another test? It might be wrong,' Molly said, her voice full of hope.

'A false negative maybe,' Gemma replied, 'but a false positive is unlikely.'

Molly knew Gemma was right. 'What am I going to do?' she asked.

'Nothing right now,' was Gemma's reply. 'I'm going to make you a piece of toast and another cup of tea. You'll eat and drink and take a breath. Take a minute.'

'This is not part of my plan.' Did she have a plan? She didn't really. Her plan had been to spend some time focusing on herself.

I should never have got involved with Theo, she thought, but she wasn't sure she really meant it.

She'd enjoyed spending time with him. Sleeping with him. Until now.

'What do I tell Theo?' she asked Gemma. 'We agreed on a summer romance, a "friends with benefits" type scenario. I don't think a baby counts as a benefit,' Molly said.

'Some people might think it does,' Gemma suggested.

Molly shook her head. 'No. We didn't plan on this. I didn't plan on this.' She'd told Theo as much.

'No kidding.' Gemma wrapped her arm around

Molly and helped her to her feet. 'Come with me, I'll put the kettle on.'

Molly collapsed onto a stool at the kitchen bench. '*Do* I tell Theo?'

'Why wouldn't you?'

'Our relationship is hardly serious. And I don't want to be tied to a man because of a mistake. I don't want to be tied to a man at all. The next relationship I'm in will be by choice, not circumstance.'

'In that case you only have one option because you can't, in all honesty, keep the baby and not tell Theo.'

'There is another option,' she said. 'Theo might not want anything to do with me or the baby.'

'But that would still mean telling him and taking that chance. Do you honestly think he wouldn't choose you and the baby?'

Molly didn't know what to think but she did know she couldn't terminate a pregnancy. She was filled with despair as she realised that a brief lapse of concentration was going to change her life. She hadn't planned on having children, but she knew she would struggle with a termination.

And that was the second time Gemma had used the word honest. Molly knew she was right. She had to be honest. She had to tell Theo.

It was only seventeen days ago that she'd told Theo she didn't want children. Could she do this? Could she raise a child? Could she do it alone?

Molly's hands were sweaty. She thought she might throw up but she knew tonight's nausea wasn't related to her pregnancy hormones, but to nerves. More than nerves. It was triggered by fear. She was going to tell Theo her news, their news, and she was terrified.

He might want nothing to do with her or the baby or he might want to be involved. Both options had pros and cons. Both options were equally terrifying. One would mean she would lose her independence. She would have to accommodate Theo in her plans and she'd be permanently tied to him through their child. They would be permanently connected and she did *not* want to be tied to a man out of obligation.

The other option would mean she would lose Theo. She was prepared to be a single mother but was that fair on a child?

Now that she was between a rock and a hard place she found that things were not so black and white. It was a lot more complicated in real life. Theory and practice were two very different things and she really had no idea how she wanted this to play out.

She'd have to put the ball in Theo's court and go from there.

She checked the time. She had ten minutes before Theo would arrive. She'd invited him for dinner. She had managed to avoid him at work—she knew she wouldn't be able to pretend everything was fine and the issue was not one she could discuss at work. Dinner was the best, the only, option and thankfully Gemma had agreed to make herself scarce for the evening and leave the apartment free for Molly and Theo.

Molly found a playlist on her phone and connected it to the speakers, using the music to settle her nerves. She lit the mosquito coils and placed one under the table and the other near the herb pots in the corner of the balcony. She finished setting the table and filled a jug with cold water. Bustling around kept her hands busy and her mind occupied.

Before leaving the house, Gemma had made a chicken salad for Molly to serve for dinner. Molly couldn't face the thought of cooking and the idea of handling raw meat brought on another bout of nausea. If it wasn't for Gemma's help Molly would be serving toast with Vegemite—

that was about all she could manage to prepare at present.

She switched on the fairy lights that were strung around the balcony and then turned on the Christmas tree lights. Gemma had decorated the house for Christmas, which was now only two weeks away.

Molly would have the apartment to herself over Christmas. Gemma was going to Brisbane but, as Molly had volunteered to work between Christmas and New Year, Matt and Levi had invited her to have Christmas dinner with them, and she was happy to have a reason not to go to Sydney. She would miss her sisters but she wasn't ready to leave Byron Bay yet. She had found some inner peace since moving here— although her peace had been shattered a little with the events of the past week—but that was another good reason to stay away from Sydney. She needed some time to work out how to announce the situation to her family. To work out how to tell them they would be grandparents and aunts.

She wasn't sure how that news would be received. She thought her sisters would be excited, she hoped her mother would be too, but there was no way of knowing. Her mother had learnt to guard her emotions a long time ago.

Molly wondered what Theo did for Christmas. He would be back in Sydney by then.

She wondered what his family would think of her news. Would he tell them?

Her musings were cut short by a knock on the door. Her heart skipped a beat when she opened it. Even though she knew it would be Theo the sight of him still took her breath away. He looked good.

He was wearing a pair of pale cotton shorts and a black T-shirt. His face was tanned and he looked healthy and strong and gorgeous. Molly knew he'd enjoyed his time in Byron and she was about to make sure it was time he'd never forget. One way or the other.

He kissed her and she closed her eyes and let herself imagine, just for a moment, a future where she could trust him not to break her heart. A future where they could be happy.

But any future they would have was now going to be complicated by her pregnancy. Things were never going to be the same. Never going to be simple.

As Theo released her she was overcome by a wave of light-headedness. 'There's beer in the fridge or water on the table. Help yourself to a drink. I'll be back in a minute,' she said as she fled to the bathroom.

She splashed her face with cold water and took two deep breaths before drying her face. She applied concealer to cover up the dark circles under her eyes and then rejoined Theo for a dinner that she couldn't face eating.

Gemma's chicken salad was delicious but Molly's appetite was non-existent. She picked at her dinner, moving food around her plate, while she tried to make conversation.

'Are you sure you're feeling better?' Theo asked. 'You're very quiet and you've barely touched your meal.'

'There's something I need to tell you,' Molly said as she put her knife and fork together on her plate and pushed it aside. She could feel her dinner pressing against her oesophagus, threatening to make a reappearance. Theo was watching her closely, waiting. She almost felt sorry for him, he had no idea what was coming, but this was as much his fault as hers. He needed to hear what she had to say. 'I didn't have a virus. I assumed that I'd caught something but it turns out that wasn't the case.' She glanced away as she summoned up her courage before returning her gaze to Theo. 'I'm pregnant.'

Theo was silent. Molly waited, willing him to speak but at the same time dreading what he might say.

'Pregnant? Not sick?'

Molly shook her head. 'Obviously I'm one of those statistics you read about in the pamphlet that comes with the morning-after pill.' She must have ovulated before they had sex. 'Our timing wasn't great.'

'Pregnant. Wow.' A smile slowly spread across his face.

Molly frowned. 'You're not upset?'

'Upset? No. This is amazing,' he said as he stood and moved around the table, taking her hands in his and pulling her to her feet. 'We're having a baby.'

He wrapped her in a hug and kissed her and for a minute, Molly forgot that she was planning on doing this alone. This was not the reaction she'd anticipated and it felt good to share this moment with Theo. But that wasn't going to be her reality.

'How is this good news?' she asked.

'I've always wanted to be a father and I think, I hope, I'll be a good one. I've had plenty of lessons in how not to raise a family,' he said, but he must have heard something in her voice because he stepped back, releasing her, and looked into her eyes. 'You're not happy about this? I know you said you didn't want children...'

She heard the note of hope in his voice and

knew he was counting on her changing her mind. 'I'm keeping it,' she told him, giving him the news she knew he wanted, 'but we didn't plan on having a baby. We barely know each other.'

'There are worse things that have happened. We're not the first ones to find ourselves in this situation. We can make it work.'

'Make what work?'

'Us.'

Molly shook her head and sat down. She needed a bit of space, physically and mentally. 'There is no us, Theo. We had no plans past the next two weeks.'

'We'll make plans.'

He made it sound so simple. But Molly knew it was far from that. Unexpected tears welled in her eyes and she blinked quickly, trying to stop them from spilling over. 'Neither of us signed up for parenthood.'

'That doesn't mean we can't do this.'

'Theo, we agreed to a summer romance. We didn't agree to raising a baby.'

'What do you suggest we do, then?'

This was moving faster than Molly had anticipated. She'd barely accepted the fact she was pregnant and she hadn't expected to start making plans tonight. 'I don't know. I'm still trying to work out how this happened.' She felt sick.

'Shall I tell you what I'm thinking?'

Molly nodded. There could be no harm in hearing Theo's thoughts. Unless he wanted to take the baby and raise it on his own. Despite not having motherhood in her future plans a week ago, Molly knew now she couldn't give her child up.

'What if you came back to Sydney with me? What if we got married?'

CHAPTER NINE

'WHAT?'

He wanted to get married?

Molly shook her head.

That was a ridiculous idea.

Unexpected and ridiculous.

'I have no plans to move to Sydney and I don't want to get married.'

'Why not?' he asked.

'We agreed to a summer romance. We hadn't talked about anything after that and suddenly you're talking about spending the rest of our lives together.' Molly paused to take a breath, she could hear a slightly panicked note creeping into her voice and she needed to calm down. 'That makes no sense. I don't want to be trapped in a marriage because of a baby. And I don't think you do either.'

'Would you prefer I went back to Sydney and left you to it?' he asked. 'That's not going to happen. I barely saw my mother and father growing up. You know I was basically raised by my grandparents. I want to be present for my child. I want to be involved.'

'I'm not saying you can't be involved.'

'Maybe not, but you are saying you're happy to have a summer romance but you don't want a relationship. You'll have my baby, but you don't want to marry me.'

'I don't want to marry anyone.'

'But I'm not just anyone,' he argued. 'I'm the father of your child. I don't want to be cut out of my child's life. If we're married that can't happen.'

'I'm not trying to cut you out.'

'But you want to make all the decisions.'

'Not all,' Molly replied, 'but I do want to be able to make some. Starting with whether or not to get married. I don't want to be told what to do, how to think, where to live.'

'I wasn't,' Theo objected.

'You just did! Literally three minutes after I told you the news you said, let's move to Sydney. Let's get married. As if I don't get a say.'

'Of course, you get a say, but would it be so awful to do this together?'

No, it wouldn't. In her heart she could see the future. But she couldn't risk it. The future wouldn't turn out as she hoped—she'd learnt that much. Happily ever after only existed in fairy tales.

Molly wiped away a tear. Theo had proposed out of honour. He hadn't proposed because he was in love with her. He hadn't proposed of his own accord. He'd proposed because of the circumstances, because he thought it was the *right* thing to do, and she couldn't accept. She would *not* end up like her mother—trapped in a marriage with a man who didn't love her.

'I don't want to lose my independence. My mother was hamstrung by her circumstances. She had no career and no money. I've worked hard to make sure I have financial independence. What I didn't always have was emotional independence. I was too busy seeking validation. Now I have both and I'm not prepared to give them up.'

'Commitment and dependence are not the same thing.'

Molly shook her head. Theo was wrong. 'I spent years being Daniel's girlfriend, Daniel's on-again-off-again girlfriend. The girl Daniel cheated on. Now I'm going to be someone's mother. I don't want to be someone's wife. I want to be me. Molly.'

'You will always be Molly. I'm not trying to change you. I'm trying to support you.'

But Molly was worried that support might end up feeling like control. She needed to breathe. She needed some space. 'We're not going to sort this out tonight.'

'I agree,' Theo said. 'We should sleep on it and talk tomorrow. But,' he said as he kissed her goodnight, 'I want you to remember this is good news and we will work it out.'

Molly collapsed on her bed after Theo left. She knew she should clean up but she was exhausted. Emotionally and physically.

Theo wanted to marry her.

For a brief mad moment she'd been tempted to say yes.

But he didn't love her. He just wanted to make sure he saw his child.

It was ludicrous to think that their story could end in marriage. In happily ever after.

She was having a baby; she was going to be a mother. She was going to co-parent with Theo. That was enough commitment for now.

Marriage was unnecessary.

And marriage without love was ridiculous.

'So, you'll let me know the date of your first ultrasound scan?' Theo confirmed as he signalled for their dinner bill. Just the thought of that first scan, of seeing his baby's heart beating on a screen for the first time, filled Theo with joy, a sense of anticipation and happiness more intense than anything he could have imagined.

'You'll come up from Sydney for it?' Molly asked and Theo nodded. 'How will you manage that?'

'I'll make it work. I'll take annual leave days. As long as you give me enough notice I can block out my diary.'

He was due to return to Sydney on Tuesday, in three days' time. His six-week stint was coming to an end and he still hadn't convinced Molly to move with him, but he had no intention of missing those milestones. He needed to show Molly he was serious about being involved and that started with the antenatal appointments. He hadn't figured out yet how he'd manage to attend antenatal classes—he assumed Molly would be going—but there was time for that. He knew there was a fine line to tread between being interested, being involved and Molly thinking he was trying to control her pregnancy. Her life.

He was so grateful that Molly had chosen to keep the baby and he was going to do everything in his power to support her, as well as make sure he was involved in the pregnancy and beyond. The huge responsibility of raising a child wasn't lost on him but it was a duty he would embrace.

He would prefer to do it side by side with Molly, as partners, not co-parents, but that outcome was still a work in progress. Molly had taken it off the table but Theo wasn't giving up yet.

He'd invited Molly to dinner and they'd spent the night talking about logistics, which was important and necessary, but Theo knew there was also plenty being left unsaid. There was no discussion about how they felt. The conversation had been practical, not emotional.

Perhaps he should have cooked for her at home. In the privacy of his house maybe they would have been more honest with each other, more forthcoming about their feelings, their hopes and dreams. Perhaps he'd suggest that for tomorrow night.

He knew he was running out of time. He knew that once he moved to Sydney it would be harder to convince Molly that they should be together. He was worried it would be out of sight, out of mind. That was another reason he was determined to travel to Byron Bay for appointments. He wanted to remain in Molly's life.

Four days after hearing Molly's news he was still overcome with emotion, excitement and nervousness. It was exhilarating but terrifying all at the same time. He was determined to be a good father, a loving father, a hands-on father—all the things he'd missed out on— but working out how to make this happen was going to be a challenge.

He'd briefly considered staying in Byron Bay but he knew that ultimately he couldn't run the family business from there and that was what was expected of him, what he expected of himself. There were three clinics in Sydney—that was where he needed to be. It was frustrating but he'd figure out a solution eventually. He was not going to be an absent father. He could see a future with Molly. He just had to figure out how to convince her.

Trust was the key.

He needed time to show her that she could depend on him.

He hadn't suggested marriage again. He knew he'd got that wrong. She'd said she wouldn't marry him. He should take comfort from the fact she'd said she wouldn't marry anyone. But he wasn't just anyone. He was the father of her child.

'So, we agree, open lines of communication are important,' he said as he paid the bill. 'We will make this work. We both want to do what's best for our child. I'm sure all parents think they'll do things differently but I really want to get this right.'

'I do—' Molly's reply was interrupted by the

sound of screeching tyres as a car rounded the corner outside the restaurant at speed. The noise level in the restaurant dropped as conversation among all the diners ceased when they heard a deafening crash and the unmistakeable sound of metal crunching and glass shattering.

There was a brief moment of absolute silence before a car horn blared and continued incessantly. Overlaying that came the sound of a second crash, duller than the first, followed by screaming.

Theo and Molly ran out to the street. A cloud of dust billowed in the air, choking the intersection.

Theo sprinted down the road, heading towards the screams and the dust, and Molly dashed after him. She rounded the corner and came to a stop, giving her brain a moment to process what she was seeing.

A car had careened up onto the footpath and was jammed between two concrete planter boxes, its nose against the wall of an old two-storey building that operated as a wine bar.

Molly knew the wine bar had an outdoor dining area on the street, under the veranda. The planter pots were supposed to act as a barrier, as protection for the outside tables, but somehow the car had flipped onto its side and slid in between the planter pots, taking out a veranda post in the process. The veranda had collapsed and she could see broken chairs and tables lying crushed under the weight of the veranda. She had to assume that, moments before, people had been sitting at those tables.

It was a confronting scene. Debris was strewn across the road as the dust began to settle and Molly's heart was in her throat at the thought of what carnage might be revealed. They needed to find out if there were people trapped under the building.

People were milling around—dazed and stunned—and Molly saw some crawling out from under the veranda. Bystanders helped them to their feet. Others had phones to their ears and Molly could hear them talking to emergency services. The police station wasn't far away and she expected they would be on the scene quickly.

She looked for Theo. They should start tending to the injured victims.

She found him clambering up onto one of the concrete planter pots to peer into the driver's car window. The window was cracked and he punched it, knocking it in, before reaching his hand inside.

Molly peered through the rear window of the

car. She could see the driver slumped over the wheel. He was covered in white powder from the airbag, bleeding from the head. Theo was feeling for a pulse. She couldn't see a passenger on the other side of the car. That didn't mean there wasn't one, but the car was jammed tight between the planter pots and the building. There was no way of opening a door. No way of getting to anyone inside.

Theo climbed down from the car. 'He's alive but unconscious,' he said as they heard sirens in the distance.

'Could you see anyone else in the car?' Molly asked.

Theo shook his head as a young man emerged from the rubble at their feet. Theo grabbed him under his armpits and helped him stand. He was covered in blood and dust.

'You have to help me. My girlfriend is in there,' he said, pointing back under the building. 'She's trapped under the car.'

Molly saw Theo's quick glance in the direction of the car. 'Is she conscious? Breathing?' he asked.

Molly knew he was really asking if the girl was alive.

'I don't know.' Tears spilt from the man's eyes,

making muddy streaks through the dirt on his face. 'Her leg is trapped; I can't get her out.'

'What's her name?' Theo asked as Molly put a hand on the man's arm, offering comfort through touch but feeling that was all too inadequate given the circumstances.

'Bree.'

Theo dropped to his knees and before Molly could ask what he was doing he had crawled under the car and into the rubble.

Molly's eyes widened. What on earth was he doing?

The veranda posts creaked and groaned and dropped another couple of inches.

What was he thinking? He was putting himself in danger. For what? What did he think he would be able to do? He couldn't move the car.

Her heart was in her throat as she sent up a silent plea in the hope someone or something was listening.

God, please let him be okay. Get him out before he gets hurt. Before anything else goes wrong.

She rested her right hand on her stomach, subconsciously shielding her baby from harm. She knew it was a reflex action, instinctive, protective. She knew her baby was okay, but her baby's father was a different matter.

Staring at the black hole into which Theo had disappeared, she knew she'd made a mistake. She'd been an idiot. So fixated on maintaining her independence, her control, that she was risking everything.

She wanted Theo in her life. She *needed* him in her life. Not just for their child's sake. But for hers.

Molly was quite prepared to be a single mother. She had no issue with raising a child on her own or making independent decisions but, confronted with the reality of the danger Theo had put himself in, she realised her plan had a few flaws. She was quite prepared to raise a child as a single mother, but she wasn't prepared for her child not to have a father at all.

Now that Theo was in danger, she realised she didn't want to think of a world without him.

She didn't want to live without him. He made her happy. He made her a better person and she liked who she was when she was with him. Why was she refusing to accept that? Why was she resisting taking a chance on a serious relationship?

She admitted it would be difficult if he was in Sydney. *She'd* made this difficult. Not impossible, but not as easy as it could have been.

What if he was right? What if she could have commitment and independence? What if she could have a relationship with him without losing her identity? Without losing control?

It had to be worth a try.

She made a promise to herself. If, when, he came back to her they would have a conversation. They would make a new plan. She would tell him how she felt.

And if she lost him?

She shook her head to clear her thoughts. She couldn't think about that now. She needed something else to think about. Something other than Theo and the danger he'd put himself in. She turned to the young man who still stood beside her. She would let him distract her from her worries about Theo.

He was pale, his eyes were wide and he was starting to shake. He was in shock.

Molly turned to one of the bystanders. 'We need a blanket,' she said. 'Can you see if any of the restaurants have something we could borrow?'

The street was full of bars and restaurants and most had outdoor seating. Molly knew they would have blankets to ward off the chill on the odd cool night.

She turned back to the young man. 'What's your name?' she asked.

'Josh.'

'Josh, my name is Molly. I'm a doctor. I think you should sit down.' She guided him away from the crash site, not far away, just away from the damaged veranda. She didn't want to put him at risk if there was a further collapse. She got him to sit on the edge of the footpath with his feet in the gutter and wrapped the blanket around his shoulders when someone brought it to her.

'Are you hurt?' she asked as she sat beside him. He didn't appear to have sustained any major injuries. She could see a few abrasions and he had blood on his hands, but she wasn't sure whose blood it was.

He shook his head. 'But Bree—' His voice cracked and he couldn't finish his sentence.

'My friend who's gone to Bree, he's a doctor as well,' Molly told him, hoping that gave him some reassurance. She had to raise her voice as the emergency vehicles turned into the street with their sirens blaring. As the police cars, fire engines and ambulances pulled to a stop the sirens were switched off, but their flashing red and blue lights lent an eerie air to the scene.

Molly stood up to introduce herself as a policewoman approached.

'Do you need assistance?' the policewoman asked.

'No. Josh's injuries are minor, and the driver

of the car was alive immediately after the accident, but my colleague—' Her voice caught as she thought about Theo. 'My colleague couldn't get to him so we don't know the extent of his injuries. We think he was alone in the car but we're not certain.'

'Where is your colleague?'

Molly pointed at the car. 'He's gone in there. There's a young woman, this man's girlfriend, trapped under the car. We don't know if there are any others.' She could see other people with bloodied heads, bloodied hands and torn and dirty clothes, but she didn't know if there were any others unaccounted for.

The policewoman nodded. 'Okay, thanks for the information.'

As she turned to leave, Molly stopped her. 'Can you take Josh to the paramedics? He's in shock and needs someone to keep an eye on him. I need to wait here.' Molly could have done it, but she wasn't leaving until she knew Theo was safe.

She paced up and down the edge of the road, her eyes glued to the crash site, willing Theo to reappear. Hadn't he heard the sirens? Didn't he know the cavalry had arrived? He could come out now, let the emergency services crew do their jobs.

Finally, he emerged.

'Theo, thank God.' Molly hurried to his side and threw her arms around him.

Over Theo's shoulder Molly saw a paramedic heading towards them. He'd obviously seen Theo emerge from the debris and assumed he was injured.

'I'm fine,' Theo said when the paramedic touched him on the arm. 'I wasn't caught up in the accident. I'm a doctor. There's a young woman trapped in the rubble and I went in to see if I could help her.'

'She's alive?'

Theo nodded. 'Barely.' He kept his voice low and Molly could see him looking around the crowd, searching for Josh.

'Her boyfriend is in one of the ambulances,' Molly told him.

Theo nodded again and gestured to a policeman and called him over. He didn't let go of Molly—was he supporting her or did he need reassurance as well? Molly tucked herself against his side, not willing to be separated from him.

'The car has pinned her against the wall of the building. She's trapped by her legs.' Theo addressed the paramedic. 'The car seems to have missed her abdomen and vital organs but I suspect she's losing blood from somewhere. Her pulse and respiration are elevated and she's drifting in and out of consciousness. It's going to be difficult and time-consuming to free her. She might not survive long enough to be freed and if she does then the process of releasing her could still prove fatal. Falling blood pressure is a major concern. I think we should have an air ambulance on standby. She's going to need to be transferred to a major hospital in Brisbane or Sydney.'

Theo turned to the policeman. 'And the veranda will have to be secured before we move the car.'

The policeman nodded. 'We've called in the engineers and the fire brigade will try to stabilise the structure while we wait. We need to clear the area now.'

'Come on, you need to get warmed up.' Theo was speaking to Molly now. She was still tucked against his side but she hadn't realised she was shaking. She hadn't realised she was cold.

Theo took her hand in his and led her away from the chaos and the trauma. There was nothing more they could do now. It was going to take some time to plan, prepare and complete the rescue and retrieval and emergency services were now in charge. 'Will you come back to my place?'

Molly nodded. She didn't want to be alone. She needed company. She needed to hold Theo, to feel that he was okay, unharmed and in one piece.

She held tight to Theo's hand. She thought it might be the only thing keeping her upright. Adrenalin continued to course through her system, making her legs shaky. Fear tainted her voice as she asked, 'What on earth did you think you were doing, going into that situation?'

Theo looked at her for a moment before he responded. 'There might have been something I could do. I had to try. All I could think of was what if that had been you trapped in there? Alone. Injured. What if I could make a difference? Imagine how terrifying it would be to be alone in a situation like that.'

Molly didn't have to imagine. She knew the level of fear. 'But it *was* you in there—I can imagine. What if you hadn't come out again?'

'But I did. I'm fine. Now we just have to hope that Bree will be too.'

'I need a shower,' Theo said as he unlocked his front door. He was still holding Molly's hand. He hadn't let go since they'd left the accident site, and she hadn't wanted him to. He stepped into the bathroom, taking her with him, and turned the taps on, running the shower.

Molly sat on the closed toilet lid as Theo fiddled with the taps, adjusting the temperature. She looked properly at him now and realised he was filthy. She hadn't noticed, she hadn't been paying attention to his clothes, she'd just been grateful that he was okay.

The bathroom was filling with steam, the fog reminiscent of the cloud of dust that had engulfed the crash site. Molly shivered as the memory tore back into her consciousness.

'I think you should have a shower too,' Theo said. 'It'll be the quickest way to warm you up.'

Molly could barely speak but she wasn't cold any more—she was numb. Frightened. Terrified. She still hadn't recovered from the idea that she could have lost him. She was well aware that he was leaving, which meant she was going to lose him in one form, but losing him to Sydney was better than losing him altogether.

Theo took her hand and helped her to her feet. As the mirror clouded with fog he began to gently remove her clothes. He unzipped her dress and Molly lifted her arms, letting him slide it over her head. The room was warm, thick with steam and moisture. He squatted down, running his hands down the length of her legs to undo the laces on her sneakers. She lifted one foot, then the other, as he slid her shoes from her feet.

His hands were on her hips now, warm against

her skin. A tingle of awareness and anticipation surged through her as Theo slipped his fingers under the elastic of her underwear and pushed it from her hips. He stood up and moved behind her to undo the clasp on her bra. He wrapped his arms around her and his hands cupped her breasts. Her breasts were full and heavy, already changed by her pregnancy. His fingers ran over her nipple and it peaked immediately under his touch. Her breasts were far more sensitive than normal too. Another side-effect of her raging hormones.

Molly's knees trembled and Theo held her up with one arm around her waist. He half lifted her and helped her into the shower.

Molly pressed a hand into the tiled wall to support herself and let the hot water run over her as she watched Theo get undressed. His clothes were filthy and one leg on his cotton chinos was torn. In contrast his chest, when he removed his shirt, was smooth and tanned and clean. He kicked off his shoes and stepped out of his ripped trousers and underwear in one movement.

When he was naked Molly reached her hand out to him and pulled him under the water with her.

He cupped his hand at the back of her neck, sliding his fingers through her hair, and pulled her to him. He bent his head and covered her lips with his. His lips were soft and Molly sighed and leant into him as she opened her mouth. She parted her lips and let his tongue explore her mouth.

Her hands skimmed over his naked buttocks. They were tight and firm and warm under her fingers. She pulled him towards her, pressing her stomach against his erection. She wanted him closer. Needed him closer.

Her breasts, plump and ripe, flattened against his chest. She arched her back and her breasts sprang free. Theo cradled one in the palm of his hand as he ran his thumb over her nipple. A throaty moan escaped from her lips as she tipped her head back and broke their kiss.

She reached down and wrapped her hand around his shaft. It throbbed under her touch, springing to life, infused with blood. She could feel every beat of his heart repeated under her fingers.

He ducked his head and took one breast in his mouth as Molly clung to him. His tongue flicked over her nipple, sending needles of desire shooting down to the junction between her thighs. It felt amazing but she wanted more. She was desperate for more.

She held onto his shoulders and arched her

back as she thrust her hips towards him. His fingers slid inside her, rubbing the sensitive bud that nestled between her thighs. Her knees were shaking. She was incapable of thinking. She was far too busy feeling. Her body was a quivering mass of nerve endings, her senses heightened, touch, taste and smell being flooded with information courtesy of Theo's lips and fingers.

'I don't think I can stand any longer,' she panted. She was barely able to find the breath to speak. 'You'll have to hold me.'

He scooped her up in one easy motion and she spread her legs, eager to welcome him. She felt the tip of his erection nudge between her legs as she wrapped her thighs around his waist. She heard him sigh as he plunged into her.

She enveloped him as he thrust into her warmth.

God, that felt good.

She moaned as he pushed deeper.

'I'm not hurting you?'

'No.' The word was a sigh, one syllable on a breath of air.

She closed her eyes as she rode him, bucking her hips against his, her back arched. She was completely oblivious to everything except the feel of him inside her as she offered herself to him. His face was buried into her neck and she tipped her head back as he thrust into her, bringing them to their peak.

'Oh, God, Molly, that feels incredible.'

Hearing her name on his lips was her undoing. Her name had never sounded so sweet and she had never felt so desired. She gave herself up to him and as he exploded into her she joined him, quivering in his arms as she climaxed.

He kissed her forehead and her lips and held her close until she stopped shaking.

Molly was lying in Theo's arms. She was emotionally spent from the events of the evening and physically exhausted after their lovemaking, but she couldn't sleep. She lay in the dark and listened to Theo breathing. It was a sound she didn't think she would ever tire of.

She didn't want to lose him. How would she find her happily ever after once he was gone? Would their baby fill that void? She didn't think so. A baby and a partner were two very different things. She'd told Theo she was happy being single, that she was working on herself, that she didn't want a partner, but she knew now that she wanted Theo. She still didn't want to be married but that didn't rule out something more serious with Theo.

She thought she might be falling in love with

him. That was unexpected but not as frightening as she might have once thought.

Should she tell him how she was feeling? No. She didn't want to be the one to take the risk. She'd told Daniel she loved him once. He hadn't said it back. She wasn't prepared to go through that pain again.

'Are you awake?' she asked.

'Yes.'

'Are you thinking about the accident? About Bree?'

'In a roundabout way. I'm thinking about our baby. About how life is short. What if something had happened to me today? I know you were worried. I should have thought about that before I rushed into trying to be a hero. If something had gone wrong I would have left you and the baby alone. I know you said you're happy to be a single mother but I don't want to be an absent father. I want to be around for our child. My father lived in the same house as me and I barely saw him. I can't stand the thought of being in Sydney if you and our child are here.'

Molly held her breath and hoped he wasn't going to ask her to move again. She didn't want to say goodbye to him, but she knew he would be gone in less than a week. And that was her doing. She had said she wouldn't move to Sydney. She'd told him she wanted to make her own decisions. But now she thought that perhaps they could have compromised, but she wasn't sure how or what she could have done. How were they going to make long-distance parenting work?

'What if I stayed here?' Theo said.

'Here?'

'Yes.'

Her heart had leapt with hope at his suggestion until reality swiftly kicked in. 'But you're supposed to be taking over your mother's business.'

'I might be able to do that from here.'

'Why would you do that?'

'Being around for my child is more important than living in Sydney. If you want to live in Byron Bay, that's where I'll be. I'm not prepared to walk away from my responsibility to my child.'

She had been terrified that she was going to lose him tonight when he'd disappeared under the building. She couldn't imagine her life without him in it. She'd be happy if he stayed but what would that mean for them?

'And what about us?' she asked. The baby was tying them together but what would have happened to them if she weren't pregnant? Was it a relationship that could have survived or would it have run its course with time?

'I'm not saying we have to be in a relationship, although I acknowledge we will have one of sorts because of our child, but what if we could have more than a summer romance?' he said. 'A proper relationship.'

'But not marriage?' Marriage was still a step too far. She wasn't prepared to give up her independence and that was how she viewed marriage. From her experience it wasn't a partnership. It involved compromise, she understood that, but from her experience one person always compromised more than the other. Theo hadn't said he loved her. If she let herself fall in love with him, she knew she would be the one to compromise. She would be the one with everything to lose.

'No,' he agreed. 'We can keep seeing each other but without pressure, without expectation. We need to find a way forward. Together. But we don't need to figure it all out tonight. We've got eight months to work out how we're going to navigate this. I just need to know if it's an idea you'd consider. If you'd be okay if I stayed?'

'Yes,' she said. 'I would.' She'd be more than okay with that. 'I think we should see what happens.'

'My mother is back in the country tomorrow after her conference. I'll call her tomorrow night and put my proposal to her.'

CHAPTER TEN

'I CAN'T BELIEVE you've done this.' Theo was on the phone to his mother. He'd called to discuss the possibility of him staying on in Byron Bay, he hadn't mentioned Molly or the pregnancy—that was a conversation best had face to face—but she had completely blindsided him with news of her own. And the news wasn't good. 'You didn't think to tell me?'

'No. It was my decision and it was too good an opportunity to pass up.'

'When are you going to tell the staff?' he asked.

'I thought you could do it tomorrow before you come back to Sydney. You won't be staying in Byron Bay now.'

'You want *me* to tell them?'

'Yes. Making tough calls is part and parcel of management. If you're going to take over the practice one day you need to be able to have these conversations. To take responsibility. Think of it as a learning experience.'

Theo wasn't sure he wanted the responsibility or the experience. In his opinion he was going to be the bearer of bad tidings without having any input into the decision. But he knew there wasn't much he could do. The decision had been made.

All his plans were unravelling.

Theo felt sick. His mother's news had cost him a night with Molly. He couldn't face her last night, not with this decision hanging over his head, and he'd made an excuse, told her a lie, and now he was hoping she didn't find out. He knew a lack of trust was a deal breaker for her.

He was the first person to arrive for the fortnightly Monday morning staff meeting. He wanted to make sure he had time to gather his thoughts and run through his announcement. No, not his announcement, his mother's.

He smiled at Molly when she arrived, only marginally late, but his smile felt forced. He then avoided looking at her, knowing he would have difficulty getting through the announcement if he caught her eye. He knew he would see disappointment in her expression.

'Most of you know that my mother, Lian Chin, is the owner of Pacific Coast Clinics. She has some news that she has asked me to pass on. It affects all of you. Some of you know that this clinic hasn't been performing as well as expected recently and Lian has decided that the Byron Bay clinic is no longer a required part of the business portfolio, and she has sold the property and is going to offer the practice as an ongoing concern to any potential purchasers.'

'What? We're losing our jobs?'

He could tell Gemma was incensed, but part of him was glad that it was Gemma who had spoken up. He wasn't game to meet Molly's gaze yet. 'The clinic will be offered as an ongoing concern, but the purchaser would have to find new premises. This site has been sold to developers.' He knew that financially the sale of the building made sense. It was a large landholding, on a corner site in the centre of town. But the decision did not sit well with him morally. 'We're hoping to find someone who wants to take the practice and the staff on.'

'And if you don't?'

'We've got three months before the site needs to be vacated. I'm hopeful that will give everyone time to find another job if we don't find a buyer for the clinic.' Theo's stomach felt as if it were lined with lead. He couldn't believe he was imparting this news and, by the look on the faces of everyone in the room, nether could they. 'I'm sorry, there's not much more I can tell you, but I'm happy to answer any questions that you might have, if I can.'

The room was silent. Nobody had anything to say. They were all stunned. Theo had been feeling included, feeling comfortable, as a member of staff, but that had all changed within the space of a few minutes, several sentences and one decision.

'I'll let you discuss this news among yourselves. You're welcome to ask me anything you need to throughout the day.' He thought the best course of action would be to leave the room and give them freedom to discuss the announcement without him present but as he headed for the door he saw Molly rise from her chair.

'Theo.' She had followed him from the room.

She closed the door behind her. 'What the hell was that all about?'

'I'm sorry, Molly.'

'You're sorry? We're going to lose our jobs and you're sorry! How long have you known about this?'

'I only found out last night. When I called Mum to discuss staying here.'

Molly laughed. 'Really. Did you ever actually intend to stay here?'

Theo frowned. 'Of course. We talked about it.'

'We talked about a lot of things. We talked about the practice and the issues it was facing. We gave you suggestions. Did you even discuss those with your mother or was this a done deal?'

'We discussed it, but she felt that selling the building made the most sense financially.'

'I thought you agreed medicine was about more than money.'

'I do. But this was her decision. I'm as upset by this as you are.'

'I don't think so. This doesn't affect you nearly as much. It's not your livelihood at stake. You have a job in Sydney.'

'What do you mean? I'm staying here.'

'Not on my account, you're not.'

'What does that mean?'

'You know how much this job means to me. This place. These people. I won't be manipulated into moving to Sydney. I can't believe you've done this to me.'

'I haven't done anything to you. And no one is asking you to move to Sydney. I was going to stay here. Why would I do that if I knew there was going to be no job? For either of us.'

'I don't think you should stay here. I think you should go back to Sydney. I think our relationship, for want of a better word, is done,' she said before she spun around and walked off, leaving him standing alone in the corridor.

The sun was shining on Sydney Harbour and it was a picture-perfect summer's day, but Theo was oblivious to his surroundings as he made his way across the city. His heart ached. He'd lost everything. Molly blamed him and he couldn't argue with her. In her eyes he'd taken everything from her and having him in her life was not enough of a consolation prize. He wasn't wanted.

He kept his head down as he walked through the clinic to his mother's office. He wasn't in the mood to make polite small talk with any of the staff. He was frustrated, heartbroken and angry. He knocked on Lian's door, his irritation manifesting in short sharp taps, loud and unapologetic. His mother owed him some more information.

'Why didn't you tell me you'd had an offer on the property before I went up to Byron?' he asked, barely able to manage a cordial greeting before launching into the root of his aggravation.

'Because I hadn't. The offer only came through once you were already there.'

'You still could have told me,' he argued. 'I thought you wanted me to look at options to make the clinic profitable and I thought we'd come up with some good ideas.'

'Many of those suggestions had merit,' Lian agreed, 'but some would have required quite a bit of capital investment. Once I got the offer to sell that made the most sense from a financial perspective as well as a time perspective. It was a lot of money tied up in the land. The site was worth far more as a development site. It didn't make financial sense to keep it.'

Try telling that to the staff, Theo felt like saying, though he knew that opinion wouldn't do him any favours.

'Can I ask why you bought the practice to begin with? Did it make financial sense at the time?' he asked.

'I wanted to expand, and I looked to invest in Byron Bay as it was a growth area, and I thought it might be a good option for retirement, but then I realised it's just a bit too far away to keep an eye on easily and your father and I decided we didn't actually want to retire, or even semi-retire, to Byron Bay. We like Sydney, our friends are here and it's convenient. It was a mistake to buy it.'

Theo's eyebrows shot up.

'What is it?' Lian asked when she saw his expression.

Theo shook his head. 'I've never heard you say you've made a mistake.'

'I've made a few,' Lian replied. 'But I hope I've learnt something from each one. If you can fix it or learn from it, it can be a positive. A mistake isn't a problem unless you repeat it.'

And that was when Theo realised that he'd made a mistake. And he'd made it twice.

Twice he'd walked away from Molly.

He'd let her down, unintentionally it had to be said, but that didn't change the fact that he hadn't supported her. He hadn't fought for her and he was ashamed of himself.

She'd pushed him away because he'd broken her trust and he couldn't blame her for that. He recognised that, for all her talk of independence, it was her fear of being let down that had led her to strive for that in the first instance. If she didn't depend on anyone she wouldn't be disappointed. His fears of rejection, of not being deemed good enough, had caused him to walk away, believing she didn't want him, only Molly had taken that to believe that he wasn't someone she could rely on. When what she really wanted was to be able to depend on someone. On him.

He should have fought harder for her.

He should have stayed.

His mother's words resonated with him. About

mistakes but also about retirement. About finding somewhere to slow down. About Byron Bay.

That was where he should be. He'd found peace, acceptance and happiness there. With Molly. He could imagine growing old there. With Molly. And that was where he wanted to be, not in forty years' time but right now. With Molly.

The woman he loved.

He loved her.

He should never have left her.

Was it possible that together they could overcome their fears? That they could be stronger together?

Was it too late to win her back? Too late to tell her how he felt? Too late to make amends?

He had to try. He'd already lost everything. There was nothing more to lose.

He knew what he had to do.

'I have a proposal for you,' he said to his mother.

Molly stood beneath the lighthouse, a solitary figure, alone with her thoughts. She was up before sunrise, unable to sleep, but her eyes were closed now. She was leaning on the railing, facing east, listening to the waves crashing onto the rocks below her. The sound reminded her of Theo. Rolling waves were the soundtrack of their lovemaking.

She opened her eyes, looking for something to distract her, something to take her mind off Theo, but the ocean was empty and the horizon was only just beginning to glow.

It was Christmas Eve and he'd been gone for almost a week. Her heart ached. He'd broken it, smashed it, but she would have to find a way to deal with that, to deal with him, because even though he was gone, even though she had sent him away, there was no escape. He was the father of her unborn child and she knew that would connect them for ever.

Had she expected too much from him?

She hadn't expected to fall in love and that was when her expectations had changed. She'd said she wanted independence but then she'd changed her mind but hadn't told him. That was hardly his fault.

A life with Theo had, for a brief time, been what she wanted but depending on someone else frightened her, so much that she'd taken the first opportunity presented to her to push him away. By accusing him of letting her down, she'd sacrificed their relationship for her independence at the first hurdle.

Had she been too quick to judge? Should she have tried harder to work things through?

Had she made a mistake?

Maybe, but now she was stuck with the consequences of her actions. Stuck with having to co-parent with Theo without being with him.

She'd acted hastily and she was as much to blame for the situation as he was. But that didn't lessen her heartache.

Would her heart ache so much if she weren't still in love with him? Unfortunately for her she couldn't turn love off like a tap. She had banished Theo but she couldn't banish her feelings and now she'd just have to find a way to manage. Given time, she might be able to do that.

She had thirty-five weeks until her due date. That might be enough time.

Or it might not.

With a little effort she pushed thoughts of Theo to one side. There were more pressing issues to deal with right now. She needed to get on with her life. The future she'd pictured briefly with Theo had changed completely. She needed to do something about finding a new job. She couldn't afford to wait. She was going to be a single mother; she needed to be settled into a job before she had the baby. She needed her new employer to find her invaluable. Her priority had to bc hcr baby. Her heartache would ease and she'd eventually work out how to co-parent with Theo.

She turned south, looking away from the horizon towards the road leading to the lighthouse, imagining, over the sound of the waves and the seagulls, that someone was calling her name. She didn't expect to see anyone, she assumed it must be a trick of the wind, so she was surprised to see a familiar figure jogging up the path.

Her heart rate quickened as her body betrayed her.

Theo.

He slowed his pace as he approached her. Was he unsure of his reception? His dark eyes showed signs of fatigue—had he been sleeping poorly too? She curled her hand into a fist, forcing herself not to reach out to him, not to smooth the worry lines from his face. She wasn't the person to console him any more.

He stopped in front of her. Just out of reach. His eyes dark with apprehension.

'What are you doing here?' she asked.

'Looking for you.' His answer was matter-of-fact but his voice was soft and filled with longing and Molly's heart lifted with hope.

He was looking at her closely, his gaze intense, and she felt the familiar and not unpleasant sensation of her insides melting, turning to warm treacle. 'How are you?'

Molly almost laughed. His question was so brief, so minuscule compared to her feelings. She was devastated over what she'd lost, feeling sorry for herself and also annoyed that her first reaction to seeing Theo had been pleasure, but she didn't tell him that. 'I'm fine.' She could do brief.

'And the baby?'

His question brought a half-smile to her lips. 'The baby is the size of a sesame seed.' She was only five weeks pregnant. She knew the baby would be getting facial features now—eyes and a nose—it was developing into a tiny human, but it was still tiny.

'I know, but I've missed a week.' He shrugged. His tone wasn't accusatory, which was just as well. His banishment was his own fault. 'It's felt like a lifetime.'

She heard the heartache in his words but he had only himself to blame for that. Her heart was aching too. She didn't want to cover old ground so she repeated her question. 'What are you doing here?'

'I need to talk to you.'

'I'm not sure there's anything we need to discuss.' Her heart was bruised, her pride dented, her trust broken and the pain made her tone sharp.

'Please,' he begged her, 'can we sit down? Can you give me five minutes? It's important.'

The sun was only just starting to peek above the horizon. Molly had nowhere else to be and, she couldn't deny it, suddenly nowhere else she wanted to be. She nodded and let Theo lead her to a bench against the lighthouse wall. She sat and folded her arms across her stomach, keeping her distance, knowing if she let him touch her she'd be in danger of believing anything he said.

He reached for her but withdrew his hands as she crossed her arms. 'It may make no difference to what happens next, but it's important that you know this,' he said. 'I know you think I colluded with my mother, but I promise you she made all the decisions regarding the practice. I'm not trying to shift the blame to her. I'm telling you the truth. She didn't consult me about the sale. I knew nothing of it until twelve hours before I told all the staff.'

Hope died in Molly's heart. Had he come back just to rehash business matters? She admitted to herself she'd been wanting more, hoping for something personal. Hoping he'd missed her as much as she'd missed him. She sighed inwardly. He'd asked about the baby—was that the best she could expect? 'Why hadn't your mother told you about the sale earlier?'

'Apparently she only received that offer from the developers when she was overseas at the conference.'

'And you believe her?'

Theo nodded. 'I've seen the emails.'

'Why didn't you say anything to me as soon as you found out? Why didn't you give me some warning?'

'I didn't know how to tell you. I was afraid of what it might mean.'

'Did you even try to talk her out of it? We came up with lots of options—did you even discuss any of those with her? Did you try to fight for us?'

Theo nodded. 'I did but the reality was the offer to sell was too good to refuse. I agreed with her on that.'

Molly opened her mouth to interject.

'But I disagreed with her next move of giving up the practice entirely,' Theo continued, as if knowing what Molly was about to say. 'The town needs the clinic. She should have considered that and realised that not every health practitioner wants to run their own practice. She could have handled that better. This whole situation has taught me a few more things about my mother and myself. It was a unilateral decision and when I questioned her she told me it was hers to make. I know she intends for me to take over the business one day but the way this decision was made makes me question whether she will ever really let go. Whether the clinics will ever be mine to run as I choose. But I think I have found a solution.'

'Which is?' Molly's voice was flat. She was going through the motions, feigning polite interest, responding to Theo's words, when in reality she wanted to know if he'd really come back just to talk about work.

'I'm going to take over the Byron Bay clinic. I'll need to find another site but I'm going to keep it going. My way. Our way.'

'Our way?'

'I understand none of this might make any difference to how you feel about me, but I want to be here. I want to be where my child is. I don't want to be a part-time father. I'm not walking away again. I want to be here, with you. I want us to do this together.'

'Do what exactly?' Molly asked.

'Work together.'

'You want me to work in the clinic? Your new clinic?' What was wrong with men? Which part of independence didn't he get? Did he think that she would be grateful to have a job? She would, that much was true, but she wasn't going to work for him.

'I know how important your job is to you,' he said. 'How much you love the town. You want financial independence, job security and to be able to stay here. I think my solution gives us both what we're looking for.'

'But you'll still control my fate. My employment. I don't want to be controlled by anyone.'

Theo shook his head. 'I want you to work in the clinic if that's what you choose, but not as an employee. I want to make you a partner in the business. I want you to have the independence you need.'

'A partnership?'

Theo nodded.

'I can't afford to buy into a practice,' she told him. A business partnership was appealing but she didn't even have money for a lawyer to draw up a contract, let alone money to start a business.

'It will be my gift to you.'

Molly frowned. 'A gift? You'd do that for me?' She tilted her head as she considered him. What did he want in exchange? she wondered.

'Yes. I want you to know you can trust me, but I thought a physical commitment would give you protection, a guarantee. No one will be able to take it away from you.'

Theo's eyes were dark and solemn, almost begging her to believe him. To trust him. Could she? She wanted to—desperately. 'Is that all you want?'

He shook his head. 'Not quite.'

She knew there would be more. There was always more.

'I want to raise our child together, not as two single parents but as a couple. I want to be in a relationship with you, if you'll have me. I made a mistake leaving here. I made a mistake leaving you. I don't want to give up on you, on us. I want to give you the world and I want to make a life with you. I want a family, people I can love without reservation. I love you, Molly.'

'You love me?' That wasn't the addition she was expecting. Once upon a time, just ten days ago, it was the extra piece she was hoping for but she'd let go of that dream. Now her heart leapt with hope.

'I love you.'

She heard the catch of emotion in his voice as he repeated his words. He loved her.

Could she possibly have everything she'd dared to dream of?

'I love you,' he repeated for the third time. He

shook his head as if he couldn't believe it himself. 'I've never said that to anyone before.'

'Have you never been in love?' she asked.

'Once. With an amazing girl,' he said, and Molly steeled herself for what was coming next. 'She was bright and beautiful and she could light up a room. And I'm still in love with her. It's you, Molly. It's always been you.'

Molly's heart soared as she broke into a smile. She'd almost convinced herself that she didn't need anyone, that she didn't need him, but she knew that wasn't true. He loved her. And she loved him.

She had sacrificed their relationship for her independence only to realise that wasn't what she wanted after all. But now Theo was offering her everything. Independence along with a commitment and, best of all, his love, and she knew she wanted to make the same promise to Theo. She wanted to be his.

She reached for his hands as she said, 'I love you too. I didn't want to fall in love, but I can't resist you. I can't live without you. When you went into that collapsed building and I thought I might lose you that was the worst moment of my life. I realised I'd fallen in love with you, but then I thought you let me down and I convinced myself that I was better off without you in my life.

I jumped to conclusions and I'm sorry. I'd been so afraid that you'd let me down that I made myself believe you had, just to prove myself right, just to make my expectations real, but I've been miserable. I've missed you. I've missed you so much.' She paused before finally uttering the words she needed to say. 'I love you too.'

Theo was beaming, his gorgeous grin stretching widely across his beautiful face. The morning sun fell on his face, turning his skin golden and making his dark eyes shine. He gathered her to him, wrapping his arms around her, and Molly lost herself in his embrace.

'What do you think?' he asked. 'Let's spend Christmas Day together and the next day and the next, and then we can celebrate a new year together and create a life for ourselves here where we can be happy. We'll have our work, our family, we'll have each other. Will you be my partner? In work and life?'

Molly sat back. She needed to clarify exactly what he was asking. 'Does your version of family look like a traditional one? I will be your partner, we will be a family, but I don't want to get married. Not yet. Maybe not ever. But that doesn't mean I don't love you. I want to be with you. I don't want anyone else, but marriage isn't for me. Can you live with that?'

'I won't deny that I would marry you in a heartbeat,' Theo replied, 'but, married or not, it won't affect how much I love you or our child. Married or not, I will still try to be the best partner, the best father, I can be. I'll be happy if I can wake up beside you every day. I want to spend the rest of my life with you. I love you and a wedding ring won't change that. I will love you just the same.'

The lighthouse towered above them, but Molly was oblivious to its beauty. All her focus was on the man in front of her. The love of her life. She was smiling now as she pulled Theo towards her.

'Then, yes, let's do this. Today, tomorrow and the next day. You and me together,' she said, before she kissed him with all her heart and soul. 'I love you.'

* * * * *

MEDICAL

Life and love in the world of modern medicine.

Subscribe and fall in love with a Mills & Boon series today!

You'll be among the first to read stories delivered to your door monthly and enjoy great savings.

WE
SIMPLY
LOVE
ROMANCE